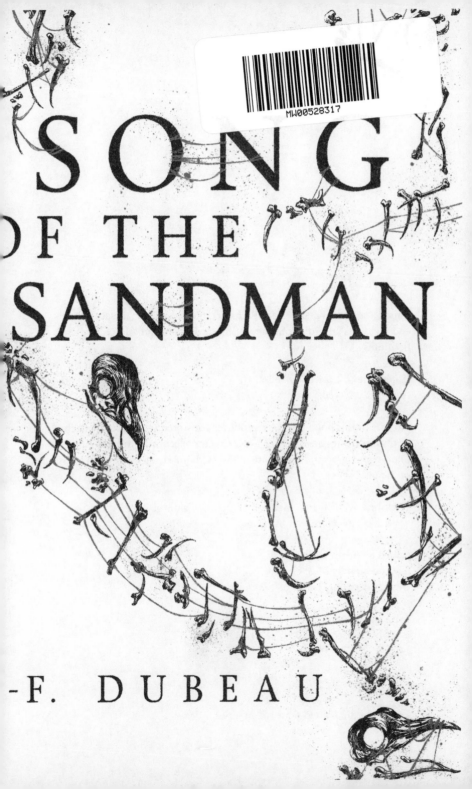

SONG
OF THE
SANDMAN

-F. DUBEAU

Published by Inkshares, Inc., San Francisco, California
www.inkshares.com

Edited by Adam Gomolin
Cover design by M.S. Corley
Interior design by Kevin G. Summers

ISBN: 9781942645962
e-ISBN: 9781947848054
LCCN: 2017955460

First edition

Printed in the United States of America

PROLOGUE

THE WORST PART about the worst things is that they can happen to anyone. There is no inoculation to catastrophe, no matter how many precautions are taken. Sometimes the fort we build to protect ourselves is the very thing that collapses and buries us alive. The thicker the walls, the heavier the masonry, the more bones get crushed, the more skulls get split. It's the sense of security that becomes the great betrayer, folding in on itself, obliterating all within.

It had taken the better part of a decade for Alice to build those walls. She'd started with nothing but the pieces of a shattered life and whatever emotional tools were available to an eight-year-old. Her shelter was flimsy at first, hastily put together from whatever leftovers of herself she could find. The largest stones her tired and wounded mind could carry were stacked together to form a fragile barricade, one that threatened to crumble at the slightest touch.

And it did crumble. Over and over throughout the years, Alice would have to build again and again. But each time, she found she had more resources to work with, that she could lift heavier materials, and that she knew how to construct a sturdier bastion. One from within which she could protect her battered spirit.

By her sixteenth birthday, Alice had built a veritable fortress. The repetitive drudgery of her routine, however unique, had made her a skilled architect. As long as she didn't step out of line, as long as she didn't think of all the things she'd never have, it was easy enough for her to endure.

The very trappings of her predicament had become symbolic of her fortress. The bars on the windows no longer served to keep her in, but instead protected her from what was outside. The scratches on the wall, each marking a day in captivity, had been painted over, as she no longer counted the time before she might be rescued or escape.

Incarceration was transfigured into security. Captors were now family; and routine, a shield. Food, lodging, and even some measure of education were provided to her. Other members of her new family had to work one or two jobs, giving up their earnings to the community; meanwhile, all that was required of Alice was that she keep her voice in perfect condition.

As far as she could tell, this was going to be her life until the day she died. Everything was arrayed to keep her safe and healthy and content. She was a delicate music box, kept in perfect working condition, stored in a velvet-lined box for its own protection.

At sixteen, eight years into her imprisonment, Alice's life took another sharp turn.

It started when she heard a loud commotion outside her room one night. Then came the screams. Neither were unusual. The refurbished storeroom Alice called her own was located in the basement of what used to be a school. Members of the family would sometimes move furniture and boxes in and out of storage down here, caring little whether they bothered her with their activities. Sometimes it would be one of her "brothers" or "sisters" who would be dragged down the stairs. Kicking and screaming, they were taken to the lonely darkness of the Reflection Room, a small custodial closet where family members would be locked in solitary confinement if they broke a rule. The Reflection Room smelled of stale blood, urine, and fear. The smell of discipline. One Alice knew from experience.

On this day, Alice had no idea what could be going on and felt no curiosity toward it. Whoever had transgressed would be punished and then welcomed back into the fold. Their sin would be bled out in fits of painful contrition. Upon hearing the sounds, her thumb quickly pressed the volume control on her earphones to drown them out. So seldom did Alice get an evening to herself; she'd be damned if this one would be ruined because someone had displeased Mother.

Prokofiev blasted loudly in her ears and she bent over her book once again. It had taken time to convince Mother to procure the Harry Potter series for her. Mother had argued that it might give her "ideas." But Alice knew where to draw the line between fantasy and reality. She knew the bars on her window were too narrow for an owl to fly through.

"Alice!"

She snapped her head up at the mention of her name, yanking her earphones off at the sight of Victor Poole. With well-combed graying hair and a dark brown goatee, he was the very picture of a schoolteacher. Or what Alice imagined one would look like. He must have been calling out her name for a moment, as he looked at the end of his wits. His skin was red from exertion and his throat was ragged as he spoke. His maroon cardigan had a large dark stain at the front that looked like spilled oil.

"Alice! Come quick!"

He stood in her doorway, waiting for her to react. But Alice never had visitors. She was kept to a strict schedule and even stricter limitations on where she was allowed to wander. What could Victor Poole possibly want with her? These questions were wandering back and forth through her mind when she heard the wail.

The wailing hadn't come from behind the door of the faraway Reflection Room; it had originated from somewhere closer. The scream had an animal quality to it, the sort of noise that might escape the belly of a wounded dog. High-pitched yet guttural, fraught with agony, it was a plea for release.

"Mister Poole, who's that screaming?" asked her tremulous voice. He didn't answer.

"Is she coming?" Mother's voice echoed down the hallway, delicate yet uncompromising. In the background a drawn-out howl attempted to drown her out.

Before she realized what her thin limbs were doing, Alice climbed out of bed and rushed past Victor, pushing him aside, the flat of her hand pressing into his soiled cardigan.

The hallway underneath the school that she called home was dimly lit by a spine of fluorescent lights. They stretched from the stairs and service elevator, all the way to the other end of the basement. There, another set of stairs was hidden behind a door that said EXIT-SORTIE in glowing red letters. Midway through the hall, a door was pulled open and a small gathering of family members crowded around it.

"You called, Mother?" Alice asked, obedient.

The tension was unmistakable. The two men closest to the door wore masks of abject horror, gray skin across their contorted features. Whatever they were looking at, the source of the tortured screams, Alice couldn't imagine. The only certain thing was that she wanted no part of it.

The third closest spectator was Mother. Hers was the demeanor of an annoyed supervisor. Arms crossed, back stiff, she glared at Alice with equal parts disdain and impatience. She might as well have been waiting for her to make her bed or get ready for school or finally mow the lawn before the weekend was over. All of this while someone was almost certainly dying a painful death mere feet away.

"This is it, Alice. Time to shine," Mother said, stepping aside and gesturing calmly toward the open door.

It took a moment for the other two witnesses to realize what Alice was doing and get out of the way. Averting her eyes, Alice stepped up to the threshold, just as another earsplitting scream—this one of a thick, wet quality—burst out of the opening.

She looked back at Mother, preferring to face her impatience than whatever was in that room. She could smell the metallic aroma of fresh blood, feel the rank humidity of sweat and bodily fluids. It was a slaughterhouse that she didn't want to face alone.

"Hurry," Mother said, letting just a hint of fear slip through her urging. "You can do this, Alice."

Taking a deep, blood-scented breath and closing her eyes, Alice turned toward the room. Moist cracking and a frantic gurgle were all she could hear. Knowing she would lose her nerve if she were to take but the smallest of peeks, she instead concentrated on the task at hand.

"Anytime, Alice," Mother said, through thinly veiled worry.

Another deep breath and Alice began to sing. The song—a sweet, slow lullaby—came out a trembling mess. Alice could picture Mother's annoyed eyes. She was better than this, more practiced. In fact, when she put her mind to it, as Mother demanded her to do at this precise moment, Alice was perfect.

Voices and noises, screams and echoes, all attempted to ripple the glassy pond of her concentration. A fine, warm mist touched her right cheek and something nudged the tip of her naked foot. But she maintained focus, thinking only of the air as it was pushed out of her lungs. Alice concentrated on how she could manipulate it with her vocal cords, her tongue, the opening of her mouth, even the tilt of her neck. Before long, she was lost in the lullaby. Her mind let go of the physical world surrounding her, abandoning all other senses. Her limbs were gone, as was the ground under her feet. If it weren't for the need to take in air so that she could sing, she may have even forgotten to breathe.

However long it had been, the room was quiet now. Her only companion was the sound of a slow and ponderous dripping.

Alice slowly cracked open her eyes. They stung from the light and they hurt from the cramped muscles that had kept them shut. While she had been prepared to see the room turned into a butcher shop, the reality far exceeded her imagination.

The singing had put a stop to the butchery, but Mother, along with every other surviving family member, had been put to sleep. They were slumped on the ground, awkward piles of humanity tossed aside with careless abandon. They were the lucky ones. Their chests moved up and down in deep slumber.

Others had been less fortunate.

Alice couldn't tell how many family members had been killed, their remains in a mess of limbs and innards. She thought, if only for a callous moment, that counting heads would do the trick, but even that seemed a challenge.

Among the carnage, she saw a stroke of pale gray in the middle of a crimson tableau—one last survivor. Nestled amid the various body parts like a bird in a nest lay the body of an old man. Ashen and wrinkled and completely naked, his eyes were covered by thick scabs of dried blood. At the center of each wound was a dark iron nail, driven into the socket. Whoever he was, the old man wasn't part of the family. In fact, judging from the viscera covering his hands, he was the one responsible for this massacre.

What Alice didn't know was that the name of the man to whom the body had once belonged was Sam Finnegan.

Feeling her fortitude waver, Alice lifted her left hand to her face. It was the one she had used to push Victor Poole out of her way. Feeling for the first time the sticky wetness between her fingers, she saw that she'd been wrong. It wasn't oil that stained Victor's cardigan, but blood. Blood that was growing stickier as it dried.

Gore, violence, the tangible remains at her fingertips . . . none were what bothered Alice most. That didn't mean she wasn't shaken by the experience, but while she'd been singing to put the old man to sleep, something had sung back to her. An echo of her lullaby. A voice without sound that only she could hear. It was dark and angry, but also wounded and sad.

Standing more alone than she'd ever felt, her emotional fortress in ruins once more, Alice struggled to decide what to do next. Mother had told her countless times that she was meant for great things. That one day she would meet an incredible destiny and her voice, her singing, would hold the key to a new age. The rest of the family believed that, but Alice had always doubted.

Until today, when she had sung to and had heard the words of a god.

VENUS

SOLITUDE, DEATH, AND DARKNESS.

The three fears of Venus McKenzie.

The subway tunnel the young girl was sneaking through felt more hollow and more foreign than it should have. Venus kept looking up at the ceiling, a reminder of the sleeping city just a few feet above.

Though she hated it, Venus could handle the solitude. She'd been raised an only child. In fact, often she chose solitude. It had been her decision to come to Montreal on her own and not involve her friends. Though, now that she marched blindly down the tunnel, she did long for some companionship.

She still feared the loneliness, but patting the cell phone in her pocket, Venus was reminded that her friends weren't really that far. She could, with one call, retreat back to humanity and find Penny and Abraham waiting there.

Her relationship with death was a longer and more complex affair. Where other children were afraid of corpses, she had been fascinated by them from a young age. She thought, in fact, that she would follow the path of her uncle Dr. Randy McKenzie, who was a medical examiner. But living in Saint-Ferdinand had taught her what death really was. It was one thing to poke and prod at a stranger's deceased form, a subject rather than an individual, but quite another to live for years among people who would routinely vanish without a trace. Not to mention the frequent news of mutilated remains discovered in the woods, an occurrence that repeated two or three times each year. One day she'd be buying candy from Cindy at the corner store, and a week later Cindy's parents were burying her in the local cemetery. It was different when the dead had a name and a face.

Then there was the time she'd danced with a god of hate and death. This, too, had left its mark.

Death had announced its presence at the Laurier station through the vilest of means. It had reached out to her, pungent tendrils of decay that snaked through the air, undetected by most but unmistakable to Venus. Saint-Ferdinand had taught her the aroma of a decomposing corpse. And the Laurier station smelled of home.

That left only the darkness.

The darkness, she simply couldn't stand. It was just another word for *shadow*, and that was something Venus had had quite enough of lately.

A shadow was supposed to be nothing more than the absence of light. But it was more than that: it was where things could hide. All manner of things. The ones that existed just on the edge of life and death, or somewhere beyond it. She'd known a being of shadow, a creature of pure darkness. It had ruined her life, gouging out part of her soul in the process. Besides, darkness amplified everything else. It made the solitude that much more isolating. It sharpened her other senses, accentuating the thick smell of death. Her hearing was also keener, letting her know exactly how quiet and lonely the tunnels were at this time.

Solitude, death, and darkness. Those were the things going through Venus McKenzie's mind when she tripped over the supine body of Sylvain Gauthier.

Her own cry of surprise echoed back to her from the concrete and stone walls of the tunnel. The high-pitched scream went down an octave with each repetition before eventually dissipating in the dark.

With a bit of luck and an embarrassing stumble, Venus managed to keep her balance and avoid falling flat on her face. She was walking near the cold, moist wall, staying clear of the rails. Her boots were disturbing puddles of stagnant water that reeked of decay and garbage, but while no sweet-smelling rose herself, she could do without being covered in muddy rainwater and rat piss.

Despite the darkness, there was no mistaking the corpse. The smell alone was quite enough to confirm it. The lump that had nearly sent her sprawling to the ground had to be Sylvain Gauthier. The stench was beyond belief, answering the question of how it had traveled so far down the subway line as to be detectable all the way back at the Laurier station. How had no one reported it? Why had the maintenance crew not stumbled upon it yet?

Their negligence was her good fortune.

Gauthier had looked something like her uncle: a little pudgy, with an easy, if pained, smile, and hair everywhere but on top of a shiny scalp. What had attracted Venus's attention to him wasn't so much his appearance but rather a handful of words tucked away in the article that had reported his disappearance.

Member of the Church of the Sandmen.

There had been a small cult of people calling themselves "Sandmen" in Saint-Ferdinand. While Venus knew very little about them, she had no doubt about a connection.

After weeks of nearly fruitless research and investigation, with nary a clue to latch on to, the forgettable article in the *Montreal Gazette* had breathed new life into Venus's mission. Still, it would have been preferable that Gauthier still had breath of his own.

Like a flare of burning magnesium, light exploded at her fingertips. Venus's phone, for all its faults, had a decent enough flashlight, though the damn thing would drain the battery so fast, it might have been a race.

The *Gazette* article had stood out because of the unusual circumstances of Gauthier's disappearance. By all accounts, he'd been inadvertently pushed in front of an oncoming subway train. An unusual delay in the schedule had caused a sizeable number of would-be passengers to accumulate on the platform, waiting for the next train. Some sort of commotion had occurred just as the subway emerged from the tunnel and, according to witnesses, there was a thud and a screeching of brakes as the train stopped suddenly.

Yet, despite hundreds of people present, some standing just a few feet from Gauthier at the moment of impact, the victim had completely vanished.

The Montreal police assumed the accident hadn't been that bad and that Sylvain Gauthier must have walked away, vanishing into the crowd, preferring not to draw attention to himself.

Already, that part of the story didn't ring quite true to Venus.

When she was about twelve, a few months before she and her parents moved to Saint-Ferdinand, the McKenzies had been on a trip to Montreal, enjoying the many festivals that took place downtown in the summer. On the subway ride home, just before transferring from the green to the yellow line that would take them to Longueuil, their train had come to a sudden halt.

After a lengthy pause, passengers were finally allowed off. The train had hit someone, a woman who'd leaned too far over the tracks. Her body had been lying on the ground, a single transit cop directing people away from her.

It didn't prevent Venus from looking. The victim's face seemed almost intact. Everything still in the right place. Her skin, however, was the color of crushed Lac Saint-Jean blueberries, a red tint at the edge of the bruising. She was lying on her side, arms in an uncomfortable but still not unnatural position. She might have been unconscious, or just wounded, if not for her eyes. Open and glassy, they seemed to be stuck on the verge of crying. Her face was frozen in a final, aborted expression of distress.

Whatever had happened to Gauthier, Venus knew he hadn't simply walked it off.

The article was quick to confirm it. Family and friends had reported him missing and now, through the media and a forgettable few paragraphs, authorities were calling on the public to report any sightings of a wounded, possibly disoriented man.

The flashlight on her phone cut through the darkness. A bright circle of illumination poured onto Gauthier's corpse. He looked identical to what Venus had expected, down to his brown jacket and striped fuchsia tie. The beam of light stopped on Gauthier's bloated face, giving Venus the final confirmation that she was on the right track.

Someone had gouged out his eyes.

The retching came suddenly. The vomit followed fast and unstoppable. One moment, Venus was looking down at the white glare blowing out the gray skin and crimson wounds, a portrait of roses upon snow; the next moment all the contents of her stomach erupted forth from her mouth. The muscles of her lower abdomen spasmed and her throat burned from the bile and stomach acid.

Why, she wondered, spitting out the dribble of half-digested food, would her stomach turn on her now? Had she not grown a thick enough skin to endure this sort of thing?

After all, she'd been witness to the execution of Nathan Cicero at the Saint-Ferdinand Circus Massacre. She'd seen Inspector Stephen Crowley gun down half a dozen performers and stage hands before being stabbed in the neck by his own son. She'd seen his body dissolve, consumed by shadows like a voracious swarm of beetles.

The aroma of decay, thick and wet like garbage on a hot summer day, combined with the gruesome bloated cheeks and lifeless skin, all adorned with the red buds of absent eyes replaced by writhing white maggots, had somehow pushed her over the edge.

My stomach is a traitor, she thought.

Gathering her wits, Venus tried to get a better look at the body and its surroundings. She'd want to take pictures, go through his pockets, and try to better understand who he was and what connection he'd had with this so-called Church of the Sandmen.

And the man she suspected of hunting its members down.

But every time she looked up, Venus would feel her insides again turn upon themselves. The floodgates were open now. The smell of her own vomit, mixed with the pungent stench of Gauthier's decomposing remains and postmortem bowel movement, made breathing difficult.

"Get it together, Venus."

Her name came back to her, hollow after bouncing on the cold walls, but it brought no comfort, only highlighting her solitude.

Gauthier, her only companion, lay silently at her feet, and with every moment he was becoming more difficult to ignore.

Upon pushing the home button on her phone to turn the light back on, Venus was met with the bright smile of two young girls on a sunny afternoon. Both were making silly faces as one extended her arm to take the picture. Venus's gray-green eyes were full of life in a way they hadn't been for a while now, Penny's a deep cerulean that would make the sky jealous.

Venus's fingers traced the few quick motions it took to unlock the phone, navigate to Penny's contact info, and call her.

"Finally come to your senses?" Penny's groggy voice answered, eschewing all preambles.

It had been their arrangement, Venus's safety net while she was in Montreal. If ever she felt in too much danger or threatened, got sick of it or scared, or any number of other situations they had discussed, all Venus had to do was call Penelope and her friend would race to Montreal to retrieve her.

"Not quite." The timid words echoed across the tunnel.

"Veen? It's three a.m. on a weeknight. I'm driving to Montreal. If it's not to pick you up, it's to kick your ass."

"I'm sorry, okay? I need someone to talk to, and you're the only person who gets why I'm even here."

Penny let out a long sigh. It wasn't yet capitulation, but they were on their way.

"Wrong, Veen. I don't get why you're there."

Venus took a deep breath, both to collect herself and to deliver her explanation in its entirety. Nerves were getting the better of her, forcing the words out faster than she'd intended.

"I don't know what else to do? That thing from my shed wiped out my—our—families! The only way I'm keeping it together is focusing on stopping that monster, and I need Peña to do that."

Lucien Peña.

It was one of the names Venus had picked out of her grandfather's notes. The name that came up the most. Peña had traveled with Neil McKenzie, explored the world with him, gathered knowledge at his side. If anyone knew about the monster from Saint-Ferdinand, it would be him.

"He won't let me get close enough, but at the same time, he's always lurking nearby, like he's hovering over my shoulder. But I think he's changed his pattern."

"What do you mean 'lurking'? You mean you're being stalked by a giant magic hobo and I'm supposed to just brush that off?"

"He's not exactly stalking me," Venus said. "But whenever things are getting dicey, he'll turn up somehow. Like last week, some real creeper was tailing me for a couple of nights, always hanging outside the hostel and giving me really gross looks. But then the guy completely vanishes and next thing I know, I'm talking to this other girl he'd been harassing and she said the guy got the shit beat out of him by"—her friend's words repeated in her mind—"a 'giant magic hobo,' as you put it."

Another deep sigh came over the line, interrupted by the terrible connection.

"Six foot five, probably knows some of the same hocus-pocus as your uncle. What else would you call him? And if that story was meant to make me feel better, it was a complete failure," said Penny.

"I'm just saying, the guy is like some sort of guardian angel to homeless kids."

"Right, a regular superhero, and you've got him figured out."

"I do! There's been a series of accidents. Weird things that pop up in newspapers about people disappearing and then being found dead a few days later. Get this: every one of these people belong to a so-called 'Church of the Sandmen,' and it all started right after the circus massacre. I've tracked down the last victim: Sylvain Gauthier. Some big-shot lawyer."

Venus could hear the sounds of mugs being moved around, a cupboard slamming shut, and coffee percolating on Penelope's end. "All right," Penny said, tired but sincere. "Where's this guy's body now? Did you already call the cops?"

"He's right here. At my feet. Unless he ran away, which I really hope he didn't. I'm not equipped to handle the undead right now."

"I'm sorry, what?"

"I mean, emotionally."

"No. I mean, you're with the body right now? Like, as we speak?"

"Yeah. That's why I'm calling. I don't know what to do next. Or rather, I know exactly what I'm supposed to do, but I can't bring myself to do it."

"Oh my god. Venus. Call the freakin' cops! What are you thinking?"

"I'm not calling the cops! I don't want to spook Peña just as I'm getting close to him. Besides, how well did the police getting involved work out at Cicero's Circus?"

Lucien Peña had vanished from society, erasing as much of himself as he could in the process. The only clue they'd found about his whereabouts was an article dating back fifteen years, deep in the online archives of the *Montreal Gazette*. Peña, described as a disgraced professor of anthropology and archeology, had attacked an unidentified man in a fast-food restaurant. Witnesses had described him as "rabid" and "unhinged." He was never apprehended, nor had he been heard from since.

"Speaking of cops," Venus continued, procrastinating. "Any news from Daniel?"

"What? No! And who cares?" Penny said. "You called me because you didn't know what to do? Well, I'm telling you. Call. The. Cops. Please."

"Fine. I just need to do something first."

It wasn't so much that she'd found her lost courage. The thought of looking at maggots crawling out of a dead man's eye sockets still made her empty stomach do acrobatics. But if there was one force in the universe that could silence even that level of revulsion in Venus McKenzie, it was curiosity.

Missing eyes were not a foreign concept to a resident of Saint-Ferdinand. They had been the calling card of Sam Finnegan, the Saint-Ferdinand Killer. Now it appeared to Venus as a signature from Peña.

"Venus?" Penny called out. "What are you doing?"

"I don't want to leave empty-handed."

With a deep breath to brace herself, Venus plunged her hand into the dead man's pants pocket, hoping to find a wallet. The fabric was cool to the touch and a little damp. All she pulled out was a set of keys that included a fob adorned with the BMW logo.

Carefully leaning over the body, trying to touch it as little as possible, Venus put her phone on the ground so she could use both hands. The light from the screen projected upward. Cables and tubes running the length of the tunnel stretched up into inky black shapes. Before she could search Gauthier's other pocket, however, Venus noticed another dark shape. Red and irregular, it seemed pulled from beneath the body. Clumsy brushstrokes of burgundy and brown traced the concrete in front of her. If there was any doubt that Lucien Peña was sending a message, it was obliterated by what she saw.

A sideways football drawn using the blood of the victim, but with a smudged spiral in the middle. Like an eye.

"Venus? Veen?" Penny's weak voice came in and out on the speaker of the phone. "What's going on?"

Venus ignored the phone, reaching out instead with a trembling hand, intent on tracing the pattern of gore on the wall. Images from the murals in her backyard shed flooded back in a traumatic torrent. The more she tried to blink them away, the more persistent they became.

Spirals within spirals of a convoluted design, framing a crude image of an eye. The mural of coagulated blood wasn't identical to the one that had been drawn on the walls of her backyard shed, but it was similar enough. This design would have been one of the last things her father had seen before he was killed by the god.

The moist walls had not permitted the blood from drying out completely, so it remained wet to the touch. Venus's stomach wanted to do another somersault but was instead gripped with cold dread. Memories of that summer were as palpable as the blood sticking to her finger, and she could almost feel the god's presence in the nearby shadows.

"Hey!" a woman's voice called out from deeper in the tunnel, accompanied by a bright light. This wasn't subway security. The voice carried with it the weight of genuine authority.

"Penny," Venus said, picking up her phone. "I don't think I'm going to need to call the cops after all."

ABRAHAM

THE CRACKS WERE like a spider's web. Thin and white, they radiated from a central point of impact. Each spoke on the wheel was randomly connected by other fissures along their length. Tiny shards had fallen off since he'd first dropped the phone a little over a week ago.

Fortunately, the damage hadn't affected the device's functionality. Abraham could still make calls, listen to music, and play the occasional game. Even through his thick, calloused skin, he could feel the texture of the cracks when he swiped over them. It bothered him. The pattern of his fingertips would map out the creases in the glass, reminding him that this new toy, already damaged, was either too fragile or that he was too much of a clumsy oaf. Knowing his luck, it would fail him when he needed it most.

With a heavy sigh, he tossed the device onto the kitchen table, half hoping it would fall apart on impact. The little piece of technological wonder was an anachronism at the Peterson farm. Right now it lay motionless next to an empty cereal bowl that was older than Abraham, on a wooden table made by Petersons three generations ago. Even the silverware, though not fancy, was an antiquity. Abraham could imagine the spoon in his bowl had once been a gleaming, polished utensil. Now, after decades of scratching against dishes and teeth and brushes, it was a pale, flat metallic gray.

Abraham shifted his heavy frame, the chair and floor responding with a chorus of creaking wood. The farmhouse itself was also ancient. Thick, sturdy hardwood floors ran throughout most rooms. They had been refinished now and again, but they still hinted at the house's history. There was a dark spot on the kitchen floor where water had seeped into the grain. A few boards had been changed in the living room, so the color of the wood didn't match the rest of the original floor.

It gave the Peterson home character.

With a grunt, Abraham got to his feet, laboriously pushing on the table with his hands. He was a large boy for his age, over six feet two inches tall, with hair the color of a maple tree's trunk, brown but dull. His eyes were a little too close together on his large face and he tended to slouch to hide his height. On his best days, he gave off the air of a gentle giant, powerful and well-meaning.

Looking around, he observed how all the cabinets in the kitchen were wide open again. They'd been doing this for a while now. The first time Abraham had noticed was a few days after the massacre. He'd been too busy to give it much thought back then, with all the coming and going and answering questions from cops. By the time things had calmed down, he'd all but gotten used to the random doors creeping open and slamming shut. For a while he'd worried it was his father, the cancer finally eating at his mind.

Strange though it might have been, it was a relief to one night see half a dozen cabinet doors yawn open in front of him while knowing his father was sleeping on the living room couch. Whatever the cause, it had nothing to do with Harry or the slow progression of his illness. In Abraham's mind, that left two possibilities: the house was settling, or there were ghosts. Sighing again, Abraham picked up a stack of papers from the table. This was Saint-Ferdinand: as long as they limited their activities to the kitchen, the ghosts could wait.

Abraham thumbed a quick text message on the phone to let Penelope know he was on his way.

There was a shortcut to Penny's place he used to take, through the fields and part of the forest. But he had neglected to take care of the grounds all summer. Fertile soil had gone unchecked, and now the whole area—from the farmhouse to the edge of the forest—was overgrown with weeds. Abraham just couldn't bring himself to step onto that part of the land. A scant couple of months earlier it had been a killing field, the site of the now notorious Saint-Ferdinand Circus Massacre. Ultimately, seven people had lost their lives after Inspector Crowley, the local chief of police, had gone on a shooting spree.

Walking to Penny's house would take him up Main Street. Though the trek would take over half an hour, Abraham didn't expect to see a single car, perhaps not even another human being.

The Richards farm was the first property Abraham walked by. The photo of a middle-aged woman's face looked back at him from a real estate sign planted on their lawn, right next to the long driveway. The word *sold* had been added atop. There were many signs like it all over town. Though few were crowned with the appended *sold*, most of the owners had already left.

The sun was bright, the sky marred by only a few wispy clouds, but Main Street still felt like it was in twilight. Abraham wasn't greeted by the smell of burgers and grease from the fast-food joint near the gas station. The restaurant, his favorite, had closed its doors for good. It wasn't the only one. As he crossed the street, Abraham could see all the way to the other end of the village. Some stores, like the flower shop, had their windows boarded up; others had signs pasted to their windows declaring that they were now closed for business. Only the grocery and convenience stores were still open, though at this hour, they remained deserted.

Abraham tripped over a pothole, his attention taken up by an effort to remember how Saint-Ferdinand had once been. The village had been many things while he'd grown up there. Bright and lively during the day, forbidding and scary as the sun went down, but one thing it had never been was depressing.

It all made Penelope's home stand out when he got there.

Penny had inherited the house from her mother and had since kept it in impeccable condition. The dark blue wood paneling and white window frames were freshly cleaned and radiant under the bright sun. Her lawn had been raked of the first few autumn leaves, and the cobblestones that led to her front door were swept. Even though the other houses in the neighborhood had been abandoned for only a couple of weeks, their FOR SALE signs a statement to that effect, they all seemed derelict compared to Penny's property.

It made Abraham feel guilty about neglecting his father's farm.

"Anything to avoid talking about ghosts," he said to himself, pressing the doorbell.

"Coffee?"

Penny had aged.

They all had over the summer. However, where events had taken their toll on Abraham throughout the aftermath of Saint-Ferdinand's demise, Penelope had suffered the worst of it—right from the onset, when her mother had been found dead, ripped to pieces in the woods. The aftershocks of the initial tragedy had left cracks in her personality. She'd become more private and deliberate, but also quieter, retreating to a position of observer. Having already lost her father five years prior, Penny was now alone. What could possibly compare to that?

"So, what should I do?" he asked, flipping through his stack of papers.

"What do you *want* to do?"

Penelope busied herself in the kitchen, having left Abraham at the dining room table with his papers and a slice of pecan pie. He'd come seeking her help in filling out college applications. Penelope had already gone through the process herself but had also navigated the legal labyrinth necessary to keep her mother's house. School applications must have been a cakewalk.

Abraham knew how difficult a decision it was for Penny, to keep the house. This was where she'd grown up and it was where she and her mother had mourned her father's passing. There were a lot of memories here for her, but how did you decide if the good ones outweighed the bad? There was no metric for this sort of thing, and Penny was someone who loved metrics.

"I want to be done with all this paperwork," he answered after a moment.

"No, you dummy," Penny said, walking back in while the coffee pecolated in the kitchen. "Long term. What do you want to do in five years? Ten?"

Abraham ignored the jab. This was how Penny talked to him. Instead he poked at the piece of pie with his fork, focusing his attention across the kitchen and into the adjoining living room.

Penny had redecorated over the last few months. He'd helped her install some of the shelves on the wall and build a bookshelf and a coffee table. It was her way of moving forward while staying in what had been her family's home.

On the couch, he could see a lump of gray fur. It looked like a stuffed animal, but Abraham knew better. Underneath the cheap faux fur was Venus's cat, Sherbet. Or whatever creature it had become. The girls insisted it was harmless, that they should keep it, and Abraham went along with the idea, even though the thing made his skin crawl.

"I don't know." He shrugged. "I need to stay close so I can take care of Dad. I used to think I'd be working on the farm, but now . . ." But now there wasn't going to be a farm for much longer. In fact, the Peterson legacy was coming to an end, with Saint-Ferdinand gasping its last breath and his father right along with it.

Abraham needed to figure out what he was going to do once everything he knew and loved had slipped through his fingers.

"Permission to be honest?" Penelope asked, taking the papers away from him.

"Granted."

"How long do you think your dad's got?"

"Pardon?"

She had asked to be candid and he'd known Penelope to be direct with him. She knew how sensitive he was about his father's health but had never been one to bring it up. "Your dad's dying and the farm is falling apart. Fine. That's terrible. I get it. But you can't keep building your life around him."

"What the hell, Penny?" he said, turning in his chair, outraged. "That's a shitty question!"

She didn't cut him off. She didn't have to. A simple index finger pointed at his face was all that was required.

The two of them stood in silence, the coffee machine dripping and gurgling from the kitchen.

Abraham looked from Penny's hand, all the way up her arm and into her pained crystal-blue eyes.

There he sat in her kitchen, pestering her for advice, complaining about his ailing father. Meanwhile, Penelope had been dealing with the death of her mother and finding herself an orphan at a time when she needed the same kind of guidance he expected from her.

It was indeed unfair, but not toward him.

His father was dying, but Harry Peterson had been dying for years and might still have weeks, months, or more ahead of him. As painful as the slow demise might be, father and son had prepared for it and enjoyed each other's company and said whatever needed saying. Twice so far, Penny had been denied that luxury.

"I'm sorry," he said, bowing his head.

"Eat your pie."

Her voice did not reflect the look she'd given him. It was calm and measured but also sweet.

Penelope walked back into the kitchen. Abraham could hear the sound of dishes clinking.

One sugar and a drop of milk, Abraham thought. *That's what she likes in her coffee.*

When she walked to the table, the tension of their exchange had washed off. She placed a steaming mug in front of him, next to his pie. She also knew what he preferred in *his* coffee, though he suspected it wouldn't be as sweet as he'd have made it himself.

Abraham looked up and smiled at her and she smiled back. It was exactly the kind of little moment he liked to savor when the two of them hung out together, but as always, something had to spoil it.

A report echoed across the room, startling them both.

It was the familiar clap of wood upon wood, immediately accompanied by a chime of rattling dishes. Penny's shoulders tensed, the jolt of her arms making her spill coffee all over Abraham's papers.

"What was that?" he asked, hoping she'd know the answer.

Penny didn't reply, putting down her mug with a quivering hand and looking slowly over her shoulder.

She didn't know.

It was happening here, too. Whatever was opening cupboards and cabinets back at the farm was doing the same in Penelope's kitchen.

After weeks of forcing himself not to think about it, all the possibilities that had been lurking at the back of Abraham's mind came flooding in.

He'd assumed these were the ghosts of the people killed at the farm. But if so, why were they also at Penny's? Was it something to do with him? Maybe it was something much more dangerous, like the creature Venus had kept in her backyard shed during the summer. The one Penny had tried to kill.

"You think it's that thing?" he asked, hoping she'd at least be able to confirm it wasn't.

"It's been going on for a few days now. Freaked the hell out of me the first time. Sherbet didn't seem bothered, so I figured it couldn't be that bad. But it keeps happening. That, or I'll take a shower and when I come out all my stuff has been moved. I'll find my toothbrush on the kitchen counter or ice trays piled up on a coffee table. It's maddening."

She sponged at his papers with a dish towel, trying uselessly to salvage them from the spilled coffee. Abraham recognized it for what it was—busywork to avoid a busy mind.

"It's happening at the farm, too," he said.

The frantic cleanup stopped as Penny froze in place. When she turned around, it was no longer worry and concern that painted her face but irritation, not unlike that of a parent facing a stubborn child.

"You didn't tell me that."

"I was going to. But I didn't want to upset you. It's not the strangest thing to happen in Saint-Ferdinand, so I figured it could wait. Besides, you didn't tell me either."

She frowned, throwing the towel over her shoulder and then crossing her arms.

"Fair enough. I know you're not a fan of Sherbet and I didn't want to upset you. What did your father have to say about this?"

"My dad?"

"Yeah, your dad. Are you telling me you didn't mention this?"

"That his house is haunted? He'd never believe me and would probably think I've lost my mind. He's fragile enough as it—"

"He's lived in Saint-Ferdinand his whole life. He knew about Crowley and this so-called god. He's not going to die over a ghost opening cupboards."

"How are you acting like this is nothing?" he said, agitated. "After the last scare, the doctors said he should avoid any kind of stress. I'm terrified just watching him go up and down the stairs on his own, and you want me to just walk up to him and say 'Oh, Dad? We have spirits in the kitchen. No big deal.'"

"You're worried about that stupid prophecy, aren't you?" Penny frowned.

"Ezekiel said that Dad would die in Saint-Ferdinand and that things that die here don't rest easy. Both of our houses are haunted. Hell, the whole town is probably haunted!"

"Prophecies aren't real, Abe."

"Neither are ghosts or gods or undead little monsters in fur coats!"

"Don't drag the cat into this."

"That," he said, pointing at Sherbet, "is not a cat, Penny. Not anymore."

"Leave Sherbet alone. He's been through enough." Penny paused, seeming to try to compose herself by pinching the bridge of her nose. "Please, talk to your father. He can help us."

Abraham got up from the table and walked back to the front door. Part of him wanted to end the conversation. It made him feel uncomfortable. His father's health had been hanging over his head for years, but never had the thread that held that particular sword ever seemed so thin.

"Where do you think you're going?" Penny asked as he pulled his shoes on.

"Home. And I think you should come with."

For a moment he hoped she would agree, but Penny didn't budge, crossing her arms again instead.

"Why would I do that?"

"So I can protect you."

"I'm no more in danger here than I would be at the farm. What are you going to do if the hauntings become violent? Punch a ghost?"

It sounded silly when she said it like that, but she was right. What could he do to protect her, or himself and his dad, if things changed? If whatever forces were opening cupboards and moving dishes decided to throw knives instead, there was little in his power to stop them.

"I'll go if we talk to your dad," Penny added. "And I need to bring Sherbet. I don't want to leave him alone."

"Leave the cat and we can talk about my dad on the way."

For a moment Penny did seem to ponder the option. Leaving Sherbet shouldn't be a deal breaker, as he wasn't even technically alive.

"Go home, Abe. Talk to your dad. I'll be fine here."

Stupid.

The temperature had dropped since his walk earlier in the day. Fresh puddles of water gave testimony that a cold front had pushed through the area and brought quick showers while he was busy damaging his friendship with Penny.

In the end, they'd accomplished nothing of what he'd set out to do. He was no closer to figuring out what to do with his life, had filled out none of his applications, and, to punctuate the failure, had left all of his paperwork at Penny's.

None of that mattered. He'd left Penelope behind, and that felt like the biggest failure. What if the phenomenon wasn't ghosts? After all, they'd never found out what had happened to the monster after it'd escaped Venus's shed. Perhaps this was a way for it to manifest. Then what? Would it strike at his father, Penny, and finally him?

But Penelope was right. What could he do about it? She'd stabbed the beast with a knife and it'd had no effect. Abraham couldn't punch a god any more than he could a ghost. It didn't make leaving his friend behind feel any better, though.

Abraham turned to give Penny's house one last look, perhaps catch a glimpse of her in the window. Maybe even see her step out, having reconsidered.

Instead all he saw were the blue walls of the house catching beams of sunlight that snuck in between clouds. Distracted, he stepped in a puddle of rainwater.

Normally, he wouldn't care so much, as he'd be wearing thick, steel-toed, waterproof boots. However, he'd worn his good sneakers. Muddy work boots wouldn't have cut it when visiting Penny.

Who am I kidding?

It was pointless. Even if he did wear the right shoes, he'd neglect to shave. If he got the grooming and the footwear right, he'd forget to change and show up smelling of sweat and fertilizer.

By the time he'd gotten home and peeled the sock off his wet foot, his calloused skin was wrinkled and moist. Not to mention the odor.

"That you, Abe?" a tired voice called from the living room.

"Nope," Abraham answered, trying to put a smile in his voice.

The answer that came sucked any sliver of joy right out of him. A wet cough with a life all its own, like something was inhabiting Harry Peterson's lungs and fighting to get out. It was too loud and lasted too long; when it did subside, it was followed by a rattling sigh of both relief and submission.

"Funny guy," Harry said, as if he hadn't been spitting out his life into a handkerchief a second earlier.

"Just got back from Penny's," Abe said, sitting down on the couch across from his old man's favorite armchair.

"Figured."

"Still don't know what I'm going to apply for."

Abraham considered bringing up his fallout with Penelope. However, much like discussing the kitchen cabinets, he worried it would put undue stress on the old man. Looking at him now in the glow of the television screen, he saw every line and every crevice in his gaunt face. He was a blue wraith whose luminescence shifted along with the programming on-screen.

"Didn't you mention cooking school at some point? You're pretty good in the kitchen. Do better than your mother. Bless her soul, she was an angel, but she couldn't even handle the microwave."

Abraham chuckled. Aside from his appearance, Harry seemed well. There was a tank of oxygen on a small cart that followed him everywhere, with tubes going up his nose, but the stubborn old man refused to let it slow him down.

He spent the lion's share of his time in his studio. Abraham always worried that the smell of oils and the fumes from the turpentine would aggravate his health, but he couldn't bring himself to do anything about it. Painting was all that Harry Peterson had left aside from his son and his pride. Taking him out of his studio would lose him two, perhaps all three, if he was resentful enough.

Besides, he had a project—one last painting, he said. He'd claim vociferously that this time, after decades of practice, he'd get it right. This time, it would be perfect.

"Done for the day?" Abraham asked, trying to kick off his remaining shoe.

"Yeah. Eyes are getting blurry. One bad brushstroke and I could be set back for a couple of days. Painting's like a woman: best to take it slow and easy."

"Don't say that."

"Bah."

"Eat anything?" Abraham asked.

"Nah. Waiting for my son the cordon bleu to get home. Have him fix me a gourmet meal."

"Steak-and-cheese sandwich fancy enough for you?"

"Depends if I get a beer with it. A fancy beer."

There had been a time when Harry's doctors would have frowned at the idea of anything but the most sensible food and drink for their patient. Alcohol was certainly out of the question with the potent cocktail of medication that was already on the menu. However, at this point, they'd all agreed there was nothing to gain by depriving a man knocking at death's door the last few pleasures he could get.

Every night, Abraham fixed what he feared would be his father's last meal and brought him his painkillers, though they seemed to have little effect.

They did have fancy beer, though. While not basking in riches, the Peterson household could still afford a few luxuries. In this case, a few bottles of Chimay always stocked the refrigerator.

They ate in silence while watching a few sitcoms on television. It was good. A reminder of the old days, days soon to be irrevocably past.

Abraham wanted to strike up a conversation, to follow Penelope's suggestion and dig into his father's knowledge. But then he'd catch Harry looking at him. He'd look at the old, squinting eyes burrowed deep in their sockets and framed by crow's feet, and he found pride in them.

What was he supposed to do? He could bring up the cabinets or ask about ghosts, but his father already looked like he had one foot in the grave. Abraham was terrified he'd be pushing him the rest of the way.

Eventually Harry fell asleep. Simply staying alive was a chore for the man. Walking to and from the studio with his oxygen tank took as much out of him as a marathon would have in his youth.

Abraham picked up the dishes, taking them to the kitchen, intent on washing them before going to bed himself. Flipping on the light switch with his free hand, his stomach sank.

Not only were the cupboards open, but every single dish, bowl, pot, and glass had been stacked on the dinner table. Neither Abraham nor his father had heard a thing, and no one had turned the lights on in the kitchen—they would have noticed from the living room.

Abraham put the dirty dishes in the sink. He'd have to put everything back. Eyes shut and head hanging from his shoulders, he could feel the full weight of the situation pushing down on him. How much longer before it broke him?

After a minute, Abraham realized he'd been gripping the edge of the sink with so much force that his knuckles hurt. It was a lot to accept for him, but he had to face facts: he was afraid. He was afraid for his dad and for Penny, but also for himself.

Looking up from the dishes and through the kitchen window, looking for his courage in the neglected fields or the outline of the barn, Abraham noticed something.

The lights in Harry Peterson's studio were on.

Either they'd been left on by accident, or Abraham had a new explanation for the cabinets. Maybe it wasn't ghosts or an ancient vengeful god. Maybe it was just a squatter with a strange sense of humor.

Harry's studio was built into the second floor of the barn. The Peterson farm hadn't raised animals in over a decade, so the bottom floor had been converted into a makeshift garage with an immense room above, one filled with dozens of easels and hundreds of canvases. The ceiling was covered with professional-quality lighting that shone upon the room like the midday sun.

He walked between the paintings. Harry had reverently covered each of them with a white linen sheet. It was tempting to peek under a few and see what wonders his father had created, but either respect or a stranger fear kept his curiosity in check. Harry Peterson's paintings were no ordinary works of art.

"Hello?" Abraham called out, listening for any sound of an intruder. There was nothing but his own echo. No shadows moving between easels or sheets rustling as someone hid behind them. A quick walk-through of the studio confirmed that he was the only one there. Him and the giant canvas his father had been toiling over since returning from the hospital.

A staggering eight feet high and easily five feet wide, it, too, was covered by linen, but this time it was the striped fabric of a bedsheet. And even that was insufficient to cover the full height.

A new thought crossed Abraham's mind.

Harry Peterson had once explained to his son that the paintings he made, or attempted to make, were meant to blur the lines of reality. So far he'd only been able to paint birds that came alive within the confines of the canvas. What if he was attempting to push further? What if Harry Peterson's current masterpiece was meant for more?

With a flourish, Abraham removed the sheet, exposing the immense canvas and the work that was consuming so much of his father's remaining days.

Considering what he knew of his father's paintings, he had expected something else. Something more . . .

Alive.

An animal or perhaps a whole menagerie of creatures. Something that might explain the strange things going on in his and Penny's kitchens.

Instead it was a gate. A stone archway built of oil and pigment, but it looked almost real enough to step through.

The landscape beyond was like nothing he'd ever seen. There were rough stones and patches of low grass that swayed in the wind. Lichen covered every rock, and just before the horizon was a turbulent ocean, dark and gray with only the occasional whitecap to break its monotony.

Something bothered Abraham about the archway, but it took a moment for him to figure out what. The gate was covered with a particular pattern, a spiral of lines with the complexity of a rosebush.

These were carved in stone, highlighted by pale moss that had grown within the recesses. He'd seen this design earlier this summer. On the walls of Venus's shed. Except it wasn't chiseled into rock. The pattern had been made of bone, blood, and viscera.

DANIEL

UNTIL A MINUTE AGO, Daniel's plan had been simple.

All he wanted to do was visit his girlfriend's grave in Sherbrooke and, if the time allowed and he felt up to it, take a detour to Saint-Ferdinand on the way back.

He'd spent weeks psyching himself up for this day, steeling his spirit against the emotional strain of finally paying his respects to Sasha and going back to face his friends.

The day had started well. The weather was sunny and warm and he felt brave enough to admit his shame and fears. For the first time in over two months, Daniel held hope he could find redemption in the Eastern Townships and in Saint-Ferdinand.

All he had to do was stay under the radar.

The sun was shining so bright that it took Daniel a moment to even notice the cop car behind him. Only when it used its siren, blaring out a quick burst of sound, did Daniel see the red and blue lights.

Daniel reluctantly put his foot on the brake of his trusty old Civic, gently turning the car away from the road and bringing it to rest on the side of the highway.

He toyed with the idea of peeling off. The glare of the sun on the cop car's chrome bumper made it difficult to see if it was highway patrol or a cruiser from a local town. Sighing in resignation, Daniel turned off the ignition and pulled out his license and registration, praying quietly that there was some mundane reason for the stop.

"Didn't think you'd pull over," the cop said, leaning down to look through the car window.

A wave of relief washed over Daniel. While he still couldn't see the officer's face, silhouetted by the sun as it was, he knew the voice. It belonged to Lieutenant Mathieux Bélanger, Stephen Crowley's second in command. Matt was a family friend. Someone Daniel had known since he was a child.

"Can't say I wasn't tempted to make a break for it," Dan said.

"Not the best car to stage your getaway in."

"Gonna arrest me?"

"Not my preference. I do have a lot of questions though."

Daniel turned down the knob on the AC. With the window open, there was no point in wasting energy. Besides, he needed a moment to think his answer through.

"Any way we can do this without going down to the station?"

Lieutenant Bélanger sat on his haunches and carefully took off his sunglasses. The boy saw for the first time that the events in Saint-Ferdinand had left their mark on Matt, too. His usually phlegmatic features were no longer so. There was fear in his eyes. Fear and a hint of sadness. *Loss too*, thought Daniel. These were all things Daniel saw in the mirror every morning.

"You mind if I sit?" Matt said, gesturing at the passenger seat with his chin.

Bélanger's question was answered by the unlocking sound of the doors as Daniel picked up the disaster of empty fast-food bags that littered the seat.

Bélanger went around and let himself in. Tall and thin, his head was almost rubbing against the roof of the Civic, forcing him to lean back.

"All right. Let's start with the most important question: You doing okay?"

Daniel sighed, stress leaving his body along with his breath. It was more of a statement than a question. It was a declaration that Lieutenant Bélanger still gave a damn. In fact, in the last two months, this was the first time Daniel was having a conversation that didn't involve paying for food or settling the rent for his shitty Brossard apartment.

"Yeah. I'm good. Good as can be expected."

The words came out choked. It was hard not to get emotional. The overwhelming relief of this small and superficial human contact gave him something to hang on to. It also reassured him that maybe, just maybe, getting taken in for questioning wouldn't be the end of the world if it came to it.

"Good. A lot of people are worried about you, yours truly chief among them."

"Who else?"

The way Daniel had left Saint-Ferdinand, he wasn't sure much good faith remained toward him. He'd ditched Penny and Venus, abandoning them to the aftermath of his father's massacre.

"Everyone, Dan. We didn't know if Stephen had kidnapped you, you'd just run away, or worse. Where did you go? Why didn't you tell anyone?"

"I just snapped, I guess. I saw my dad execute a man in cold blood and then fire into a crowd. I didn't know what to do. So I just ran."

Daniel stared straight ahead while giving his explanation. He didn't want to look Matt in the eye and have him spot the deception.

"You should have come to me."

"How? He's my dad, Matt. We're the Crowley Boys. Even if I had anything to say, I don't know that I could have betrayed him."

His voice shook with the last few words. In the end, Daniel had betrayed his father in the deepest way possible.

"He killed seven people. Eight, including William Bergeron." Matt turned his upper body to face Daniel, forcing him to look back. "You understand? Your dad killed his best friend. I don't know what happened to Stephen, but he's not safe to be around. Not even for you."

"I know what you're getting at, but I have no idea where he is," Daniel lied again.

Along with his friends and all the surviving performers and stagehands who were at the circus that day, Daniel knew what had happened to Stephen Crowley. He was dead. Slain by the only person who truly grieved for the man.

His son.

What could Daniel say? *I stabbed him with a supernaturally imbued kitchen knife and his body dissolved into shadows before my eyes?*

He'd had that discussion with the mirror a few times. Did what he remember really happen? Could it have? Or had Daniel lost his mind somewhere during the spring? Relying on his mirror for therapy should have been enough of an answer, but it made him wonder: Wouldn't it be better if he *were* mad? How many of his loved ones would still be alive if it were all part of some twisted fever dream? The lieutenant sighed deeply and shook his head. He looked left and right, as if expecting someone to show up and overhear what he was about to say. Daniel could tell that Matt didn't believe him.

"Don't protect him, Dan. We . . ." Matt hesitated, struggling with what he had to say next. "We have reasons to suspect he killed Sasha."

Daniel didn't know if he was supposed to act surprised at this. He'd learned of his girlfriend's death from Chris Hagen and, after the massacre, come to his own conclusion on the subject.

"I think I already knew that," he said, his tone flat to keep the emotions under control.

"What about Erica Hazelwood? Any idea where she might be?"

Daniel shook his head.

"And Dr. McKenzie or Venus?"

"What about Venus?"

"She's gone. Stuck around a few days and then vanished. You sure you've got no idea where she is? Where any of these people went?"

"I don't know, Matt. I swear."

The genuine surprise at hearing of Venus's disappearance seemed to strike a chord with Matt. The sliver of undeniable honesty gave him purchase enough to believe the rest.

They sat there in silence for a while. For Bélanger, this kind of contemplative silence was nothing out of the ordinary. To Dan, it was a chance to enjoy company for a moment. It was comfortable and reassuring. Which meant, of course, that it couldn't last.

"No way I can convince you to come in for questioning?"

"I won't try to run if you order me, but I'd rather not right now. I'd take it as a favor if you didn't force it."

"Do you swear you have nothing to add at this moment in time that would help us find your father? Nothing at all?"

"I've had no contact with him since he shot up the circus."

Lieutenant Bélanger nodded, satisfied with the answer. He then shuffled his feet and opened the door, stretching one leg out of the car.

"Matt?"

"Dan?"

"Did they ever find Sasha's remains?"

The lieutenant's jaw shifted and set, and his brow knitted itself over his eyes. "We found her body in an old hangar on the Richards property."

"Tell me," Daniel said after a moment of silence. "Tell me how you found her."

Bélanger put his sunglasses back on, but said nothing.

"Matt. He was my dad. I heard about every case you guys worked in the last five years. If you really think he did this, then I want to know what you found."

Daniel could see the man close his eyes even through his glasses. "She was in so many pieces, they buried her in bags."

Standing over the grave of his dead girlfriend, Daniel felt a cold wind cut through Elmwood Cemetery. Occasional drops heralded the coming of rain, but it wasn't enough to shake him from his reverie.

They buried her in bags.

The words reverberated through Daniel's mind, drowning out all the heartfelt words of mourning he had planned for this moment.

He saw instead, as vividly as the recently turned earth, the contents of her coffin.

Clear, hermetically sealed sacs, like morbid sandwich bags, all piled up in a silk-lined box. Each containing some organ or part of a limb, soaking in blood and the fluid that oozed from decomposing corpses.

This wasn't how he wanted to remember Sasha. He'd gone through all the tropes. Buying flowers to leave by her headstone, getting his first haircut since he'd fled Saint-Ferdinand. Even purchasing a cheap suit when he arrived in Sherbrooke. He'd forgotten to get new shoes, wearing his worn sneakers instead.

Daniel tried to conjure up an image of Sasha's intact body, but his mind couldn't keep a firm grasp on it. Her athletic limbs would fall apart and her near-perfect skin would tear and slide off. Organs would slough to the floor in his mind, where they would collect into pools that would then be swallowed by hungry plastic bags. Her face was last to go. Having avoided the predations of age, it now stretched and tightened over her skull, unable to resist the pull of decomposition. Her warm and welcoming smile distorted into a rictus of teeth that would immediately fall out of rotting gums. His imagination, strengthened by weeks of isolation, was poisoned.

Suddenly his right leg pulled back, and with a swing he kicked at a small bouquet of flowers that sat over the grave. It was an act of pure rage, followed by a scream equal parts torture and anger. If there were other people in the cemetery, they'd have thought him mad with grief and they would have been half right.

It wasn't only the hole left in his heart that prompted the outburst, but the possibility that his father had had a hand in it.

Daniel had assumed that it was the monster in Venus's shed who was responsible, and in a way, it very well might have been. In the end, if Stephen Crowley had indeed murdered Sasha, then the creature had been the guiding hand that had made him do it.

This fact only added to the pain and confusion.

How much had his dad been warped so that he would do such a thing? How conscious was he of the corruption? Did he try to resist?

Daniel readied himself to kick another bouquet, but before he could swing his foot, the energy drained from him. Instead he collapsed onto his knees and stared at the scattered white azalea petals.

"You're late," a familiar voice called out from behind Daniel.

The cruel wind played tricks with his hearing, giving the impression that it was his father who had spoken. His heart twisted in place on hearing the subtle Crowley drawl. It was a smoother voice than he remembered. And the question had been asked with more kindness than Daniel was used to from his father. This wasn't Stephen Crowley, just a sadistic trick of his imagination.

Stephen Crowley was dead.

"The funeral was weeks ago."

Daniel turned around, recognition pouring into his grieving mind with the slow drip of suffocating tar.

"Hagen."

Standing a few yards back, hands in his pockets and a bored smile on his face. The strange man who had arrived in Saint-Ferdinand days before the massacre that claimed his father's life was the spitting image of Daniel.

No, not a spitting image. A cleaner, sharper reflection. Hagen's hair was similar but refused to succumb to the winds tousling Daniel's. They both wore black suits that hung from bodies of about the same build, but Hagen had an ease to how he wore his. In fact, Daniel had never seen the man without a tie and jacket.

"Daniel," Hagen said. "Just like a Crowley to be so difficult to find."

Hagen smiled as he walked closer, a hand already extended toward him. He seemed genuinely pleased to see Daniel, something that struck him as strange. Then again, many things about Chris Hagen were strange.

Hagen's odd demeanor momentarily distracted Daniel from the spark of white-hot anger that flared inside him at the mention of his father.

"What are you doing here?" Daniel asked, shaking the cool hand mechanically.

"I'm here to see you, of course," Hagen replied. He read Daniel's face. "I paid off the groundskeeper to give me a call if he ever saw your car parked here," Hagen answered.

"That's a little creepy."

"I know, right? But you didn't leave me any other option, and I think you'll agree that this is important. Dare I say, momentous."

Daniel tried to read the man's eyes, but all he saw were brown pools of emptiness.

"I tried to find that article you said you were going to write about Sam Finnegan. The one you said you were going to interview my dad for. I couldn't find anything by the name Chris Hagen. What happened?"

"Well, for starters, I have to confess that my name isn't Chris Hagen. Also, I was never a reporter."

The news didn't surprise Daniel. He'd given the man the benefit of the doubt, but he'd always suspected something dishonest lurking under the oil-slick facade.

"Then who are you? What do you want from me?"

"Who am I?" His smile broadened to reveal perfect white teeth. "Come on, Daniel, you're the son of a police inspector. Can't you figure it out?"

Daniel tried and it seemed as if the answer were dancing at the tip of his mind, there but elusive.

"My name's Francis Lambert-Crowley. I guess you could say I'm one of the Crowley Boys." The facsimile paused, staring at—nearly through—Daniel. "I'm here to take you home."

Lambert-Crowley. The name struck Daniel. The idea was preposterous, one more layer of deceit. But he knew there was truth to it. In front of him stood a faded memory, the grown version of a face he knew from photos that had long ago been taken off the walls by his father.

"I really can't believe you didn't put two and two together yourself. The name, our ages, and physical appearance? I'm your brother, Daniel."

With these words, the man who had been Chris Hagen spread his arms, as if expecting an embrace. But it never came. The gesture hung there, unrequited.

"You're lying," Daniel said, knowing he wasn't.

"Come on, Daniel. Look at me and tell me you don't see it."

The resemblance was written in every one of their features. The age difference wiped clean some of the similarities, but enough remained that it should have been obvious.

"Why didn't you just tell me?"

"It's complicated," he answered with regret. "I didn't want Dad to know I was in town, but I also wanted to see my brother again."

"What the hell do you want?"

Daniel made no attempt to hide his contempt. Perhaps it was frustration at himself for being so blind or maybe it was the masquerade perpetuated by this "Francis" that got to him, but he was fully prepared to take it out on the man. His balled fist and scarlet face made no secret of that.

"Whoa there, buddy." Francis's hands came up in a show of peace, but his smile, his infuriating smile, remained. "Remember what I said: I'm here to take you home."

"I already have a home."

"No, you don't. At best, you have a house. A cold, empty house. What I'm offering is home. You'd get a roof and a bed and all that, but mostly, you'd have a family."

"No," Daniel answered without hesitation. "You're no brother of mine and you're not a Crowley Boy. You can keep your 'family.'"

Francis looked him up and down, casting an air of judgment at his wrinkled suit and his dark, tired eyes.

"Are you sure?" The question was weighted with disappointment that, under any other circumstances, Daniel might have thought was genuine. "I'm not just talking about myself, you know?"

"Get away from me."

"Suit yourself. If you happen to change your mind, I believe you have my card?"

"Go away!"

Daniel took a step forward, ready and eager to follow through on his implied threat. From the corner of his eye he saw an old couple turn at his scream, but he didn't care. After a moment, Francis waved his hands in a subtle, dismissive gesture before putting them back into his pockets. He turned and, without so much as a backward glance, made his way down the path and toward the gate, leaving Daniel to mourn over plastic bags.

There were several places that Daniel had thought of visiting on his way back to his apartment. After all, Saint-Ferdinand sat between Sherbrooke, where Sasha was buried, and Brossard.

The conversation with Francis had sparked a desire to go home. His real home. He longed to lie on his own bed and walk through the kitchen and living room and find comfort there. Daniel wanted to feel his father's presence, not as he had become, but as he had been, before the world had caved in on itself.

But while one part of him craved this simple solution, another knew that it would be too much. That he wasn't ready. In that house were all the memories of his dad as the dedicated father he'd been for years. The fishing boat in the driveway and the front porch where they'd sat and talked about their respective days would be crushing reminders of all that had been lost. And what if Francis was right, and the moment he crossed the threshold, Daniel would realize it was no longer home?

Seeking out Bélanger also crossed Daniel's mind. It was the logical choice. Matt had known his father for a long time. Maybe he knew about Francis. Maybe they could run a background check and get more information. Sooner or later though, he'd have to explain how his father had died. And how long after that would Daniel try to convince Bélanger that there was indeed an ancient god loose in Saint-Ferdinand?

In the end, he settled on someone who would understand.

"Daniel?" Penelope said through a crack in the door.

All Daniel could see of her was an eye, bluer than he remembered, lost in unkempt blond hair. Daniel hadn't expected his heart to beat this fast. Like a schoolboy, all he wanted in that moment was to pick up and run.

"Where the hell have you been?" she asked, opening the door a few more inches.

Daniel just stood there like an idiot. Staring. He didn't realize it at that moment, but a goofy grin had sculpted itself onto his face.

Penelope waited, a concerned frown hiding in the shadow of her disheveled hair, her blue irises still noticeable despite her squinting eyes. She was pretty, there was no question, but Daniel couldn't be bothered to notice her physical appearance. His mind had instead latched on to something much more important, like a lost sailor disregarding the stars in favor of a lighthouse.

Concern.

"Are you okay?" Penelope asked.

He nodded, still the fool, before being able to articulate a simple "Yes."

She contemplated him a moment longer, the grinning idiot at her doorstep late at night. While she wasn't exactly rejoicing at his presence, the concern, the precious concern, remained.

"Are you going to come in or are you spending the night on my porch?"

"I'd love to come in," he said. "It's freezing out here."

Penny had him sit in her living room and she brought him some hot tea. Daniel and Penny had never been close enough that he'd visit her at home. Looking around, he couldn't quite tell if she'd redecorated since her mother's passing. There did seem to be a mix of old and new, and a lingering smell of fresh paint. It made him wonder, if he ever got back to his own home, how would he handle casting out the ghost of his father? Would he try to keep the good parts of Stephen Crowley echoing between the walls?

"I thought you were more the coffee type," Daniel said, forcing a smile.

"I have work tomorrow. If I drink caffeine, I won't be able to get any sleep at this point."

"What do you do?"

"Who fucking cares what I do, Daniel? Where the hell have you been?"

As much as Daniel hungered for mundane conversation, Penny wasn't going to indulge him in petty comforts. The concern was still on her face, but now it was overshadowed by irritation.

"I've been renting an apartment in Brossard. I couldn't exactly give any references, so it's a pretty shitty place. It's got a bed and running water, but the bathroom is communal and there are definitely rats. It's a dump."

Penelope looked up at him from her mug. She was pissed, and the guilt in Daniel's gut told him she was right to be.

"And the suit?" she asked.

"I was out visiting Sasha's grave."

He didn't really want to play the sympathy card. Penny had also lost her family. While she should be able to relate to his own loss, she just sat there, staring at him, a scientist observing a particularly confusing specimen. She didn't lean in for a hug or offer condolences.

"Why did you leave, Dan?"

"At first I told myself I was protecting you guys. That, if I stayed away, everyone might leave you alone and focus on me."

"My hero," Penny said, sipping from her tea.

The sarcasm didn't go unnoticed. Daniel frowned, tempted to snap back. The weeks hadn't been kind to his moods. He'd realized he had a much deeper connection to the Crowley temper, the quick fuse that had gotten his father in so much trouble throughout his life.

"Hey," he said, "I'm baring my heart out here. So I wussed out. I saw my old man randomly kill a bunch of people. That messes with a guy. I don't know what else to tell you."

"We needed you here," Penelope explained, still calm. "Everyone had your back. Venus, me, Cicero's people. We all covered for you. We kept you out of everything. As far as Lieutenant Bélanger knows, there were two murderers, Sam Finnegan and your dad, and he thinks they're both still at large.

"I get it. You needed time. I guess I just imagined you'd get in touch with us. Plan our next move."

Daniel pressed his palms into his eyes. He hadn't considered a "next move."

"I'm sorry," he said. "I know it's a bad excuse, but I've only just come to terms with everything. Hell, I couldn't bring myself to visit Sasha's grave until today. But you're right. That thing is still out there, isn't it?"

Penny nodded.

Daniel looked around the living room again. He and Penny had followed a strange, parallel path where they'd each lost their only remaining parent. They'd both been orphaned, their plans for the future falling apart in their hands. That one catalyzing event was traumatic enough for each of them, and while he'd run away from the reality, Penny had stayed put and begun rebuilding.

"So, what is the plan?"

"The plan? The plan is you stay over tonight and I'll have Abraham come over tomorrow. Between the three of us, we can come up with a plan."

"What about Venus?"

"Venus decided she couldn't wait for the band to get back together, so she went off on her own."

By the time Daniel woke up the next day, the morning sun was filtering through the thin teal curtains of the living room.

To his surprise, he'd slept well. Better than he had all summer. Ever since Sam Finnegan, the Saint-Ferdinand Killer, had been apprehended, worries and suspicions had bothered him like an irregular background noise. Waking up on Penny's couch, still wrapped in the comforter she'd been using, was an unexpected and welcome relief.

Penny was right. He should have come back sooner.

Daniel yawned and allowed himself a hint of a smile. His home-coming hadn't gone as well as it could have, but it certainly wasn't the catastrophe he'd expected. His initial plan to discuss the revelation Francis had burdened him with, that they were brothers, fell apart. Instead Penny had reminded him that he had purpose. That he had friends. Together, they would make the world normal again.

Turning to his side, Daniel was startled as he felt something leap onto his hip. Surprised at first, his smile widened as he recognized the feeling of Penny's cat, climbing up to demand attention. For a heartbeat, he felt a knot in his stomach. Sasha had owned two cats. But he managed to focus on the pleasant memory of watching her play with her pets instead of picturing the current state of her remains.

"Hey there, buddy," Daniel said, reaching out to pet the creature.

The fur felt strange. It was cool, and thicker than it should have been. It was also loose, but not in any natural way. It didn't slide around the muscles smoothly but rather pulled off of the animal.

Curious, he turned his head to look. What he saw crushed his newborn optimism, and his stomach sank.

Instead of a cat sitting calmly on his side, there was a grotesque creature. A hollowed-out stuffed animal animated by what appeared to be a skinless demon. It looked like a gremlin wearing a fur coat and an awkward cat mask.

Daniel took a deep breath, intent on screaming out in terror as he scrambled to pull himself from underneath the unnatural horror.

Then the thing started purring.

ALICE

THE MIDDLE OF the afternoon was cold and dark to Alice. She could still feel the sun hitting her face during the brief intervals in which it managed to punch a small hole through the clouds. All it did for her sight was intensify the dancing spots that swayed to their own choreography behind her eyelids. Warmth would briefly flirt with the surface of her skin before slowly fading as the light was swallowed up by the sky once more.

Her sense of smell remained sharp, with the cool air carrying hints of leaves on the verge of falling.

Her ears, on the other hand, sensed nothing of her surroundings. Her entire skull vibrated with the steady melody that she sang. The small bones that translated vibrations into coherent sounds suffocated under the onslaught of music. An orchestra of her own biology labored to play the song that Simon, her teacher, had selected for her that afternoon.

At that very moment in time, Alice felt alone. Not the dark and terrible loneliness of her youth; back then she was kept in a room for days on end, like a forgotten doll. When she was bad, Mother would punish her by locking her in the Reflection Room. The lack of light and lack of sound would drive her to the border of insanity.

But while she sang, out here in the woods, the isolation became a blessing. Even with Simon steps away from her, she was completely on her own. All the worries from the compound and the family, all the complaints from Mother about her lack of progress, all the demons, would leave her be. Only the musicians of bone and cartilage and the dancing spots of light in her eyes kept her company. An orchestra and ballet of her own flesh.

Singing was like an adventure. Alice would first fumble and trip as she found her footing, but soon the odyssey would begin and she would be transported along the story the composer had laid out for her and that she was now telling herself. There would be ups and downs, moments of joy and moments of dread. The pure enjoyment of a strong finale would offer a positive denouement and satisfying climax, completing the parallel.

As the last notes of her rendition of Vivaldi's "Winter" departed her throat, leaving behind nothing but the slightest vibration at the tips of her lips, she could feel her lungs burn from exhaustion.

Reality gripped her sense of touch, one limb at a time. First her knuckles demanded release from the tension they were under, then it was her knees that begged to be allowed to bend once more. Her eyes stung as she peeled back her eyelids to see the sun.

When her eyes were able to focus again, she saw Simon still standing in front of her, exactly where he'd been when she'd started. His face was, as always, a buffet of expressions crowned by hair more unruly than Beethoven's. His brow was locked in a permanent expression of judgment that only deepened whenever he heard music. Alice expected it to one day collapse under its own weight. His eyes, on the other hand, were looking glasses that reflected his deep inner fears. Alice knew how scared Simon was of Mother and the other Sandmen. Sometimes she saw the same thing in her own eyes, a background chorus of anxieties and doubts. Of all that went on with Simon's features, this was what she understood best.

Standing there in the cool fall afternoon, Simon's mouth was slack, his lips parted and his jaw sitting a little loose. Without even trying, she'd gotten him just a little under her spell. It wouldn't be the first time. When Alice had first begun to truly brush with perfection, she'd push the line on purpose, seeing how much she could get away with, eager to discover what she could do with the sound of her voice. Simon's mild stupor wouldn't last long, but she knew that a tug on her vocal cords would be a pull on his strings. She knew that, but he didn't.

After a moment longer than he probably realized, Simon shook his head, trying to shrug off the cobwebs in his mind. Alice suppressed a laugh, biting her lower lip in the process.

"Good. Very good," he said, suppressing a yawn. "But you're still trying to replace the instruments of the arrangement with your voice. Make the music your own instead of molding yourself to it."

This was what happened when the student far exceeded the master. Simon would wrestle to find any crumb of criticism just so he'd have something to say. While she had indeed attempted to follow the fast pace of the violins in the original arrangement, it had not been a failure. Her pace and rhythm hadn't faltered. But by that point, Simon was probably too entranced already. He couldn't admit that. The other criticisms were often more technical. Tips and lessons that had resonated well at first. Control your breathing. Open your mouth and be confident. Rely more on your diaphragm. She'd long ago transcended the need for such help.

Alice shrugged, trying not to seem too dismissive. Her training for today was just about done. She would have loved to keep on singing for hours, but what she wanted was irrelevant.

"Maybe this piece just doesn't work," she said.

"It's not meant to," he answered, gesturing for them to start walking back to the compound. "But Mother wants to hear you take on more challenges and expand your repertoire."

"I'm doing my best. My voice is still changing and the season doesn't help. One day it's cold and dry and the next it's warm and humid."

They crested the small hill that gave them the pretense of isolation, hiding the compound from their sight. Trees had started to lose their foliage and looked more naked every day. Jeremy and his wife, Clementine, could be seen sweeping leaves of red, yellow, and brown from the long-abandoned basketball court at the back of the compound. It had been an elementary school once. Built in the seventies or eighties, the place offered spacious grounds, classrooms that were repurposed into dormitories for those who lived on-site, and of course—Mother's favorite—a large gymnasium that could accommodate the entire Church of the Sandmen. There she held her sermons, the spotlight on her and her alone.

From this angle, Alice could see the parking lot. It was filled with cars, as it always was on the days when Mother gathered the congregation. Among them, she could pick out Simon's ancient silver Datsun.

There was a time when, after coming back from practice in the woods, she'd begged Simon to take her with him. To drive her back to her family or to an orphanage, or even abandon her on the streets of Montreal. He'd refused again and again, but she'd begged again and again, until the day he relented and Mother caught him.

She'd spent a solid week locked inside the Reflection Room, a gag in her mouth so she couldn't damage her vocal cords with her screams. It was only removed so she could eat and drink. The torment didn't even afford her time to use the bathroom.

The worst of it, however, was the loneliness. Alice's captivity afforded her very little time alone. Even when hidden in her room, she was always monitored somehow.

The Reflection Room had been designed too small to lie down and sleep in, with too low a ceiling to stand up in, and too dark to see within. It was an echo chamber for one's own thoughts, amplifying the sense of loneliness and isolation.

Simon, too, had paid a price. He'd spent plenty of time in the Reflection Room too, but this offense deserved harsher punishment. Before the incident, Simon would occasionally bring up his family. Alice would live vicariously through his stories of his wife and son. After, Simon never brought them up again and if Alice asked about them, the music teacher would grow quiet and distant. It took some time, but she eventually figured out that Mother had taken that away from him too.

There was a strange hum of excitement as Alice walked into the repurposed school that served as the Sandmen's compound. From the exterior, it might as well have looked abandoned. A squat one-story building with dark brown bricks and intermittent aluminum paneling. Every surface was dusty and water-stained, though the windows were clean, catching the morning sun and blue sky in their reflection. Once over the threshold, however, one couldn't escape the hum of activity. The Sandmen, as a family, were always busy. Outside of curfew, her brothers and sisters would come and go, each preoccupied with their duties.

Alice had always been more fascinated by those who got to leave the grounds. They had the freedom she'd been denied since childhood. Mother called them her "hierophants," and only she stood above them. They got the cars and jobs, but also wore colored sashes denoting their ranks within the family. Simon said it was because they were paying more to be part of the Sandmen.

Mother discouraged Alice from interacting with the hierophants, or anyone who spent much time outside the compound. She'd warned about the temptations of the outside world and the corruption it represented. Only the strongest had the spiritual fortitude to walk outside of Mother's light.

Alice was the weakest. She knew this because of the constant temptation to leave the family. To try to go back into the normal world and away from the safety of the Church. Her curiosity, while encouraged, was tainted by unwelcome desires for freedom. Her sinful nature was so strong that even after having suffered so long for each inch of privilege she had managed to accrue, the voice begging her to flee would not be silenced.

The people she did interact with most, outside of Mother, Francis, and Simon, were the family members who, like her, never left the compound: the cooks and maids and groundskeepers. Like her, they depended on their betters for both survival and salvation. Their lives were as tedious and repetitive as her own. They woke, went about their routine, then went to bed again at curfew, content to have contributed to the cause and moved an inch closer to salvation, whatever that may be.

Except today. Something was different today. The air had the same electricity as when new members joined the family. The excitement of embracing new people and swelling the ranks of the Sandmen, but also the refreshing taste of something new in their lives. Something different to break up the monotony of routine and, perhaps, have a glimpse of the outside world through their eyes.

There were few things that Alice loved more than to sit at the dinner table and eavesdrop on the conversations of the neophytes. Someone else would have worried about their past and the troubles that had brought them to the doorsteps of the Sandmen, but all she wanted to hear about was the real world. Alice knew it was sinful, but she couldn't help dreaming of one day being allowed to leave the compound.

Normally, Alice would have made her way down to her room after practice. Two months prior they had brought a monster in the shape of an old man back to the compound and she had lured it to sleep. Ever since, the rest of the family had started to treat her in a strange new way. She couldn't put her finger on what it meant, and thought it better to remain discreet.

It was a different atmosphere that greeted her today. The usual murmur that rippled through the halls of the compound were at once louder and softer. They were like whispers too pregnant with excitement and curiosity to remain unheard.

Members of the family barely paid attention to her as she walked among them. The temptation to use this opportunity was difficult to ignore. Alice was curious to catch up on any gossip that might have passed over the previous weeks, even at the risk of being asked about the old man again.

She split the difference and went to the cafeteria. There, she could get some tea and lemon juice, perhaps a cookie or two. If confronted, she could claim that her throat felt a little raw and then retreat to her room.

Her voice was always a good excuse behind which she could hide. It was all she was good for. To sing the songs that kept the world spinning. Or the ones that could end it.

The cafeteria was buzzing with people and filled with the smell of roasting coffee and homemade doughnuts. Everyone was gossiping and chatting, clustered in small groups and cliques. A hush came over the gathering when she walked in. For a paranoid moment Alice thought that every single conversation, suddenly aborted by her proximity, had been about her. As talk slowly resumed and eyes were averted from her, she decided she was wrong. They were just afraid. Or they suddenly respected her for her abilities. Maybe these were one and the same.

The strangest thing was how the family was starting to treat her the same way they treated Mother. They would step aside to let her pass. Where she'd once gone mostly ignored by the congregation, no worthier of their notice than the cracked paint on the walls or the streaks on the linoleum, even the highest members of the Church would now nod in her direction.

As was often the case during her singing practice, Mother had conducted a service. Every morning on weekends and once on Wednesday nights, she would gather her flock and improvise her sermons. Inevitably, these events generated chatter. Usually she'd proclaimed a promise or inducted some new recruits. Occasionally the whole sermon would be devoted to the admonishment of a deserter, a member of the Sandmen who'd returned to civilian life. These loud rants would go on later than most and Mother would invite anyone with a grievance toward the deserter to voice their thoughts out loud and in public. These drawn-out complaints would go on for hours, with each new participant doing their best to top the previous speaker with a more fiery accusation. How much was true, and how much was fabrication perfectly tailored to gain Mother's love and attention, was anybody's guess.

Alice weaved through the crowd in the cafeteria. She took particular care to avoid anyone wearing the colors of the hierophants, while nodding to anyone else she knew well enough to. Her goal was the food table. All she wanted was tea and cookies. A lot of cookies. Mother didn't let her indulge in treats too often, even though she kept telling Alice how skinny she was.

There were more than cookies available and more than just tea, but Alice had modest tastes, reaching to fill a plate with oatmeal cookies and a cup with steaming orange pekoe. Satisfied with her feast, excited even, she turned around, hoping to retreat to her room.

"What the hell!" a man's voice cried out.

Alice had just spilled most of her hot tea on Robert Anderson. The red sash over his gray jacket marked him as one of Mother's hierophants. She also knew him as the family's accountant, a powerful man within the Church and outside of its walls as well. There he stood, outraged and furious as the tea cooled and dripped from a stain on his pants.

"I'm sorry, Mr. Anderson. I didn't see you there. I . . ."

She wanted to fill her cup back up and go to her room, but this wasn't something she could voice to Mr. Anderson.

While struggling to find the proper apology, Alice noticed a change in Anderson's features. They seemed to smooth over. The creases and lines that painted his frustration were being erased, and instead a picture of calm came into focus. Before she could figure out what to say next, Robert Anderson's demeanor had become almost fatherly.

He reached around and behind her, grabbing a handful of napkins from the table.

"No need to apologize, Alice," he said, smiling now as he dabbed at his pant leg. "I was just startled. That's all. I didn't know you were here. We hardly see you around anymore."

The incident had drawn the attention of others in the cafeteria. Eileen Fleisher, another of the family's higher-ranked members, looked on from farther down the table. She was one of Anderson's friends—all the hierophants were friends—and seemed curious how Alice would react next.

She felt like an insect trapped in a jar, with enormous faces peering in, hungry to learn of her behavior.

"I . . ." She hesitated, unsure if she should apologize for hesitating or just change the subject. "I should go."

Eyes wide like a scared deer among wolves, Alice tried to sidestep Anderson, hoping to weave out of the cafeteria and away from the crowd. She didn't make it two steps.

"Alice," Anderson said, putting his hand on her shoulder. "Why the hurry? Stay. We'd love to know more about you."

"You have such a beautiful voice, Alice," Eileen cut in, her own voice soothing. "We do all wish we could hear it more."

She must have sensed Alice's fears, complimenting her on something so she'd forget how out of place she really was.

"Thank you," Alice said. Her voice was weak and low. Why were they all being so nice? Why did they even pay attention to her? Usually Mother had to bring her up onstage during sermons to remind everyone Alice even existed.

It was the old man. They all knew how she'd put him to sleep with a song. Looking up and around, exploring the eyes of every silent observer, Alice could see it. The same respect in their eyes that they gave Mother.

"You should sing something for us," Eileen continued, drawing some disapproving glances from those around her. "Just a little."

There was something predatory in her request. Eileen wanted to hear her sing for the same reason she'd slow down at the sight of a car crash. Idle curiosity. Alice was about to politely refuse when Robert Anderson added his opinion.

"Don't put us to sleep," he said with an insincere chuckle. "But we'd love to hear a little song."

"Yes," someone else in the back piped up. "Sing for us."

"Sing!" another voice joined in.

Soon the cafeteria had become its own chorus of demand. Dozens of family members who wouldn't have noticed Alice standing right in front of them a few weeks ago, demanding that she sing for them.

Alice closed her eyes tight, wanting to escape but unable to do more than wish the situation away.

Then, the same way it started, the chorus ended. Each voice went silent, their calls for a song aborted. The quiet washed over the cafeteria like a wave until Alice could hear the squeaking of shoes on the linoleum and the shifting of bodies in the crowd.

"Now, now," said a familiar voice. "Why are we bothering our most important little sister?"

It was Francis. Mother's actual, biological son. By birthright he stood at her side and atop the hierarchy of the Sandmen. The rest of the family feared Francis, even though he never acted anything but pleasantly.

"Alice?" he said from the cafeteria door.

She looked up and through the parting crowd to see him. He wore a black suit and white shirt, like she'd seen him wear every single day for eight years. As always, he was smiling. Hands in his pockets, he beckoned her with a nod, like one would a dog. And like an obedient hound, Alice went to him.

Francis was her savior, her knight in suit and tie. Just like the rest of the congregation, Alice feared him. Not because of his ties to Mother or what they all thought him capable of, but rather because of what she knew he had done.

Eight years ago, Francis had been the one to take Alice from her mother, father, and sister, stealing her in the name of the Sandmen.

JODIE

"YOU PUT HER WHERE?"

Constable Jodie LeSage was already in a dreadful mood. The night had been, up to this point, a complete disaster, and her partner seemed to be on a mission to make it worse.

"A cell? Don't worry—there's no one else in there. I'm not an idiot," Ben said.

"Those two statements contradict each other. Christ, Ben! She's not a goddamn perp."

"You said to put her anywhere but a conference room."

The point was to keep a low profile while they decided what to do with the girl. They'd caught her trespassing on municipal property, but she was both a minor and a first offender. The unspoken policy was to give a stern warning and release, or drive the kid home and let the parents bring down their own wrath. In this case, however, there were other considerations to account for.

"I meant for you to take her to the caf. Get some snacks out of the vending machine. Not stick her in jail. Kinnison is gonna be handing out pink slips when he finds out."

"Nah. The commander wouldn't do that. Besides, he adores you. I'm sure he'll let it slide."

Jodie grumbled a half-hearted acknowledgment. Commander Kinnison did let a lot of things slide. At least a lot of the dumb things Ben would pull off or her own indiscretions when out on patrol.

The two walked through the station toward the small cell block. The whole place felt deserted. They were on the tail end of a shift, and soon everyone on patrol would swarm back in. Until then, apart from civilian personnel and another couple of constables filling out reports, they had the station to themselves. The more important people, like detectives, were in the tunnel near the Laurier metro.

To his credit, Ben hadn't closed or locked the door to the cell, removing the shadow of wrongful incarceration from his deeds. He'd still broken from protocol in half a dozen places, but the girl didn't seem bothered by her predicament. She was still nervous, but compared to when they'd caught her in the subway, or on the ride back to the station, she seemed almost serene.

Perhaps now she'd be comfortable enough to talk.

"Hey." Ben nodded at her as he walked into the cell.

He took a seat next to her on the painted concrete slab that served as a cot and picked up a handful of candy bar wrappers. The girl barely seemed to notice, keeping her eyes on Ben, apprehensive and on her guard.

"Didn't leave me anything?" Ben asked, inspecting the contents of his hands. He had a disappointed look on his face that Jodie knew to be sincere. Like a kid who'd been told he'd miss a school trip. Ben was the archetypal good cop. He had this goofball nature and knee-jerk optimism that could get on Jodie's nerves. He also had a knack for leveraging these qualities to build rapport with people, and she had to admit it made their job a lot easier.

If he took on the mantle of the nice one, that only left Jodie to fill in the shoes of the mean one. She was, despite herself, the bad cop.

Crossing her arms, Jodie leaned on the frame of the cell door and tried to put on her best maternal frown. She doubted that it had the intended gravitas. Closing in on her twenty-sixth birthday, starting a family was the furthest thing from her mind. But she tried her best imitation of parental authority.

"Venus?" she asked. "You still haven't told us what you were doing in the tunnels."

She wasn't the first kid the two constables had caught in the bowels of the transit system. Sneaking down into the subway tunnels to tag the walls or leave graffiti was a popular activity among the teens and troublemakers of Montreal. Venus didn't quite fit the portrait, however. She wore the right clothes: secondhand army fatigues from one of the many surplus stores on Saint Laurent Boulevard, black leather boots, and a thick gray wool shirt. The kind that was fitted to her body, with a tight collar. She even had the typical backpack that hitchhikers favored, the kind meant for camping or traveling.

But everything was a little off. Her hair was too clean, though not by much, and all the clothes, while appearing secondhand, were well maintained. She also looked better fed than most and had no visible tattoos or piercings apart from two empty pinpricks in her earlobes.

Venus busied her fingers with a package of single-serving cookies, looking up to meet Jodie's eyes but then averting them immediately after.

"Some friends of mine dared me to tag a wall." She shrugged. "I thought a subway tunnel would get me extra points."

She was a terrible liar. Every word that fell out of her mouth was forced and hesitant, and within two sentences she'd adjusted her seating position twice.

"Oh yeah," Ben said. "I did dumb stuff like that when I was your age. Peer pressure is a bitch, ain't it?"

Ben followed up his attempt at sympathy with a wink and a nudge of his elbow, but Venus recoiled from him, pulling all of her limbs in a few inches. Jodie doubted that Venus even realized how she was acting. The furtive looks around the room, the short breaths and unblinking eyes, along with the instinctive flinching whenever she or Ben made a sudden move, they were all signs of something.

And Jodie knew what.

She'd left Venus in her partner's care so she could look something up. The name Venus McKenzie rang a bell. It was, after all, a memorable name. Not many people named their kids after Roman goddesses these days. But because of her age, it was unlikely that Venus had been mentioned in the news, which meant Jodie had probably read it in an internal report or while looking up files of high-profile crimes.

Nothing in the past year had been more high profile than the Saint-Ferdinand Circus Massacre, and Jodie had made copies of everything she was allowed to. It wasn't much. The case files were in the hands of the detectives in charge. All Jodie was able to scrounge up were internal memos, APBs, and general-interest reports. It made for about thirty pages of various materials, printed and neatly stapled at the corner. Not much, but she wasn't part of the task force looking for Stephen Crowley. Though everything she needed was in the papers rolled up in her hand.

"What kind of paint were you going to use?" Jodie asked, settling into her role of the hard-ass police constable.

"What?"

"For your tag. What kind of paint did you bring? Or were you going to use a marker?"

"I don't know."

"Show me."

Jodie nudged her chin at the large bag near Venus's feet. But the girl didn't even make a show of looking through it. Instead she set her jaw and attempted to make eye contact again, shying away at the last moment.

"You weren't there to tag anything or paint any graffiti," Jodie said, her fist closing tighter on the printouts. "You were there looking for that dead body. Right?"

The body of Sylvain Gauthier. He'd disappeared only a few days prior, but his body had never been found. Security footage and witness testimony said that he'd fallen to the tracks, but when the tunnels were searched, nothing was found. Someone had taken him, killed him, and brought back his corpse to the scene of the crime.

"No. I found that guy by accident."

"Listen," Ben said, turning toward Venus but keeping a respectable distance this time. "You're not under arrest and you're not in trouble, but you've got to tell us how you knew that body was going to be there and why you were looking for it."

Venus's right hand reached up to her shoulders, pulling at strands of her red hair, her body nervously trying to distract itself from the pressures of the questioning.

Jodie wasn't happy about putting the nails to her like this. It was one thing to interrogate a suspect or ask questions of a witness, but Venus had all the symptoms of trauma. Trauma caused by a cop. She'd had first-row seats to Inspector Crowley executing a man and then pouring gunfire into a crowd. It was tempting to back off and tell Ben to do the same. Drop the whole routine and turn Venus over to a social worker. Kim would be the one on call at this time of night. She was a good one. She genuinely cared about the runaways and delinquents put in her care. Kim would handle this with the attention it deserved.

But Jodie wouldn't do that. Not so long as she thought Venus had information that she wanted.

"I know what you've been through," she said instead. "The circus. Stephen Crowley. Sam Finnegan. That's some scary stuff."

Jodie brandished the rolled-up printouts as a way of making her point. This time Venus did meet her gaze, green eyes locking into her own dark brown ones. There was a surprising intensity in them. A fierce focus and intelligence but also a sort of hollow quality that was unsettling.

"I remember the first time I saw a guy get shot," she continued. "I was working in Toronto at the time. A guy called Richard Clayton. Standard traffic stop. But he had a warrant for drug possession. When Clayton tried to make a break for it, my supervisor pulled his sidearm and ordered him to stop. Of all things Clayton could have done, surrendering or running faster or ducking into an alley, he pulled out a pistol. I heard two shots. Clayton missed, but my super didn't.

"It wasn't what I expected. Clayton didn't just fall to the ground quietly. He crumpled up like a dropped garbage bag. He started screaming. Just nonstop, earsplitting yells. When the pain subsided and shock settled in, he started begging for his mother. It sounds pathetic, but it was terrifying. He was hit in the leg. Artery. There was a thick pool of blood all around him by the time we stopped the bleeding. He barely survived. It all happened in about two minutes. I'll never forget all the screaming, and that was just one guy."

Ben nodded to Venus, acknowledging that it was true and that he knew the tale.

"I know it's not exactly the same thing, but I think I understand how you feel. At least a little."

Jodie expected some resistance to that. After all, what teenager ever agreed to anyone understanding how they felt? Regardless, she hoped that it might help lower Venus's guard. To know that even the cops she seemed to fear also experienced trauma. That what she was feeling was normal.

Instead Venus cocked her head and raised an eyebrow as if she'd just come to her own epiphany.

"Why were you guys there?" she asked.

Before she could stop herself, Jodie turned to Ben, who returned her look. Like two accomplices caught in the act, they exchanged a glance and immediately pretended they didn't.

"Looking for trespassers," Ben said, almost convincingly.

"Doesn't the STM have their own security for that sort of thing?" Venus asked.

"Fine. We were looking for the body. We're cops. It's what we do."

"Okay, but neither of you is a detective. And why are they having you babysit if you're part of the investigation?"

"Hey!" Jodie cut in, surprised at her own tone. "We're not the ones being questioned."

"Is that what this is? 'Cause I'm pretty sure interrogating a minor without her legal guardian is unlawful."

Venus rose to her feet and crouched to pick up her bag, never taking her eyes off Jodie. She'd gone from flight to fight in an instant, but Jodie still recognized the signs of fear.

She could keep Venus at the station. Demand that her legal guardian come and get her—or, failing that, hand her over to Kim.

But that meant processing her and ultimately putting her in someone else's care. There would be no opportunity to get the answers she wanted.

Jodie looked to Ben for a solution and realized what their mistake had been. They were Constable LeSage and Constable Neale demanding answers while in the bowels of Station 38 of the SPVM.

"Ben? Are there still any good burger places open at this time?"

VENUS

THE GIRL IN the mirror was frozen and silent. Her green eyes looked back at Venus while time stood still. Without the passage of time, there was no rush to leave the comfort and safety of the bathroom. There was no pressure to put any clothes on and go back to her would-be benefactors. Venus could stand here forever, warmed by the fading humidity of the shower and the large soft towel wrapped around her.

The emptiness in her eyes was back. It had probably never left. Ever since her first communion with the thing in her backyard shed, she'd had this hollowed-out part of her soul. A cold spot where light didn't refract properly and the darkness was gouged just a little bit deeper than it should be. It was a barely visible scar that stood out to her. A reminder that she was no longer the same Venus who had found the god over the summer.

Part of her longed for the chance to see the magnificent horror again, to have it fill that part of her that had been left empty. If she let her imagination get the better of her, Venus could hear the dark thing calling.

Venus leaned toward the mirror, breaking the spell and starting time once more. It felt odd to be clean after so many weeks of living in cheap motels and student hostels. Had her skin always been this pink? She didn't remember her hair being quite that red, either. She looked like a cartoon character.

Ben had given her a pair of flannel pajama pants and a faded black T-shirt with the name of some obscure metal band screen-printed on the front. Picking it up, she thought about the circumstances that had brought her to accepting his hospitality.

The two cops had taken her to eat after leaving the police station. Both were trying to shed their skin and no longer be constables Neale and LeSage. Wearing instead the shape of Ben and Jodie, average Montreal citizens just trying to help.

Ben made a good show of it and Venus couldn't help taking a liking to him. He had devoured his own meal, quickly stealing fries from both his partner and Venus. His mouth refused to ever close, alternating between chewing and talking. He reminded her of Abraham, who was also a stranger to table manners.

This made it easier to accept their invitation to continue their conversation at Ben's apartment, which was only a few blocks away. Jodie had sweetened the deal by promising Venus she could take a shower there, and have some tea.

Venus had given up so many things to chase after her so-called destiny. She was reluctant to accept the prophecy spoken by her grandmother. Like a bad play on words, it said that Venus would be the one to fight the god she'd held prisoner. There was no promise of victory. Between her natural skepticism and the weight of her friends' lives in her hands, Venus just wanted it all to be over with.

Both the T-shirt and pants she'd been loaned were too big. It didn't matter so much for the former, but the latter felt loose no matter how tight she pulled the string at her waist.

With the used towel neatly folded in one hand and holding her pants up with the other, Venus stepped out of the bathroom. She half expected it to be sunrise or maybe to find the world a hundred years older, but time hadn't slipped through her fingers quite that swiftly. It was late, but it was still just a normal night.

"Toss all that in a corner. I'll put it in with my next load of laundry," Ben told her.

He and Jodie were sitting at a kitchen table. One of those terrible prefab pressed-pine kits bought out of a Swedish warehouse. It was the kind of furniture that her dad had hated. He had a thing for handmade furniture and lamented these things that were built by machines.

"Tea?" Ben asked, pouring hot water into a large mug before she could answer.

"I thought cops were more of the coffee-and-doughnut types," she said, sitting down in front of the steaming mug.

"Makes him fat," Jodie said, sliding a tea bag across the table to her.

Venus sat, looking at the two cops who'd adopted her for the evening. They'd been kind to her. The sort of kindness that made her question their motives. She didn't like being their charity case and suspected some kind of ulterior motive, but at the same time, she didn't want to see every cop as yet another Stephen Crowley. She could tell Jodie had seen the fear in her, so she tried to bury it and prove her wrong.

"So, what do you guys want?" Venus asked, stirring some honey into her tea.

Jodie cleared her throat. "Tomorrow we'll be handing you over to a social worker. You'll love Kim. She's great with kids your age. But before we do that, I wanted to give you a chance to unburden yourself."

"Wait," Ben said. "When did we agree to hand her over to anyone?"

"Well, you're not going to keep her. No pets allowed. Besides, she's a minor. Unless we can get our hands on a legal guardian, we have to hand her over to youth protection."

Constable Ben shook his head with a weak smile.

"I'm not trying to adopt her. But we took her out of the station. We can't simply waltz her back in. I thought maybe we could just bring her back to her parents or an aunt or something. Didn't you say she has an uncle?"

"She's not our—"

"Hey," Venus interrupted. "I'm right here. And I already have a legal guardian."

This wasn't entirely true. Venus had planned, once back in Saint-Ferdinand, that she could meet with the people who'd helped Penelope get back on her feet. Matt Bélanger's sister was a lawyer and had essentially taken Penny under her care, referring her to all the proper authorities. She'd been instrumental in helping her navigate the maze that allowed Penny to remain independent until her eighteenth birthday. "As soon as I'm done with—"

Weariness and the glow of warm comfort loosened Venus's tongue.

"Done with what?" Jodie asked.

"Nothing." Venus clammed up.

"Come on, Venus," Jodie pressed. "Start with Gauthier. You didn't just find him by accident. You were looking, weren't you?"

She leaned back, scrutinizing Venus with her dark brown eyes. The constable looked tired but alert. If Venus were to venture a guess, she'd say that Jodie was invested. Her questions went beyond idle curiosity and just doing her job.

"Fine," she began, putting her face in her hands. "You're not going to believe me anyways."

Ben leaned in, hungry for the tale. Two months prior most people in Montreal wouldn't have known the village even existed.

"You know about the massacre at the circus. You know it was Stephen Crowley who went berserk and shot all those people," Venus continued.

"Everyone from the Saint-Ferdinand police to the RCMP is looking for him and Sam Finnegan." She didn't mention that her uncle was also probably on that list. "But that's because they don't know that Stephen Crowley is dead. And I expect Sam Finnegan is too."

Jodie leaned over to dig into her bag, fishing out the papers she'd been brandishing back at the station. She leafed through them, pausing to lick her thumb every two pages, until she stopped and put the document flat on the table. She pointed at a paragraph near the bottom of the page.

"Here. And next page too. All testimonies saying that Crowley fled from the scene."

"He didn't. He never left Abraham's . . . the Peterson farm."

A brief moment of silence passed across the table. Even Ben didn't dare break it with a comment or question.

"Okay," said Jodie. "Let's assume you're telling the truth. What does that have to do with Gauthier?"

Venus could feel the tips of her fingers burning at the prolonged touch of her mug. White knuckles, strained by the effort, kept them in place despite the pain.

"Stephen Crowley was at the head of a group in Saint-Ferdinand, a cult calling themselves—"

"The Sandmen," Jodie interrupted. "Or the Church of the Sandmen."

The way she was leaning over the table, Jodie might as well have been a panther ready to pounce. Whatever it was that interested her about the Sandmen, it must have been important, even personal. The hunger in her face made Venus hesitate. Only after stealing a glance at Ben, seeing how he remained interested but relatively calm, did she choose to push on.

"The Sandmen," she repeated back to Jodie. "Why are you interested in them?"

"Well," Ben jumped in, "it's a common thread between the deaths that they were all known members of the Church. Also . . ."

He didn't finish his thought, turning to his partner to elaborate further.

Jodie's eyes had broken from Venus's somewhere during the conversation. Instead they drowned in the shallow remains at the bottom of her mug, reflecting on an inner focus. She took a deep breath, as if she were ready to dive into dark waters, and started her own tale.

"My sister was, or is, Alice LeSage . . ." she began, leaving a pause to gauge whether Venus knew who she was talking about.

"When I was maybe a few years older than you, Alice was kidnapped from my parents' house. I was away at my first year of uni and not home, but whoever's responsible, they took her right under my parents' nose.

"Two years ago, before I got partnered with Ben or started work-ing in Montreal, I was doing traffic in Laval. Someone called in say-ing they'd seen a girl of about thirteen walking along the side of the road, looking scared and disoriented. The guy gave a description of the girl, and I got it in my head that it was my sister."

A lot of conflicting emotions seemed to fight for dominion over Jodie's features during her explanation. Anger and loss were caught in a duel that the constable's stoicism struggled to hide.

"How does that tie back to the Sandmen?" Venus asked.

"After a few hours of searching, we were told to assume she'd been picked up and that she must have been some hitchhiker. But I kept looking. There were a few places within walking distance of where she was seen, but there was one place that stood out. One building that was closer yet more isolated than any of the residences we looked at. I went to that place. I talked to the residents. Everyone was pleasant and friendly, but they all stank of lies. Maybe I just don't deal well with the zealot types, but I couldn't accept anything they were saying when they assured me that no one matching the descrip-tion of the hitchhiker lived with them."

Jodie's jaw started to tremble and her eyes closed tight. She wres-tled with the memory a moment longer before she reopened her eyes and continued.

"I got reprimanded for acting above my authority and was given strict orders to never again go anywhere near those people or I'd lose my job. I was told that it wasn't my sister and to put the matter out of my head. Venus, that place was the Church of the Sandmen."

Venus remembered Alice LeSage. There had been a lot of news and media around her disappearance. Most parents had kept a closer eye on their kids after Alice vanished. Most, but not Venus's.

"In the eyes of the law, the Church of the Sandmen is a legitimate religious organization," Ben said. "If you ask me, though, they're just another end-of-days cult, like the Order of the Solar Temple."

There was no love for the Sandmen around Ben's kitchen table, that much was clear. Venus could feel a softening of her resolve, its integrity melting under the warmth and sudden connection with

Ben and Jodie. She and her friends had resisted going to the authorities in Saint-Ferdinand and with everything that had happened with Crowley, she thought that option was permanently off the table.

Her tea had cooled along with her apprehension. She parted her lips, ready to lay down a full confession of what she knew of the Sandmen and what had really happened in her little village. But Jodie beat her to it.

"Well, the good news is that now you can put all of this out of your mind," she said.

"Pardon?"

"Your little investigation," Ben picked up after his partner. "I gotta say, I'm impressed by how resourceful you've been, but Jodie's right—you have to give it up now."

"What? No! I'm way more a part of this than she is!"

Jodie shook her head and tried to force the condescension out of her smile. "You're just a kid. Whoever killed Gauthier is clearly dangerous and remorseless. We can't, in good conscience, allow you to keep playing junior detective."

"'Junior detective'?" Venus was outraged. "You just said you were little more than traffic cops. At least *I* know what happened to Inspector Crowley."

Ben tapped his mug on the table twice. "About that, we're going to need you to give us every detail you can. And anything else you might know about the killer."

This time it was Venus who put her mug down, albeit in a more forceful manner. With a crash, she stood, sending her chair falling backward, and slammed her hand flat on the surface of the table.

"Screw that!"

"Venus, please," Jodie said, attempting to soothe her.

It didn't work.

"For a second I thought you guys were going to help me out. I know more about this than you do. More than whoever's in charge of the investigation. I don't need your help!"

It was like an epiphany. Through the rage she could see that she really didn't need their help. She knew about the god, about what had really happened to Crowley, and who Sam Finnegan truly was.

"You need *my* help."

It wasn't quite accepting the prophecy spoken by her grand-mother. The whole concept of destiny still rubbed Venus the wrong way, but she could suddenly see the role she had to play. Sheepishly, she turned to pick up her chair, righting it and sitting down again, embarrassed by her outburst.

"Venus. Whatever you tell us, we'll bring it to the task force and they'll handle it." Jodie tapped on the stack of papers in front of her. "It says you lost your dad over the summer. Wouldn't you prefer to have some time to grieve properly? What could possibly be more important than that?"

She did want to grieve her father. Her relationship with Paul had been a strange one, but he was a good man and he had loved her. Above all else, however, she wanted revenge, and every time she allowed that hate to bloom, she could trace its roots all the way back to the god. She could still hear it calling to her.

ABRAHAM

ABRAHAM HAD ALREADY been awake and busy in the kitchen by the time he got Penny's message.

As per his daily routine, he'd gotten up at the crack of dawn, checked in on his old man, and went down to prepare some breakfast for the both of them. To his relief, every cupboard had remained closed overnight and the dishes he'd put back in place for the umpteenth time had stayed put.

Breakfast wasn't a complicated affair in the Peterson home. Eggs and either ham or bacon, with a side of toast. His father's portion was smaller, but also came with a generous side dish of medications.

Hey. Come over? 8-ish?

Abraham smiled. He'd been looking for an excuse to check up on her. He also wanted her opinion on his father's painting. She'd insist they include Harry in the conversation, but maybe that wasn't such a bad thing.

Sounds good.

When Abraham got to her driveway, however, his attitude quickly soured.

There was a white Civic sedan parked behind Penelope's car. He knew that car as well as anyone in Saint-Ferdinand. It was Daniel Crowley's Civic. The boy who'd killed his own father.

Abraham and Daniel had never been friends, the same way most coworkers aren't. They shared the same spaces: school, their hometown. But they hardly ever talked.

Venus and Penny had explained Daniel's role in the massacre. How he'd saved the circus performers by killing Stephen Crowley. From a logical perspective, Abraham understood. Crowley had done what he'd had to do. However, he couldn't bring himself to imagine doing the same, and from an emotional point of view, couldn't understand what Daniel had done.

Worse was the disappointment of realizing that this was about Daniel, not him. Crowley had reentered the picture and that was why Penny wanted him over.

"Why are you standing out there?" he heard Penny call out.

While he'd been procrastinating, she'd spotted him and opened the door. Her hair was messed up and she was still wearing a thick terry cloth bathrobe. The morning sun caught on her blond mop, giving it a strawberry tint as she frowned at him.

"I wanted to apologize," he said after walking in, holding two brown paper bags in front of him.

Penny took the packages, raising an eyebrow in the process.

"Apologize for what?"

"Calling Sherbet a monster."

"The cat is what you want to apologize for?"

"Not really. It's just the easiest thing to start with."

She gave him a little smile, which he took to mean that she understood. Something about the morning light made her eyes look even bluer than usual, which in turn made his heart melt.

"Don't worry about it," she said, leading him inside. "You're not the only wuss."

Abraham walked in and kicked off his boots. Stepping out of the entrance, he saw what she meant.

Daniel Crowley sat on Penny's couch, fully dressed in a wrinkled suit, minus the jacket. He looked like he'd just come back from a bachelor party or a particularly rowdy wedding. The teen who had, at one time, been *the* guy at their school, had his feet raised from the floor and his back firmly pushed into the back cushion of the couch. He seemed caught between running for the door and digging into the cushions for safety. It was a hilarious image, but Abraham couldn't bring himself to laugh.

On the floor, the source of Crowley's fears stalked back and forth. Sherbet, the cat who had been turned into a mockery of life, was now hunting Crowley's toes. It had been a sweet and adorable creature when alive, proud of its thick coat of silky charcoal fur. Venus had loved that cat more than Abraham could understand anyone loving a pet.

Sherbet had been Venus's only friend when moving to Saint-Ferdinand and that, at least, made some sense.

The thing that prowled around Penelope's house, however, was no longer an adorable and affectionate feline. It was an abomination. Stripped of skin, fur, and life, Sherbet walked around with exposed muscles, pawing at everything and fixing guests with his unblinking eyes.

Penny had fashioned a sort of costume out of an old stuffed animal, but the accoutrement was unconvincing and made the cat look even creepier. A four-legged flayed zombie was hard enough to stomach, but the fake fur gave it the appearance of a demonic marionette. If nothing else, Abraham and Daniel could bond over their revulsion for the thing.

"Oh! What's this?" Penny asked in a singsong voice. She'd dug through one of the bags he'd handed her and pulled out a sack of cat treats and a foam ball infused with catnip. "Look at what Uncle Abe brought you, baby. Look!"

Penny crouched down and bounced the ball in front of her feet, attracting the animal's attention. Sherbet pounced toward the new toy, forgetting all about Daniel Crowley's toes.

When the cat got close enough, Penelope grabbed it from the floor and swung it into her arms. Abraham could hear the thing purr from across the room. She cooed at the little beast with a disturbing amount of affection. It was too weird. His mind couldn't process that level of strange.

"I brought us some breakfast," he said, hoping she'd leave the cat alone for a moment. "Didn't know you had company."

His voice felt impotent as he pointed weakly toward the second bag. This one was larger. A brown paper bag speckled with grease stains. It looked like a bag of fries from a cheap fast-food joint.

Penelope ignored him for a few more seconds, focusing on playing with Sherbet and offering the cat some of the treats Abraham had brought. She whispered into the holes where his ears would have been, telling him how he was the "pwettiest widdle kitty."

Eventually, and to both boys' obvious relief, she put Sherbet down and gave him a pat on the rump to send him along. Penelope's eyes shifted between the two of them, contempt and amusement fighting for dominance.

"You cowards want coffee?"

Both he and Daniel nodded like a pair of synchronized idiots.

Abraham unzipped his coat and went to sit down in the living room. He'd always been able to allow events to wash over him. He was a stone. A boulder that let the river flow around it undisturbed. Anchored by boundless—some would call it naive—optimism, he never faltered in his role as a friend. He was there when needed, absent when not.

Something had changed and it was impossible to put his finger on what. Certainly, tragic events had had their transformative effect, but this was Saint-Ferdinand. Tragedy would have been the name of the village's baseball team if it had been big enough to have one. He and Penny had gone through this before, too. Five years ago, when her father had disappeared. Abe had been there for her. When his own father had gone through chemotherapy for the first time, she'd accompanied him to and from the hospital. None of this was new. Things should still be the same.

Except they weren't.

There had been a monster in Venus's backyard shed, her pet was an undead abomination, and now Penny was hosting a murderer in her house.

Daniel was sitting on Penny's favorite comforter. From the flat creases and how it was partially stuffed into the cracks and recesses of the sofa, it was obvious someone had slept in it.

"Abe? Abraham?" Penny's voice finally broke through.

She was holding a mug of coffee in front of him. It steamed in the cold air. It was an odd thing to notice. The heating hadn't been turned on in the house yet and he was still wearing his coat. He mumbled an apology before taking the mug.

"So, what are you doing here?" he finally asked Daniel.

The other boy was mid-drink and seemed lost in his own thoughts. His eyes tracked Sherbet's movements like a swimmer would a shark's fin in the water.

"You have to kill that thing." Daniel ignored Abraham's question.

"Pardon me?" Penny answered, outraged.

"It's been touched by the same god that made my dad into a monster. It's going to turn on you."

"I am not killing Venus's cat," she declared.

"I'll do it for you if it's too difficult," Daniel said.

He stood up, signaling that all she had to do was say the word. To Abraham's relief and perhaps even surprise, there was no joy or eagerness in Dan's actions. This was duty, and duty Abraham could understand.

"Can he . . . it . . . be killed?" Abraham asked.

"That's a good point," Daniel said. "It's probably not even technically alive right now."

"You are not having this discussion in my house," Penny said.

"It's not like I want to harm the little guy, Penny. But what if he becomes dangerous? It's probably not a bad idea—"

"No. Not in my house."

Then a realization seemed to hit Daniel. A painful eureka moment for the current situation.

"The knife. I still have the knife. It's in my car," he said.

"What knife?" Abraham asked, a moment before it dawned on him. "Oh. The knife."

Abraham had seen a god only once in his lifetime and it had been locked in Venus McKenzie's backyard shed. On that night, Penny had tried to kill the thing, stabbing it with a chef's knife.

"No," Penny repeated.

She threw her mug at Daniel.

It hit him square in the left temple and shattered on impact. Scalding brown liquid covered his face and the collar of his shirt. Shards of ceramic fell to the ground in a crash as a bloom of red flowered just above his eye. Coffee was everywhere, staining her favorite comforter. Penelope wasn't one to back down from smacking someone, usually Abraham, behind the ears, but she'd never thrown anything, let alone a ceramic mug, at anyone.

"Get out of my house, Crowley!" Her voice trembled with rage.

"What the hell?" Daniel rubbed his head and looked at the blood on his hand.

"Out!" Penelope screamed.

There was something in her crystal-blue eyes, in the way she stood and how her fists were clenched in tight white-knuckled balls, that stopped Daniel's protests before they made it out of his mouth. Sherbet, standing between her feet, hissed for emphasis. Daniel froze for a moment, his own outrage draining out of him along with the color in his features. He was seeing something in Penny that Abraham couldn't recognize, or perhaps coming to some other realization, but it was enough to make him shut up and walk to the door.

"Fine," he said.

Without further protests, but never taking his eyes off Penelope, Daniel put on his sneakers, not bothering to tie the laces, and silently backed out through the door.

Both Abraham and Penny stood in silence, listening to the sound of the Civic's engine coming to life. It took a few minutes before they heard the car pull out of the driveway and fade into the distance. All the while, Abraham watched his oldest and dearest friend shivering with a fury he'd never seen. No, not fury. Nothing so transitory. Hatred.

Yet, like a simple-minded fool, the wrong words were tumbling out of his mouth before he could stop them.

"He's not wrong, you know," he said, loathing himself for it.

She didn't throw any coffee at him as he'd feared. In fact, his statement seemed to calm her down a little. Her muscles relaxed and her features evened out for a second before melting into melancholy.

"What that thing did to Sherbet ain't natural. Best put him out of his misery."

"What about me, Abe?" she said, swallowing an aborted sob.

He scrambled to think of how to pull his foot from his mouth. While he tripped all over his tongue trying to find the right words, his brain was also tying itself into a knot, chasing the proper course of action. "Take my hand," she said, offering up the limb. "Go ahead. Take it."

Comfort, then. He sighed and tried to offer a sympathetic smile. Comfort, he could provide. No one had ever accused him of being a charmer and he was too awkward to be suave. To call him socially clumsy would be generous. However, if nothing else, he had perfected the art of giving comfort. Long arms and big hands attached to a soft but powerful body made him perfect for long, reassuring hugs that he was more than happy to provide.

Abraham reached out and took Penelope's hand in his. Her fingers were minuscule in his paws, delicate but beautiful with a touch of color at the ends, where her nail polish was chipping. He expected her skin to be warm, heated up by the mug she'd just thrown at Daniel and the anger that had coursed through her veins.

However, when their skin touched, her flesh was ice, colder even, somehow. So cold, in fact, that it burned. It reminded him of touching carbon ice in science class. The brick they'd been given to experiment with constantly gave off a thin mist instead of melting into a liquid. They all took turns applying house keys to its surface and listening to the metal squeal as it cooled.

That was how cold Penelope's hand felt. He yelped and tried to pull away, but she quickly grabbed him, nabbing his index and thumb in her fingers.

"What about me, Abraham?" she repeated, tightening her grip and her features. The irises of her eyes almost glowing with the intensity of their cobalt hue. "The god bled on me when I stabbed it. Everywhere its blood touched me feels like this now. Are you going to put me out of my misery too?"

"Penny . . ." Abraham pleaded.

Her tears were flowing, but her grip was that of a titan. The pain in Abraham's fingers had gone from a scalding sensation to a numbing cold and unhealthy tingle.

"Do you think I'm a threat? That I'm going to turn on you? Am I too much of a risk to be allowed to live?"

The questions were manic and increasingly difficult to make out. His hearing felt like he'd been plunged underwater, muted as he sank deeper into the pain of his hand.

"No!" he screamed, both as an answer and final plea to be released.

And so, she did.

Abraham fell to his knees, clutching his fingers, attempting to rub some sensation back into them. He tried to bend them, but the knuckles felt like they were going to explode. When he looked up at his friend, she was still standing there, looking down at him. Her eyes were puffy, her lower lip quivering.

When he started pulling himself back to his feet, she took the handful of steps needed to get to the front door, which she swung open. After unceremoniously kicking his sneakers out onto the porch, she stuffed her hands back into the pockets of her terry cloth bathrobe and stared back at him.

"Out."

In no conceivable way could that have gone worse.

Abraham went back and forth on what had gone wrong as he started the long walk home. The easy answer was to blame Daniel. His attitude toward Sherbet made sense to Abraham. But it was too much to ask that Penny allow the cat to be killed. They just needed to lock it in a cage, preferably in a separate house.

But things were more complicated than that. Something was terribly wrong with Penny herself and he'd somehow failed to notice.

He'd seen the black blood coating his friend's forearms after she'd stabbed the monster. He'd been the one to push her out of harm's way at the very last second. The insidious infection that had been left behind, however, had failed to register with him, and now it might cost him his friend. It was one more item in the list of things Abraham felt powerless to handle.

"Hey, Peterson." The familiar voice interrupted his pity party.

It was Daniel Crowley. He'd parked around the bend on the side of the road, a defeated look tarnishing his otherwise enviable features. He'd been waiting there for Abraham, who'd been so caught up in his own world that he'd almost missed the familiar car.

"Here." Crowley reached out of the car window, handing Abraham a folded oil-stained dishrag. He held it with reverence and care as if it were a precious artifact.

"What's this?"

"Check it out for yourself," Crowley answered. "Careful. It's sharp."

Abraham knew without unfolding the cloth. It was the knife. It had never dawned on him the significance of the object. It was a murder weapon but also the instrument of vengeance Penny had tried to use against the god.

When he did unfold the rag, oil staining his fingertips in the process, Abraham marveled at how mundane the blade looked. If what Penny had told him was true, this was a weapon that could cut the flesh of ghosts and had put an end to Stephen Crowley when shotgun blasts had failed.

"Feels heavy," Abraham said.

"It does, doesn't it?"

Abraham tried to hand the kitchen utensil turned murder weapon back to Crowley, but the other boy refused, backing a few inches into the interior of his car, hands up and open, as if to avoid taking the knife back by accident.

"Nope. It's yours now."

"I don't want it, Crowley."

"You're gonna need it, Peterson," Daniel continued, leaning out again from the driver's-side window. "Listen. I see how you look at her. I get it. If you feel that way, you can't let that cat stay in her house. You just can't."

"I'm not gonna just go in there and stab her cat. Hell, it ain't even hers. It's Venus's, and she'd murder me if I so much as touched a whisker on its face."

But all Crowley could do was shake his head and give a small, disappointed smile. It was as if Abraham had given the wrong answer to an obvious question.

"You don't get it. Do you really feel safe knowing that something touched by that evil thing lives under the same roof as Penny?" Crowley frowned out his windshield as he marshaled his thoughts. "Look, you don't want to lose someone you love just because you couldn't do something difficult. That cat was touched by that demon. It's why it won't die." He turned back toward Abe now, ready to finish the thought. "Like my dad."

He gripped the steering wheel, knuckles white with the effort, eager to leave. He closed his eyes, but Abraham could see it as a weak effort to shut in his tears.

Abraham took a step back, folding the cloth over the blade.

"You can't be afraid of doing something difficult for the greater good. Do you understand?" Crowley said.

Abraham didn't think Daniel expected an answer, but he nodded anyway. Venus's cat, the god that had been locked in her shed, Sam Finnegan, and the circus massacre—they were all things that wouldn't simply go away. The ghosts of Saint-Ferdinand wouldn't rest without help.

Daniel averted his eyes and pulled one hand from the wheel, letting it drop to the ignition key. For the first time, Abraham got a good look inside the car. The passenger seat was littered with empty bags of fast food, some grease-stained and others with the tops of disposable cups poking out from the opening. While he didn't know Daniel well, he was as aware as anyone of how obsessive he'd been about his Civic.

"How about you?" Abraham asked. "What are you going to do? Gonna disappear again?"

Daniel Crowley didn't bother to turn his head to answer, leaving the window open only a crack so he could be heard.

"Yes and no. I think," he said, "I think I have a family reunion to attend."

Abraham's thoughts were in a dark place when he got to the bend in the road in front of the Richards farm.

Crowley had driven off without any further ceremony. For a second, Abe had thought of asking him to come stay at the farm. It was the charitable thing to do, but there was something about Daniel's attitude that had made him keep the offer to himself.

There was a dullness in Daniel's eyes that had made Abraham sad for the boy. Though he'd mentioned a family reunion, he looked like someone heading to a funeral. Slow of thought and decision, the opportunity to make the offer had slipped and Crowley had driven off, leaving Abe with a dirty rag and a murder weapon.

He was in no hurry to go home, or anywhere for that matter. Daniel and Penny were right: Abraham had to do something, even if it meant losing the people he loved. It wasn't just Daniel who'd placed the knife in his hands. It was destiny.

Across the road from where he walked, dragging his feet on the way home, one of Saint-Ferdinand's most tragic calamities had occurred. Within days of the Saint-Ferdinand Killer being caught, as the village had sighed in relief, another victim had been discovered: Penelope's mother. He'd heard that the scene was like a slaughterhouse. Some had compared the carnage to a bear attack. While Abraham got shivers just thinking about it, something was compelling him to take a step forward. Then another. So, he went, barely looking to the street for oncoming traffic.

Abraham hadn't bothered to visit the site himself. At this point, it would be just like any other patch of forest. Every piece of evidence and all remains would have been removed by the authorities. Maybe a stray length of yellow plastic tape or a discarded blue rubber glove, but nothing to mark the area as anything special. Morbid curiosity had a draw of its own, however, and there was an almost supernatural pull to the murder site. Or perhaps he was still procrastinating getting home.

Don't.

A voice, probably his imagination, warned him away. Or was it guilt at his own curiosity?

You're scaring me.

His pace didn't slow, despite the strange new voice echoing from his subconscious. Abraham chose to interpret it as a manifestation of his own fears. It had been a long twenty-four hours rife with oddities. This new twist shouldn't come as any surprise.

Abraham. Please.

A gust of wind blew between the trees. While the weather was getting colder, it wasn't quite so deep in autumn yet. Leaves were still on their branches and the sun was strong enough that by midday he wouldn't need his coat any longer. The wind shouldn't reach this far into the woods and certainly shouldn't be this glacial. He could see his own breath as he exhaled, a hallmark of the coming winter that should still have been several weeks away.

Puddles of rainwater from the previous day rippled for a moment and were soon covered in frost. Abraham's cheeks stung with the cold and his lungs burned as he inhaled. The fingers that had suffered in Penelope's grasp ignited with freezing pain all over again, nearly forcing him to drop the knife.

Unease turned to fear and Abraham tried to backpedal. His eyes watered in the cold, but he refused to blink, terrified of what might happen if he did.

"You're scaring me."

The voice wasn't his own. He realized that now. It was small and rang like bells. A shy, scared little thing that echoed in harmony with the arctic gusts weaving between the trees. He knew that voice. He'd helped Penny babysit its owner. He'd given her piggyback rides and played Candy Land with her.

"Audrey?" he asked.

And there she was, stepping out from behind a tree. Pale and fragile, like a forgotten porcelain doll. Still the same eight-year-old girl she'd been on the day she'd died, but ethereal and luminescent.

She wore the same elaborate white dress her parents had buried her in. Wisps of her platinum hair, now glowing in the shadows, seemed to flow in a different wind. Her naked feet were buried half an inch into the hard soil, bare and immaterial.

"Help me, Abraham . . . ." she pleaded, turning to face him.

Abraham had been told of Audrey's ghost, but despite expecting her visage, he was still taken aback. Where her eyes should have been were two empty holes. She looked alive if not for that and the paleness of her skin. The only touch of color a red felt hat on a teddy bear she clutched in her small arms and a streak of blood from a cut on her left cheek.

Driven by concern, Abraham took a step forward, hiding the rag and knife behind his back. "It's okay, Audrey. I won't hurt you. It'll be okay."

"I can't see, Abraham." Her voice was choked with terror, every word almost a sob. "Help me. Help all of us."

DANIEL

PUTTING THE KNIFE in Peterson's hands had been like closing a door. Having held on to the patricidal blade had been more of a burden than Daniel had realized at the time. Even out of sight, wrapped in a rag on the back seat of his car, the mundane chef's knife had kept the events at the circus fresh in his mind.

Reuniting with his friends from Saint-Ferdinand hadn't helped. Having killed his father, Daniel had crossed the proverbial Rubicon. Sliding that blade into Stephen Crowley's neck had changed Daniel and set him apart. He could see that now.

It wasn't simply that Penny didn't have what it took to fight back against the monster they'd faced during the summer. The stakes were different. The god from Venus's shed was woven into the Crowley family's fabric, but Daniel had only ever known a fraction of that family.

Maybe that was why Venus, too, had left Saint-Ferdinand. She was chasing after her own family's past. Hopefully the knife would make it into her hands and all that prophecy garbage could sort itself out. It wasn't like Daniel to pass on a burden like this, but it wasn't something he could carry where he was going.

Keeping one hand on the wheel, Daniel fished out a business card from his pocket. It had seen better days, traveling from his nightstand back in Saint-Ferdinand to his glove compartment and then eventually to his wallet. The ink had faded, rubbed off from weeks stuck between a student ID and a seldom-used credit card.

Thoughtfully, Daniel rubbed his thumb on the sigil of an hourglass with wings. The logo of the Sandmen had been the first thing that had pulled the rug out from under his feet and sent him tumbling down the hellhole his life had soon become.

Chris Hagen, the card read in unassuming lettering. Except the *s* was almost completely swallowed by a deep crease. Underneath the name was a perfectly legible phone number.

With a shaking hand, Daniel pulled out his cell phone. His eyes darted from the phone to the road as he punched in the number. For a moment he considered canceling the call. He still had money stashed away, enough to move across the country if he needed to. Or he could go back and make good on his promise to talk with Matt. Maybe he could make the lieutenant believe all the crazy shit from the circus. Instead he put the phone on speaker and tossed it onto the dashboard.

"Daniel?" the phone squawked weakly.

"Hagen?"

"Call me Francis."

Daniel thought back to the previous day. He'd been standing over Sasha's grave, bemoaning his loss and drowning in self-pity. It was Francis who'd shocked him out of it by revealing who he really was.

"I gave it some thought," Daniel said, speaking loudly so as to be heard over the engine. "I'm in."

"Are you sure? I thought you were going back to your friends."

"I am. I did." Daniel hesitated. "I wanted to check in on them first."

"Dan. I can call you Dan? You make it sound like you're moving to another planet. You'll see your buddies again. In time."

It didn't feel that way to Daniel. Even if he'd left on better terms, there was a certain finality to accepting the offer. Francis had been ambiguous about the whole thing. He'd talked of a place to live and a family, but what had put its hooks into Daniel was the mention of his mother.

Marguerite Crowley had left him and his father when he was little more than a baby. Any memories he had of her were from the few photos Stephen Crowley had reluctantly showed him. She was the woman who'd abandoned them. In a way she was the reason they called themselves the Crowley Boys.

Now she'd sent a brother who Daniel didn't know he had to retrieve him. There were so many unanswered questions, how could he refuse?

"Daniel?" the voice came from over the phone, shaking him from the memory.

"Sorry. I was just thinking."

"Not getting cold feet, are you?"

"No. Not at all. I've got nowhere else to go anyways."

Daniel could almost hear the smile stretch over Chris Hagen's face through the phone. It was the subtle, unheard sound of victory.

"Well, that's what family is for, Daniel. When you hit rock bottom, we'll always be there to pull you back up."

It was too much to ask that Daniel's reunion with his estranged mother be somewhat normal.

There was no house at the address Francis had given him. There was barely a neighborhood. Someone had clearly planned for a development of some sort in the area, but something had aborted the project in its early stages. Streets had been paved and plots outlined, and electrical lines had been drawn, but if anyone had bought property here, they'd never bothered to build on the land.

Only one structure stood in the area: a school that, judging from the architecture, had been built in the early eighties. If it was meant to entice families to move to the area, it had failed.

Daniel slowed his car to a crawl before turning into the parking lot. There he saw, in bold blue letters, the words CHURCH OF THE SANDMEN on a sign. They were printed over milky-white plexiglass, along with the motto SERVING A GREATER GOOD. And to the far left of the text was the image of the winged hourglass.

Just like the ornate decoration atop the chest hidden in his father's bedroom, and the logo on Francis's business card.

Like most schools, the compound had a large perimeter fence that gave access to the parking lot and playground. All of it was dilapidated, worn by decades of neglect. The only sign that the school wasn't completely abandoned were the many cars in the parking lot. An eclectic blend of makes, brands, and years mixed together. There were perhaps two dozen: a black Lexus RX here, a rusty Elantra there. Some were luxury vehicles, but most were of standard suburban stock.

As he parked, Daniel could see a man standing in front of the school's main doors. He was wearing a familiar black suit and he waved at Daniel.

It took a moment to cross the parking lot; all the while Francis, hands nonchalantly tucked into his pockets, watched him with a blank smile.

"Did you have any trouble finding the place?" Francis asked, once they were within earshot.

"I thought I had the wrong address."

"Not quite what you were expecting?" Francis said, his smile broadening a little as he opened the glass door, allowing Daniel inside.

"Not even a little."

The interior of the compound wasn't that much different from its original purpose, at least aesthetically speaking. All traces of the original academic vocation had been stripped, however, leaving the walls barren and sterile. The black-and-white linoleum floors were still pristine and polished, and the dull blue paint on the lockers that lined the walls looked as fresh as the day it had been brushed on.

There was a smell of incense and disinfectant that didn't seem quite at home in a school. Most disturbing was the distorted sound of a singsong speech resonating through the empty halls. If there were so many cars, Daniel wondered, then where was everyone? And whose voice kept echoing through the school?

"I hope you don't mind my misleading you a little, Daniel. You can probably guess that when I said 'family,' I wasn't referring strictly to you, Mother, and me."

Daniel shrugged. He couldn't quite say what he'd been expecting, though this was certainly not it. He was here to see his mother and to get answers. Francis didn't seem to register that.

Daniel stopped in the middle of the hallway. There was a trophy case along the wall, across from a pair of large doors. The school had presumably planned on displaying awards and accolades for their athletic and debate teams. Instead it now housed a number of framed photos and artifacts. While the items made no sense to Daniel—a link of chain here, a rodent's skull there—the majority of the pictures featured a familiar face.

"Good ole Mother," Francis said.

The resemblance was undeniable. Side by side with Francis's face, reflected in the glass, Marguerite Lambert-Crowley's features beamed back at them with a beatific smile. She looked older than in any of the pictures Daniel's father had shown him, but there was no mistake about the lineage. If anything, the crow's feet and lines around her mouth gave her an air of confidence and authority. This was no longer the happy young mother getting her picture taken at the circus. This was the face of a leader.

There were images of her standing in front of a crowd, arms raised high and eyes turned to the heavens. Others were taken as she bestowed colored sashes to important-looking men and women, like a queen during a knighting ceremony. In every photo, standing next to her or not far in the shadows, was Francis, always with his black suit.

"When do I get to meet her?"

Francis gave the question some thought in his own detached manner, theatrically rubbing his bare chin as if calculating myriad possible answers.

"If you don't mind meeting her in your current accoutrement, then there's no harm in having you sit in on today's sermon."

Daniel surprised himself by immediately wanting to say no. He'd just seen his own face in the trophy case's glass. He was unshaven and disheveled. His clothes were obviously slept in. Yet it was his shoes he was most ashamed of. The worn sneakers might have been sufficient when working on his car or hanging with his friends, but they seemed wholly inappropriate, even sacrilegious, for a rendezvous over a decade in the making.

"I . . . I'd need to freshen up a little first."

Francis raised an eyebrow and curled his lip in a half smile. Daniel couldn't decide if his brother was amused or annoyed by his self-conscious worry.

"There's a bathroom right up the hall where you can comb your hair and splash some water on your face."

Getting a good look at himself in the mirror and under the bright fluorescent lights of the bathroom, Daniel realized there wasn't much that could be done about his clothes. The best he could muster was combing his hair with wet fingers so it wouldn't look quite as messy, and wash his face in the sink. The results were far from perfect, well below how he would have wanted to present himself to a long-lost mother.

Studying his reflection, he tried to put on a mask of happiness. He wanted to show that he was glad to have a family after all, but the most he could do was put on an insincere grin.

Why would he have anything to celebrate? Who were these people who'd vanished for most of his life and only now extended their hands to welcome him back? His own mother had abandoned him, and there he was worried about making a good first impression. She should be nothing to him.

Never had Daniel realized how much he'd relied on his two strongest allies. His father had always been there to guide him on any important coming-of-age decision. Meanwhile, Sasha had been the one to hold his hand as he'd navigated more personal issues.

The thought of Sasha sent a shiver down Daniel's spine, despite the hot air blowing loudly from the dryer on his hands. So potent was the chill that he almost thought he saw his breath in the air.

With what little damage control he had managed, Daniel gave himself one last look in the mirror before stepping out into the hall to meet Francis.

"Hey!"

So lost in his thoughts was Daniel that he didn't notice when someone else walked into the bathroom. Then again, she was almost invisible. Not only was she short and thin, wearing loose gray sweatpants and an equally nondescript gray hoodie, she seemed to naturally shrink into herself.

"I'm sorry," she said, averting her eyes. The hurried apology and scurrying reminded Daniel of a frightened mouse. It was said so quickly that he didn't even have time to give an apology of his own.

Walking back into the hall, Daniel struggled to even remember the girl's face, having noticed only her large terrified eyes framed by long dark hair. Yet he couldn't get the echo of her voice to leave him, the words *hey* and *I'm sorry* stuck in his head like a pop song.

If any effort had been put into remodeling the school to better fit the Church of the Sandmen's purposes, it had all been poured into the gymnasium. In fact, one had to look to the ceiling to find any remnants of the room's original purpose: two retractable basketball hoops fixed into the rafters. Everything else had been arranged into a high school drama teacher's wet dream.

Theater-style seating covered a full third of the floor space. At the front, a stage had been erected, picked out in bright beams from spotlights above.

The auditorium could comfortably sit around five hundred people, but less than half were filled. Yet, instead of taking up one of the empty seats near the front, Francis guided them to the back and into the shadows, farther from the rest of the crowd.

"Don't worry," Francis reassured him. "You won't miss a thing."

He then pointed toward large speakers, the kind you'd find at the movies, positioned at the corners of the gymnasium.

As if on cue, a hiss of static popped to life, followed by the shrill cry of audio feedback. The lights in the auditorium faded, leaving only the stage as the sole focus of everyone's attention.

"Oops. Sorry," said a woman onstage, half embarrassed, half commanding. "You'd think I'd have the hang of this by now."

The congregation allowed a short polite laugh.

His mother looked identical to her photos from the trophy case, though a little older and maybe a little more tired.

Marguerite Crowley, née Lambert, was a short dynamo with curly shoulder-length black hair. She seemed a little less austere in person but just as elegant. From her business-casual black dress that wouldn't be out of place on Wall Street, to the understated silver earrings and coordinated jewelry, she radiated class. It was easy to see where Francis had gotten his taste in fashion.

Her demeanor matched her sense of style. She walked the line between strict and relaxed in her posture. The fluidity of her walk suggested a dancer's practiced movement. From the tilt of her hips and the angle of her neck down to where she chose to throw her gaze, every act was a sentence in the grand essay that was her presence onstage. Even her little faux pas with the microphone seemed part of the act. Marguerite Crowley wove her appearances with purpose and direction. Her performance had a goal, and every step was meant to serve it.

"Good morning, everyone," she said. "I see a few people are missing," she continued. "That's disappointing."

Daniel looked around. While there were a lot of empty seats, considering the room's capacity, he thought it was a pretty good crowd. How many people were supposed to attend this weird little church? Back in Saint-Ferdinand, he'd witnessed a different gathering of the Sandmen, or rather the sad little cult that borrowed the name.

His father's version of the cult had been a gathering of bickering villagers wearing silly robes and indulging in animal sacrifice. This assembly seemed inspired by church revivals. Every time his mother spoke, her audience responded with clapping, laughing, and gasping. They were participants in the sermon. To this, Mother would smile, signaling that she was pleased with her congregation.

"Some of you might have noticed something in the papers."

A disapproving rumble passed through the crowd.

"Now, now. Not all papers are bad. Or rather, they're not always bad. If you did read the news over the last few days, you might have noticed something about Sylvain Gauthier. I know Gauthier had a few very close friends here, Maria in the back for instance, and Claude here. Well . . ."

She hesitated, pausing to collect herself.

"I regret to inform you that Gauthier was killed."

Marguerite let the news sink in. A wave of grief in various degrees swept through the crowd. The woman in front of Daniel, whom he only now recognized as Beatrice Bergeron, began an aborted sign of the cross that was replaced by a gasp of indignation. Francis remained unmoved and looked even a little amused.

"The papers are covering it up as an accident. That he fell in front of a subway car. I think we all know different, don't we?"

A hint of anger flared up and what had been murmurs a moment before quickly escalated to a vocal frenzy. Everyone had an opinion, and each of them seemed to feel they were in a one-on-one conversation with their leader. The necessity of the speakers was becoming apparent to Daniel.

"Did I not warn that the closer we came to the appointed time, the more perilous things would become? That our enemies would no longer lie in wait but rather slither out of the shadows, intent on our destruction?"

Despite her dire words, Mother seemed to keep her absolute calm. She paced the stage, only bringing her microphone to her mouth when she spoke.

"But we are the righteous," she continued, once her audience had quieted some. "And they are the wicked. Gauthier was one of us. A member of this family. And he will be rewarded for his work and for his sacrifice. As will you all. Because little do our enemies know that we've already won. They fear us because they know, maybe not as a fact, but deep inside their empty souls, that we don't worship an absentee god."

A hush fell over the audience. A knowing silence shared by everyone, like a secret that they feared might escape the walls of the gymnasium. Mother nodded with a broad but humble smile, basking in the quiet approval of the Sandmen.

It's here, Daniel realized. *The god is here.*

He could feel the blood drain from his features, the tips of his fingers tremble. The remembered weight of the knife was suddenly heavy in his palm and the image of it plunging into his father's throat vivid before his eyes.

Anger warmed him from within, flaring bright at the thought that he was in the same location as the thing that had eradicated everything he held dear. The Crowley temper, but his own interpretation of it. Not the explosive furor Stephen Crowley had so often openly displayed, bursting into fits of red-faced rage at any irritation, but the slow seething of a forge. Less immediate, but so much hotter and more capable of damage.

"I'm sorry, Mother," a woman standing a few rows closer to the stage said. Her voice was hesitant and trembling, almost afraid.

"What is it, Cassandra?" Mother asked. She took a few steps toward the edge of the stage. There, the lights lost just a little of their intensity, painting the illusion of intimacy for the discussion to follow.

"I . . . It's just that . . ." Cassandra stumbled, unable to put the words to her idea. A sniffle and then a sob escaped her before she could go on.

"Let it out," Mother demanded softly.

"The . . . Our Lord is not what I expected Him to be."

"This is about Victor, isn't it?"

Cassandra nodded vigorously, holding her shirtsleeve to her nose.

Mother stood and backed up into the light once more, bringing the microphone to her lips. She boomed through the speakers, dominating the gymnasium.

"Ours is a god of Love and Life, but He is not without fault. Before His salvation at our hands, He had been imprisoned and tortured. Shackled against His will by those who lacked the vision and compassion to care for Him.

"I understand your loss, Cassandra. I, too, had to abandon much to be here. We all knew there would be sacrifices, and where you lost Victor, I had to leave a husband and child behind."

That was not how Stephen Crowley had described things. There was never any mention of selfless sacrifice, just a variety of ways of saying, *She abandoned us, Dan.*

"I know that our Lord taketh," Mother continued. "But our Lord also giveth back. The lives that were tragically, accidentally lost at His hands can be brought forth once more. All that is required of us is faith."

Mother let her words sit, bleeding into their own echo. She then crouched down on her haunches, bringing her eyes level with those of the grieving woman. She let the microphone hang from her limp fingers, speaking with her own voice, soft yet audible in the reverential silence.

"Do you understand, Cassandra?" she asked, with infinite compassion. "Are you still with us? To the end, like Victor was?"

Cassandra didn't answer with words, nodding vigorously instead.

"A lot of you fear to voice your opinions and concerns," Marguerite said, rising to her feet and using the microphone once again. "Don't. For over a decade, have I not guided you well? Have I not kept this Church strong, growing our numbers every year? Have I not, at long last, delivered on the near-impossible promises that I made?"

The crowd mumbled its agreement. Some nodding, others grunting a shy yes.

"Cassandra Poole hasn't just shown incredible courage of conviction by voicing her worries, but a faith that challenges my own by standing firm against adversity. Our Lord demands much of her. He took her husband, but believe me, this will make her and Victor's rewards that much more glorious."

A slow applause started from the far right, near the stage. It spread like a bacterial infection, growing exponentially in reach and volume.

Soon, Sandmen were standing in the dark, showering Daniel's mother, their Mother, with praise from a standing ovation. Barely visible anymore through the crowd in front of him, Daniel could see her first avert her eyes from the adulation, briefly self-conscious of the worship lavished on her. Turning back to her devotees, she soon drank in their cheers and feasted on their gratitude.

Daniel cast an eye toward Francis, looking to anchor himself amid all that was happening. But Francis simply sat there, in the dark, his own amused eyes riveted on Mother. A smile of detached mirth hung from his lips.

As he listened to the crowd clapping and cheering, it dawned on Daniel what his purpose reuniting with his mother and brother truly was. He'd had no expectations as to what kind of woman Marguerite Lambert-Crowley would be, but he now knew two things about her: she was formidable and she had to be stopped.

ABRAHAM

WHEN THE DOORBELL RANG, Abraham was still unprepared. It might as well have been another Abraham who'd sent Penny the invitation.

After being kicked out of her house, he'd wanted to wait before fixing things. It still seemed like the wisest course of action, but he no longer had the luxury. His conversation with Daniel, followed by Audrey's apparition, had turned him around about asking his father for help, but he wasn't up to facing this task alone. Also, Penny would probably do a better job of explaining everything they knew so far.

Now, like an idiot, he stood in front of the door, gripped by doubt over his decision. He remained paralyzed for a solid minute before the door clicked and swung open on its own.

"Forgot how to use a doorknob?" Penny asked, the sass returned to her voice, as if the previous day had never happened.

Abraham smiled and shook his head.

She was joking again. Well, the kind of mocking humor that passed for jokes with Penny. Things were going better than he'd hoped.

"Come in?" he said, moving out of the way and extending his arm as an invitation.

"No," she answered. "Not yet."

Abraham's smile wavered and he bit his lip. The temperature outside had warmed a little, but nothing like how it had been just a few days prior. The rains had brought a cold front and it was here to stay. Unlike him, Penelope knew to dress for the weather and she'd apparently walked her way here from work. It was a long trek. It was the kind of walk that allowed someone to get introspective and come to terms with important decisions. Abe didn't want to consider what those might be.

"We have to be on the same page, Abe," she continued. "I need to know that I can trust you."

"What? Of course you can trust me. Penny, this is me. I got your back."

Since they'd been kids, he'd been more than willing to take blows for her, rather than stand by and watch her take blows she insisted were hers to take. As they grew up, Abe decided that she was one of a handful of people, including his dad, for whom he'd lay down his life without hesitation. Did that mean he loved her? Maybe. He'd certainly had his fair share of crushes on Penny over the years. Yet Daniel had given him that knife and he'd taken it, knowing full well what purpose it might serve.

"But you didn't," Penny said, taking a half step back. "Maybe I brought this on myself. I should have told you about my hands sooner. But the way you and Crowley were talking about Sherbet . . ."

"Penny," Abraham said, failing to keep the pleading out of his voice. "If I'd known, I'd never have said those things. I was trying to protect you! Come inside and we'll talk about it over dinner."

"I know." She sighed. "But when do you go from saying to doing something wrong? I need you to promise me one thing. Promise me that, and we'll have dinner and we'll figure things out."

"Anything."

"Say you'll keep your hands off Sherbet."

A simple request, but Abraham, in a rare moment of perspicacity, heard the deeper meaning behind it.

She wasn't talking about Venus's cat. Or, if she was, it was symbolically. Of course, if he promised to leave Sherbet alone, Penny would hold him to that, but what she really needed to hear was an assurance that she, too, would be safe.

Abraham looked down at his hand, slowly flexing the fingers that her grip had nearly frozen off. The pain was gone, but the memory remained sharp. Something had happened to his friend. A terrible change neither of them could explain was taking place in her. She needed him on her side.

He smiled and extended the hand to her.

"Deal. You've got my word."

It took her a moment to put the gesture together. She looked at his hand—open, naked, and vulnerable—then at her own, gloved against the cold outside and within. With a smile, she grabbed his palm and shook it.

Then she pulled him into a tight embrace. Squeezing him hard against her.

"Shut up," she said, anticipating that he was going to try to say something and knowing it would ruin the moment.

They ate the meal Abraham had prepared in what was a surreal bubble of normalcy, even if their conversation took the occasional shallow dive into the bizarre.

Abraham was a better baker than he was a cook. Pastries and cakes came naturally to him, which he always credited to his sweet tooth. He had to put a little more effort into the main course, going out of his way to pick up fresh ingredients, including a detour to one of the local farms for fresh pork. There were live hogs there and he thought of Venus. Not because of the swine, but because he knew his friend hated to see farm animals destined for the slaughter.

Even with the best ingredients, Abraham wasn't quite satisfied. The meat, in his opinion, had turned out too dry. If he ever got accepted into cooking school, he'd have to work on that. Get a better understanding of roasting meats so that his pork loins wouldn't be so dry. And he'd have to study sauces so that the wine-and-pepper reduction would be thicker.

Penny made no complaints, congratulating him on his work instead. As he put a portion of leftovers into a plastic container for his father, he caught her giving him a warm look that could pass for admiration. Or maybe more, he hoped.

"What do you feed it anyways?" he asked over angel food cake. There had been a series of questions about Sherbet that bothered him and while they had been discussing more mundane subjects, Abraham had decided to satisfy his nagging curiosity. If he was to accept the little zombified feline, he might as well understand it.

"It's still Sherbet, so he eats the same things. Dried food with the occasional wet stuff. Mostly seafood flavored. Though I'm really cutting back on the wet food."

"Too expensive?"

"No. Too disgusting. You see, he doesn't digest the food like a living cat. It just sits in his stomach and his guts for a day, and when he poops it out, it's a mess of rotting fish and shrimp. It's the worst, and so disgusting that it spooks him out of his litter. Then he just trails it all over the house."

Abraham nodded, putting another spoonful of cake and strawberries into his mouth. Penny shook her head.

"Amazing. This is literally the most disgusting thing I've ever described and there you are, still shoveling food into your mouth."

"Sowwy," he mumbled, crumbs dropping from his lips.

As the half-pronounced word left his mouth, along with a few crumbs of food, Abraham braced himself for more admonishments. Table manners, or rather his lack of etiquette, had always been a sticking point between them. However, she just smiled and shook her head again. The world had lost its mind, taking life in Saint-Ferdinand's unique flavor and spinning it out of control, but their friendship had endured. Or so Abraham liked to think.

As far as he was concerned, the moment could have lasted forever. Penny on the verge of laughter, him wiping his face with a napkin. It was perfect, warm, and comfortable, but most of all it was normal. But normal was a rare commodity in Saint-Ferdinand and had a tendency not to last.

An explosion of sound, short but loud, erupted all around them.

Penny screamed. Abraham nearly jumped out of his skin, not from fear so much as shock. All at once, every cupboard in the kitchen had been thrown open. Eighteen wooden doors, swinging on their hinges and slamming into one another, leaving dishes and glasses to clatter.

Mouth open but without a word, Penny looked around the kitchen, drawing an arc to take it all in and ending with her eyes on Abraham. Her spoon rattled as she dropped it onto her plate. *What the hell was that?* she silently demanded to know.

The shock wore off of Abraham first. Once the initial surprise dissipated, he seemed more disappointed than terrified, like a child who'd had his toy taken away.

"Yeah . . . I guess we should talk about the ghosts, shouldn't we?" he said as she still stared with her mouth agape.

"This is not a good idea," Penny said.

She stood on the moonlit grass of the Saint-Ferdinand Cemetery. Earlier in the season, the burial site was beautiful, gorgeous even. The heavy humidity and generous sunlight had nurtured both the manicured lawns and the tall weeping willows to grow lush and verdant. It was a local joke that William Bergeron could have practiced his putting on the graves of the dead.

Now Bergeron was buried here and the village was almost abandoned. No one made that joke anymore.

It still spoke to how long the shadow of death had stretched over Saint-Ferdinand. The dead now easily outnumbered the living at least two to one. Lavish headstones, some dating back over a century, were all meticulously maintained, and wrought-iron fences gave the place an air of nobility that went far beyond the rural atmosphere in the village.

"Well, for once, it's not one of mine," Abraham said.

He stood a few feet beyond the gate. With his work boots and a thick flannel jacket, he looked like a lumberjack's caricature. Except instead of an ax and beard, he had a shovel and a heavy-duty yellow flashlight.

Abraham felt his attire inappropriate for such hallowed grounds. His navy-blue suit would have been more dignified, and now that he knew the dead were watching, it seemed irreverent to wear anything less, but the work ahead demanded it.

"If you come up with anything better, I'll be glad to hear it," Penny said.

"I thought you wanted us to talk to my dad."

After all the time Abraham had spent psyching himself up to ask his father for help, Penny had been the one to stay his hand when he went to wake the old man.

"I'm meeting you halfway. You wanted to know more before we went to him? Well, here we are."

"This isn't even where I saw Audrey," Abraham said, his fingers drumming nervously on the handle of his shovel.

"No. But this is where she's buried. Aren't you curious to know what Randy did to keep her ghost around?"

"Not particularly, no."

Abraham's phlegmatic nature made him difficult to creep out. He certainly wasn't afraid of the dark and could walk through a spiderweb without flinching, never going into fits of panic like most people.

However, what they were planning was, beyond its illegality, an affront to all decency. He'd worked hard to get Penny's trust back. If she thought a little bit of digging could help their cause, then so be it. He'd do a little digging.

It wasn't as if she was enamored with the prospect either.

"You said she looked afraid and she told you that Saint-Ferdinand was full of ghosts?" Penny reminded him. "Cemeteries and ghosts go together pretty well."

"Like fudge and ice cream."

The simile escaped him before he could stop himself. It was the kind of comment at the wrong time that usually got Penny riled up at him. But she was too enveloped in her own thoughts to even notice.

"Something must have happened after Cicero's Circus," she said. "Audrey was the only dead person I saw when . . . when I . . . She was the only one."

Penny was reluctant to talk about her out-of-body experience. Earlier that summer, Randall McKenzie had hijacked her body, pushing her soul to its edge for a brief period of time. She'd seen where spirits wandered after death, but by her recollection, the place had been empty. No ghosts or restless dead, only the presence of a vast and ravenous god of hate and death. Abraham shivered at the thought.

"I remember you saying she had nails in her eyes," Abraham said, "but when I saw her yesterday, there was nothing. Well, not nothing. I mean, there were eyes, but ya know, poked out? Like there were nails at some point and—"

"Okay, stop. I get it," Penny said, waving her hand.

They made it to the back of the graveyard. Low-hanging condensation formed a thin layer of fog hovering a few inches above the grass. It lent an atmosphere both forbidding and soothing. Abraham could just as easily imagine a rotting arm exploding from the ground and through the fog as he could see himself lying on his back, staring at the stars.

"Well, here we are," he said, stabbing the head of his shovel into the ground.

The two stood on either side of a gorgeous white granite headstone. The name Audrey Bergeron had been carved into its surface, along with the dates 2004–2012 and the simple statement AN ANGEL TOO BRIEFLY AMONG US. The statue of a cherub clung to the upper left corner of the headstone, looking beatifically at the soil below. The ground still bulged where the tiny white casket had been lowered below. Small shoots of grass had begun to cover the earth but would be unsuccessful before the first freeze of late fall. They'd get another chance in the spring.

"Are we sure we want to do this?" Penny asked, touching a gloved hand to his arm and giving his flannel jacket a gentle tug.

"I'm sure we don't. But I think you're right. We gotta figure out what Randy did. Can't exactly ask him directly, so . . . Maybe Venus could help find him?"

Penny shook her head. It wasn't the first time they'd spoken of finding Randal Mackenzie. But he might as well have vanished off the face of the Earth. Venus had gone off on her own, looking for a man named Lucien Peña. He was another member of the Craftsmen, like Randal, and an associate of Venus's grandfather. With heavy resignation, he let out a sigh before handing Penny the massive flashlight.

After a final pause to take stock of what he was about to do, Abraham plunged his shovel into the ground. He pulled out a generous bit of soil, which he tossed aside with a grunt. Then another. Abraham kept excavating and digging in silence.

Occasionally Penelope would pipe up to softly suggest he dig a more even hole, but digging was one of the few things he knew better than she did.

If asked, Abraham would have estimated that he dug like this for an hour at the very least. In truth, he'd been at it for little more than thirty minutes. Once done, he and Penny had a clear view of the white casket that housed the mortal remains of Audrey Bergeron. The polished box appeared to glow in the night, catching as much of the moon's light as it could, making it its own. Only a shovel-wide crack on the surface of the lid marred the ivory finish of the casket.

"Well . . . at least we won't have to fight too hard to open it," Abraham said, trying to ignore the creeping smell of rot and fungus rising around him.

"Small blessings," Penny added.

Always the utilitarian, Abraham decided that Penny's hesitant comment was his signal to act. He bent down to pull open the lid. The casket had filled with dirt, having poured in from the crack on top. Only a few strands and folds of a white dress poked out of the black earth.

Already emotionally exhausted, Abraham let out a heavy sigh. He'd always been like this. Doing the unpleasant things that needed doing while hiding how it eroded him. Three years earlier he'd been the one to pick up and toss the carcass of a dead groundhog that had been run over and flattened like a pancake. Penny and Venus, who'd been walking with him on one of their frequent summer trips to the ice cream parlor, had both protested: Venus more out of sadness for the poor woodland creature and Penny in horror that her friend would grab a rotting, sunbaked carcass with his bare hands. She didn't let him touch her for two days, even after he'd aggressively cleaned up.

After some hesitation, Abraham plunged his hands into the dark soil. Letting his fingers slip down the silk lining of the casket, he rummaged his way around the dirt until he found folds of thin linen and what felt like a broken xylophone. Touching the length of a tiny fragile spine until he had a secure hold, Abraham pulled the body of Audrey Bergeron from the earth and into the moonlight.

He had imagined that, somehow, she would be no different from her ghostly apparition, a reflection of her body on the day she'd been buried. He'd envisioned a frail porcelain doll still wrapped in her funeral dress, delicate hands and features picking up the moon in a way that would make her glow like her ghost and casket had.

That was naive of him. Audrey's body was suffering from the same assault of nature as any of the dead would. Her face came forth from the soil first, lips pulled back and broken eyes sunken. Her skin was gray and stretched where it wasn't split. Worms and beetles crawled away from the light, falling to the earth or scurrying back into the wounds they'd dug. Audrey's beautiful platinum hair had kept its ethereal white hues, but was now dirty and pulling at a scalp that seemed all too willing to give out. There was evidence of a battle between the cosmetics applied by the funeral home and the ravages of nature, but the fight had been long lost, decomposition the clear victor.

"Oh my god," Penny sobbed.

The beam from the flashlight shook and Abraham tried to convince himself that his friend wasn't having a nervous breakdown.

"All right," he said, trying to sound as level as he could. He wondered what it said about him how he could remain so calm while witnessing such things. "What now?"

It took a minute for Penny to reply. Abraham's eye was attracted by a hint of red buried in the dirt.

"Are there nails in her eyes?" Penny called down before he could inspect further.

"Nah. Nothing. Just wounds. Like her ghost," Abraham answered. "You think there should be?"

"I don't know. I assumed that if her apparition had had them at some point, maybe her body would too? What about her feet?"

Indeed, after clearing off the soil, Abraham found two nails, old and black, impaled through Audrey's tiny naked feet.

"Yeah. One in each foot."

Out of idle curiosity, Abraham pinched one of the nails between his fingers and pulled at it, testing how secure it was in the dead flesh. It felt stuck, like the blood and embalming fluid had sealed it in as glue.

A deep chill filled the open grave as he gave the nail a slight twist, intent on dislodging it so he could inspect it better. The tips of his fingers felt frozen by the iron they were gripping, a sensation all too reminiscent of Penny's grasp.

"Don't! Leave those in," Penny demanded. "Whatever happened to her ghost is happening to her here. What if it works both ways? I don't want to mess with things we don't understand yet."

"One for my dad?"

"Yeah. I almost wish Randy were still around so we could ask him directly though."

"Hey, what about the bear? When I saw her, she had her favorite teddy bear in her hands."

Penny shook her head. "You must have seen some sort of emotional resonance or memory of hers that she projected or something. Her bear wasn't buried with her. I saw it over the summer. Randy made me use it to summon Audrey."

Abraham scratched the top of his head. He remembered Penny talking about that. It confirmed that the bear meant something in the grand scheme of things, and it was worth making sure it had not also been buried with Audrey. He tried to dust Audrey's body off with as much reverence as could be mustered under the circumstances. As he removed the dirt from her dress, he came upon a soft lump. He had to wrestle it from the crone-like fingers of Audrey's hands, which clutched at the thing with a vigor only reserved to the dead or the desperate.

A bear. It was a teddy bear with a faded-red felt top hat. He knew that bear. It had been Audrey's favorite toy out of her vast collection of stuffed animals.

"Hey, Penny!" he said, waving the toy in the air like a prize. "Look what I found."

But Penny didn't answer. Instead she reached down and gently plucked the bear from his hand. The moon caught a brief image of her expression, afraid and astonished.

"That's impossible," she said. "I left that at the police station two months ago."

VENUS

VENUS OPENED HER eyes to a sideways television. A black window into nothing but her own weary face staring back. Alternating bands of shadows and sunlight filtering in from the window blinds were projected on its surface.

There was always a moment of discomfort when she first woke. A few seconds where she would feel naked. Like a knight going into battle before putting on armor. She was vulnerable to memories she'd sooner forget.

She'd lost her father but couldn't afford to grieve for him yet. Her mother had vanished, abandoning her when she was needed most, but Venus would have to process that anger later. Even the strange emotion she couldn't name—a mix of confusion and loss at having met her grandmother for the first time, only to lose her within a few hours—would have to wait before being sorted through.

Venus had to push these concerns away every morning, burying the emotions anew with every sunrise. They distracted from the mission.

On a glass-top coffee table, between her and the television, her clothes waited for her. They weren't neatly folded, but they were folded. More important, they were clean and dry.

Venus tried to remember when she had dragged herself to the couch, wrapped the bedsheets around her, and fallen asleep.

Sometime after Jodie had finished describing the other so-called accidents involving members of this Church of the Sandmen. How, like Sylvain Gauthier, each of the victims had been found hidden away from where they'd been murdered a few days after the fact.

Reluctantly, she pulled her left hand out from under the covers and reached to touch the clothes. They were cool, so Ben must have put them there during the night, before he and Jodie went to sleep.

Ears perked, she tried to determine if anyone else in Ben's small apartment was awake. Perhaps the sound of newspaper pages flipping or a coffee machine percolating would betray their presence. Aside from a loud, roaring snore from the bedroom and the occasional car that drove by under the living room window, the whole world seemed to remain asleep for now.

Unwilling to abandon the warmth of the bedsheet burrito she'd wrapped around herself, Venus grabbed her clothes and, with the sheet still hanging from her shoulders, made her way to the bathroom.

She changed and relieved herself, folding the pajama pants, T-shirt, and bedsheet as neatly as she could, knowing full well they'd likely be thrown in the wash anyway. It just seemed like what a good guest would do.

At the risk of waking Ben and Jodie up, she splashed some water onto her face. As she dried her skin with a towel, Venus caught her own reflection.

The image averted its gaze this time, unwilling to see the cold place in her eyes. This hollowness left by the god would swallow all these emotions, making a feast of guilt and grief.

This was how Venus put her armor on. It felt like ice on a bruise. Instead of a physical wound, however, it was her emotions that Venus wanted to dull. Her pain was guilt and her aches were regrets. Either by purpose or accident, the monster in her backyard shed had left Venus with a piece of itself that had manifested as a vacuum inside her. With a little effort, she could feed her feelings to the hungry void and, after an initial shiver, be able to think clearly and act unhindered. Every morning since the circus, she would rid herself of the anger toward her mother and the grief for her dad, but also steel herself with the focus needed for that day.

She stepped out of the bathroom and carefully put the pile of laundry on the kitchen table.

The snoring kept rumbling from the bedroom, reassuring her that she was still the only one awake.

Venus thought of leaving a thank-you note. Something to let Ben and Jodie know that she appreciated their help and hospitality. Perhaps adding a line wishing Jodie luck on finding her sister. Instead she walked to the door and grabbed her bag, intent on going back out on the hunt for Lucien Peña.

"Take this."

Ben's voice came from the living room. It was followed by the sound of leather decompressing as he got up from the couch that only minutes before had been Venus's bed. Silhouetted by the morning sun, she couldn't see what he was holding. But judging from the way he held his hand out, she could make an educated guess.

"I don't need money," she said, almost as an apology.

"Take it." Ben approached until he was near the kitchen table, only a few feet from Venus.

"I don't need it."

"Jodie is going to lose her goddamn mind when she finds out you left. I don't want her to think I let you go empty-handed." He took another step forward and Venus could see the small bundle of cash he was offering her. "You lucked out. Any other cop would have given you over to the youth court or social services. But Jodie really thinks you can help find her sister."

"She didn't seem to believe much of what I had to say last night."

"Jodie believes that you believe what you said about Saint-Ferdinand."

The sigh Venus let out sounded more exasperated than she'd intended it to. So they thought she was crazy. Who could blame them? Sometimes she couldn't trust her own memories of the summer either. It had all sounded so outlandish coming out of her mouth.

"For what it's worth, I believe you," Ben said, lowering his voice. "Can I at least make you an offer before you go?"

"No," she answered, pushing aside any sympathy she had for Jodie. Whether she believed in the prophecy or not, this was her mission. If she was going to be the one who fought the god, she'd need help, but as far as Venus was concerned, the only help that mattered was Lucien Peña. Single-minded focus was her best and only weapon, and she needed every inch she could get if she hoped to catch Peña again before the trail got too cold.

"Hear me out," Ben continued, ignoring her rejection. "Give us a couple of days—just through Friday—and we'll help you look for your guy."

"You can't help me. In two months I've only seen him twice. He shows up when I'm in trouble. With you guys around, he's bound to stay away."

Constable Ben pocketed the money, taking yet another step forward.

"But you don't have access to the tools we have. We can ride in a squad car, keep an eye out, listen on the radio for anything suspicious. Meanwhile, you can tell us everything you know about the Sandmen, and we'll give you pointers on how to continue hunting. I'll even tell you how to best avoid getting caught by the cops again. Worst-case scenario, you get a few days with a roof over your head, some warm meals, and the privilege of hanging out with the coolest cops in town."

It was tempting. Venus surprised herself with a shy smile. "The coolest cops in town," she repeated. They kind of were, she thought. Which was another reason she didn't want to drag them into this.

"Nah. I'm good." She spoke the words, or rather her sense of independence spoke them for her. It was Venus's understanding that her grandfather had been the same way. That he had shared a similar focus and drive. The thought had occurred to her that it might have been what killed him in the end. Regardless, even the stern Neil McKenzie had surrounded himself with people. He'd rallied his own cult to stand against the god of death and hate.

These ruminations worked their way through her thoughts as she twisted her boots around and did an about-face, hands firmly grasping the straps of her backpack. If she stayed too long, she might take Ben's offer. So far, everyone who'd been involved with

Saint-Ferdinand, its cults, and its god had suffered or died or both. She didn't want the coolest cops in town to join those numbers.

She tried to take a step and get out the door, eager to be away from the officer and his tempting offer, but her foot wouldn't hit the ground and her backpack pulled her up.

"Whoa!"

"I'm not done talking, Veen," Ben said, holding her up by her bag.

"Let go! And don't call me Veen!"

Venus tried to pull away, but the cop's grip was too firm. Her arms impotently attempted to reach the hand holding her backpack's handle.

"What's going on here?" Jodie's voice called from behind.

The snoring had stopped. All Venus's yelling had woken her up.

"Venus doesn't want to stay for breakfast," Ben explained.

"Then she doesn't have to stay for breakfast. Let her go."

"But she's hilarious. Look at her," Ben said. Venus could hear the smile in his voice before he pulled her up another half inch into the air. He was strong for his size.

"Ben, you're being an asshole. Put her down."

Almost immediately he complied, but he made sure to turn Venus around before he let go. She could have spun back toward the door and bolted. Ben wouldn't have grabbed at her again and she could have been on her way. But she'd seen Jodie.

If she'd looked at Venus with pity or anger, she could have still walked out. What she saw instead was a deep disappointment in her eyes. If she walked out, she'd be taking something important away from Jodie: the best opportunity she'd ever had to find her sister.

"Go on," Jodie said, her words flat. "Try to be careful out there. I don't want to be finding your body in a subway tunnel."

Venus tried to stand her ground. She made a half-hearted attempt to use her connection to the god to numb her feelings again, but it was too late. Her overwhelming loneliness and fear had worn out her determination. The armor had failed. Hopefully, this weakness wouldn't backfire on the two nicest people she'd met since coming to Montreal.

She shrugged the bag off her shoulders and sighed.

"What's for breakfast?"

"I hate to be the naysayer—"

It was Jodie who spoke while sitting in the passenger seat. She'd been in a mood since they'd left the apartment.

"You love being the naysayer," Ben cut in, eliciting a long exasperated sigh from his partner.

Venus sat silently in the back of the car. She'd taken the opportunity to charge her phone while at Ben's apartment but had only now bothered to turn it on. When she did, the thing started buzzing like an angry beehive. Her messages displayed a handful of photos of an open grave. Venus tapped into the cold place the god had left, numbing the dread and pain the photos summoned. They were pictures of Audrey's grave. At the very end of the string of photos was just one name followed by a question mark: *Randy?*

"Someone has to be the voice of reason, Ben, but how long do you figure Kinnison's going to tolerate this?"

"This" was the arrangement they'd made to take Venus with them on the job. Ben had been smart about the whole thing, showing just how determined he was to keep her around. He'd contacted Kim, the social worker they'd threatened to call when they'd first met, and explained the broad strokes of the situation. He told her that Venus was curious about police work and that taking her along would be good for her. He skipped over the juicy parts about cults, murders, and chasing down a street shaman. That was the stuff that seemed to really grab Ben's attention.

Venus didn't get the details, but it must have worked well enough to get approval.

"I told Kinnison it was your idea. And, since he absolutely adores you . . ." There was mischief in Ben's voice.

"Ugh! Of course you did," Jodie said, annoyed. "So, Venus? This guy we're looking for? If he's a regular in the area, he shouldn't be that hard to find. Whatever details you have on him, now's the time to share."

Venus's phone buzzed with a new message and she looked down at it before answering the cop.

We need to find Randy.

"His name is Lucien Peña," she said as Jodie immediately started punching the name into the car's laptop. "I don't think he's got a record. Not under that name. He's made it his business to not exist anymore."

"Right, a lot of people who live on the streets try to be as anonymous as possible, but we've still probably seen him around."

"I doubt it. I told you: he's not just some regular guy living off the grid. We won't find him by conventional means."

Venus could see Jodie roll her eyes through the rearview mirror. The constable wasn't subtle about her skepticism on the whole magic angle of Lucien Peña and all that had happened in Saint-Ferdinand. It was hard to blame her. Venus herself would have laughed at the idea if she hadn't witnessed it with her own eyes.

"We can start with the basics and work our way from there. You say he vanished for over a decade and only now he's killing Church of the Sandmen members. He's changing his behavior. Maybe he'll slip up."

"Maybe. He's old but big. Six four, six five. Broad shoulders and a thick Santa beard, but yellow-gray instead of white. Bald on the top of his head, with thick coal-black eyebrows. I've seen him with an old Expos cap once."

"So, generic hobo then?" Ben asked.

"I dunno. I think he'd probably stand out in a crowd. But he dresses to draw attention away from himself. Long beige coat. Dirty turtleneck. That sort of thing."

Jodie twisted in her seat to look back at Venus. She noticed that Venus was poking around on her cell phone, and it seemed to remind her of something, prompting her to pull out her own phone.

"Not much of a disguise, if you ask me."

Nothing she was saying made Lucien Peña stand out from the many other homeless men who walked the city's streets. That particular description didn't ring a bell because it was so common.

"We're not going to catch and corner him if he doesn't want us to. Like I told you, I've been at it for two months and I've barely seen a hint of him. It's like he's doing something to the city.

"Nathan Cicero, the owner of the circus in Saint-Ferdinand, he tried to explain it to me. It's like Peña is exploiting errors in how reality is built and then hacking them. My uncle does something similar."

Jodie listened attentively, but still looked mired in doubt, trying to decide if Venus was lying or crazy.

"I think I get it," Ben said. "They're cheat codes. Used to be with old console games you could buy these devices, GameSharks or whatever, that you'd put between your box and the cartridge. Then you'd enter codes and you'd get infinite lives or skip to a specific level. So it's like Peña has one of these devices between himself and reality. Makes sense."

"You read too many fantasy novels," Jodie said. "Maybe Peña just doesn't hang out in Montreal full time. Maybe he was in a completely different part of the country for fifteen years. Hell, maybe he's dead and this is someone else entirely. The only thing I'm sure of is that he's not a *magic hobo*."

Ben laughed as if it were Jodie who was talking nonsense. Having filled out a parking ticket, he stepped out of the cruiser, put the ticket on the windshield of a car, and calmly walked back.

Venus was trying to get ahold of a man with cheat codes to the fabric of the world in order to track down and defeat an ancient and terrible god along with the cult that harbored it. She needed Sherlock Holmes. She needed Superman. She needed Gandalf. Preferably all three rolled into one. What she had were a couple of traffic cops.

Ben sat back in the car, tossing his pad at Jodie, who was still thumbing at her phone. She then handed it to Venus, unlocked to a fresh contact page for her to fill out.

"Okay," Jodie said. "Let's assume for a moment that there is something to what you're saying. All we have to do is take away his GameShark and he should be easier to find and catch."

"I don't know if it's something we can just take away. Besides, I need him on my side. He was there when it all started. What he knows can solve everything. I hope."

"Solve everything" implied finding Jodie's sister, and the constable seemed to grasp that, nodding at Venus.

"All right," Ben said, starting to drive south down Union Avenue. "Different plan. What if we use the magic against him?"

There was a strange intensity to Ben that hadn't been there the previous evening. It hadn't been there this morning over breakfast, either. His eyebrows were a flat horizontal line above his eyes and his jaw was tense. Every muscle in his face was an expression of the effort going on inside his skull as the idea was taking form.

"I don't think that's a good idea. I don't know much about what he can do."

"How sure are you that he's trying to protect you?" Ben continued, ignoring her protest.

"I . . . It's the only reason he's shown up so far. Whether he's doing it because he was a friend of my grandfather's or because of that stupid prophecy, he's keeping an eye on me and protecting me from creeps. Like some weird, smelly guardian angel. But he never sticks around to talk."

Venus was starting to see where Constable Ben was going. At the same time, they took a turn onto René-Lévesque Boulevard. It was a busy street, three lanes wide in each direction, that delineated Montreal's downtown core from the old part of town. Pedestrians and motorists shared the asphalt in an uneasy truce, each leaving the other just enough room to navigate.

Ben kept accelerating.

"And this guy is aware of the city in a way that transcends reality. Would you say there's a good chance he knows we took you in and that we're helping you find him?"

Venus nodded again at Ben's reflection. Her heart was racing, keeping pace with the patrol car's increasing speed. Both were reaching a dangerous velocity.

"Ben?" Jodie asked as they narrowly avoided running over a pedestrian.

A black Audi had just missed their back bumper by less than an inch, its driver having the gall to honk at a police cruiser. At this rate, without the car's lights flashing their presence, they were going to crash.

"Ben! Slow the hell down! What do you think you're doing?" Jodie seemed like she was starting to panic. Her movements spoke of a hesitation, trying to decide if she should grab the wheel from her partner or pull the hand brake, anything to stop Ben's suicidal race down the boulevard.

Then it happened.

Every traffic light as far as the eye could see turned green simultaneously. Montreal itself seemed to lean in and accommodate Ben's reckless behavior.

It had to be Lucien. The green lights were too much of a coincidence, creating a hallway of safety for their breakneck race. When Venus looked back, she could see that, in the opposite direction, they were all red. Soon the only cars moving were the ones cruising alongside them. Everything else, even the pedestrians, had stopped.

In the rearview mirror, Constable Ben smiled. Their prey had taken the bait. Lucien Peña, her self-appointed guardian angel, had flinched and shown his hand. Ben's dangerous plan had worked, drawing the old magician out of hiding. Even Jodie seemed to realize what she was witnessing, teetering between disbelief and admiration.

In the blink of an eye, Constable Jodie's expression changed, crumbling into shock and then horror. With a deafening crash, her partner's body was violently shoved into her. Ben's side of the car caved in, obliterated by the impact of a speeding vehicle, twisting metal, and shattering glass.

Brown.

Venus noted before the force of the crash knocked her senseless. The truck that had hit them was brown. It was a strange detail to register, considering the circumstances.

Venus didn't exactly lose consciousness. After all, she wasn't the one whose body had suffered the blow of the impact. While she was sitting directly behind Ben, the truck had only plowed into the front portion of the patrol car, sending the police cruiser spinning clockwise. Physics were unkind to objects making sharp trades in vector and velocity.

Eyes closed and fueled by adrenaline, Venus's hearing sharpened. She heard Jodie's short cry of horror and pain before the wind was knocked out of her. Every detail of metal bending and glass breaking also registered with uncanny precision. She heard the pop and hiss of airbags being deployed. A wet crunch informed her that something was getting broken in Ben's body. Probably a large bone like a femur, or maybe his hip. These were the only sounds his body made, his wits and perhaps the life having been punched out of him instantly.

The commotion must have lasted less than a second. For Venus, it was followed by nothing but darkness and silence. Her eyes were kept shut by the primitive desire to stay ignorant of what had happened.

Squinting, she parted her eyelids. The light wasn't blinding. She'd barely blinked for a few seconds, never leaving her irises time to adjust to the dark. Reality thus came in with complete clarity.

In the front passenger seat, Jodie was still conscious, though the left side of her face was red with blood, probably hit by Ben's skull in the impact. She was trapped under her partner, whose upper body had been shoved into her lap. It looked like she was cradling his torso, her left arm wrapped around his shoulder, which hung at an odd angle. Ben's right hand was resting on the dashboard, the wrist twitching violently every half second or so. Venus couldn't see from her position, but judging from the part of the delivery truck that now sat in the driver's seat, she imagined there must be little left of his pelvis and legs.

A loud metallic scream pulled Venus's attention away from the two cops who'd been so kind to her. The car door whined open, having been popped out of place by the car's sudden change of shape.

Before she could react, a thick, grimy hand closed on her upper arm, pulling her out of the car with a violent yank. She felt her other arm jerk as it pulled the weight of her backpack with it, fingers frozen in a fist around the strap.

The immense old man who'd taken her out of the wreckage forced her to her feet. Venus quickly discovered that something was wrong with her left ankle. It wouldn't hold her straight. There was no pain yet; that would surely come later.

Dazed, her eyes fell on the brown delivery truck that had smashed into their car. The driver hadn't gone through his windshield. Instead he'd cracked it with his head, his face now resting on the steering wheel.

Sound came back to Venus. A bystander screaming in panic. Cars in the distance roaring in a faint echo. There were no sirens yet, unlike in the movies, where they would have instantly been heard. In their stead was an increasing commotion. People either rushed to the scene to offer help or stood around, filming or gawking.

"Idiot kids," grumbled Lucien Peña, pulling a still stunned Venus away from the crash site. "All right, McKenzie. You want to talk? We're gonna talk."

ALICE

IT WAKES.

So I must put it back to sleep.

Alice knew how wrong it was to rejoice at the stirring of the beast next door, but she couldn't help it. Every two days, it would stir and every two days, she would have to sing slumber to a god.

It wasn't a pure joy. If the happiness she felt could be compared to a song, it would be an overly complicated amalgam of dissonant melodies. A symphonic experiment that bristled with ambition but ultimately fell flat.

Hers was the joy of feeling important.

Alice's education was limited to what fellow Sandmen had taught her over the years. What she knew of math she learned from Mr. Philibert, who slaved in the kitchen making the family's meals. Alice was allowed to work with him over a few summers, but he'd had to patiently teach her basic arithmetic or otherwise she'd have been useless to him. She'd been taught the basics of how to read and write, knowledge she'd later sharpened through books. Alice had negoti-ated her way to owning a few of her own. At first she got things that would help further her education, leftovers from the aborted school. An outdated atlas and dictionaries along with the occasional textbook. Eventually she discovered novels. Imaginary places printed on paper and bound in cardboard where she could escape while still caged within the Sandmen's compound. When she was fourteen, Alice surprised herself with being able to hold a somewhat coherent conversation with other members of the Church about the works of R. L. Stine. There were still things she remained appallingly ignorant of, like physics and chemistry, along with philosophy and politics, but at least she had the tools to ask questions now. Though she knew not to do so too often.

There was one thing, however, that Alice knew better than anyone else. She knew how to sing. And the songs she knew best were lullabies.

As with everything else, the songs she studied and practiced had been handpicked by Simon and approved by Mother to serve the Sandmen. She didn't mind. The lullabies made her useful. She was doing the one thing she was good at. Better than anyone in the family, better perhaps than anyone in the world.

That point of pride, that moment when she knew that her abilities weren't only prized, but unique and unparalleled, was her biggest source of joy outside of the singing itself. She knew such feelings were wrong. That to bask in such narcissistic glee was a sign of a deeper inner corruption. The awe and envy others felt when they heard her sing was obvious. Even Mother's practiced manners and elegant posture were insufficient to hide the admiration she felt.

She'd once told Alice that this was the very reason why they called themselves the Sandmen. That it was their job to help their god find rest. Everything the family did was to support this secret goal of guiding their all-powerful Lord with song. It was a sacred duty that only a perfect voice could carry out. A voice like Alice's.

So, when the alarm clock on her nightstand chimed, reminding her that she had to take care of the creature from across the hall, Alice was happy.

Besides, she wasn't limited to singing to the god; she could listen to him sing back. What it sang was terrible and monstrous. Songs of the apocalypse and hymns of vengeance wrought upon all of humanity. Like a bird in a cage, it sang of its captivity and desire for freedom, and only Alice could hear the song in her head. They were songs that she understood all too well.

She hurried out of bed and, scratching her rump in an act she knew to be devoid of class and poise, made her way to her own private bathroom. It smelled of stale piss and moldering sewer. Something in the plumbing must have been put together wrong, letting the septic tank breathe right back at her. She'd have to ask Francis for a new air freshener cartridge, but that could wait.

"Bah!" she said, testing her voice.

It was scratchy, as expected. She poured herself a glass of tepid water to help warm it up.

She drank half while looking at herself in the mirror. The face that looked back was unpleasant. Her dark hair was a catastrophe, built high above her scalp upon a scaffolding of tangles and untamed bangs. The oversize faded pink T-shirt she wore in lieu of a night-gown hung on her bony frame like the clothes on a scarecrow. Her eyes were too big, her nose too small, her lips too thin, and her face too round. At least she didn't have to worry about smeared makeup, on account of she never wore any. It didn't matter, she told herself; as Mother would say, the only thing of any importance was her singing voice.

Alice grinned at the girl in the mirror and finished her water. Briefly, she considered brushing her teeth but decided against it. Who cared if her mouth stank of last night's dinner? If this was like any of the other days she'd put the god to sleep, it would just be her and the old man who served as its host.

She poured another glass of water, put on the worn fleece and sheepskin slippers next to the door, and went to serenade the monster back to sleep.

Cold air welcomed her as she stepped out of her room. The halls in the basement of the compound were heated just enough to keep the pipes from freezing in winter. A small discomfort wasn't going to keep her from her duties, and she walked out into the hallway with purpose, only then hearing the voices echo through the hall.

" . . . perfectly harmless. For the most part."

It was Francis, with his nonchalant posture, black suit, and per-fectly coiffed hair as always, standing back from the open door to the god's prison. The person he was talking to stood next to him, a step behind and knees bent, ready to run. He looked either appalled or terrified, and Francis seemed not to notice.

Alice knew the boy. She'd run into him the previous day while going to the bathroom. He'd changed into the family uniform: track pants and a T-shirt with white sneakers. Everyone who wasn't Alice, Mother, or Francis wore the same thing while in the compound. Aside from the colored sashes that denoted rank, it made them all look alike. Bees sharing a hive.

The stranger looked like a more handsome and muscular version of Francis. A sudden wave of self-consciousness about her appearance crept up her spine and she was about to turn and hide back in her room when Francis called out.

"Alice!" he said, an unsettling imitation of sincerity coloring his voice. "I was just about to come and get you. It's showtime."

He smiled. His unique configuration of lips and teeth had for years given her nightmares. That mirthless grin was the first thing she knew of the Sandmen. Before meeting Mother and becoming part of the family, and before this was home, Francis's smile was her entire world. For a while she even told herself that there might be something genuine about it. She knew better now. Francis didn't have an ounce of human warmth in him.

These days she saw him for what he was: a strange flesh puppet doing the best interpretation of humanity it could pull off. His was a perfect smile because Francis overcompensated, not knowing exactly why real people used that particular facial expression. All he understood was what was expected of him. In many ways, he was just as much a creature in a skin suit as the god she was meant to serenade into slumber.

"I thought I was going to be alone," she said, taking a step back. "I'm just going to go wash up?"

"No time for that," Francis said.

The other boy turned around at the sound of her voice and she could finally see his eyes; her knees felt like soft putty for a moment.

He gave her a nervous, lopsided smile that was effortless in a way that Francis couldn't hope to imitate. He extended a hand for her to shake. It felt warm and sincere.

"Have I introduced you to my brother, Daniel?"

"Pleased to meet you . . ." Daniel said, leaving her to complete the sentence.

"Alice. Alice LeSage," she answered.

Daniel's face grew a little pale at the mention of her last name and his pupils danced around in his eyes. Could he have heard of her? The thought was as fleeting as it was ridiculous.

The cold suddenly reminded her that aside from a T-shirt and slippers, Alice was essentially naked. The thought made her blush and she quickly pulled her hand away.

"I . . . I should really get to work."

She skirted around the two men and into the room.

In the two months since Francis had dragged the dying body of an old man into the basement of the school, Alice had had plenty of time to work through her aversion to the morbid sight. She got used to singing to a corpse, and kept the thing within it buried in dreams.

In life, his name had been Sam Finnegan. In death, there was some debate over what to call him. Francis still called him Old Sam, but Mother claimed that the person who'd been Finnegan had left the flesh some time ago. She hadn't yet offered any alternative for whatever was left. So Alice had opted for "Sam."

And Sam was a gruesome sight.

They'd dressed him up in a small white T-shirt that hung loose over his emaciated frame, along with a pair of black jeans that only remained on his person by virtue of a leather belt through which several extra holes had been punched.

His skin looked like stretched rubber over a brittle-boned skeleton. The thin layer of flesh revealing too much detail of his skull and joints. His lips were thin and pulled back in a permanent and morbid grin, and whatever hair he had left was long, white, and disheveled. Despite all of this, his eyes were what truly made Alice gag.

Two long dark iron nails had been plunged into his eyes and through his frontal lobe, obliterating both his sight and parts of his brain. Francis had assured Alice that the old man was quite dead, despite the movements of his limbs and the words he occasionally spoke in dry rasps.

The first time she'd sung to Sam, a practiced lullaby she had no reason to think would work, her hesitation and fear had cost the lives of Victor Poole and five others. It was only by chance that she'd managed to get the notes right before she could be torn apart with them.

"Sam's going to be your patient, your neighbor, and your new best friend," Francis had explained while others mopped up the blood and gore from the old man's room. "I need you to be as comfortable around him as you are around me. It wouldn't do to have your voice tremble when you sing to him. Mother would be disappointed. Oh! And the world might end."

Mother would be dead. We'd all be dead.

On that day, she'd learned why she'd been taught to sing her whole life. Why she had been instructed on how to use her voice and form the perfect inflections in her tone. Why she had been taken from her parents. Francis, waxing poetic, had once described his hopes for her as being able to "sing reality apart."

For the time being, Alice would have to settle for bringing slumber, and perhaps succor, to a god.

No, not exactly *a* god. The thing inside Sam was *the* god. The very entity that Mother had promised to the Sandmen. A creature born of eternity that they, as a family, would bind into servitude and use to bring forth a new age.

It was ironic, thought Alice as she went through a few quick vocal warm-ups, that the very thing they worshipped, they were also enslaving. There was a cruel practicality to their version of worship. A congregation that would not beg for favors from their Lord, but rather demand and obtain its grace.

And she, ugly and stupid little Alice, was the key to it all.

Alice opened her eyes, taking in the details of Sam's dungeon. Where her own remodeled storeroom was warm, even cozy, the perfect template of a gilded cage, the prison in which the Sandmen kept their god was little more than cinder-block walls and a concrete floor. A thin mattress and a few cotton sheets had been tossed onto the ground. Someone had dragged in a ratty old sofa for her to sit on when she wasn't singing. It still bore the maroon stains of dried blood.

It was cold in Sam's room, and the bare floor seemed to pull the warmth from her skin. Her naked legs were quickly covered in goose bumps as she made her way to where Sam lay on his weak excuse for a bed.

What a way to treat a god, she thought. Tossing him aside like an unwanted piece of furniture, only pulling him out when needed and keeping its maintenance to the bare minimum. Mother's sermons talked about a god of love and light whom the Sandmen should adore. Sam should be sat upon a golden throne in a room awash with sunlight and decorated with elaborate tapestries. What kind of worship was this?

Alice sat on her haunches, taking a moment to brush the old man's scant few hairs from his face. It was a pointless, ridiculous gesture. One that she felt self-conscious doing under Francis's watchful eye. She was, after all, bringing comfort to an unfeeling corpse. She wondered if the creature within could comprehend her intentions. Yet she couldn't help it. Maybe she felt sorry for the old man Sam had been. Maybe this was what she would have wanted for herself in this situation. More likely, this was about her. A gesture meant to settle her own nerves. Care designed to connect with her audience, alien though it might be.

"Shhh . . ." she whispered, pressing the back of her fingers to Sam's cheek.

The creature flinched and groaned. She was running out of time.

Taking a final sip of water before setting the glass down onto the floor, Alice rose to her feet and stepped back. She cleared her throat and took a moment to steady her breathing. She ran through a mental list of the various lullabies in her repertoire. The god was moving, its flesh prison stirring to life.

"You might want to sit down for this," Francis said to his brother.

"I'm fine," Daniel answered, but his voice was tinged with fear. Alice pictured him as a rabbit pawing around a sleeping wolf. He was afraid. Not of her, of course, but of Sam, like he understood that this wasn't just some incapacitated old man on the floor.

Alice shushed them both. This was the one situation where she had any kind of authority among the Sandmen. No one wanted Sam to wake up before his time. Even Daniel, who likely had no idea what was going on, obeyed without question.

With the room finally quiet, the unsettling comfort with her morbid audience reestablished, and a suitable song selected, Alice began.

Calmly pulling in one final breath of air, the girl who could sing reality apart began her lullaby.

"I'm cold."

Alice's voice had a tremble to it. The muscles in her jaw quivered with the nearly overwhelming need to set her teeth chattering.

She'd suffered none of these symptoms while singing. Making music put Alice in a trance, severing her connection to the real world. It wasn't only because of the impossible demand of singing a perfect song—there were memories attached to that particular lullaby. Memories of a loving mother whose face she couldn't remember, only her voice whispering a melody to put her to sleep.

Alice had let the last note slip slowly from her lips. Like a gourmet licking the back of his teeth for a final hit of flavor, she held on to that final vibration. Only once she was completely finished, any hint of the music having left her, had she heard a loud thump from behind her.

Daniel had fallen.

It was a side effect of her singing. Simon had suffered a similar fate when Alice had first begun to master the lullabies, brought down by the very magic he was training her to achieve. It was an unfortunate property of sound that it was indiscriminate. To be within earshot of her singing meant to be affected by the intent of the melody. She had, so far, mostly practiced lullabies, very simple and ultimately inoffensive songs. Yet, it had been enough to move her training outdoors and away from the compound. Only during the very coldest months was she allowed to sing inside, and only deep in the chill basement, where she could go unheard.

They'd brought Daniel to the couch, and now she sat there, his head on her lap, wondering if she should just try to wake him up before she froze to death. Francis hadn't been too keen on her approaching his brother like this. In fact, she wasn't very comfortable with it either, but something about the unconscious boy tugged at her, making her worry about his well-being in ways that were unfamiliar.

"I can get you something from your room if you want," Francis said.

He stood there, looking down at his brother, his emotionless smile hanging higher on the right side of his face.

"I'll be fine," she said.

"Are you sure? You're shivering. Wouldn't want the world to end because you caught a cold, would we?"

The worry was as close to a genuine human emotion as Francis could display. It fell short, his words hovering too close to the wonder of a child pulling the wings off a fly.

No, that wasn't accurate either. It was the opposite. Through the years, Alice had learned that Francis was no sadist. He lacked the passion for it. If he were to dismember an insect, it wouldn't be to see it suffer, but rather because he didn't care that it did. His curiosity was devoid of emotion, compassion—even desire. It was a mechanical drive and whenever she witnessed it, Alice felt an old fear creep back into the marrow of her bones.

"I want to make sure he's okay."

"He'll be fine. He didn't hit his head. You must have sung particularly well. Even the fall didn't wake him up."

It was true: She was improving with every performance. The lullabies weren't a spell. The slumber they induced was no more than it appeared—sleep. The better she sang, the deeper the slumber, but there was no magic keeping the victims from awakening.

Sam's corpse was different because it was, well, a corpse. But others were simply human beings succumbing to a biological urge. It had happened to Simon. It had happened to a few others. Even

Mother had made a point of staying away or wearing earplugs whenever Alice sang. No one was immune.

No one but Francis.

"We should wake him."

Alice idly moved a strand of hair from Daniel's face, much like she had Sam's. Part of her was busy admiring his handsome face, appreciating his thick dark hair and symmetrical features. But another segment of her mind was much more preoccupied with noticing the subtle differences between his living slumber and Sam's dead sleep.

When she'd first sung the corpse back to sleep, almost too late to save herself and those around her, she'd felt the presence trying to break free of the flesh. There was no physical change apart from increased animation in the dead, but on a more metaphysical level, it felt like the body of Sam Finnegan was filled with maggots and ready to explode.

Daniel, on the other hand, inspired warmth. The vulnerability that emanated from him while he snored had an endearing quality. For a moment Alice wondered if perhaps . . . but quickly she remembered her place.

"I didn't know you had a brother," she said to distract herself from the thought. "Why haven't we seen him before? Doesn't Mother love him?"

"Ah, you haven't been to the sermons in too long," Francis said, putting his hands in his pockets. "Mom loves all her children. If you'd attend, you'd know that by now. It gets repeated. Endlessly."

"I have singing classes during the sermons. Mother says it's easier to keep people away from me that way."

Francis shrugged. "Maybe, but I'm sure if you asked, she'd get Simon to reschedule. You have no idea how proud she is of her time on the soapbox. It's like she's the movie star she never got to be up there. Not that I blame you. As far as I'm concerned, you've heard one of those rants and you've heard them all. Believe me though, Mom adores that boy more than she'll ever let on."

"Then where has he been all this time?"

A few of the books Alice had been given over the years were romance novels. For a while she thought it was a taunt. A cruel joke.

But when she dug into the likes of *Romeo and Juliet*, *Jane Eyre*, and *The Notebook*, she found herself less envious of the characters and their complex emotional lives. She enjoyed the simplicity of her existence, and having it disrupted by things like longing and desire was an unnecessary distraction.

When she did allow a stray fantasy to touch on the subject, however, it felt like stepping in a puddle of cold water. It was jarring and unpleasant. It startled her with the realization of how devoid of warmth and comfort her life truly was. Dread would soak her heart and it would take days for it to completely dry off. All the while, she had to endure it silently.

Mother often spoke of love. How she loved the family and how they worshipped a god of life and love. She'd gift all those around her with her kind smile, which seemed to confirm that love. Even Alice had been the recipient of that kindness on occasion.

She knew it was all hollow and empty. Alice couldn't remember how it felt to be loved. She mostly forgot what it even meant to crave affection. For some cruel reason, Daniel brought back that need in her.

"Somewhere safer than here," Francis said.

"Why?"

"Because." Francis smiled. This wasn't his usual mirthless grin, however. There was something old and sinister to it. The perfect teeth showed just a little bit more and his lips seemed to curl up above his canines. This was the smile of a predator. A smile she'd seen once before, while standing by the front door to her home when she was a child.

"Mom loves us all," he continued. "But you and me? The rest of the Sandmen? She keeps us around. She has you living across the hall from a god imprisoned in a dead man's body. We tend her gardens and make her food while living with a thing that eats souls for breakfast.

"Mom loves us, all right, but Daniel was the only one she loved enough to leave behind."

DANIEL

"SO YOU'VE MET our little Alice, have you?" a woman's voice intruded from behind him.

Daniel was having breakfast. The Church did not fail to provide its members when it came to food and drink, but even the copious amounts of coffee failed to shake his drowsiness. The familiar voice, however, cut cleanly through the remaining tendrils of sleep.

Details of the previous day were fleeting. Daniel could remember Francis showing him around the compound, finishing his tour with a trip to the basement. It was all so strange, yet fit in perfectly with his notion of the home for a cult. Everything was communal, from the cafeteria he was now sitting in to the bedrooms, which housed up to six Church members at a time. They shared meals, showers, and chores. On the surface, it all seemed almost wholesome.

The basement was where things took a more sinister turn. Daniel had suspected the Church of the Sandmen to have the god of Saint-Ferdinand locked away somewhere; Mother had said as much in her sermon. But he hadn't expected the beast would be locked in Sam Finnegan's wasted body. Or that it wasn't the only captive.

"May I sit down?" the voice intruded again.

Daniel's heart caught in his throat. It was Mother. Even without the filter of speakers and a microphone, there remained a commanding quality to her words. To put her request in the form of a question was etiquette, not respect.

He'd asked that Francis arrange this audience for him. A meeting with his own flesh and blood. To Daniel, this was meant to be a life-changing moment. A time to have all the questions his father had ignored, finally answered.

How did Mother eventually decide to spare some of her precious time for her youngest son? By joining him for breakfast in a school cafeteria.

The elegant Marguerite Lambert-Crowley pulled up a chair in front of him. She cast an apprehensive look at the orange plastic seat before sitting down and leaning her elbows on the painted aluminum table.

As if on cue, the half dozen or so cult members who were quietly sharing their meal all stood. No longer hungry, each picked up his or her tray and glass to depart. They left the room in such quiet discipline that Daniel could hear the polyester of their pants swishing as they walked out.

"Daniel?"

Mother's soft hazelnut eyes looked into him with infinite yet manufactured care. It was the kind of look that came with practice and intent. She had planned this encounter, he could tell, accosting him while he was still half asleep and unprepared.

"M—" Daniel started, but cut himself short. What was he supposed to call this woman who'd abandoned him over a decade prior? Mom? Mother? Marguerite?

"'Mother' will do," she answered, reading his intent.

After her sermon in the gymnasium, Mother had given Daniel a radiant—almost tearful, he thought—smile from across the room while tending to her congregation. However, that was all the welcome he'd received until now.

Francis had taken him from the crowd almost immediately, hurrying him away like a shameful secret. The refugees from Saint-Ferdinand had recognized him, casting their own curious glances in his direction. Others noticed the uncanny resemblance with Francis and Mother. The Sandmen's "royal family" was expanding, and the devout didn't quite know how to feel about it. Most likely, they were waiting to take their cue from their leader, and act accordingly.

The distant stares and furtive, curious glances continued through the afternoon as Francis walked him around the compound, explaining the various rules of the Church. Daniel had been given a room, a "uniform," and even a short list of janitorial chores he was expected to perform. His contribution to the Sandmen until he was given duties more suited to his skills. They were a cult after all, not a charity.

"Why?" Daniel asked.

It was as simple a question as he could muster, but pregnant with implications. The very simplicity tilling fertile ground for a variety of answers.

"Why did I leave? Why the Sandmen? Why did I take Francis but not you? Which 'why' do you want me to answer?"

"How about all of them?"

She leaned in to push Daniel's tray to the side, making room to further lean across the table on her elbows. Daniel pulled back a moment when she reached to take his hand, unsure of what to make of the sudden familiarity.

"I'm trying to save the world, Daniel," she said, squeezing his hand. "Yesterday, when you were standing in my auditorium? That was the last thing I ever wanted to see."

She let go of him and sat back, the plastic of her chair creaking as she settled.

"Truth be told, Daniel, I don't want you here."

This was a scenario Daniel had played many times in his head while growing up. He'd always imagined his mother apologizing and explaining the contrived reasons why she'd simply had to abandon him and his father. There had to be a logical excuse. They'd had a fight or there was another man. Surely, leaving her son behind would be the one thing she regretted most, he'd told himself.

Anger filled the gap left by drowsiness, flaring up in that familiar Crowley way.

"I guess I shouldn't be surprised by that."

"Don't be melodramatic, Daniel. You're mistaking action for intent."

"What's that supposed to mean?"

"You think that my wanting you away from here is some attack on your person somehow. You want me to say I left your father because of you? Fine. That is exactly why I did it."

"What the hell?"

Daniel stood up, toppling the cheap plastic chair to the linoleum floor. He could see himself reflected in the large windows that gave out to the abandoned schoolyard. His shoulders were pulled back and his fists were at his sides. It was a familiar posture to Daniel, one he'd seen his father adopt on many occasions.

"You're doing it again, Daniel," Mother said, her calm unwavering.

She stared him down. A tiny woman perhaps half his weight, but unperturbed by his outburst. She was familiar with the Crowley temper and, even after more than a decade away, remained unimpressed by it.

Daniel took a deep breath, first unclenching his fists and then picking up his chair from the floor. There was no dignified way of doing so, and he couldn't help but suspect that it was as Mother had intended.

"Tell me," she said as he sat down again. "How did your father die?"

The question felt like a trap, another means by which to test his anger, but Daniel wouldn't fall for it.

"I killed him," he said, trying for nonchalance. He was hoping that it would be his turn to draw a reaction from her.

He did, but it wasn't the reaction he'd expected. There was no outrage or frustration. She didn't seem shocked or flustered. Instead her features cracked to reveal a deep anguish. If Daniel would have gambled on it, he would have guessed she mourned for his father, her husband.

"This is what they don't know," she said, gesturing to the walls to indicate the rest of the cult. "But you and I, we understand.

"I promised them a god of life and love, but I brought them the exact opposite. You didn't kill your father, Daniel. It did. That's what it does. It took everything Stephen held dear and twisted it against him. His love of Saint-Ferdinand. His vow to protect. His son."

Mother took a moment to compose herself, misty-eyed at her own explanation.

"It did the same to my father. It will probably do the same to me in time, if I fail."

"So you took Francis and left me and Dad to face it."

"No." Mother shook her head and twisted in her chair. "I took Francis because I needed him. I left you, and I left Stephen to protect you. It's only later that I realized your father would find the god on his own."

"You expect me to believe that all of this was for my own good?"

It sounded like excuses to Daniel. His father had led his own branch of the Sandmen to hunt for the god. Couldn't they have worked together?

"It doesn't matter what you believe. Chasing gods is dangerous business. I didn't want you anywhere near it."

"But Francis is up to the task?"

Mother inspected her blouse, picking out a piece of stray lint as she thought her answer over. Daniel tried to play her game, to see if there was anything of his mother in him that he could use in his favor. He squinted as he concentrated on reading her body language, to spot the cracks that might reveal the subtext of the woman. He knew the alphabet of her movements, but couldn't figure out the vocabulary.

"Are you jealous of him?" she answered, now satisfied that her attire was flawless again.

"No," Daniel lied.

"Good. You shouldn't be. You were an infant when I left your father and of no use to me. Even now you could never do the things Francis has done for me."

"Like kidnap Alice LeSage from her family."

Daniel leveled the comment like an accusation, but at this point he knew she would sweep even this crime under the rug, claiming it as a necessity.

"Alice is special too. Taking her wasn't optional. Surely, you recognize that by now. But you're still appalled that I did. It's that kind of sentiment that makes you more a liability than an asset.

"When I say the god is what killed your father, it's not only out of kindness. This creature, it makes us do things. It twists us against ourselves. It's no coincidence that you were the one to take down Stephen. I don't know if it planned it that way, but it certainly fed on it. That's why Francis is so special.

"Everyone is part of the Sandmen because they want something, but not Francis. Your brother has no desires, no wants. Ever since he was a child, I knew there was something about him.

"Did you know we used to have a dog?"

Daniel shook his head. His father had never allowed him to have pets, calling them a useless burden.

"Some spaniel mix," Mother continued. "We named it Charlie. Disobedient animal, but adorable. Charlie had large floppy black ears and would bark at anything that moved. One day your brother took Charlie for a walk, but that dumb dog slipped its leash and ran in front of a car. I think it was one of the Richards boys driving, but they never confessed to it. Doesn't matter. Francis brought Charlie home under his arm like he was carrying a sack of potatoes back from the store.

"He put the dog's carcass on the dinner table and when I asked him why, Francis simply said he didn't know what to do with a dead dog. He never cried or even said he was sad, and he never mentioned Charlie again after that day."

She sighed and pulled herself from the plastic chair. For a brief, ephemeral moment her composure slipped and she looked tired.

"I'm sorry if this isn't the heartwarming reunion you were expecting. Or maybe you thought I'd be some bitch who'd abandoned you out of indifferent neglect. I don't know."

The sun broke through the cloud cover and burst through the cafeteria window. Mother's face was suddenly silhouetted, unreadable in the shadows.

"What now?" Daniel asked.

He fully expected to be kicked out. His stay would have been brief, but worst, it would have been fruitless. Mother had been clear, however: she had no use for him, and that made his expulsion inevitable.

"Now?" she said, mirroring his tone. "Francis tells me that you're good with people, and you seem to worry about the welfare of our little Alice. I can't protect you by keeping you away, so instead I'm going to give you a promotion."

When Daniel first set foot in Alice LeSage's room, he was appalled by the conditions the girl was forced to live in.

There was a smell to her room that had faint hints of a backed-up sewer. It took a moment, but he was eventually able to link it to a small attached bathroom. Whoever had installed the plumbing had done a poor job of it, and now his nose was paying the price.

The next thing that struck him were the bars on the windows. She was in a basement, so already daylight was a precious resource in short supply. The bars, however, cast a forbidding shadow on the opposite wall, an inescapable reminder that she was a prisoner.

Otherwise, the room might as well have been that of any sixteen-year-old girl. It was messy, with laundry strewn across the double bed, and the walls were covered in posters. Except, they weren't of boy bands or rock stars, but classic musicians and pretty landscapes. Also, she had a small kitchen table pushed into a corner. A place for her to take her meals instead of going up to the cafeteria.

At first Daniel had to force himself to remember that she wasn't like the other Sandmen. Alice stood apart from the desperate and the gullible who fell into Mother's web. She was a prisoner. Once he began to notice the resemblance to the Missing posters he'd seen in his youth, that distinction became impossible to ignore.

"I remember my father talking about you," Daniel said as he was picking up their dishes.

They had sat in silence as they ate. Alice uncomfortable with this stranger in her room, and Daniel trying to ignore the background odor.

"What does your father have to do with me?" she asked, raising an eyebrow.

She'd retreated to her bed and sat with her back to the concrete wall, cradling her knees close to her chest. She reminded Daniel of a trapped animal and, as far as he could tell, that was exactly how she thought of herself.

"My dad was an inspector in Saint-Ferdinand. A cop. When you disappeared, there was a lot of news on television and in newspapers about you. He volunteered his department to help canvas the Eastern Townships, and they put up posters and flyers and everything. The whole thing lasted for a few years."

Daniel thought back to Mother's story about Charlie the dog.

Once, when he was a kid, he'd found a dog, little more than a puppy, under the front porch. It had been midsummer and the pup had probably been from the spring litter of a stray. Its breed was hard to determine, though he could see a bit of schnauzer under the matted gray fur. The poor thing was no larger than a cat, a malnourished collection of skin and bones. There had also been a smell coming out from under the porch. Like rotting meat. Both Daniel and his father had assumed the animal had dragged some prey underneath with it.

The dog had the same trapped but unyielding gaze as Alice. A creature who knew its situation was miserable and unsustainable but remained ever suspicious of anything that could damage the status quo.

They'd tried to goad the animal out with food and treats. There were attempts to scare it out with loud noises. Daniel had wanted to smoke it out, but his father didn't want any fire that close to the house. All attempts to crawl under and fetch the pup were met with barking, growling, and a snapping jaw.

This had lasted for a day and a half before Stephen Crowley called in Donna Miller, a veterinarian from Sherbrooke. It took her less than a minute to decide the dog was probably rabid and the smell it carried was from a festering wound on its hind leg. At least his father had the sensitivity to send Daniel inside the house before he shot the animal.

"They shouldn't have," Alice said after a lengthy pause.

"Shouldn't have what?"

"Looked for me."

"He was a cop." Daniel tried to bury the pain of talking about his father, uncertain of how successful he was. "It was his job. Besides, you were a missing little girl. The whole province was looking for you."

She pulled her knees closer to her chin and looked up to her barred window.

"Well, I'm glad they never found me."

The dishes rattled in the tray as Daniel put it down on the table. He didn't so much slam it on the surface, but the noise was enough to startle Alice.

"That's crazy. Your real family is probably still worried sick about you! Are you telling me you're fine living like this?" Daniel waved his hand across the room, lingering a moment in the direction of the bathroom. "You could have lived a normal life instead of being trapped here in this crazy cult!"

Something changed in Alice at that moment. In one fluid movement, she shed her awkwardness and slipped out of bed to stand in front of him. Daniel had never met anyone so ready for a fight. For a second he was reminded of Penny before she'd kicked him out of her house.

"You can't talk about Mother's family like that."

"You're defending her? She stole your life!"

"She gave me purpose! What do you think would have happened if I hadn't been here to put that creature to sleep when they brought it back? Here, I matter. Here, I'm important."

"Here, you're a tool."

Daniel didn't so much regret what he said. It was true, after all. He wanted his words to break through the brainwashing. But Alice was obviously hurt by the way he'd said it. He wasn't simply attacking her. He was striking at her very purpose, which was probably the only thing she had. He'd been too brazen and hurried. Daniel had expected a captive eager for escape, but the cult indoctrination was thicker than he'd anticipated. He'd have to take much smaller steps if he was going to get to her, and through her, maybe to the god.

"Listen," he said in a measured tone. "I'm sorry. You're not a tool, but my mom is using you. She doesn't care about you, only what you can do for her."

A trembling in Alice's lower lip told Daniel that he was far from having mended the damage of his words. The girl, whom he barely knew, was wavering between anger and hurt, on the verge of either crying or hitting him in the face.

"Oh really? You think you know so much, Daniel Crowley? Two days and you're an expert on Mother and *my* family? You say she doesn't care about me? Then who does, Daniel? My parents? The police? You?"

She was the dog from under the porch. Too hurt and afraid to accept any aid, but too damaged to abandon. Except, Daniel couldn't simply put her out of her misery.

"Maybe I do."

The anger seemed to slip from her, like a layer of dust blown clean from a neglected bookshelf. There was still enough to drive the tension in her fist and in her shoulder, but he had her attention.

"My car is right outside. We could leave right now. I could have you with your real family before these people even know we're gone."

He wanted his plea to come out as a confident offer of freedom. He needed Alice to see reassurance and comfort in him. Instead the words came out with desperate insistence.

Like a cool wave of relief, a confident calm seemed to sweep over Alice. She unclenched her fists and her shoulders relaxed. Even her features lost some of their edge. There was a sliver of hope that perhaps he was wrong and, unlike the dog, Alice could be saved.

"I am with my family," she said, a soft curl to her lips showing how comfortable she was with the statement.

Without urgency, she turned Daniel's pity on him. Her eyes spoke of a compassion marbled with condescension. *You don't get it, do you?* they seemed to ask.

"They're your family too. You'll see."

The door to Alice's room clicked shut behind him. Daniel stood outside the threshold, the tray of stacked empty food dishes in his hands. He could feel the weight of the keys he'd been given in his pocket and the pull of exhaustion demanding that he get some sleep. As much as he'd love to think he was resilient, his stamina was faltering. It had been an emotionally draining day, leaving his nerves exposed. Like his father, he could hide behind irritability and anger, but after spending so much of his life avoiding the Crowley anger, it was an option he'd rather avoid.

Later he'd blame the exhaustion, but in the moment, Daniel couldn't get his legs to move. He should have been going up the stairs, taking the dishes to the cafeteria, and finding his way to the small dorm room he'd been assigned. Instead his thoughts kept wandering between the keys in his pocket and the door across the hall.

Daniel shook his head like a wet dog. His hair, greasy from a few days without a shower, waved back and forth with the movement. To no avail, he tried to blink away the confusion. The only thing he did manage was to finally get his feet moving.

Instead of heading toward the stairs, however, he ended up taking a few short steps across the hall.

Drawing a deep breath, Daniel knelt down to put the tray on the floor. As he bent his knees and felt the back of his thighs touch the heels of his feet, the smell of copper filtered through the chemical scent of cleaning products on the linoleum.

His fingers traced over dark lines on the floor. Maroon stains that had hidden in the grooves between tiles. There was little doubt in Daniel's mind what their origin was.

He stood up and then tried the door handle. It rattled in his hands as if to give him one last chance to back away and quiet the curiosity that masqueraded as duty in his mind.

Instead, unbidden, his hand found its way into his pocket. Tired but nimble fingers fished out the keys. They were linked together on a janitor's ring, the kind with a retractable chain and belt clip. Daniel flipped through the dozen keys in his arsenal, settling on the one marked *004*. The number on the door before him. The key was clean and new, shining bright even under the dim fluorescent light. Whoever had owned this key ring had probably never set foot in room *004*.

The hinges barely complained as he pushed the door open, but Daniel didn't need the sound effect. There were plenty of other things in Sam Finnegan's prison to make his skin crawl.

Careful to avoid the clicking of the latch bolt, Daniel closed the door behind him. He told himself that it was so no one could catch him in the act, but in effect, Daniel was locking himself in a cage. One with a thirsting god already inside.

The first time he'd visited this room and seen the conditions in which Sam was kept, Francis had been his guide. His dispassionate confidence had reassured Daniel. Even as he realized what the creature on the ratty mattress really was, as long as he stayed calm, it was easy to follow Francis's lead. Now, alone in the dimly lit room, a single fluorescent tube fixed overhead, Daniel could much better appreciate the caged power within Sam Finnegan.

His legs carried him forward, passing the decrepit old couch and the half-empty glass of water Alice had forgotten earlier that day.

"Hey, Sam," he whispered.

What reaction did he expect? Was there even anything of Finnegan left in this pale husk?

Sam didn't answer.

But something else did.

"Stephen . . . Crowley . . ."

The voice was a bucket of ice water tossed at Daniel's face. They were words without sound, spawned within his thoughts, both starting and stopping in his own mind. He might have imagined them but instead knew with certainty that he hadn't. Their alien quality left no question.

"No . . ." the voice continued, correcting itself. "Not Stephen."

Sam hadn't moved a hair on his white head and his lips were still and dry. He couldn't have been more inert if he'd been made of clay. If he still breathed, Daniel was hard-pressed to see any proof. That didn't stop the creature within from speaking to him. It was struggling to figure him out and find purchase in his mind.

The thought terrified Daniel. Even bound in human flesh, shackled by the chains of sleep, the god of the Sandmen retained enough power to speak to him. It inspired a deep primal fear, but also resonated a sort of majesty. If this was the kind of creature that primitive humans had worshiped as gods, there was little doubt as to why.

"My name is Daniel," he caught himself saying out loud.

There was no immediate answer. He could somehow feel the god smiling, even if he couldn't see it on Sam's lips. The intent was there, just as tangible.

"Daniel," it thought, etching the name in the boy's brain. "Are you here to bargain?"

Stephen Crowley had made a bargain. The god had unshackled his anger and given him near invulnerability. Fury reknit his flesh against wounds that should have killed him. Daniel had only put an end to it because he'd wielded a weapon touched by that god.

Daniel had no such weapons now, a fact he deeply regretted.

"Your father, my servant, kept his end of our bargain. Your lineage is in good standing."

The entity sounded pleased. Satisfied. The truth of the sentiment unwavering.

"I'm not here to bargain."

The entity recoiled from his brain a moment and for the first time Daniel noticed that it wasn't simply transmitting thoughts into his mind, but rather extending its own presence there. No sooner had it left, however, it was back.

"You disagree with Stephen's end."

Disagree? Daniel almost laughed. The being's implanted thoughts left so little room for ambiguity, but its alien perspective created an odd and unsettling language barrier. *Disagree* was both incredibly accurate, yet so far from the scope of how Daniel felt. The word could have been a taunt.

"I was my father's end," Daniel stated, his voice firm, an attempt to take ownership of the dialogue.

The god remained unimpressed.

"You killed Stephen, my creation. You did it wielding a part of me against him. You were an instrument. A single word in a conversation I was having with myself."

The truth of that statement resonated tragically with Daniel. Ever since the circus, he had thought of his father's death as the result of his own rage gaining a supernatural hold on him. While that may have been the seed of it, the god had just stated in no uncertain terms that it had had much more of a hand in the matter than that.

"You killed my father," he stated flatly.

"You say it like it matters."

The Crowley anger flared inside Daniel. Of course it mattered! How could this creature think otherwise? It was so much more than Stephen Crowley who'd died on that day. Aside from Nathan Cicero and the other victims from the circus, every witness had had their lives damaged by the event. Saint-Ferdinand had been dealt a fatal wound and was bleeding out to this day. And whatever innocence Daniel had had left had been ripped from him.

Fists clenched and teeth gritting, Daniel was almost blind to how the entity took notice of the anger. Like a dog, curiously sniffing at a fresh tennis ball, it circled the white-hot rage, poking it with its nose. Pushing it around with its paws. Daniel could feel its desire to grab at his fury, sink its teeth in, and run away to bury it somewhere secret. A place where it could go dig it up later when it suited its purpose.

A deep, practiced breath brought Daniel's temper back under control, taking away the object of the god's curiosity.

"Are you sure you would not bargain, Daniel Crowley?"

Another breath, and Daniel was able to unfold his fingers. Taking one more look at Sam's immobile form, he released his jaw and took a step back.

"I can be the salve to all your troubles, Daniel Crowley. Your reality is so malleable. Like clay at my fingertips. It would be as little effort for me to put all your worries to rest as it would be for you to pull the nails from Samuel Finnegan's eyes."

"There's nothing you can offer me that would make me do that," Daniel said, assurance creeping back into his words.

"Are you so sure? Stephen Crowley gave himself to me . . . . Don't you want him returned?"

The thoughts it implanted in Daniel's mind were louder somehow, etched deeper into his gray matter. They branded themselves with a deafening urgency. It was an image, imbued by emotion, of Stephen Crowley. Not the one from the day he died, but rather an amalgam of all the good days Daniel had spent with his father. A flood of memories from old fishing trips on sweltering sunny days or hockey practices his father used to coach, all showing an idealized version of the past. In those images, they were the Crowley Boys again.

"God taketh, but god can also giveth back."

ABRAHAM

"GHOSTS, HUH?" Harry Peterson said.

The old man sat on a stool in his studio. The afternoon Eastern Township light cascaded around him. Harry was busy mixing oils and paints, adding in little of this color and a little of that pigment, looking for the perfect hue.

Penny gave Abraham a nudge of the shoulder and a look that translated to *I told you so*. The hesitation to bring all of this ghost and god business to Harry's attention was driven purely by fear. Death scare after death scare had left Abraham's heart raw. It was a wound with most of the skin shorn off. It was agony to think what it might do to his father to add more to his worries.

Penny, as always, had been much more rational. They were, after all, dealing with things far beyond their understanding. A god who existed both in life and in death, straddling the worlds, its power divided. The spirits of the deceased, walking restless and confused across Saint-Ferdinand. Venus leaving for Montreal, hoping to connect with one of her grandfather's associates, only a few vague clues to guide her. In fact, this was the great irony of their situation: Harry had a buffet of intelligence at his fingertips, but Abraham remained starved for answers. Too worried that if he touched any of it, the whole meal might crumble to ashes.

Harry Peterson didn't evaporate or die when his son approached him. Instead he picked up some dark green from his palette and used a painting knife to mix it in with the moss color he was creating.

He adjusted his wire-framed glasses and leaned into his painting while making a wet murmur with his throat as he considered the question.

"You're both seeing this little dead girl appear, distressed and confused, so you just want to run off half-cocked and save her, don't you?"

Penelope and Abraham gave each other a grim look. That was exactly the plan. Audrey had been under their care on multiple occasions in life, and it only seemed right to continue in that direction for her in death. Wasn't that what funerals were for? To stretch our care for others beyond the grave, just in case there was some speck of comfort that the deceased might benefit from? Knowing for an absolute fact that Audrey's spirit lingered on only added weight to that responsibility. The problem was, they had no idea how to help her. You couldn't call 9-1-1 for this sort of thing. Besides, Audrey wasn't the only restless spirit in Saint-Ferdinand.

"That bear didn't end up in her grave by accident," Harry continued, meticulously mixing a drop of ivory into the moss-green dab of paint.

"Mr. Peterson," Penny explained, "I held that bear in my hands two months ago and used it to bring Audrey's ghost to me. Nobody's disturbed the soil on top of her grave since then."

With a small fan brush, Harry Peterson picked at the new hue he'd composed for his work. He then crouched down with pain and effort until he was but a couple of feet off the ground. For a moment, he considered the painting as he did the question, then he began to apply the color.

Abraham winced when his father did this sort of thing. He could see the old man's trembling legs and shaking knees. But it was what he wanted, so the boy bit his tongue. There were many things he would do to keep his father's health from failing any further, but depriving him of his greatest joy in life wasn't one of them.

"What's this?" the old man asked, pointing at the spot his fan brush had just caressed.

"Rocks," Abraham said, then caught himself, seeing a trap in the question. "Moss on rocks!"

Harry shook his head. "It's paint. Oil and pigment on canvas. Magritte taught us that." He tapped the rim of his glasses thoughtfully with the handle of the brush. "For now it's only a projection of the moss and rocks that I have in my head. It's enough that you see it as what I'm trying to show, but it's still just—"

"The bear never left the grave."

Penelope interrupted with understanding passing between her lips. Harry twisted his head around and looked up at her with a proud if tired smile.

"The bear I held to call her. That was just a projection. Audrey painting her toy on the real world."

Harry didn't waste any of his precious breath answering, relying on his smile and gentle nodding to convey his satisfaction at her reasoning.

The mural had evolved since Abraham had last seen it. Not in the composition and subject, but rather in the level of detail and complexity. It was the same painting, a sunset or sunrise framed by an ancient stone arch. But the previous version might as well have been a rough sketch. It had gone from a crude rendering to a formidable expression of realism. Warm oranges illuminated the sky and bounced off waves in the distance, yet the setting remained cold. Meticulous attention in choosing the scarce few fern leaves along with the abundant lichen and moss told a long tale about where the scene might be located. It seemed so plain and empty.

"But what about the nails?" Abraham asked, eager to be part of the conversation. "She had nails in her eyes but now they're gone."

From the corner of his eye, Abraham noticed Penny give a shudder as he drudged up the memory.

Harry teased paint onto the lichen, adding near-imperceptible highlights that gave it a hint more dimension and texture.

"Penelope?" Harry prompted.

"The bear isn't the only projection," Penny continued. "The god in Venus's shed is also a projection of sorts. When I had my out-of-body experience this summer, I saw, or rather, I felt it. What we're seeing is just a piece of it poking through a hole in reality. So . . . if the line between reality is fudgeable and blurry and all that . . . then . . ."

"Then?" Abraham urged her on.

"Then I don't know!" Penelope's irritation seemed aimed at herself and Abraham both. He'd noticed that she was wearing gloves. His father's studio was large and had a tendency to be cold during the fall, but not nearly enough to justify covering her hands. She wasn't protecting herself from the cold, but rather others from her hands.

His own fingers twitched at the memory.

"What if the nails aren't a projection though? Dad, you said your painting was just a projection of what you're imagining, but you have half a dozen paintings with live birds in them. What if . . ." Abraham stopped. "Never mind. This is stupid."

Penny cocked her head and furrowed her brow. It was an expression she often wore when she thought he'd said something majestically dumb. He knew those moments well, when he hadn't thought through what he'd said and even his best friend just didn't know what to make of him anymore.

"No," Harry said. "Go on, son."

Abraham hesitated. His idea was far-fetched and connected dots he didn't feel had any business having a line between them, but it felt right.

"If a projection of an idea from the living . . . in a painting . . . can become real, why not a projection of something important to the dead? I mean, where did the bear appear last time? You said Erica Hazelwood found it at the site of your mother's death. That's where I saw Audrey."

The frown on Penelope's forehead evaporated. Her mouth hung slightly open in silent surprise as she tried to catch up to his thinking. Her right hand pulling at the fingers on the left, trying to tease the solution out of the leather of her gloves. It wasn't a Sherlock

Holmes–level deduction, but he'd gotten there first and that was a rare feat for Abraham.

"Maybe she could push her projection of the bear through at that spot because of the god. It was there too. Maybe she's reaching through the same hole that monster used to kill my mom." Her voice was cold, heavy with sadness.

"So all we need is to find another place where something horrible happened? Should be easy enough," Abraham said.

"No, no. Not necessarily." She stepped closer to him, as if the proximity allowed their thoughts to work better in concert. "Just somewhere that the veil has been thinned down enough."

"Then we're looking for a place where something violent and supernatural happened!" It felt like they were finally making some progress. Abraham's thoughts stumbled over one another as he tried to think of a good spot to investigate first. The cell block at the police station? Venus's shed? Right here on the farm, where the massacre had occurred?

"That would narrow it down, except . . ." Penny frowned.

"Except that we live in Saint-Ferdinand," concluded Harry, snuffing out Abraham's excitement. "Might as well be looking for a specific blade of grass on a golf course."

Occasional surges of guilt kept popping up for Abraham throughout the day. This was an important task, more dire than life and death. They were in the business of saving a soul, perhaps many souls. The weight of responsibility should have pressed more heavily on his shoulders.

Instead it felt to Abraham like a noble quest, and it spoke to his spirit as a caretaker. He wanted to help. He wanted to be the hero, but most of all, he wanted to impress Penny.

So far, they'd wasted all of the day's dusk and a few hours of night looking through the fields behind the Peterson farm. They sifted through the overgrown weeds trying to remember where everything had been set up only a few weeks prior. Eventually, having found no bear or other artifacts from Audrey, they moved on to the site of Gabrielle LaForest's murder.

"You don't have to go," Abraham said, trying his best to be protective.

Penny hesitated. They stood across the road from the patch of woods. Maples and firs cast sinister shadows with only an orange streetlamp attempting to banish them. This was where her mother had breathed her last breath, and Abraham wasn't looking forward to the trauma that going back might cause his friend.

"No. It's fine," she said. "This is where I saw her the first time. She scared me and I hurt her. I wasn't there for my mom's death. I know it's not much better, but Audrey is what I associate with this place. Maybe that will help?"

Despite her assurances, Penny did suffer a bit of a breakdown. As they got to the clearing where Abraham had seen Audrey, Penny let a trembling hand brush over gouges left in the trunk of a maple tree. Deep and savage, they might have been made by a bear, but both knew they hadn't been. She allowed a soft sob to escape, only to catch herself, trying to pretend it never happened.

Finally they stopped by Venus's house to inspect the backyard. Unfortunately, nothing was left of the notorious shed. Every piece of it had been taken into evidence during the investigation. If there was anything to find there, it failed to reveal itself.

In contrast to their visit to the woods, here they took time to reminisce about their first time seeing the creature, and how Penelope had had the gall to stab a god. It was an empowering, but also terrifying, memory. One made worse by the sight of her gloved hands.

"I can't believe I'm about to say this, but we're about to run out of locations with traumatic backstories—in Saint-Ferdinand," she complained. "What about Finnegan's trailer? Or the spot on the road where Audrey died? How much more emotionally charged does a place need to be for her to give us a sign?"

"I'm not sure," Abraham answered, tired and frustrated but ever greedy to be in Penelope's company.

To be out so late in Saint-Ferdinand was oddly intoxicating. They'd all done it at one time or another, of course. Daring one another to sneak out past curfew and wander through the darkness. It would have sounded strange to an outsider, but Saint-Ferdinand had its own boogeyman. A serial killer had lurked among them and no parent wanted their child out after dark.

Tonight was different. There was no permission needed, no breaking of curfew, no need to constantly look over their shoulders. With the earthly killer gone, the threat of the nighttime had vanished.

They knew that wasn't technically true. Sam Finnegan had vanished from jail soon after the circus massacre and although it was presumed that Inspector Crowley had killed and hidden his body, there was no proof of that. If Finnegan had indeed escaped, then he was still lurking around somewhere, unhinged and with decades of experience in luring and disposing of victims.

Penelope in particular had every reason to hate and fear Finnegan. She had made that fact obvious as they'd stepped out of the farmhouse after dinner. In an act that echoed deeply of her actions earlier that summer, she'd reached for the knife block and pulled out the largest carving knife she could find.

It wasn't her knife and it wasn't her house, but she didn't bother to ask permission or explain. Abraham didn't complain. He had decided some time ago that his friend carried a much heavier burden than he did, and had thus accepted that there were certain behaviors of hers he'd never understand. At least this time he knew she was armed.

"What are you smiling at this time, you goof?" she asked, after catching him with a grin on his face for the umpteenth time.

"I dunno. I just like walking around, ya know? Gotta find some fun in all this."

She seemed unconvinced by his explanation. He wanted to admit that he appreciated their time together, but he knew it would sound like a confession, not the matter of fact he wanted it to be.

"Not everything has to be a string of traumatic events. Even in this stupid village," he tried to further explain.

This time, however, her stare didn't waver. A small smile of her own crept onto her lips, pushing her rosy-chilled cheeks upward. She squinted as if trying to see inside him. Her eyes made him uncomfortable, the blue in them appearing to almost have a light of their own.

"What?"

"Nothing. I'm just thinking maybe you're right. Maybe it shouldn't always be about the traumatic events."

"Exactly! Why can't it be about the—"

Abraham cut himself off, interrupting his walk dead in his own steps. So sudden was his stop that he almost lost his balance and fell over. Instead, after a breath, he used the momentum to do an about-face, grabbing Penny's arm and pulling her back toward Main Street, as if he'd forgotten something there.

"Abe! What are you doing?"

"It doesn't have to be about the trauma, Penny!" he said with renewed excitement.

"Skip to where you make sense, please?"

"We've gone to all these places with murders and death, and maybe that's where the wall between life and death is thinnest. But what if that's not where Audrey prefers to hang out? What if instead we should be thinking of her happy places? Where she felt safe."

Penny didn't share his enthusiasm. She frowned and looked around, rediscovering where in Saint-Ferdinand they'd wound up. He was taking her toward Hemingford Road, where the nicer part of town was.

"And I guess you figured that there's no place like home?" she said, deciding that they were walking toward the Bergeron house.

"Exactly!"

He wasn't exactly sure how much faith he'd put into the idea of finding Audrey's "happy place," but he liked the idea that perhaps not everything had to be doom and gloom. That maybe for once they could find a lighter side to their quest.

The house, by far the most luxurious in the village, had been left behind. Beatrice Bergeron had gone who knows where after losing her child and husband. The screens on the windows were caked with the remains of dandelion seeds. The long stone path that led to the front door was dusty and under assault by weeds, while reeds had begun to spread from the nearby ditch and onto the vast lawn. The local homeowner organization would have had a fit at this level of negligence, except that most of them had also left the village.

"Here," Penelope said, stopping at the threshold of the empty driveway. "This is where William died."

It was a large driveway, over two cars wide. Yet the spot she'd picked to stand on seemed arbitrary.

"How do you know?"

"I'm not sure," she said, rubbing her gloved hands for a warmth that would never come. "Just a feeling, I guess."

Penelope shuffled in place, wringing her hands and pulling at the leather of her gloves without ever removing them.

Nervous would have been an acceptable term for her demeanor, but there seemed to be more to it than that. She looked like a trapped hare: too panicked to stand still, but too terrified to run. Every muscle and nerve twitching in an effort to find a way out of her skin.

"I don't see any sign of her," she said after a moment of cursory inspection.

"You, uh . . . You want to check out the house?" he asked, hoping that perhaps his initial optimistic idea still had merit.

While jittery and even more on the edge of hysteria, Penelope nodded and followed his lead.

Abraham lifted the same yellow flashlight he'd had the previous night, waving it at Penny, trying to reassure her that he was prepared.

"One question though: What do we do if there's an alarm system?"

"I don't know," Penny answered. "Nothing, I guess. If they have an alarm, it's probably a silent one, and the only way we'll know we've tripped it is when Matt shows up to arrest us."

Hopefully, if they did get caught, the whole thing would be written off as two teens looking for a quiet, solitary place to share an intimate moment. Abraham could live with that. But if they went to jail, that would be another problem entirely. Who would take care of his father? How would Penelope deal with sitting in the same cell as the man who'd butchered her whole family?

Without worry of disturbing any occupants and in blissful, willful ignorance of any potential security system, Abraham gave a few good kicks to the back door, breaking the lock. A heart-stopping crack was followed again by absolute silence.

The house was full of ghosts.

Not real ghosts. Abraham knew what those felt like by now. The ghosts in the Bergeron house were all made of sheets. Tall ones draped over the lean skeletons of lamps and chairs. Squat and fat ones shrouded the tables and sofas. Every piece of furniture was thus protected from dust and sunlight.

This unintentional haunted-house motif shouldn't have been any creepier than a Saturday morning cartoon. But the distant light from the neighbors' houses turned the apparitions into forbidding shadows and specters. Occasional cobwebs swayed eerily in the displaced air as Abe and Penny walked by.

"Cheery place," Abraham remarked, trying to fill the silence.

Penny didn't answer as she walked across the living room, arms outstretched to caress the armchair and sofa as she passed by them, her silhouette outlined by the minimal light filtering in through the thick blinds. Even after several minutes, Abe's eyes refused to adjust any further.

"Where do you think we should look?" Penny asked, her feet taking her to the kitchen.

"Not sure. Her bedroom closet?"

"She's not playing hide-and-seek, Abe. Let's pretend you're right: Where do you think she'd go for her most pleasant memories?"

Penelope had babysat Audrey here and although the house now felt alien and strange, it was easy to remember it as it once was. It was a large home, but not a complicated one. A lot of open spaces on the main floor, with bedrooms on the second, and one huge playroom in the basement. The Bergerons had made their home into the perfect place to entertain friends. The backyard had two picnic tables and a grill that would make most steakhouses envious.

Hockey viewing parties and birthday events were all frequently held at the Bergerons' home. At least, they had been during the eight years Audrey had been alive. Her presence had made William and Beatrice into the happiest and most generous couple in town.

Abraham followed Penny to the kitchen, thinking for a moment that little Audrey's love of ice cream might make it the right place to look first. Alas, still no sign of the girl or her spirit. Only the dark backyard and the hum of the refrigerator.

Seeing the flashing numbers on the microwave did shake loose some cobwebs in his mind. Popcorn. When Penelope would babysit Audrey, they'd make popcorn and watch movies in the home theater downstairs. If there was any pleasant memory of Audrey's that involved him and Penny, it would be how they'd watch animated Disney movies until the little tike fell asleep and they had to carry her upstairs to her bed.

"How about the basement, in the game room?" he suggested.

The Bergerons had made their home into the perfect place to entertain friends. Every conceivable luxury could be found: an arcade cabinet, Ping-Pong and pool tables, as well as several couches arranged in front of an immense TV projection screen, and a small kitchen that always smelled of fresh popcorn or hot wings.

The door to the basement creaked with a high-pitched whine when they pushed it open. In absolute silence and with his senses heightened, Abraham felt as if he could hear everything.

Without even thinking, he extended his left arm to flick the light switch just outside the stairwell.

The beeping of the arcade cabinet booting up and the humming of dozens of halogen bulbs broke the careful silence. A warm green hue tickled the corner of Abraham's eye from the fixture above the pool table.

He should have known. The appliances in the kitchen had power—why would the basement be any different?

"Well, at least it isn't as spooky anymore," he said with a light laugh, attempting to bring levity to his clumsiness.

"Right. Wouldn't want that, now would we?" came a voice, raspy and out of practice, from around the corner of the stairs.

It was the voice of someone who'd barely spoken in days, perhaps weeks, but it was also a familiar voice, one that Abraham was glad to hear, if only for a second. But before they could turn the corner, he saw how Penny's spine had gone rigid, her fists clenched. He remembered that she had her own history with the owner of that voice, and how it didn't belong here.

"Dr. McKenzie?" Penelope asked, the suggestion of a threat under her breath.

They turned the corner toward the hallway that led to the television room. Along the wall was the door to the legendary Bergeron wine cellar. William was well known for his drinking and expensive tastes. The large refrigerated, humidity-controlled room filled from floor to ceiling with pricey bottles had been a point of pride for him. After clicking the door behind him, Dr. Randall McKenzie emerged from the cellar.

"Penelope," he said, stepping under one of the halogen lights.

The man had wasted away since Abraham had last seen him. His features didn't simply lack in fat and muscles but also in the joie de vivre that had animated Venus's uncle. Once, he'd been the one to sneak them details about the many murder scenes in Saint-Ferdinand, or share tidbits about criminal pathology and autopsies. He was the cool uncle. The guy Venus had always assumed would let her try her first beer.

Now there was little left of that person. Instead of the loud Hawaiian shirts and cargo shorts or the brown slacks and jacket, he wore large black denim pants, some generic T-shirt salvaged from who knew where, and an oversize gray hooded sweatshirt.

His steps were hesitant and his posture was that of a dog caught in a car's headlights.

"Well . . . you got me," he said, taking full advantage of the dramatic lighting. "Now go away."

The disgraced medical examiner waited for a reaction in an almost theatrical pause. Apart from the new clothes, there was now something abrasive about him. A sarcastic impatience that scratched at Abraham. The boy had seen his own father's wisdom increase and his demeanor become softer the more hardships he faced, but Randy seemed to have been sharpened to an edge by his own trials.

He turned on his heel, revealing a bit of a limp in his step, and put his hands into his pockets and acted as if Penny and Abe were already gone.

"What the hell, Randy?" Penny yelled after him. Her anger as hot as her hands were cold. "How long have you been squatting here? Do you have any idea what we've been through while you were cowering away?"

McKenzie stopped, his hooded head straightening by a degree before he turned around again.

"No, Penny, I don't know. And ya know what? I don't care. I've got my own shit to deal with. Haven't you kids meddled enough already?"

"Have we . . . you monster!" Penny stepped past Abraham, walking to within two feet of Randy. She towered over him. Taller, more athletic, and pulling at the fingers of her gloves with threatening jerks of her wrists. "We were just in the cemetery yesterday! We know what you did to Audrey. You're the reason she can't rest!"

"You don't have the briefest comprehension of what I did for that child. In fact, your collective ignorance is half the reason everything is so messed up—"

Penny, her hand now naked, slapped Randy's face with her open palm. The shock of pain and outrage in his face was ephemeral, almost immediately replaced by bulging eyes and gritted teeth. Even in that brief moment of contact, the cold had bitten into him.

"Tell me again how bad you have it, Randy? C'mon. I'm all ears."

VENUS

HER ANKLE WAS AGONY.

After a few hours, Venus was confident that nothing was broken and all she had was a bad sprain. That being said, her captor was forcing her to walk at a pitiless pace and it did her ankle no favors.

The moments immediately after the "accident" were a messy blur. Venus didn't want to admit it, but in all likelihood, she'd been in shock. She'd been nabbed from the wreckage by Lucien Peña himself.

A fist the size of a bear paw pulled at her wrist, forcing her to walk on her injured leg, leading her away from the wreck of the delivery truck and the police cruiser. By the time she could think straight enough to wonder about Constable Ben's fate, they were clear across town.

It had been the strong, cold breeze off the Prairies River, the body of water that separates Montreal and the suburb of Laval, that had knocked Venus back to her senses. Over three hours of walking and stumbling and limping were brought into sharp focus, including the crash.

"You killed Ben," she said, shaking off the large paw that had pulled on her hand as they'd traversed the city. "Oh my god . . . You killed him! Why?"

Lucien shrugged at her question and something snapped. Venus hit him. First with her right fist, then her left. She had no delusion that she was going to hurt the huge man. He was as big and heavy as the rumors had suggested. Judging from the roll of his eyes, her punches barely registered.

It wasn't even at him that Venus was angry. Rather, her violent outburst had more to do with her anger at herself for how she'd allowed Ben and Jodie to convince her to stick around with them. She'd known the risk she would inevitably put them in, but her hunger for companionship had clouded her judgment.

Her fists pounded into Peña's chest. This could have gone on for a while, and Venus certainly would have been fine with that, but something in the back of her mind reached out. Like a voice, dark and familiar, it whispered soothing, wordless thoughts, begging to be fed the anger.

The hollow left by the god was growing. She could feel the connection becoming stronger. There was reason for worry in that, but also no denying the advantage it provided. Now was no time for emotional outbursts, so she allowed her anger and guilt to drain from her and into the cold place in her soul.

Seeing the calm wash over Venus's face, Lucien put his hands into his pockets, fishing out a pack of cigarettes and a plastic lighter. He sat smoking, nonchalant and uncaring, on one of the park benches that lined the bike path that ran under Viau Bridge.

"Why?" she asked again, with a numbness to her calm.

"I leave a trail of dead bodies and you drag a couple of cops into it. How else did you think that would play out? Besides, that was a hell of a stupid way to try to corner me."

She wanted to kill him then. She had no means to do it, but the desire was no less palpable. Thoughts of waiting for him to fall asleep or let his guard down so she could choke him crossed her mind. What would that achieve, though? After weeks, she had finally found Lucien Peña, the man who she thought would help her defeat a god, and she hated him.

"You didn't have to kill them."

"You certainly are your father's daughter, aren't you?"

Peña pulled on his cigarette, watching with disdain as the smoke caught in the cold wind.

Fresh anger blossomed in Venus's heart, but she was quick to quell its fury, calling again on the emptiness gouged out of her soul. The potential of the god's blessing was becoming more and more apparent to her. The creature's touch could temper the fires of her anger. It dulled her grief and muted her pain. Looking at Lucien Peña, she saw the cruel killer, a man who murdered Sandmen without a second thought and had now probably killed her new friends. But when she called on the god's "power," all she saw was a tool. Lucien Peña boiled down, becoming a means to an end.

"How do you do it?" she asked.

Lucien gave her a half smile. He looked at Venus as a lion tamer would a big cat he didn't know. Arrogant experience in a struggle against careful wariness.

"Oh, the city and I, we go way back, ya know."

"I don't," she said, allowing her earnest curiosity to filter through. "But I need to learn."

"Right. The prophecy." He pulled on his cigarette for effect. "I guess I shouldn't be surprised Neil didn't bother teaching his kids."

"He taught my uncle Randy, but none of that made it down to me."

"Figures. Bet your dad forbade him. Paul was always a bit of a pussy."

Venus had been pulling off her boot, a worn black leather thing she'd gotten at a military surplus on Saint Laurent. She wanted to inspect her ankle and see how bad the swelling was. Any thought of that was slapped out of her at the second mention of her father.

"How dare you?" she said, her voice calmer and flatter than she'd intended. "My father sacrificed himself. Wasn't it the Craftsmen's job to stop that god? How long have you been hiding here, waiting for someone else to clean up Saint-Ferdinand?"

Lucien didn't answer, not with words. Instead he turned his head, furrowing his thick brow in an effort to be menacing. It failed to rattle Venus.

"How dare you?" she repeated, hoping to force an explanation or at least some amount of shame onto the man.

The stare-down didn't last very long. After a few heartbeats of silence, Venus opted to turn back to her foot and ankle to assess the damage. She didn't feel anything out of place aside from the hot water balloon that had replaced her muscles. She'd heal in time.

"You know about Katrina's prophecy, so you know why I sought you out. Sandmen, Craftsmen, my grandfather, the circus. I need to know as much as possible," she said, pulling off her thick gray sock and pushing her toes back into her boot.

"'Katrina'?" Peña scoffed. "Is that what she's calling herself? Really committing to the whole fortuneteller bit, ain't she? I guess 'Elizabeth' lacked flair."

"She's dead," Venus said, hoping to tug at some emotion in him.

It almost worked. For a moment Lucien Peña was quiet and perhaps even contemplative. He tossed the butt of his cigarette onto the bike path and lost himself looking over the river.

"She must have known it was coming," he murmured, mostly to himself.

"She did," Venus said, following Peña's gaze to the river. "So did Cicero, and my dad. They all just accepted their destiny like they had no choice."

The same way she was expected to accept her own without a fight.

"That's the part stories don't tell us. Who we are is one of the building blocks of our destinies." Peña looked at his hands. He seemed to dwell back on his own actions and how they might have brought him to where he is now. "A man is the result of the impact between himself and his circumstances. Same for a woman. Same for a god."

"Cicero told me about that. He said that's how he knew my father was dead. Because, if given a choice between running from death or trying to save someone, even if the attempt was futile, Paul would try saving a life. And as much as it hurts, that was my dad. That's who he was."

Peña turned his black eyes toward Venus, scrutinizing her as if for the first time. He had the look of someone reassessing a complex situation.

"Maybe Paul wasn't that much of a pussy after all."

The implied apology hit home more than Venus had expected. But it did nothing to erase Peña's actions or his attitude. Ben and Jodie were still either dead or gravely wounded.

After a while, Peña looked at his watch and cursed. He leaned in over Venus, grabbing her calf with one hand and wrapping his finger the whole way around her slender limb; then, pinching the back of her boot with the other, he yanked the footwear into place.

"Ow!" she screamed, the sprain in her ankle awakened anew. "What the hell?"

"I'll be your mentor, McKenzie, but I ain't your nurse. We have a schedule to respect."

"What? Where are we going?"

"C'mon." He sighed, motioning for Venus to follow. They walked for perhaps five minutes, heading toward Ville Saint-Laurent, a borough to the northwest of the island with a large industrial park near the airport, before he continued his belated answer. "We're killing someone."

For a moment it felt like everything she'd hidden in the cold hollow of her soul would spill out. Lucien had stated his intention with such callous disregard that it was difficult to accept the words at face value.

"I'm sorry, what?" she asked, barely keeping her stutter in check.

"That thing you think makes me a monster? We're doing that. We're off to kill a member of the Church of the Sandmen. Isn't that how you were tracking me down? Figuring out my involvement in those deaths? Well, there you are, McKenzie: front-row seats and a backstage tour."

"How?" Her question was twofold. She was curious about the technicalities. She knew that Peña used his mastery over the city to commit his murders.

It wasn't that much different from what Randy did for the dead, except Lucien Peña was applying it to Montreal as a whole. Manipulating objects to influence events that would, through some sort of convoluted incantation, result in a very specific accident, one that would either kill or incapacitate a member of the Sandmen. The entire city was a Rube Goldberg machine of murder. Peña was casting a spell, and the whole of Montreal was the surface on which he drew his enchantment.

This was how he'd killed Gauthier and it was how he'd caused the crash that likely killed Ben.

Venus needed to know more. She had no love for the Sandmen, or the Craftsmen for that matter. Both cults had been instrumental in not only unleashing but also creating the monster that had already caused so much anguish in Saint-Ferdinand, with the potential to do so much worse.

But Lucien wasn't just systematically eliminating the cult members. He'd been able to calculate his attack on Ben's car down to a foot in either direction. The delivery truck had missed her by a hair. If he had that level of control, then how did Gauthier stumble away from the accident in the subway?

Because he wasn't simply killing them. If she was correct in her assumption, he was interrogating them first.

For the next few hours, Venus quietly followed Lucien, observing his actions. The two of them spent the night going back and forth across the greater metropolitan area of Montreal. They rode buses or the subway, but mostly they walked. They traveled all the way to Anjou in the north, only to turn around and immediately go back downtown. At each stop, Lucien would make a subtle modification to the landscape. On Viger Avenue he twisted a stop sign so it'd be a little harder to see from the road. Downtown, at the corner of Crescent and Sainte-Catherine, he gave a vigorous, violent kick to a circuit box on a traffic light. For the life of her, Venus could not fathom how each of these seemingly random maneuvers would unlock what Lucien needed to sabotage the Sandmen.

Still, she watched as Lucien counted down the precise seconds on his watch, timing each bizarre movement with a life-and-death intensity.

They made two more stops, but again, they were separated by kilometers of inconvenient transit.

The first was in front of the Hôpital du Sacré-Coeur. Located to the north of the island, it was an imposing brown-brick building with verdigris rooftops. It could probably house upward of five hundred patients. Venus didn't get a good idea of what it was that Lucien had done there, what piece of his mystical machinery he'd put in place. Her thoughts were too scrambled, the juggling act of necessity, duty, and guilt a circus performance she had never even considered would be hers to accomplish.

There was nothing she could do to stop Lucien directly. The old man may have been used up and damaged, but he towered over her and could break her with a twist of his wrist if he chose to.

She could hope to slip away, but what then? It wouldn't stop what he was up to. She wasn't even sure she wanted to stop him. The Sandmen were their common foe. All she had to do was weather the guilt and watch Peña weave his murderous spell. With luck, maybe she'd learn a trick or two, and a little ruthlessness might come in handy.

When morning came back around and the streets stirred to life again, Peña and Venus finally stopped. They had returned downtown, at the site of the accident. Except, it was as if nothing had ever happened. Even the asphalt where the delivery truck had T-boned Ben's police cruiser was clean of any debris. Montreal had swallowed all the evidence and moved on from the tragedy.

"All right," Peña said, sitting on a granite slab decorating the entrance of a government building. "We got a few hours if you want to get some rest."

The idea was ridiculous. While Venus was exhausted, both by lack of sleep and from the constant walking on her injured ankle, her mind was awash with questions. It was a cacophony that needed voice.

"What have we been doing all night?"

Peña patted his pockets and found his pack of cigarettes, pulling one out and placing it between his lips.

"Causing another accident," he said, but quickly added: "Something a little more subtle and a lot less vulgar than what I did to your friends. Nothing fatal. Just part of the greater plan."

He probably expected her to ask what the "greater plan" was, but she already knew, after a fashion. They were killing a member of the Sandmen. Maybe she knew all she needed to. Maybe she didn't want to know more. Either way, there was a bigger question that loomed over her.

"What happened? With the Sandmen and Craftsmen and the circus and all."

Venus leaned on the granite slab, trying to decide what to do with her foot.

"Idiots happened. Me chief among them, I suppose," Lucien offered as a vague explanation.

Venus raised an eyebrow. Peña was slipping back into philosophical melancholy. She could sense a hunger in him, not so much to unburden himself but to speak with someone who'd at least understand the circumstances, if not the man himself.

"At least you're being honest," she said.

"Oh, don't get me wrong. The story doesn't lack for fools. Your grandfather, Sophie, me . . . and that insufferable, incompetent Elijah. It's just that when you strip it all down, everything started with me. Whatever you do, McKenzie, never let your heart do the thinking."

This, too, was unexpected. Lucien was brutal, decisive, and cruel. So far he'd been an urban legend, a ruthless vigilante, and a monster stalking the Sandmen, executing those he could find with pitiless efficiency.

As a result, Venus hadn't even considered that the man could have a heart, let alone one that might overtake his mind. She wanted to press but decided instead to let him set his own rhythm.

After a while of staring at the passing cars, Lucien smiled.

"Have you ever been in love, McKenzie? I mean, really in love. Not just a 'crush' or some 'coming-of-age hormone-infused moment of self-discovery as you're noticing that the school quarterback's sweat smells good' kind of way. I'm not talking about whatever asshole you lose your virginity to on prom night.

"I'm talking about the real thing. The kind of love where you'd drop everything for just one more minute with 'him.' The kind that clouds your judgment to the point where you're both too scared to touch each other but want to be together forever. That if there was a way to make them part of you permanently, you would do it. Even if it meant eating them whole so that they're yours, and yours alone."

"What does that have to do with anything?" she asked.

It all sounded so strange coming out of his mouth. His voice was too coarse and his appearance too dirty and tattered to be bringing up a subject so intimate. Yet here they were.

"It's everything, McKenzie. In your what, fifteen, sixteen years on this lonely planet, can you tell me you've ever experienced that kind of thing?" Lucien insisted.

Venus shook her head. Even without the cold echo of the empty place in her soul, she knew that this wasn't the kind of thing she'd ever felt. Even the mild crushes he mentioned so dismissively had been rare and forgettable occurrences in her life. No, she had never experienced anything that intense. She'd always expected it to be something for other people, despite her auspicious name.

"Right. Well, try to get a grasp of it in your head. It's important. One day you'll find someone who makes you feel like that and if you're very, very lucky, they'll feel the same for you. A little tip, though: don't hold your goddamn breath. Chances are, you're just going to do stupid, dangerous things for some idiot who won't give a damn."

"I guess you had someone like that? Can't imagine who the lucky lady was."

A stray smile manifested on his cracked and weathered lips. The shape of his mouth spoke of melancholy and nostalgia.

Fondness, Venus thought. She knew that smile because she'd seen it on all the people closest to her. She'd seen it on Abraham when he spoke of his father, and on Penny as she remembered her parents. The unique twist of the lips, just enough to nudge the cheekbones without showing teeth. Along with the calm, arched eyebrows and distant stare, all of it spoke of a fondness for those lost. It had been on her mother's face every time she told Venus she loved her.

"No. I never had *him*." Even admitting this, he seemed rejuvenated. "I never managed to lay claim to the man. I wasn't exactly his type, if you know what I mean. Back in those days, it wasn't something you could easily bring up."

The smile faded. A different memory snuck into his eyes, turning off the lights from its predecessor. Pulling closed the curtains to his vulnerability.

"He meant well," Lucien continued. "But good intentions, ya know?"

She did. Wasn't that how her uncle had been drawn into this? Inspector Crowley? William Bergeron, who only wanted to have his daughter back? Does anyone really wake up with the desire to do evil?

"What happened?" she asked again, but with a sincere empathy that surprised her. The hollow was failing her.

"Back then there wasn't any of that Sandmen bullshit. It was just us, the Craftsmen. We inherited the name from a gentlemen-and-cigar club, a sort of 'chambers of commerce' type thing started a long time ago in Saint-Ferdinand. Apart from me, we had Neil, your grandfather, that idiot Elijah Byrd, Nathan Cicero, Samuel Finnegan, Sophie Courtier, and Edouard.

"We had it all figured out, you see. Did your parents tell you about Finnegan's wife, Amanda? She could paint things so vividly, they'd become real."

"They didn't," she answered, feeling a pang of resentment that they'd never bothered to tell her anything while they still could. She could feel hints of anger toward her mother, who'd simply run away when her daughter needed her most, but that feeling was quieted quickly. "But I've seen some of Harry Peterson's paintings."

"An amateur. Amanda was the one with the real talent. The god couldn't move when observed, you see. Part of an oath with Cicero. So Amanda painted a living eye that we used to keep the god trapped in a cave. We could have kept that going forever. But Edouard, that beautiful, ambitious fool . . ."

Venus was struggling to see the point, but at least they were getting to the relevant part of the story.

"Edouard had always thought that we were wasting the god's potential. 'What if we could control it?' he kept asking. He thought that thing was the key to elevating humanity to a new level of spirituality.

"Of course, I believed him. I hung on every word that fell from his mouth. I got it in my foolish mind that I could give that to him. Not because I thought he'd jump in my arms in gratitude, but just because I couldn't not do it.

"Byrd also had a thing for Edouard, which I guess made us competitors in a way. How stupid and juvenile is that? Lambert was married. Had a daughter. What exactly did we expect would happen? That one of us would impress him enough that he'd *switch teams*? I used to be handsome, believe it or not, but not that handsome."

Lucien's eyes were fixed in the distance. Beyond the passing cars now, beyond the sidewalk on the other side of the boulevard.

He glanced at his watch. A throwaway gesture, making sure they were still on schedule.

"I was always the one who knew things. I read the books and translated the scrolls. I was the one who picked our destinations and studied the artifacts. During our travels I found this design. Spirals within spirals that folded onto themselves in a fractal pattern. Older cultures would use these designs to guide spirits or trap their own gods. So I designed a trick based on that pattern. A sort of prison. Elizabeth—"

"My grandmother."

"That's right. Foolish woman. Though only half the fool we ever were." His words lacked sincerity.

"Anyways, Elizabeth, your grandmother, was one of the first to mess around with the god's power. She made a deal with it and it gave her some sort of second sight, though she paid a price for it. She predicted that Elijah would one day make a weapon that'd rid the world of the god. Thinking this was the prison I designed, I had him build the thing. But it didn't work."

Venus gave Lucien a sideways glance. Nothing he'd notice, but that her grandmother's prediction had been wrong. That she was fallible in her precognition was a source of hope. Not that they would never stop the creature, but that maybe she didn't have to be the one to shoulder the burden.

"Elijah took my design and made it into an amulet. It looked accurate enough at a glance and I thought he'd done a good job of it. We got together, all three of us, at the god's cave. Neil and the others tried to stop us, but they were too late.

"Edouard was so sure he knew what he was doing, he just walked up to the god. I'll give him credit: he tried to be reverent about it. He showed respect and deference, but that beautiful fool understood even less about the forces he was trying to control than the rest of us.

"The walls to the cave were covered in the same spiral pattern. As if the god were also trying to trap and manipulate spirits. I learned later that it was using the patterns to capture the spirits of the dead. Like a trapper setting snares to catch a meal. Did they tell you that? That the god eats the souls of the dead? The pattern is only part of it. The size, shape, materials used all have a different effect on how the design behaves."

Lucien traced a spiral pattern in the air with his thick, calloused finger. Despite the crude instrument, there was elegance in his movement. It reminded Venus of the Craftsmen's symbol, but also of the murals the god had painted on the walls of her shed.

"Byrd messed it up though. Edouard put the talisman around the thing's neck, but it had exactly zero effect. The god tore it off and threw the damned thing through Amanda's painting. Then everything went straight to hell."

Lucien closed his eyes, thick charcoal brows meeting in the middle of his forehead. It was as if he were trying to keep tears in or crush the images of his memories. Venus almost felt bad for the man.

"Neil and the others. They arrived. They . . . they knew what we were up to because 'someone' had gone to them. Lambert's daughter, Marguerite. She went to get Neil's help and stop her father. She got there just in time to see the monster tearing the flesh from his face.

"Took three of us to keep her from getting too close. We tried to drag her out so she wouldn't have to see, but even outside the cave, she heard the echoes of Edouard screaming. His body was disassembled, rebuilt, and destroyed all over again, always in a different and creative way. All the time the god laughed. A strange, artificial laughter, like it was trying to imitate a human laugh. All those sounds just spilled from that hole in the ground. We lost Neil and Amanda that night too. And, in a way, we also lost Sophie and Sam."

"How?" Venus mouthed the question more than spoke it, her imagination rapt with images conjured from Lucien's story, but mixed in with her own memories.

"Someone had to stay. Someone had to stay and watch as we dragged Marguerite to safety. The god couldn't leave the cave if it was being watched. Sophie and Finnegan remained. For days they stayed in the cave, unable to look away as an all-powerful god took revenge for a century's worth of captivity on the three victims who'd ventured too close."

Lucien's face was still a mask of serenity. His old, worn features seemed to be at peace with the tale he'd just told, but his hands betrayed another truth. His dirty and gnarled fingers were caught by a nervous palsy.

At long last, Venus knew the answer to the question every kid in Saint-Ferdinand had asked at one point or another: What was wrong with old Sam Finnegan? Everyone had a theory. Kind, gentle theories at first, harsher and more morbid ones after the old simpleton had been found with dozens of bodies on his property. Nothing even remotely like what Lucien had just told her.

"The thing eventually got bored and let the bodies die," Lucien continued. "Though there's no reason to think it allowed the souls the same rest. Your grandfather, my friends, and the man I loved are suffering what I can only imagine is eternal torment. All because I was stupid enough to follow through on a plan I should have known couldn't work.

"Byrd blamed my design for failing, and I blamed his craftsmanship. We haven't spoken since."

The story didn't explain everything. It certainly didn't give Venus any clue on how to defeat a god. The only thing she could distill out of the story was a better understanding of Peña as a person, whatever good that did.

"What about Gauthier?"

This had been a nagging issue for Venus. She'd figured out why Peña wasn't eliminating Sandmen at random and why they vanished for a few days before their bodies were found, but what information did he pull from them?

"What about him?"

"You interrogated him. Why? What did he know that was worth killing him for?"

The question seemed to amuse Peña, and it did snap him out of the melancholy of his tale.

"I killed him because he was a Sandman. But he did tell me how they control their god."

Venus waited for him to continue. It was astonishing enough to learn where the god had ended up after escaping her backyard shed, but to find out the Sandmen had a way to control it?

"They have someone sing to it," Peña explained, reading the curiosity in her eyes.

"Sing to it?"

Venus imagined a group of cultists, clad in robes and surrounded by candles, chanting hymns in unison to keep the god of hate and death complacent. But that didn't seem right.

"It's like Amanda's painting of the eye. Perfection is incompatible with reality. When something is perfect, it becomes real, because that's the only way the universe can reconcile things. A perfect enough song will do what every song does, but perfectly. Sad songs make you sad. Happy songs make your feet tap. A perfect song does all that to a level that can only be described as magic. The Sandmen have found someone who can sing a perfect lullaby. One that can put a god to sleep."

Cicero had explained that sort of magic to her. He might even have mentioned songs in his description, but Venus had never thought of it being used on the god. What other forms of art could be leveraged to manipulate it?

What if they could sing more than just lullabies to the god?

She wanted to ask more, but before she could and just as she had finally found a comfortable position for her injured ankle, Lucien gave another glance at his wristwatch. He sniffled like a man nursing the beginning of a cold, then started walking off.

"C'mon, McKenzie. We got a place to be."

A little more than two hours later, Venus's hands would be soaked with blood—but she would feel nothing.

It started with the sound of screeching tires and breaking glass as Venus and Lucien were stepping away from the corner. Her head snapped around like a broken elastic, her heart skipping a beat at the triggered memory.

It was by no means the same kind of collision that had totaled Ben and Jodie's police cruiser. In fact, by the time Venus had figured out which vehicles were involved, both drivers were already out and assessing the damage while trying to blame each other.

A white van with the words *Zip Courier: Express Messenger* applied in bright blue vinyl letters had rear-ended a dull silver Mercedes. The damage was minimal and no one was hurt, but the two drivers were still going at it with all their might. The accident would exacerbate the already suffocating traffic on the boulevard, but apart from inconvenience and insurance claims, there would be no other consequences. At least, none that the world would ever know.

It was just one cog in the clockwork. A piece prompted into movement by the many other tiny adjustments Peña had been performing all over Montreal.

"No time to rubberneck. We have a place to be," Peña urged her, pulling at her arm. "You won't want to miss our next stop."

Through constant badgering for most of their walk, Peña eventually explained the functioning of the grand machine they'd set in motion.

All the pieces they'd put in place over the course of the night had the sole purpose of causing the minor fender bender that Venus had witnessed.

As evidenced by the slogan on their van, Zip Courier guaranteed delivery of packages in the greater Montreal metropolitan area within four hours or your money back.

There was a package on that truck that was to be delivered to their eventual destination. A ten-story office tower incongruously attached to Place Vertu mall, its modern octagonal design and glass sidings contrasting with the shopping center's beige brick and squat two-story layout.

It took over an hour for them to get there, but they did so long before the truck. The two of them snuck in through a delivery ramp in the mall and navigated the bowels under the shops and restaurants until they stood in front of two elevator doors. Industrial in purpose, their surfaces were covered by dirty brushed metal surfaces stained in handprints. The exposed ducts and pipes in the ceiling and cinder-block walls blurrily reflected on the doors as if seen through cataracts. All Venus's senses could pick up were the humming of machines and the smell of burned metal in the air.

"You and I are both looking for answers, McKenzie," Peña explained without prompting. "We're on the same side, both trying to do the same thing."

He gave her a pat on the shoulder, the meaty hand pressing hard on her fragile arm, the first sign of any form of camaraderie he'd offered so far. It felt empty to Venus, as the realization of what his plan was slowly sank in.

"Look at us," he said. "Aren't we a couple of unlikely heroes? Still, here we are, pitting our wits against that of a god. You wanted to know how I do this sort of magic?"

She felt her curiosity dwindling from sheer exhaustion. But Venus nodded, wanting to know how Peña did what he did and how she'd ended up where she was at that moment.

"See, you can't do my kind of magic," he explained. "It's a lot like what your uncle does. A bunch of rote tricks and easy-to-repeat rituals, but knowing them isn't enough. You need familiarity. Obsessive, insane levels of familiarity. I've only been able to do the things I do, to perform the rituals I perform, for less than three years, but I've been exiled from Saint-Ferdinand for two decades. Montreal is my summoning circle. It's my Ouija board. But it only works because I know the city on a damn near genetic level. That's the difficulty of this kind of magic. The beauty of it is that everything I do is in harmony with the natural rhythm of Montreal. I don't kill Sandmen. Montreal kills them for me. I just set things up.

"Do you know what was in that white van on the bridge?"

Venus shook her head, listening to the vibrations of powerful motors coming to life and reversing course ten stories above. She could feel in her gut what was going to happen next and she was powerless and even somewhat unwilling to stop it.

"Among other things, there was a control board. A piece of electronic that needs replacing in this elevator." He pointed to the door on the left. "Don't worry. It'll make it here despite the accident. But the technician who was supposed to switch it out from the old, defective one, is already gone for the day. He thinks it can wait till tomorrow."

The motor's vibrations started increasing in pitch and intensity. Using the whole elevator shaft as an echo chamber, the sound was amplified a dozen fold by the time it reached the basement. The screeching was strained and agonized, louder with every moment, until Peña almost had to yell.

"No big deal, right?"

The deafening whine that reverberated through the elevator shaft suddenly stopped with a loud snap, the metallic whiplash of yards of steel cable finally freed from tons of tension.

Peña grasped Venus's shoulder and pulled her back a few feet. The last thing she heard, before the metal doors buckled outward and a cloud of dust and debris exploded from the newly formed opening, was a brief cry of panic from within the shaft.

Whatever malfunction was supposed to have been repaired had instead dropped the elevator car, letting it crash to the bottom of the shaft without any of the safety mechanisms kicking in.

Venus looked at Peña in that moment, his arm still extended to hold on to her shoulder, his eyes as emotionless as a shark's. He surveyed his work with alien detachment, unfeeling and unempathetic to the damage caused. This was how Lucien Peña had been waging war against the Sandmen.

"We don't have much time," he said, walking into the cloud of debris, oblivious to whatever dangerous particulate might be floating in there. Venus followed, hypnotized.

They were greeted by the eerie sound of an instrumental rendition of Frank Sinatra's classic "The Girl from Ipanema," which was drooling out of the car's speakers. The music was half swallowed by the dust. To Venus, it sounded as if the song were being played by ghosts.

Accompanying the song were the dissonant lyrics of a woman in agony. The familiar voice reached out to Venus as she held her breath, both to keep the white dust from her lungs and in dreaded anticipation of what she'd see on the elevator car's floor.

It was almost exactly what she'd expected. The weak ventilation system in the office tower's basement was finally pulling at the debris cloud, dispersing it as it drifted to the ground. It left a fine, snow-like dusting over every surface.

The woman, whimpering in pain, wore an emerald-green crushed-velvet dress that might have been half a size too small for her generous body. Though it was now covered in white dust, Venus could recognize it from a Christmas party held at the Bergerons' house two years prior. There was also a pair of earrings, large and gold, that flanked a head of short fading blond hair.

"Mrs. Bergeron?" Venus pleaded, hoping she was wrong.

"Hold her down, McKenzie," Peña demanded.

"We shouldn't move her. Not before the paramedics get here."

It was an automatic response. The paramedics weren't coming. Peña had been clear on that point: they were here to kill a member of the Sandmen. Venus just hadn't expected it to be someone she knew.

Both of Beatrice's legs were broken, the bones of her ankles sticking out of open wounds, piercing skin and pantyhose in the process. Blood was pooling, mixing pink with the white powder on the floor. "Venus?"

The voice cut like a scalpel, making an incision deep enough to hit Venus's suppressed guilt. Beatrice had called her name in both disbelief and hope. What she should have felt was fear.

This was not some random, faceless stranger. This was Audrey's mother.

"We can't kill her," Venus murmured, her voice choked by dust and guilt.

"If she gives us the answers we want, maybe we won't have to. Ask her how they keep the god sedated," Peña ordered Venus. "Ask her where they keep it. At their compound? Somewhere else? Ask her."

When Venus failed to so much as acknowledge the order, let alone ask the questions, Peña sighed his disappointment and took matters into his own hands.

"Beatrice?" he said, leaning down and laying a hand, the same hand he'd put on Venus's shoulder, on the wounded woman's left knee. His thick fingers were inches above the bleeding puncture. "Do you remember me, Beatrice?"

Beatrice shook her head, still struggling to blink out the dust from her eyes. Bloodshot and tear-filled, they were the source of narrow channels of ruddy flesh revealed from under the white dust.

"Well, I remember you, Beatrice. I've seen you go back and forth from Laval. I know you're one of the Sandmen, and you know what that makes us?"

She shook her head again, but this time there was also a quivering of her lower lip. She may not have known the facts, but she understood the implication.

Peña still took the opportunity to confirm.

"Enemies," he said, sliding his hand to her exposed tibia and giving it a brusque yank to the side.

Beatrice cried out, her scream reaching high up into the elevator shaft.

"Stop!" Venus shouted. She could almost feel the pain that Peña was imposing on Beatrice, an empathic echo of the sharp jab.

"Tell me how you keep the god sedated. I know you have it. Gauthier told me at least that much. But tell me how you keep it under control."

Peña twisted the blood-slick bone again, pulling out another agonized wail from Beatrice. The sound bounced off the concrete walls of the elevator shaft, amplified on its way up to Heaven.

"Stop it!" Venus stepped forward. "She has a daughter!"

It wasn't clear what Venus had expected this revelation might do to sway Peña. She'd seen his softer side. Perhaps she could guilt him into sparing a life.

Lucien did give pause, and twisted his neck to look at her. His eyes were impregnable black steel, unimpressed by her entreaty. He was the visage of determination. A predator with his jaws around the prey's neck, unwilling to give up his meal.

"We're in the business of hunting gods, McKenzie. What do I care if she's got a kid or two? Or twelve?"

"Audrey." Venus hoped that putting a name to the girl would somehow help give her words more sway. "Her name was Audrey. She died in Saint-Ferdinand. She . . ."

This was torture, pure and simple. It was evil and she would not stand by and allow it to happen, but the words failed her.

"Then it'll be a blessing for her to be reunited with her little girl, won't it?"

The question was intentionally cruel, meant both to shut Venus up and intimidate Beatrice. It only served to anger the young girl. After everything Lucien Peña had put her through, all the pain he'd caused in the last two days alone, Venus could see herself killing the man. From the god-touched part of her soul, she imagined a knife, the handle in her hand and the blade in Peña's heart.

But she had no such weapon and couldn't hope to stop him. He was too strong and had made no secret that he tolerated her, at best.

"Venus . . . please!" Beatrice begged.

"Pick a side, McKenzie," Peña said with lethal impatience. "You don't get to be a conscientious objector in a war against gods."

Prophecy had already spoken on her behalf. Venus was to be no bystander. Drawing on the hollow in her soul, the very wound left by the god, she buried her compassion for Beatrice Bergeron, and nodded to Lucien.

She then watched, calm and numb, as he extracted information from the dying woman while "The Girl from Ipanema" finished playing.

JODIE

AFTER TWENTY-FOUR HOURS in the hospital, Jodie had had her fill of the anesthetic blur. She'd walked away from the accident under her own power, though it was clear to any onlooker that she was not well. They'd forced her to ride in the ambulance, strapped to a gurney with a morphine drip. Once at Sacré-Coeur, they subjected her to a battery of tests ranging from a CAT scan to a full cognitive evaluation. They might have gone so far as to give her a colonoscopy if she hadn't put a stop to all of it.

Uniforms took care of one another. That was just how it was. You worked on the streets in an official vehicle, others like you were going to have your back. This was just how the EMTs had handled their part of that unspoken agreement. They were taking care of her the only way they knew how.

It was exhausting. Perhaps by design, the series of tests and constant feasts of drugs had kept her from thinking too much about Ben.

Once in a while she'd remember him, his head lulling senseless on her shoulder. The only reason she'd known he wasn't dead was his blurry-eyed blinking.

The head nurse, Nathalie or Natalia or something, had been able to give her precious little information above that. Ben had been taken into surgery. He was stable. She was told that Dr. Blouin, the surgeon in charge, was one of the best. They were always "one of the best."

They'd offered her a room, but lying down made her head spin. Instead Jodie had taken a chair in the waiting room of the ER. Watching people go in and out kept her awake. As pain slowly took hold of her head, it also cleared her thoughts. She wanted to hunt down this Dr. Blouin and grill him about Ben's condition. Hell, she wanted to be allowed to see Ben and be there when he woke up.

"LeSage?" came a familiar voice.

Henry Dickson. Or rather Senior Constable Dickson, but he wasn't one to be hung up on formalities.

"Hey there, Hank," she answered, making a show of pressing her palm to her aching head. "Not sure I'm in any condition to do an official report yet."

"No sweat. Didn't even know you were here. You look like hell by the way."

"Thanks. You should see the other guy."

Jodie had thought she was making a joke, but Dickson's face contracted, suggesting his thoughts had gone somewhere different.

"I assume Ben is here too?"

"Yeah. In surgery. Or just out of it. I don't know; they won't tell me much."

Dickson took a seat next to her. He was in full uniform: utility belt, cap, and all. Meanwhile, Jodie had dressed and undressed so many times that half her clothes hung off her like a misused store mannequin. She'd relinquished her firearm and assorted gear to the officer who'd initially escorted her in.

"Here on business?" she asked.

Her colleague was fixated on the waiting room television. There was a news report of an elevator failure in Ville Saint-Laurent. One of those freak accidents that reporters were always hungry for. A pretty blonde with perfect teeth smiled as she introduced herself, then she quickly shifted to her serious face when discussing the tragedy.

"Her. We escorted the body here," Dickson answered while fixated.

"The reporter?" Jodie's brain was still foggy.

"No. The woman from the elevator. Kinnison requested an autopsy. Actually, the task force investigating Gauthier's death was the one to put in the request."

"Wait. Say that again?"

"The woman who was in the elevator, apparently she was part of that Church of the Sandmen, just like Gauthier and Decker and . . . who was the other one?"

Jodie didn't bother answering. Her mind was racing, as much as a runner sprinting through syrup could race, trying to connect the dots. The killer—Lucien Peña if Venus could be believed—had struck again. Within a day of causing a near-fatal car crash to abduct Venus, he'd somehow also caused this woman's death.

Except, this time, something was different. The body hadn't disappeared. Unlike Gauthier, Decker, and Marcil (that was her name!), Peña had no need to take his victim away.

Something had changed, and the only thing Jodie could think of was Venus.

"Who was she?" Jodie asked, doing a poor job of hiding the tremor in her voice.

"See, that's where it gets really interesting," Dickson explained. "Her name is Beatrice Bergeron. She was the wife of one of the Saint-Ferdinand victims. Can you imagine how much the task force is losing its collective mind?"

"Yeah."

She could imagine it all too well. They would be jumping to the same conclusions she and Ben had after Venus had linked Saint-Ferdinand to the Sandmen for them. Except, the task force didn't know Stephen Crowley was dead, or that the real killer was a "giant magic hobo."

That last part was still hard to swallow. She'd seen the unique kind of urban miracle Peña could create. Sure, it was the kind of thing that could be done with computers, she supposed. But that would only explain the lights. What got Jodie was the eerie accuracy of the attack. When she came to, Venus had vanished, with witnesses stating she'd been taken by a man matching Peña's description.

She was a far cry from believing in shamans and sorcery, but Jodie's skepticism had cracked.

She couldn't bring any of this to the task force. A constable storming into their office after a head injury, screaming about street wizards and cults, would be on a fast-track to medical leave. If she were lucky.

After a while, Dickson got bored of her silence and excused himself so he could get back to work. He gave her the usual "get well" and "try to get some rest," to which she politely nodded.

Once Dickson was out the door and out of sight, Jodie pulled herself to her feet. Her head still throbbed, making her long for pills or an injection or something, but she was pleased to notice her dizziness was almost gone.

She wandered into the gift shop, browsing aimlessly through flowers and balloons. She noticed that the narrow rows of cards and knickknacks mapped a perfect progression through life. Near the register, cheerful puppy-eyed plush toys were arrayed to welcome babies into the world. Get-well cards for various light injuries or routine surgeries followed. Farther back, things got more somber. Photos of sunsets and dried leaves adorned the cards destined to those with serious or terminal illness. Finally, at the back, she found the condolences gifts. The things meant for the families of patients, rather than the patients themselves.

If all had gone well, she wouldn't be shopping this far in when it came to Ben.

"Can I help you, ma'am?" the cashier asked.

Jodie shook her head and tried to blink the fog away. It took a moment to come to her senses, but she had been staring at a particular get-well card for a while. Probably longer than what seemed healthy.

"Do you need me to get you some help?"

The cashier, an elderly woman who was the very portrait of a doting grandmother, complete with flower-pattern dress and pearl necklace, seemed genuinely concerned.

"I'm fine," Jodie answered.

She bought the card, along with a bag of chips and a small pendant of a scallop shell. She couldn't put her finger on why that last item seemed important at the time. Her hungry stomach and subconscious had made those purchases.

Trancelike, Jodie made her way back to the waiting room, intent on eating her chips and hoping for news of Ben. She growled a whispered curse seeing that someone had taken her chair. She was stuck standing with her chips, pendant, and get-well card.

She flipped the envelope between her fingers, tracing the embossed letters on the surface. *To my loving sister. Get better soon.*

Next, it was the scallop shell she held up between thumb and index finger. The cheap piece of jewelry was cast in pewter and attached to a leather cord. There was a small tag that she assumed said *Made in China* somewhere on it.

"Venus."

Jodie reached into her pocket for her phone to call the girl, or at least send her a message. Between the drugs and gnawing worry for her partner, she'd almost forgotten about Venus. She could very well be in danger. She could remember handing her phone to Venus so she could input her contact information, but as her hand came back empty, she realized the girl had never returned it.

A pang of shooting pain lanced through her skull, the signal that the last of the painkillers was finally gone. Only hunger and lack of sleep still obscured her judgment. She'd given her phone to Venus and now had no means to contact the girl.

But she could track the phone.

"Dickson? Dickson!"

Clutching her chips, card, and pendant, Jodie ran to the exit of the ER waiting room. Hopefully, she'd catch her colleague before he could leave the parking lot.

ALICE

LEAVES CRUNCHED UNDER Alice's feet. Through the playground and into the woods she and Simon had walked. The sound reminded her of chewing on cornflakes. Both had the same crispness followed by a sort of wet echo caused by milk for the breakfast, and mud for the dry foliage.

"I skipped breakfast, you know," Alice whined.

Normally, she would have eaten with Francis. She was his responsibility and he would be the one to make sure she got up on time for her lessons. His cold and uncaring pleasantries were her only company while she ate. That was better than the alternative. She hated how the rest of the family gawked at her on those rare occasions when she ate alone, their expressions caught between awe and pity.

Recently it was Daniel who had taken over her care. So far it didn't look like that arrangement was going to work out. He didn't seem to understand the Sandmen or her role within the family. He didn't fit in. It came as no surprise that he did not show up to escort her to breakfast and then to her lessons.

She'd waited and waited, and eventually it was Simon who'd come to get her. Instead of her usual bowl of cereal, though, he took her directly outside for her training.

"I'm hungry," she said, as if more complaining would somehow change the situation.

The complaint didn't even register with Simon. Of the handful of people she knew, her music teacher was the one who'd been around the longest. Even before the Sandmen, Alice could remember Simon. The faces of her mother and father were blurry and vague in her mind, leaving only the feeling that she'd been loved once. And Simon, who had always been there, like an unwavering constant. Babysitters, friends, and even her older sister were all but erased.

It was odd, then, that out of everyone, he was the one who seemed the least comfortable with her. Whereas Mother enjoyed the distance provided by authority and Francis lived in a world devoid of emotions, Simon exhibited a constant low-grade fear of her. Like a murderer living with the ghosts of his victims whispering in his ear day and night.

She felt like a monster in his presence.

"We'll grab a bite when we're done," he said after a moment. "Ms. Lambert wants you to learn a few new songs and she seems in a hurry."

Simon was the only one who could get away with calling Mother by her real name.

The air was warming up again, the cold front from the past few days finally giving way to more comfortable weather.

Aside from being able to leave her coat behind, it also meant that the increasingly red and orange leaves in the trees picked up amazing hues. With a little imagination, the forest looked ablaze.

They settled in their usual spot. Alice liked the little clearing they had chosen for these outdoor sessions. It was close enough to the school that it could almost be seen between the trees, and they'd dragged some old logs to serve as seats. Simon had even built a small firepit out of some rocks so that they could keep warm and practice longer during the colder months. Most of all, it felt like it was their private area. Away from Mother's and Francis's watchful eyes.

Simon pulled out an old leather-bound tome from his satchel. Alice knew the book well, though she'd never laid eyes on the contents. As a child, she imagined it was a grimoire, containing all the spells Simon would teach her. In time, she learned that the "spells" were only musical arrangements and that they were written on the loose pieces of paper pressed between the tome's pages. Her mastery of her perfect voice was where the true magic lay.

"Here," he said, handing her a piece of paper, his hand shaky.

On it was scrawlings of musical arrangements in Simon's nervous handwriting. Tiny letters and lines that were as much dug into the sheet as they were written on the surface.

The curious new music made Alice forget the low growl of her stomach. Even though she breathed and drank music day and night, she never seemed to tire of it. Especially now that she'd seen how much power she could draw from it.

Singing the god to sleep on the day of Victor Poole's death had been a revelation. She'd seen her true purpose in the family and could now fully understand how Mother's prophecy about her was coming true.

Focus eluded Alice as she tried to sing. Her voice was on point, pouring out of her in smooth waves that rose and crashed with the swelling of each movement. However, she couldn't seem to keep from improvising. She sang from the heart, falling prey to her emotions and using music as a form of expression, instead of a tool to be leveraged. Alice would slip into a minor key, often breaking from the soothing purpose of her song and instead broadcasting her own melancholy.

Twice Simon interrupted her to bring her back on track. After a while, however, he didn't seem to even notice. The only other interruption was from the sound of his sobs.

Alice no longer followed the formula, straying far from the usual recipe, but the divergence took nothing away from the potency of her music. The vibrations of her perfect voice, expressed in perfect melodies, still captured the heart and mind of the listener, bending them to her will.

Noticing the effect she was having on Simon, she shifted her tone one octave up and then down, studying the emotional responses of her tutor.

At first she kept the changes subtle, going back and forth between the soothing ballad she was learning and a more sorrowful version of the same song. However, with comfort came confidence, and she soon found herself trying different keys and eventually changing songs completely. What a thrill it was to have so much control! Not only over her voice but over another person. She was a conductor, moving her baton to compel a person's orchestra of feelings. Commanding the joy section to swell while the fear section would quiet down. Then, with a dramatic gesture, everything went silent and the humor section would slowly rise, building from mild amusement to a crescendo of all-out laughter.

Left to her own devices, Alice might have kept this up forever, and she was well on her way toward doing just that. It was only when she caught a glimpse of fear on Simon's face that she faltered. An unintended emotion had slipped in between two heartbeats as she was shifting from longing to satisfaction, pressing her luck with coaxing more subtle and complex feelings.

Alice hadn't intended fear. Fear wasn't her design. She stopped. The only place the emotion could have come from was Simon himself.

Being stripped of control was a common thread between her and Simon. Aside from music, being under Mother's thumb was the thing that united them. Through her singing though, Alice had broken that order and taken the wheel of her teacher's emotions, stealing that most private part of him. The only reaction he could have had was terror, but even that she'd taken, only letting it slip through in brief moments.

The ensuing silence was unbearable. Like an elastic stretched too far and suddenly let go, Simon's emotions snapped back into place. Too quick, too violent, they left him stunned with a cruel whiplash.

Bewildered, terrified, and awestruck, the music teacher could do nothing but stare wide-eyed at his student. It had been a long time since Alice had started to exceed what he was capable of teaching. He was now more of a guide or an informed audience than a teacher. He might offer notes on her progress, or research techniques that might help her maintain her voice, but Alice was the maestro.

Her voice was reaching a degree of perfection that couldn't be consciously perceived by human ears. Simon had never expected to see this level of mastery from his student. Alice wanted desperately to reach out to Simon, to reassure him. She took a step, putting out her hand, eager to touch his arm, to take his hand and apologize. Tell him she was sorry for treating him like a puppet. That she didn't know! She didn't realize what it was she was doing.

She wanted to tell him: *I will not use this for evil.* But Simon stepped back. The fear, his one true state of mind, was painted upon his face. His shaking hands creeping up to cup his ears in a desperate gesture of self-preservation. He flinched with every twitch of her lips.

"I'm sorry," she murmured. But still he pressed his palms to the sides of his head and shut his eyes tight.

He'd taught her to sing a god to sleep and she'd shown him just how much more power she could wield with her breath.

"What did you do?"

Daniel's voice cut through her rising panic. His words were flat and uncertain, adopting a neutral tone while he seemed to figure out the best reaction to what he was seeing.

Simon had crouched into a ball, hands still clasped tightly over his ears and eyes riveted on Alice. He was a man she knew had little control over his life. Like her, the Sandmen needed him, and what the family needed they controlled. But he had always been the master of his own emotions. Whether fear or rage, the feelings had been his. Until Alice had stripped even those away from him.

"Is he okay?" Daniel asked, rushing past her to squat next to Simon. "What did you do to him?"

The music teacher didn't seem to even notice Daniel near him, numb to the touch of hands on his shoulders.

"I don't know," she lied, taking a few steps back.

The curtains parted to show the enormity of what she had done. She'd taken hold of Simon's emotions and, with her singing, reshaped them to her will. With the right choice of music, Alice could twist a listener's feelings into whatever form her song called for. It was an imperfect science, but so much more than the simple lullabies Mother had tasked Simon to teach her. Songs of joy had made Simon smile and dirges had brought him near to tears. This was a facet to her singing that no one had explained. The possibilities were terrifying and intoxicating.

Time felt thick and slow as Daniel came to an apparent decision. Whatever his goal had been in coming here, everything had changed. He stood up from Simon's side and walked toward her with determination, barely slowing as he grabbed her wrist and pulled her along.

By the time Alice snapped out of her stunned torpor, she was sitting in a strange car, trees slipping past her window in a blur of green, red, and orange.

Her breath came in short, laborious gasps, threatening a full-blown panic attack as she realized what was going on.

When was the last time she'd been this far from the compound? Daniel had taken advantage of her moment of confusion to strap her into the passenger seat of his car and take her away. Was this a rescue or a kidnapping? To Alice, it didn't matter. Both were the same.

Everything she knew and understood fit in the tiny square of the rearview mirror. The old school was somewhere behind her now, containing the only family she knew. Just as she had found her place within the ranks of the Sandmen, she was being taken away.

A fleeting thought of jumping from the moving vehicle crossed her mind. The sound of the air rushing around the car, testifying to their speed, dissuaded her from it.

She dared a glance in the driver's direction. Daniel was at the wheel, silent and intense. His eyes were fixed on the road except for the occasional furtive glance he shot her way. The noble idiot saving her from the evil queen's castle on his white steed.

Alice would have found it romantic if she really wanted to be rescued. Daniel had every hallmark of the handsome hero, too, and she'd be lying if she pretended to have never dreamed up this kind of fantasy, but the real thing wasn't what she'd expected. The Sandmen were family. Not an ideal family, but the only one she could remember and the only one she knew would never abandon her.

"Turn back," she said, the timid words barely audible over the engine.

Daniel didn't hear. His perception was shielded by noise and his implacable determination. Alice couldn't understand why this was so important to him. It was in the setting of his jaw and the way he held the wheel. There was something of Mother in him. An inherited passion somehow directed at Alice.

"Turn back!" she repeated louder, to be heard at last.

This time Daniel did glance her way, but his expression was one of shock, as if he didn't expect the shy little creature he'd saved to have a voice outside of uncompromised gratitude.

"Are you insane?" he said, eyes darting between her and the road.

"I can't leave Simon out there like that."

"He'll be fine. That's the first place Francis will look when they notice you've gone missing. They'll find him."

"Gone missing? I can't leave! That's my home. Take me back!"

"Your home? These people kidnapped you and you want to go back?"

Two months ago Alice would have asked the same question of herself. But now that she knew her purpose within the family, there was nowhere else that made sense for her.

"I need them and"—she hesitated, tasting the concept of her next words carefully for the first time—"they need me."

"No," Daniel answered, giving no thought to the idea. "They don't, and we are not turning back. Trust me, once you're out of there long enough, you'll see that this is for the best."

He sounded so sure that Alice was tempted to believe him. Wouldn't it be nice? To run away with the pretty boy and be returned to a loving mother and father? She could settle back into a normal life, perhaps marry and have children with her savior. But the whole idea was more ridiculous than appealing.

Reality took her side, channeling its opinion through the ringing of Daniel's phone.

FRANCIS was written on its screen in bold white letters. Daniel made to pick up the device, but Alice snatched it from the dashboard before his fingers had even left the wheel.

"Don't!" he said, trying to stop her from answering, but she'd already answered.

What came out of the phone wasn't Francis's smooth and glacial voice. Instead a cacophony of screams flooded the car's interior, a sound straight out of hell.

"Daniel?" Francis finally said through the pandemonium. "Have you seen Alice?"

Tires screamed in protest as Daniel brought his car to a stop in front of the school's entrance. The smell of burned rubber greeted Alice as she opened her door. Daniel's phone was still wrapped between her fingers. Mercifully, Francis had ended the call a few minutes earlier, after calmly informing them that the god was awake and Alice's services were required.

The sounds that had accompanied the call painted a grim picture. They had a ring of familiarity to them. The wet cracking was like a song she'd only recently heard on the radio, familiar but new. Each scream was a lyric she'd only vaguely remembered. All over the backdrop of the liquid tearing of muscles and skin.

They rushed into the compound, and a live version of the symphony played itself in echoes down the halls to greet them. It was a struggle to keep pace with Daniel and, when she saw him freeze in his steps on the threshold of the cafeteria, Alice immediately wished she could turn back.

The sounds had made a promise of carnage and they did not fail to deliver.

Menacing and tall, the Sam-creature stood atop one of the tables. It held aloft the limp body of Alexis Petrov, paying no mind to the other human insects that swarmed around it. Instead it focused all its attention on the various tortures it could perform on Alexis's body.

Thin fingers pinched at the man's skin until it broke, pulling long strands of epidermis off for the god to study. Alice thought that this might be what a sculptor looked like as they inspected a block of marble before striking it with their chisel.

The Sam-creature was less human than Alice remembered. Hate and death animated the thin arms and legs as instruments of carnage, having twisted their anatomy to that purpose. The god's movements had an alien quality to them. Even though it wore the body of a fragile old man, its unnatural power was evident in its sinewy limbs, leaving no doubt that it could tear through the entire cult if it so desired.

It seemed temporarily mollified by its new toy, plucking at this or that part of Alexis's anatomy. Curiosity made Alice hesitate. Just as the god found itself rapt by the pulling of a bone from the forearm of its victim, she, too, remained enthralled. Not by the carnage and blood, but rather by the perpetrator of these atrocities.

Alice could have stood there for hours, watching the monster do its work, if not for Alexis's eyes finding hers. Despite the wounds and lost blood, he lived; and despite his mouth being open, he could not scream.

Morbid fascination drained out of Alice like a barrel with the bottom cut out. Her voice was ragged from running after Daniel and it trembled at the sight of Alexis's torment. She had precious little time to put the Sam-creature to sleep before it got bored of its toy and found another victim, perhaps even her.

But Alice didn't go for one of her tried and trusted lullabies. Instead she went for a slow vocal rendition of a Rachmaninoff concerto. What if she could do to the god what she had done to Simon earlier? What if, instead of slumber, she tried to soothe the monster and bring it to heel?

The song came out as perfect as she could have hoped under the circumstances and Alice surprised herself at how steady each note was.

At first she seemed to be getting the desired effect. The Sam-creature lost interest in Alexis, looking blindly toward Alice through its metal-studded eyes.

A low moan from Alexis was all it took for the weak spell to break and the god to forget all about her. A gasp erupted from Alice's

throat in the middle of her song as she watched Sam Finnegan reach
into Alexis's mouth, snapping the jaw open to increase its access, and
pull out his tongue and, with it, a generous length of trachea.

And still, Alexis would not die.

The god held the organ aloft, studying it with its nose, tasting it
with its tongue, and even putting it to its ear, listening for a voice it
could no longer carry. The Sam-creature was growing bored.

Alice panicked. She fumbled for the first few notes of "Twinkle,
Twinkle, Little Star." It was the simplest lullaby she knew, and the
one most forgiving of her tired lungs.

She closed her eyes to concentrate, focusing to push away the
strain and lack of breath, forcing herself into a trance. The magic
was in the perfection, not the song, but never had conditions been
further from perfect.

There was a crash and more screaming, but Alice had to put the
carnage out of her mind if she had any hope of putting a stop to it.

Time blurred and sounds were drowned, reality vanishing into
an abstract mess. Alice might as well have fallen asleep or into a
trance, or died—or all three for all she knew. She sang with more
desperation than skill and more fear than talent.

Would Daniel be dead when she ultimately opened her eyes
again? The whole Church of the Sandmen might have been slaugh-
tered around her as she provided the soundtrack to their annihila-
tion. Or perhaps it would be the whole world that would be reduced
to ash.

The only way not to know was to keep singing.

And as before, the god sang back to her.

Its voice was clearer, louder, and closer. There was an intimacy
to its presence that hadn't been there before. Just as it had reforged
Sam's body to accommodate its growing power, the god felt more
substantial, almost tangible in her mind.

Whatever hole separated its world from the reality of the living
was growing larger, allowing more of the god to push through.

"You came back," the god sang. *"I thought Crowley had stolen you
from me."*

Alice didn't answer; she didn't need to. The god was listening to her through her music, hearing everything it needed to from the melody.

"With each death, I draw closer," it said. *"I look forward to hearing your voice with my own ears instead of through this vessel."*

With that, the god relinquished wakefulness. But not before showing her six iridescent figures, each caught in a vortex of shadow and blood—the souls of those who had been slain that day.

Standing in gore and swallowed by silence, the bodies of the dead and sleeping surrounding her, Alice shivered. The god had wanted her to see and to know that each victim would go on after death. That they would serve to pave the road it would walk to cross over from its realm into living reality.

DANIEL

THE SCENE THAT greeted Daniel upon waking up was one of unexpected chaos. Not that he'd fallen asleep in circumstances that were any better. Alice's song had had its effect on him, just as it'd had on the Sandmen and, to everyone's relief, on the monster that had rampaged through the school.

While it was pandemonium he'd left, and pandemonium he rejoined, they were of different breeds. The butchery that painted the cafeteria's floors and walls, and even ceiling in some places, was no longer a work in progress. This was the aftermath. Gone were the screams of fear and panic, the pleading and begging and the hurried prayers to higher forces. What replaced them was the mournful weeping of survivors, the agonized moans of the wounded, and the perfect, beautiful shrieking of Alice as she was held by two fellow Church members.

Alice struggled against her captors. Her thin pale limbs flailing impotently at the arms that held her.

Daniel didn't know the names of her two assailants, but it didn't matter. They were goons in his mother's service and little more.

Both men were cut from the same rough cloth. Stocky and barrel-chested, they were the kind of men who'd worked manual labor for decades before finding the Church. One of them had a cut above his right eye and blood stained his blond hair. They'd been witness to the massacre, probably had friends among the victims. They'd be quick to find someone to blame. It showed in how roughly they handled the girl.

They didn't so much as flinch when Mother ordered them to take her to the "Reflection Room."

Daniel had no idea what the Reflection Room was. Francis had omitted that part of the compound during their tour. It sounded like someplace one might retreat to for meditation and solitary thought. A peaceful room to ponder one's actions. Perhaps even somewhere that a devout Sandman could absolve and cleanse themselves of their sins.

Judging by Alice's frantic clawing at the limbs that were lifting her from the ground, that was unlikely to be the case.

"Don't."

A hand, gentle but firm, took hold of Daniel's elbow just as he was about to intervene.

It was Francis.

He looked as fresh and relaxed as if he'd just now come back from a replenishing stroll through the neighborhood. His faint, almost mocking smile was a party balloon at a funeral. An out-of-place portrait of serenity hung in a gallery of violence.

"You don't want to go where she's going," Francis explained, pulling harder.

"It's not her fault," Daniel tried to explain.

"She attempted to escape and because of that, the god escaped. And now six people are dead."

The last statement elicited no more emotion out of Francis than reciting a grocery list.

"I'm the one who took her, Francis! She didn't even want to go."

The hand on Daniel's arm tightened, crushing his radius and ulna into one another. The fingers shook with the effort and Daniel could have sworn he saw a tremor in Francis's features.

"No. You didn't," Francis countered, his smile broadening. "She charmed you with her singing, the same way she did with Simon. Thankfully, the spell broke when I called you and you were able to bring her back. How fortunate, don't you agree?"

A tense second hung between the brothers. Francis had lied to cover for him. Mother was across the cafeteria, overseeing her flock in their moment of need. She watched with unchecked fury as Alice was being led screaming down the hall. "Ouch!"

The grip had tightened again, this time making the bones feel as if they were an ounce from snapping beneath his flesh.

"Don't you agree?" Francis insisted.

Daniel nodded. What else was there to do? This olive branch offered was as strange as the man offering it, but Daniel wasn't in a position to refuse. Nor was he entirely sure he would if he were.

"Okay, fine, but we can't just lock her up! Isn't that a little overreacting?"

Francis didn't reply. Instead he took a step back from Daniel. The heavy clicking of angry heels hurried toward them, filling the gap of his retreat.

"Overreacting?" Mother said, interrupting the two brothers.

Despite being almost a foot shorter than Francis, she bullied him farther away, pushing her small frame between him and Daniel. She was a ball of fury and thunder, growling quietly with the potential for violence.

"Six people are dead, Daniel!"

She let the words sink in, and the reality they carried took root. In their place grew indignation first. How dare this woman, who led a doomsday cult and manipulated people into giving their lives to her, admonish him? These people would still be alive if she hadn't been exploiting them in the first place. But there was no way of voicing this, not if Daniel wanted to keep his place within the Sandmen. So he bit his tongue, remaining quiet like a wordless idiot.

Stunned silence did nothing to slow Mother's momentum.

"This isn't the Order of the Solar Temple! I'm no Jim Jones or Charles Manson! When I speak of end times, it's not simply some vague scare tactic to keep my people in line!"

But through the stiff back and unblinking eyes, Daniel could see something else. Her well-manicured accusing finger was shaking with something more than anger. For a moment Mother reminded him of his other parent.

Though Stephen Crowley had been prone to a legendary anger, he'd never unleashed it on his son out of spite or malice. Every time Daniel's father would scream his face red, swear up a storm, or, on the rare occasion, threaten him with a belt, it had always been because Daniel had done something to endanger himself.

Maybe he was mistaken, or still on the weird emotional high of having his brother take his side, but Daniel could have sworn he saw echoes of his father in Marguerite Lambert-Crowley.

"I didn't gather the Sandmen so I could have my own personal harem or run some stupid pyramid scheme," she continued, her tone frustrated still, but her volume going back to a more reasonable number of decibels. "We're in the business of saving the world. You have the luxury of not realizing what that means, but not Alice. Never Alice."

She kept staring at him, her lower lip quivering but her stance and eyes carved in granite. Mother expected an answer and was ready for whatever counterpoint Daniel might want to say in his defense. But there was nothing.

What if she was right? What if Daniel had misjudged Mother in his resentment for abandoning him? The evidence of the power she was dealing with dripped from the walls and coagulated on the floor around him. She'd warned him off already. What were the chances he would be among the victims the next time there was an incident? Who was he to question the methods used to control a god that had to be contained by any means necessary?

"Do you understand?"

Her fingers came to within a quarter inch of his nose and, in that moment, Mother's stature far exceeded his own.

Again, Daniel nodded, fearing that any words out of his mouth would be the wrong ones.

Mother's demeanor didn't relax as she took a step back. In fact, this confrontation seemed to have been a welcome distraction from the weight of other responsibilities.

Dark circles were apparent beneath Mother's eyes as she looked around again, reassessing the damage done to her school and her congregation. The weight on her shoulders almost could have been seen manifesting as it crushed her.

For Daniel, it was guilt that put a heavy hand on his heart. Francis couldn't grasp the enormity of what had happened and while Mother certainly could, she didn't know Daniel's hand in it. Surveying the splatters of blood, almost artistic in their distribution across the cafeteria, Daniel thought again about that number. Six. Six people had died. And now Alice was being punished for it.

No matter how many times he tried to remind himself that they were just Sandmen, pawns in an evil doomsday cult, it wouldn't stick.

"Daniel!"

Mother was back at his side. Shaking his head, Daniel realized that she'd been calling out to him for a while now, trying to get his attention.

"I need you to take Simon home," she said once she finally did get his attention.

"Home?"

"Yes. In Notre-Dame-de-Grâce. Clear across Montreal. Can you do that?"

What she meant to ask was: *Can you get as far away from here as possible right now?*

Daniel didn't argue.

Someone who knew him well could have picked up on the suppressed fury that pulled at his muscles in impotent complaint. It wasn't very subtle, but then again, the bloodbath and ensuing tension that lingered were a good pretext for odd behavior.

The massacre had other uses to Daniel. It served as a visible reminder of what could happen if he allowed himself further heroics.

Whether Mother was honest in her ideal to save the world and contain the monster didn't matter. Her followers were earnest. Sure, they wanted something from the god, but that didn't make them villains. At least not deserving of being torn apart and broken like Alexis had been.

Daniel didn't quite know what was in store for Alice, but he knew that Mother needed her hale and healthy enough to sing. Whatever the cult had in mind for their wayward child, it wouldn't endanger the Sandmen's goals.

Like a visitor at a museum, Daniel walked by the painted walls of the cafeteria, taking in each tableau of spent life. The room was being cleared of the human debris, a hushed silence having fallen over the tables and chairs.

A wet sloshing accompanied by a staccato sigh of both fear and resignation attracted his attention as Daniel crossed in front of the stairwell that led to the floor below.

Sean Dover, a man who'd come to the Sandmen after Mother had promised his sister's cancer could be cured, was mopping up the blood dripping down the basement stairs. His hands and shoes were stained crimson and the water in his bucket had become a sudsy red soup. All he was doing now was sloshing the blood around, but he was too deep in shock to notice his water needed changing.

Daniel found Simon waiting for him just outside the cafeteria. Perhaps *waiting* was too strong of a word. The survivors had been a parade of hollowed faces. Each had the look that came when fear reached its ultimate conclusion.

Simon's condition was on an entirely different scale. The trauma of the forest had accompanied him back to the compound. Whatever it was Alice had done remained carved onto him. Daniel couldn't even be sure the music teacher had witnessed much if anything of the events in the cafeteria, but the results were much the same, yet worse. Erratic things were happening behind Simon's eyes and he would occasionally break into an unwelcome smile or suppressed giggle.

"Mr. Martel?" Daniel whispered, extending a hand to lightly touch Simon on the shoulder.

The teacher didn't flinch. He only locked eyes with Daniel and clutched at his notebook ever harder.

"C'mon. Let's get you home."

The drive was a quiet one. The evening was only setting in and traffic was still heavy in some places, slowing the ride to a crawl on certain roads.

Neither Daniel nor his passenger seemed to mind. They'd left a palace of horror and, while Simon was certainly eager to get home, he seemed to appreciate having company.

"Got anyone you need to call? Let them know you'll be late?" Daniel asked.

From the corner of his eye, he caught Simon shaking his head ever so slightly. His hands held on to his notebook, fingers shaking with the constant effort.

Only once or twice did he shift position, allowing Daniel to see the familiar image of an eye with a spiral for a pupil, carved into the notebook's cover. Just this simple icon confirmed to Daniel that this book, like him, was a relic of Saint-Ferdinand.

"What's in there?" He pointed at it with his chin.

For a moment Simon looked around and outside his window. It was with a hint of surprise that he noticed the book he'd been cradling with such force for the entirety of their trip. He lifted it up, discovering it anew, before answering.

"Art," he said. "Or at least aborted attempts at art."

Thoughtfully, Simon flipped through a few pages. Daniel could glimpse charcoal sketches, copious notes, lists upon lists and endless lines of tight-scripted text.

"Drawings, coordinates, songs, and descriptions of places that don't exist," Simon explained. "It's like a madman's travel guide to an imaginary world. But it has some insight. I've been deciphering the songs and this is where I got the idea to sing lullabies to the god in the first place. Art. It's all about Art."

Talking about the book seemed distraction enough for Simon. It was a simple balm, but one effective enough to loosen his tongue.

"Where did you get it?"

"Ms. Lambert gave it to me when she first demanded I train Alice."

Regret colored Simon's words. With each of them came the quiet desire to turn back the clock and refuse whatever payment or promises had put this book into his hands.

He finished flipping to the end and closed the cover with reverence. Now calm, Simon set the book back on his lap, much of the trauma washed away.

"Why did you say yes? Why do you stay?"

Daniel stopped at a traffic light. They were getting close to the music teacher's home. He wanted to know more about this man who could live away from the compound yet who seemed to be as much Mother's thrall as any other cult member. He wanted to learn what Simon knew. He wanted to take the book away from him.

Simon wet his lips with the tip of his tongue, eyes fixated on the red glow that commanded the intersection. Night had fully enveloped Montreal by now, and the hellish glow was all that illuminated his face.

"I accepted Marguerite's offer because I thought I had something to gain. Then I stayed because I had so much to lose. Now . . . Now I don't have anything left, so what would be the point? My house is around the next corner."

"Hey," Daniel asked. "You okay there, buddy?"

Sean Dover didn't answer. The trip to Simon's place and back had taken upward of two hours. The afternoon had spent itself and night had fallen, yet Sean had barely made an inch of progress. Only when Daniel reached out to take the mop from his hand, gently pulling it away, did Sean seem to realize he was no longer alone.

"Why don't I take care of this and you can get some rest?" Daniel said, trying to keep his voice even. "It's almost done anyways."

Sean nodded his limited understanding. He looked around for a moment, having difficulty remembering where he was and what he'd been doing. The man, Daniel decided, would have difficulty finding sleep, and whatever slumber he did manage to get would be troubled and useless.

For his part, Daniel was glad for the busywork. He had some thinking of his own to do and, much like Sean, the images from the cafeteria would haunt his dreams. He was in no hurry to close his eyes and let the memories play themselves out.

Most of all, it allowed him to work within line of sight of the so-called Reflection Room.

Carrying bucket after bucket of water from one end of the basement to the other, soaping, mopping, rinsing, and repeating allowed Daniel to let his mind wander.

He'd come to this place for revenge. To sabotage the Sandmen as punishment for what they'd done to him, to his father, and to Saint-Ferdinand. Scenarios where he'd figure out how to kill their god or expose the Sandmen to the world had floated in his mind ever since Francis had extended the invitation.

Daniel glanced up at Alice's door between mop strokes. But silly him, he'd never accounted for another victim to be locked up here.

That girl was the key to his revenge or saving the world, but possibly not both.

By the time Daniel had emptied and rinsed the last bucketful of bloody water and put away the soap, disinfectant, and mop, morning was coloring the sky a bruised purple. Pulling bright yellow rubber gloves off his fingers before washing his hands in the industrial sink of the janitorial closet, Daniel felt a strange sort of satisfaction. If he couldn't defeat the god yet, at least he could undo some of what it had done. It lacked the finality of destroying the thing, but it was empowering. A way to fight back, no matter how small.

Walking through the lonely hallway that spanned the length of the school, his jeans damp with soap, water, and bodily fluids, Daniel struggled to hold on to that feeling of satisfaction.

Bed, even with the many promises of nightmares, beckoned seductively. If he hurried, Daniel might get two or three hours of sleep, and every minute would be welcome. But just as he was about to make his way back up the stairs, something caught his eye.

The room across from the janitorial closet was locked. He didn't have to try the handle. The otherwise innocuous door was decorated with an extra padlock inches above the doorknob. It wasn't one of those small inch-wide locks that could be purchased two for a dollar, either. This thing meant business. Even at a distance, it had an unmistakable weight. The god's room didn't boast such security. Then again, who in their right mind would want to break into that prison?

A quick inventory of his keys revealed that Daniel had none that matched the brand of the padlock. Mother had been comfortable giving him full access to the compound. Except for this one room.

"Alice?" he whispered, his lips almost touching the faux wood that covered the mysterious door.

His own pulse answered him as his heartbeat hastened, made more obvious in the deathly silence of the compound. If he was right, this would be the mysterious Reflection Room and, in it, the poor Alice LeSage.

For an uncomfortable amount of time, the only answer he got was the sound of the ventilation system kicking in. The metallic boom and subsequent hum damn near killing him on the spot. As Daniel was about to give up, pulled again by the call of sleep, a faint whisper reached out to him, carrying over the hissing ventilation.

There were no words, simply the rhythmic repetition of three knocks on the other side of the door.

"Alice? Are you okay?"

Again, three soft knocks were his only answer.

"Alice. I'm going to try to get you out of there, okay?"

The overwhelming drive to be the hero—to be the Stephen Crowley he had known—was swelling up inside him again. A muffled whine managed to pierce through the thick door and be overheard above the ventilation. Desperate and pleading, it begged, wordlessly, for him to do nothing.

She was gagged, Daniel realized or decided. Either too tired or too guilty, it had become undeniable to him that this was the prison Mother and Francis called the Reflection Room.

"Hang in there, Alice," he said, louder than intended. "I'm going to get you out."

With renewed determination that overrode his need for sleep, Daniel stomped off, ignoring the gagged, muffled cries from behind the locked door.

"Absolutely not."

Mother was slumped over her desk. Her spine had lost its rigidity, a victim to the trials that plagued her. Surrounded by all the lavish accoutrements in her office, from the antique desk to the walls of books and plush carpeting, she was the one piece that no longer fit.

Anywhere else, Marguerite was the light in the room, the pinnacle of taste and class. Tonight, she was a wreck. A fancy dress hanging on a hook behind a door. Hollow, waiting to be filled once more.

"We can't just let her rot in that room."

Daniel hadn't expected this confrontation. He'd snuck up to Mother's office fully intent on finding and stealing the key to the imposing padlock and finishing what he'd started the previous afternoon.

Instead he found his mother sitting at her desk, face buried in her hands and fingers woven into her black hair. She was quick to regain a measure of composure after noticing her son on her threshold, but no amount of stiff upper lip could hide the bags under her eyes.

"She's not rotting, Daniel." Marguerite gave her son a look of mild condescension. "But we have to make her understand that escape isn't an option. We've had this talk already."

"You're keeping her gagged in there! Does she even have any light?"

"I have her gagged so she won't scream herself raw. You've seen what happens if we don't have her voice to keep things under control."

He had, and the thought still sent waves of nausea up his throat. Just thinking of Sean mopping the same step on the stairs, over and over, was a harsh reminder of that.

"Look, I get it. If Alice can't sing, people die. But she has to be more than a tool. We have to be better than that, don't we?"

Marguerite stood from her plush leather chair, each of her years showing for the first time with the effort. She'd worn a tweed wool skirt to complement an electric-blue blouse. Now standing, Daniel could see the deep scarlet stain, the size of a handprint, that had been left on the skirt. Blood that was unlikely to wash off. She turned to look out one of the large windows, focusing deep into the forest, searching for something beyond the trees.

"Nine of my followers are buried out there in unmarked graves. Five days ago Sylvain Gauthier, a member of this church, was found dead in a subway tunnel with his eyes gouged out. His was the third death to happen under suspicious circumstances. Beatrice Bergeron never made it back from her meeting in Montreal yesterday, and Cassandra Poole is dying in her room as we speak.

"I have two more members threatening to pack their possessions and leave. Obviously, I'm going to talk them out of it, and obviously, I'm going to attend to Cassandra myself."

She turned her eyes to look into his. The condescension was gone, or rather dulled at the edges, replaced instead by an almost academic curiosity. He was like a specimen, and she studied him, waiting to gauge his reaction.

"You're asking me to put aside my concerns for the sake of one selfish girl?"

"You can't expect her to perform on cue if you keep treating her like this. Can't someone else take over part of her responsibilities? What if something happens to—"

"Don't you think we've tried? I've been at this for over a decade, Daniel! We've tried training other singers, but we always start when they're too old or they just don't have the proper dedication or talent. This isn't simply memorizing spells from a book. This has to be perfect. *She* has to be perfect."

The thought dawned on Daniel that Mother wasn't strictly speaking about Alice, but was also referring, in part, to herself. For the first time, he thought he had a measure of the woman behind the cult leader, a hint of who Marguerite Lambert-Crowley was when not wearing the mask of "Mother."

"The Sandmen aren't the only ones who need her to step up and assume her responsibilities," she insisted. "It's the world that's at stake. This thing that we amusingly call a god isn't just angry at Saint-Ferdinand. It's not going to stop at killing Cicero or your father or the fucking McKenzies. We are dealing with the closest thing to the literal devil anyone has ever seen. We are standing at the threshold separating Hell from the Garden of Eden, and Alice is the door. Now you want to, what? Take her shopping? Go see a movie?"

Through her agitation, Marguerite had slowly slipped into her stage persona. She wasn't Marguerite anymore, not in that moment. She was Mother.

The brief moment of vulnerability was gone. She was Jim Jones. She was Shoko Asahara. Except that, instead of promises and rhetoric, Marguerite Lambert-Crowley had an actual god tucked away and the coming apocalypse was real.

"You've tried the stick, Mom. Now let me try the carrot."

"What is this about, Daniel?" she asked, struggling to keep the irritation from her voice. "Look at you. You can't possibly have a crush on that girl. Why do you want to play the hero?"

Daniel had still held out hope that the Sandmen here were different from their Saint-Ferdinand counterpart. As it turned out, everything in the Church of the Sandmen was stained with blood. Those dealing with the god of Saint-Ferdinand weren't any different from Sean Dover: all they did was move the blood around, unable to ever be rid of its stain.

Daniel turned from Marguerite. His left hand wrapped around the fist of his right, crushing it as if to squeeze focus and courage out of his fingers. His eyes darted around the room, desperate to find something to cling to.

"Dad's not the only one I lost in Saint-Ferdinand," he finally said. "My girlfriend, Sasha, was also murdered."

"I know," Marguerite answered, genuine sympathy cutting through her preaching. "Francis told me. He mentioned you were unusually close for your age."

It was the first time Daniel had heard it described that way. Usually people assumed that the young couple was just that, a fling of youth naively taken too seriously by the lovebirds. It was adorable, but never given much credit. Of all people though, Francis seemed to have found the most understanding description. *Unusually close for their age.*

"We were." Daniel turned back around to face his mother.

"But the god killed her." Marguerite stood, walking slowly around her desk toward her son. "Forgive me. I don't want to assume you see Alice as a surrogate, but you have to understand . . ."

She paused, reaching out to take his hands into hers and gently pull the fingers loose, liberating his right hand with the care of someone untying a particularly stubborn knot.

"Of all of us here, Alice is the only one who can defend herself against this demon. You think of her as a victim to protect when she's actually the safest one of all."

Marguerite held on to her son's hands, allowing him to feel the connection between them, the long-forgotten comfort of a mother's touch.

"She doesn't need saving," he said to show he understood.

"No. She doesn't. We do."

Abruptly, she let go of his hands, making a point of looking at her watch.

As if on cue, a knock came at the door, signaling that the Church members Mother intended to convince to remain within the congregation were here, and that it was time for Daniel to go. "Before you leave, Daniel?" she said, without turning to look in his direction. "Can you not call me 'Mom' in the future? It's undignified and I don't want the others hearing you say it."

He nodded, knowing she couldn't see.

Daniel walked out of the posh office and back into the linoleum-floored reality of the Sandmen's compound. He couldn't help but wonder if his mother knew it wasn't the god who'd killed Sasha.

ABRAHAM

PENNY HAD EXPRESSLY forbidden him from returning to the Bergeron house. Instead she wanted to report Randy's presence there to Lieutenant Bélanger. It had taken no small amount of negotiation for Abraham to convince her not to.

"Don't you dare go back."

Penny was adamant on the subject. After their return from the Bergeron house, a walk punctuated by much huffing and grumbling on her part, she'd laid down the law for him.

"Under no circumstances are you to contact that man," she explained, hand flat on the kitchen counter and pushing up on her toes. "The only reason I'm not calling Matt right this minute is out of respect for Venus. Promise me you won't go back."

Abraham had seldom seen her so dramatic about something that seemed trivial to him. What was the big deal about talking with Dr. McKenzie? He knew things, obviously, and that was a resource to exploit.

"I promise," he'd answered without hesitation.

After seeing Randy's reaction to Penny's touch, it was clear that whatever the god's blood was doing to her, it was getting worse. If there was even a sliver of a chance that Randy could help, Abraham would shoulder any risk involved.

Abraham should have expected this. If he was to save Penny, he'd have to go against her wishes. Wasn't that how it always happened in movies? The ends would ultimately justify the means. Besides, who better to put Audrey's spirit to rest than the man who'd allowed it to remain restless in the first place?

The very next day, while Penny was at work, Abraham broke his promise.

The street leading up to the Bergeron's property was as deserted during the day as it had been during the night, echoing Saint-Ferdinand's slow march toward the status of ghost town. In fact, it had been the most well-to-do who had led the charge in the real estate evacuation of the village. Others, like the Petersons, simply couldn't afford to move.

Abraham knocked on the door to the kitchen at the back, the same one he'd broken the night before. As he waited, he took stock of the property. Someone had already drained and covered the pool and put away all the patio furniture and lawn games. On any other late summer day, he would have heard the sound of lawn mowers and leaf blowers, and children running in the streets.

He was half lost in his contemplation when he realized no one was answering the door. Feeling a little silly for even knocking in the first place, Abraham let himself in. The house was much less spooky during the day. The living room was no longer populated by ghosts but rather simple linen-covered furniture. The glow of the overcast sun let every object stand out clearly, banishing the shadows so that the imagination could no longer exploit them.

"Dr. McKenzie?" he called out.

As if by habit, Abraham went over to the refrigerator and opened the door. He scanned the contents while waiting for someone to answer him. Penny would have mocked him for instinctively going to where the food was.

He made his way down the stairs. Maybe Venus's uncle was wearing headphones or sleeping, or simply too focused on whatever he was doing here to listen.

Dried mud stains on the carpeting at the bottom of the stairs made Abraham cringe. They were incriminating evidence of last night's trespass. He'd have to come back and clean that up before Beatrice came home from wherever she'd vanished to. That, and repair the kitchen door.

Abraham continued his exploration of the basement, walking leisurely through the gaming room and then circling back to the home theater. This was where he'd found the first unmistakable traces of Randy McKenzie's presence.

The medical examiner hadn't been so bold as to commandeer any of the bedrooms upstairs. Instead he'd made a bed out of a large sofa in the home theater. There were comforters and pillows and even an empty dish with dirty cutlery, the remains of a recent meal.

Abraham had expected more. From the stories told to him by Penelope and even Venus before she left for Montreal, Dr. McKenzie had been a sort of necromancer. He was the one who'd saved Audrey's spirit from falling into the jaws of a hungry god. He was the one who had commandeered Penny's body using astral projection or whatever. He'd also confirmed that he was indeed responsible for what they'd found in Audrey's grave. If all of that was true, then where were the summoning circles? The sacrificial knives? Shouldn't there be candles or a Ouija board? Abraham suspected that not all of these things were the tools of a necromancer, but surely some of it had to be real. He'd seen the gory mural painted on the walls of Venus's shed, and it was all about arcane imagery, blood, and bones.

It was only disappointing until he realized he hadn't explored the whole basement. There was still one room to inspect. The one the underaged like him had always been discouraged from entering.

The wine cellar.

Not that the Bergerons didn't trust him and Penny to stay out of the bottles, but some of the wines and liquors in there were expensive and, truth be told, everyone knew Abraham was kind of a klutz. Keeping him out of the cold room with all the tightly packed fragile bottles was probably for the best.

With half a smile and a sudden purpose and certainty, Abe went over to the cellar door and, putting a large hand over the handle, tried to open it.

The stubborn knob refused to turn, clicking in position instead. Locked. When did the Bergerons get a lock for that door? Maybe Beatrice didn't trust the house sitters? No, that couldn't be it. Otherwise, how did Randy have access to it?

At a glance, it wasn't a very sturdy door and, if done right, Abraham was fairly confident he could break in with a good shove of his shoulder. He'd crack the frame in the process, but it might be worth it.

"What the hell are you doing back here?"

Randy's voice came as a shock. Between the carpeting and Dr. McKenzie's diminished frame, Abe hadn't heard him sneak in.

"Dr. McKenzie!" Abe said. "Just the doctor I've been looking for."

"I gathered that," Randy answered. "But what the hell for? I thought you kids had declared me persona non grata."

Abraham tried to put on his most pleasant and apologetic face, the one Penny had told him looked like he was trying to pass a kidney stone.

"Well, Penny has her own ax to grind, but I'm trying to see the bigger picture. I think there's a lot that needs fixing and I think you're the one to fix it."

The former medical examiner gestured wildly around, signifying not only the house and immediate surroundings, but the whole of Saint-Ferdinand and perhaps the world.

"Sure! Why not? Let's fix things. Where would you like to start, Abraham? The people who died at the circus? Maybe get my brother back? And Crowley? What about the dozens of people Finnegan had to kill? Maybe we can go all the way back and stuff the genie into the bottle again? Which, of all the irreversible things that have happened over the last twenty years, do you think I have the power to 'fix'?"

"Well . . ." Abraham started, seemingly oblivious to the sarcastic annoyance Randy was venting, but not the smell of liquor on his breath. "We could start with Audrey?"

It was, in the end, the garage that Randy had set up as his workshop. During his life, William Bergeron, like many men, had had a tumultuous on-and-off affair with the dream of being a handyman. At regular intervals, he would get it in his head to build something. At one point, it had been birdhouses, as evidenced by the six or seven hung at the far side of the garage. A more widely known episode was the summer he'd decided to refurbish a 1977 Ford Mustang. Being no mechanic, the project consisted of William fussing over a part of the engine or the transmission for a weekend, trying to make heads or tails of the manuals, then giving up and having a professional take care of it for him. To his credit, the finished product was a beauty. Painted black with dramatic white stripes running over the hood, roof, and trunk, it was taken out for a drive perhaps twice every summer. Ultimately, the car vanished into limbo days following Audrey's troubled birth.

While deserted more often than not, William Bergeron's workshop had been the envy of every middle-aged man in Saint-Ferdinand.

If anyone had it in mind to set up a place to do supernatural research, William Bergeron's workshop was as good a choice as any.

Randy opened the garage door, allowing Abraham to walk into his sanctum of the mystic arts. It stank of burned metal and wood shavings. The boy had expected something like he'd seen in horror movies—salt spilled in circles on the ground, huge pillar candles ready to be lit and illuminate the dark sacrifices needed to conjure up the forces of darkness and corral the dead.

As things turned out, when Randy switched on the large, powerful fluorescent tubes hanging from the cathedral ceiling of the three-car garage, the only thing that stood out was the canvas-covered ghost of the good ole Ford Mustang.

"This it?" Abraham asked, incredulous and a little disappointed.

"I'm sorry, did you expect anything more? Maybe a hospital bed wired to a Tesla coil in the corner? Perhaps a bloody pentagram on the floor?"

"I don't know. I just expected . . . something. I thought magic would be a little more dramatic."

A deep sigh escaped Randy as he walked, hands lodged deep in his jean pockets, toward the workbench at the back of the garage. Another flick of a different switch and the whole garage-wide table lit up from a chain of LEDs. Power tools and workstations interrupted the workbench at regular intervals. A circular saw, press drill, and even a small anvil were all screwed into the countertop.

"What's in your dad's wizard sanctum? Does he wear robes when he works? Sings incantations or boils pigments into a cauldron during the new moon to make his paints?"

"He doesn't, but my dad—"

"Is more of a sorcerer than I'll ever be. I'm sure you've seen what he can do. Learned it as an apprentice from another of his order of what you call 'magic.' She might have been better than he'll ever be, but your old man, he waves brushes instead of a wand and mixes colors instead of potions.

"Magic is boring and tedious. It's either years of practice with little results or memorizing trivial bullshit that closes more doors than it opens. You want magic? The closest thing you'll get to a pentagram here is this . . . ."

Dr. McKenzie pulled a dirty rag from a large object sitting on the workbench. From a distance, it seemed to be a slab of rock or concrete. Randy beckoned Abraham over.

At close range, the object's appearance grabbed Abraham's guts and twisted them in a knot. He'd seen enough bones and viscera in his life that it wasn't the animal parts that bothered him. It was how familiar the tableau was.

"Is that . . . is that from Venus's shed?"

While there was a definite resemblance to the mural he'd noticed on that fateful night when Penny had played at god-slayer, it couldn't possibly be the same. For one, it was applied, or rather grotesquely melded into, a piece of concrete. Venus's shed had been made of wood paneling. Also, Abraham couldn't recognize any of the animal skeletons in this particular mural, whereas the one he'd originally seen was built from bird skulls and bones, the viscera of rodents, and the feathers of the unfortunate avian.

"It's not. I got this out from the foundation underneath the old Parker house."

Bewildered, Abraham reached out, running his index finger over the surface of a large bone. It was held on to the smooth concrete with dried blood, supported by its own foundation of desiccated tendons and sinew. It felt like plastic to the touch, smooth and slippery.

"Wow . . . there were two of these things?" asked Abraham. "What animal went into making this one?"

"Mm? Brad Ludwig if I'm not mistaken."

Abraham pulled his finger away from the gruesome mural as if it were suddenly poisonous. He'd known Brad. In fact, he'd threatened to beat up the little shit on more than one occasion as payback for bullying Venus. Still, he'd never wished for worse than a bloody nose on the guy. Nothing resembling this.

"I'm pretty sure there were three murals in total in the end, but only one was made by the actual living god of Saint-Ferdinand," Randy continued, poking at the mural with his left pinkie, testing the resistance of a particularly gnarly knob of red-marbled yellow flesh.

"What are they?" Abraham asked, struggling to banish Brad's face from his mind, or stop himself from imagining the boy's final moments.

"Psychopomps. Or rather, ritualistic representations that act as psychopomps."

Abraham couldn't suppress a chuckle at the word. It sounded silly, made-up. Before he could ask for further explanation, Randy sighed and elaborated.

"A psychopomp, according to Greek mythology, is a 'spirit guide.' They help dead souls to the afterlife. This thing, as far as I can tell, served two purposes. First, it was made from someone in the process of dying. A fresh soul to guide. Then, because of the pattern here"—he pointed to the intersecting and nested spirals—"it 'guides' the soul in a specific direction."

Leaning in, Abraham noticed human teeth that he'd missed before, embedded into the congealed muscle.

"What direction did that one point?"

"That's what I'm trying to figure out."

Randy seemed lost in thought. The way he ran his finger atop the dried-out tissue had an almost apologetic tenderness.

"Could you use one of these to help Audrey?" Abraham asked. "I mean, you said these psychopomps are supposed to guide souls to the afterlife, or do the nails you put in her eyes and feet keep her from passing on?"

Randy stood up, walking to the other end of the workbench. Near the anvil, he reached down and picked up a nail, studying it with curious, clinical intent. As Abraham got close, he recognized what sort of nail this was. An old, oily black iron nail. Like the ones in Audrey's feet.

"It's complicated," the doctor explained. "The dead don't see very well. Their eyes don't work the way ours do because, as far as I've read, once you're dead, there's nothing to see."

He brought the nail up to his own eye, angling the point toward his pupil, bringing it to within a quarter of an inch of his cornea. It made Abraham nervous.

"They say the eyes are the windows to the soul, and iron . . . well, according to mythology, is a material that's anathema to things supernatural. So, by putting nails in a dead person's eyes, it attaches their perception to the land of the living. Remove the nails and the ghost is essentially blind. Blind to the living, at least."

"That's what someone did to Audrey!"

Abraham was distressed. He could see the apparition of little Audrey, lost in the woods across the street from the Richards farm. She'd been asking for his help, begging him to save her from the ghosts that surrounded her. Her eyes, punctured and blind, that ever-bleeding cut on her cheek, and all she could see of him was the knife that had sliced her face. To think she'd been in that condition for months now, a living hell of fear and confusion in place of fire and brimstone.

But all Randy could do was shake his head, as if it were Abraham who didn't grasp the specifics of the situation.

"No one pulled those out of her eyes for her, Abraham," he said, putting the nail back down on the workbench. "She pulled those out herself, and then I put them in Sam Finnegan's eyes instead."

"Where did you learn to do all that?"

Abraham's mouth was full as he spoke, but unlike Penny, Dr. McKenzie didn't seem to mind as much.

The two of them had chatted for another hour before Randy got bored and declared he was hungry. Abraham, on a steady diet of information and knowledge, had barely noticed the time pass and his own stomach growing empty.

He'd suggested they order a pizza, but the idea was met with a disappointed look from the doctor. Of course they wouldn't be ordering anything. They weren't supposed to be there.

They did end up eating pizza, however, something picked out of the Bergerons' freezer that they ate in the basement.

"A book."

"Not something I can pick up at the library, I'm guessing?"

This drew a wry smile from Randy.

"Not likely. It was my father's book. His travel notes. Everything he and his friends learned, he put in that book."

Abraham sat, slack-jawed, with his slice of half-eaten pizza hanging from his fingers.

"You mean, like a spell book?" he asked after a moment.

"More like a very disorganized diary," Randy answered, a little amused by the idea. "Anything he and his buddies would learn during their travels, they wrote down in there. Very little of it makes much sense, but there are a few useful bits and pieces. He wanted me to learn about controlling the dead, so that's what I focused on."

In an unprecedented move, Abraham put the unfinished slice back on his plate, leaning forward in the recliner. He gently pushed his can of soda aside on the coffee table, as if its presence interfered with the important conversation he was having.

"But there were other things, right? Other secrets?"

Randy seemed more annoyed than interested in the line of questioning, as if he'd gone through it a million times already. He leaned back, away from his interrogator.

"Sure, it holds plenty of secrets. Parlor tricks mostly. Nothing big enough, like how to banish a god."

The doctor bent over, putting his plate on the coffee table, spilling uneaten crust as he did so. But he didn't get back up, leaning his elbows on his knees and pinching the bridge of his nose instead. There was a weight, almost visible, pushing down on the man's shoulders.

"You learned enough to keep Audrey from suffering like other people who've died in Saint-Ferdinand," Abraham said, a weak effort at consoling Randy. "That's got to count for something."

Without looking up, Dr. McKenzie shook his head. His shoulders jerked and Abraham could have sworn the movement was caused by a sob.

"It wasn't enough to keep her from suffering. It's not enough to bring her back or to fix her."

Abraham gave the doctor a moment to collect himself. He and Randy were at odds. Where Abraham saw nothing but good news in what they could do using the psychopomps, Randy saw only limitations, grieving the fact that he couldn't do more. Then again, Abe had dealt with the living beating the odds to remain alive, while the doctor had dealt with nothing but the dead, telling the sad tale of how they'd died. Their entire worldviews were different.

"Well," Abe said, waiting a moment for Randy to look up and give a sign that he was listening. "We can at least put some people to rest, right?"

Dr. McKenzie pushed his right palm into his eye, as if he could push back his tears. With effort, he pulled his lips into an uneasy smile and nodded with half-hearted agreement.

"Yeah. Yeah, maybe we can. How would you like to learn a little bit of necromancy?"

Abraham ended up staying at the Bergeron house much longer than anticipated. Of his many self-admitted flaws, he'd always been able to boast about his strict punctuality.

Now, double-stepping home under the gray cover of twilight, he thought about his father waiting for dinner. While Harry could certainly get himself a beer and some leftovers if he was hungry enough, Abraham didn't like his father to worry. With his fragile constitution, it wouldn't do to put the old man under unnecessary stress.

Not that he had much left to worry about, but fear for one's children was an ingrained trait of parents in Saint-Ferdinand.

After the circus massacre, news media had made a big deal of Sam Finnegan's escape and the role of Stephen Crowley in the murders. In the aftermath of such a bloodbath, it was no mystery why the village was hemorrhaging residents.

Abraham knew better. Stephen Crowley had perished, not escaped. Randy McKenzie was at large, but as he had discovered, held no murderous intent. As for Sam Finnegan himself, the old man, possessed by the god, had been taken away, hopefully as far from the village as possible.

Abraham had learned such a dizzying amount over the course of the afternoon that it was tempting to bring Penny in on the secret. She was the kind of person who devoured information the way he could gorge himself on ice cream. Abraham had but touched the brittle surface of ice atop a deep lake of knowledge that was Randy McKenzie. Once he'd dived deep enough and was confident that his gambit had paid off, he'd confess to his lie. Penny would be livid and curse him out, but she'd have to concede that he'd been right. Her curiosity would do the rest.

As he approached his home, Abraham was on a sort of high. His feet felt light and his steps were brisk, energized by the thrill of secrecy and the sharp, cold air of the evening.

Penny's mother's car was in the driveway, which was a welcome surprise. He bit his tongue in anticipation of having to pretend he'd been out walking or looking for work or helping a neighbor.

The lights to the studio were on and he could see shadows moving around between the easels. Harry was working late and Penny was keeping him company while they waited for him.

At no time did it cross his mind that Penny might not be here for him.

Still high on his success, Abraham made it almost to the top of the stairs before noticing that something was wrong. Echoing through the vast studio, he heard a choked-back sob.

It was a familiar anguish, one he'd heard a handful of times. The most recent instance of which was on the day Penny had learned of her mother's death.

But Penny wasn't usually one to cry. As she put it, she was too busy to cry. When they went to the movies, Abraham was usually the one who'd mist up at the sad parts.

Whatever it was that had brought her here to weep in his father's studio must be big, and it paralyzed Abraham to consider the possibilities.

Had something happened to Venus?

Abraham was about to take the last few steps to the studio level when his father's voice interrupted him.

"You asked me not to hold back," Harry said, tired and apologetic. "I, myself, prefer to hear the honest truth. Only fair I pay you the same courtesy."

There came a loud sniffing followed by embarrassed swallowing. Then Penny's exhausted voice rang through the studio, making its way down to where Abraham waited.

"No. It's fine," she said, sniffing again. "Well, not 'fine,' but you're right. Better the truth. It's been weeks of this and I feel like it's all just catching up to me."

Abraham was about to race up the stairs and offer his comfort. It was the perfect time to come clean. He'd broken his promise to her, sure, but in exchange he was coming back with solutions, or possible solutions. Before he could even lift a knee, Harry's voice came through once again.

"I can't tell you what to do, but I'd appreciate if you didn't tell Abe any of this."

Any of what? Why was his father hiding things from him? Abraham carefully put a booted foot on the next step of the stairs, pulling his massive weight behind it, crouching to remain in the shadows.

"He'll figure it out, you know. He's not stupid," Penny said, the words warming Abe's heart but also surprising him a little.

"Oh, I know. He puts on a show of it, but he's a clever one, like his old man. But he fusses like me too. You come running to him with that and he's liable to do something rash."

Abraham was finally able to look over the landing, confident that he was out of sight. Harry was on his work stool, a bucket of painting tools—brushes, knives, and palettes—near his feet. The cart that carried his oxygen tank was also close by, keeping him tethered. Penny sat on the floor, wearing her wool jacket and leather gloves. Abraham caught a glimpse of her eyes. They were so blue as to seem unnatural, glowing under the shadow of her brow.

"What are you afraid he'll do?"

Harry sighed. "Something dumb. Like try to kill a god."

Penny looked down at her hands, flexing the fingers, probably remembering the night she'd tried just such a thing, appreciating the consequences that had been dealt to her.

"Right," she said, something thick in her throat. "But we already agreed he's not stupid and he knows the consequences. So why would he try something like that?"

"Because it might work." Harry adjusted his seating on the bench, seemingly nervous about the subject. "Who knows? It's probably just optimistic folklore, but maybe it's like killing the head vampire and all the other vampires are cured? Wouldn't be the craziest thing I read in that book."

With a final sniffle that signaled an end to her crying, Penny looked up at Harry Peterson's current work. The painting had evolved further. There were more details and the textures had a near-tangible quality to them. Abraham could swear that if he walked up to the canvas and brushed his hand against the rocks, he would feel their cool surface on his fingers.

For all the near-perfection of the painting, it was still unfinished. The space across from the enormous stone archway remained empty.

"Did you find this in the book too?" Penny asked, nodding her chin toward the canvas.

"Mm-hmm," Harry mumbled, raising his own head to appraise his handiwork. "I'm basing it off the memory of a charcoal sketch made by Neil McKenzie almost half a century ago."

What book? Abraham couldn't think of any book or grimoire that his father might have had with drawings from Neil McKenzie. And what was this archway? Judging from what his father could do with paintings of birds, it was easy to figure out his plan was to make this painting come alive too. But why?

"What's on the other side?" Penny asked, a mirror of Abraham's own thoughts.

"Hope."

"Good. I could use a refill."

What hope? Where was Penny's curiosity now? What a time for her to become philosophical and introspective!

Harry and Penny contemplated the painting for a few more minutes. A strange pang of jealousy hit Abraham, like an unexpected slap to the back of his head. It was unwelcome and gross, but he wanted to be in his father's place at that moment, enjoying a silent pause with Penny.

"Isn't Venus supposed to be the one to best the god, or whatever that silly prophecy says?"

Harry shook his head like a man who'd already gone through this same explanation a half dozen times.

"I doubt it's that simple. You can't just kill a god. You of all people should know that. They play by their own rules, and death just ain't one of them."

"What about other gods? Did Cicero or Neil say anything about how we could summon one? They can't all be evil, can they? Maybe we can get our hands on one that'll help us?"

Abraham could recognize that, like him, Penny was grasping at straws, looking for new solutions in what they knew was well-trod territory. It was what they had all been reduced to. The same sort of desperate wishful thinking had driven Venus to Montreal and Abraham to bargain with the devil.

"Well, there was this story about this one god that loved people. Loved humanity. According to Cicero, most legends of benevolent gods come from Him . . . Her . . . It. Where all the other gods treated us like toys or nuisances, that one fought *for* us.

"Neil McKenzie traveled the world looking for any hint of that god."

"Did he find anything? Anything at all?"

With a huff of effort and a grunt of pain, Harry lifted himself from his stool. When he started to pick up his brushes and tools, Penny jumped to her feet to help him. Abraham knew this was his cue to make a stealthy exit. Perhaps retreat to the house and start dinner. He could pretend he hadn't noticed Penny's car and act innocent.

As Abraham was about to backpedal down the stairs, Harry paused again. Penny was taking tubes of paint from his old, gnarled hands. Abraham's father looked from her to his painting again, his grateful smile fading into something more wistful.

"I like to think," he said in hushed tones, "that maybe he did."

JODIE

"HERE!"

Jodie's left hand grabbed Dickson's arm while she held his phone in front of her face with her right. The car jerked to a sudden stop and the driver let slip a curse.

"Dammit, LeSage!" Dickson's tone was exasperated. "All that for a phone?"

After Jodie had barely caught up to him in the hospital parking lot, out of kindness for his injured colleague, he'd driven her around the Ahuntsic-Cartierville borough. She'd given him precious little information apart from saying she was tracking down her lost phone, promising that she'd explain everything later. A promise she had every intention of breaking. Dickson had been accommodating, but his patience was wearing thin.

"Sorry! I'm sorry," she said. "We're very close and . . ."

Her voice trailed off. The dots representing Jodie's position and that of her phone were almost overlapping on the screen. But that wasn't what made the color drain from her face.

In the distance and as far as the eye could see, all the traffic lights on Thimens Boulevard had turned yellow and refused to change. The scene was eerie and reminiscent of the seconds that preceded the crash that had nearly killed Ben. It made Jodie's blood run cold and her throat contract into a dry swallow.

"What the hell?" Dickson asked, more complaint than question.

Failing to appreciate the importance of the phenomena, the senior officer reached for the car radio. His eyes were still riveted on the endless string of yellow globes that glared right back at him.

With slow, deliberate calm, Jodie pressed the lock button on the phone in her hand and put it down on the dashboard. She moved as if she were being watched by a predator, avoiding any sudden movement that might provoke it. Her right hand found the handle to her door while her left struggled with the latch to her seat belt. Lucien Peña had bared his fangs and she would be damned if she let another fellow officer be bitten.

"Where are you going?" Dickson interrupted his report to ask.

"Getting my phone."

And Venus, she thought, but kept that part to herself.

"Wait! Let me park and we'll get it together."

Jodie was already standing next to the car and shutting the door. The window started to go down.

"LeSage? Are you okay? Maybe we should get you back to Sacré-Coeur. You can get a new phone."

All the lights suddenly turned red and, for a moment, it seemed like everything was going back to normal. Cars were starting to honk with the impatience of their drivers and traffic began to accumulate, an odd sight for the neighborhood at this time of night.

The red lights persisted longer than they should have, and then longer still. The color felt like a warning, but of what? Was it a threat to her or to Dickson, or both?

There was only one possibility she was willing to risk.

"Dickson?" she said, leaning in the window. "I'll find my phone by myself. Looks like you're going to have other fish to fry."

Jodie looked up and down Thimens, inviting Dickson to do the same. Pedestrians were starting to gather at street corners and cars were forming longer and longer lines as more of them trickled in from intersections. People were taking pictures with their phones, so far amused by the odd malfunction of traffic lights.

The senior constable hesitated, eyes jumping from the situation outside his police car to his radio and then back to Jodie. He was worried about her, which was a good thing from a coworker, but right now he was the one who needed to leave for his own safety. For the millionth time, Jodie wanted to try to explain the cause of the crash that had wounded her; then everything would make sense to Dickson. For the millionth time, she reminded herself how ridiculous her explanation would sound.

In a moment of near-epiphany, she understood why Venus hadn't tried to work with the cops to find Peña in the first place.

"I'll be fine! I bet whoever took my phone ditched it when they saw it was being tracked, and it's going to be in some bushes or something." She wanted to sound comforting. "Or I won't find it and I'll take a cab home. Either way, don't worry about me."

Dickson hesitated, radio still firmly in his hand.

"Fine," he said, resigned. "Call me when you get home, though. And don't you dare come into the office tomorrow."

Jodie smiled and nodded, stepping back to watch the window crawl back up. She saw her reflection in the glass before Dickson switched on his siren, slowly dodging his way around other cars. It was obvious why he was so worried. She looked like a mess. Her dress shirt was buttoned up, but each button was offset by one. Her belt looped around her pants but remained unfastened. Both of her boots were unlaced. In a fit of self-consciousness, she frenzied to correct as much as she could before getting back on her search.

"Shit!"

By the time she got back from crudely tying her laces, Dickson's car was long gone and with him, his phone.

How the hell am I going to track Venus down now? Jodie asked, cursing herself in the process.

The dots had been on top of each other. Her phone had to be close, and with it, Venus. If Peña had been able to threaten with the traffic lights, he, too, had to be close, didn't he?

Jodie paced back and forth on the sidewalk, dodging the accumulating crowd of curious onlookers. To their disappointment, and the almost audible relief of every driver on Thimens, the lights all returned to their normal behavior. First by switching to a random pattern of green, red, and occasionally yellow, and then switching at the predictable intervals.

A bubble of panic formed in Jodie's stomach as she realized that Peña may have very well caused her to be stranded on purpose. A less violent but no less effective way to get rid of her sniffing around. For all she knew, her phone was indeed lying in a bush by the sidewalk, waiting like spent bait to be found, all traces of Venus erased.

The bubble burst the moment she saw them.

An enormous man wearing a trench coat, his stature that of a bear, was holding the hand of a short teen with shoulder-length hair that filtered orange under the streetlamp. They both stood, immobile among the disappointed and retreating throngs of pedestrians. She expected them to turn around and vanish in the thinning crowd, their ominous warning delivered.

Instead they stood still, letting people wash around them like flowing water, unperturbed.

"Pig!" the large man shouted.

It took Jodie a moment to realize he was calling to her. No one called cops "pigs" anymore, at least not to their faces. The insult was more embarrassing for how much it lacked in imagination. To make sure she understood, he waved a cell phone over his head. Her cell phone.

"Venus!" Jodie called out, closing the distance between them with the longest strides she could manage.

The girl looked healthy enough, though her posture suggested she might be favoring her left leg a little. Considering the scope of the accident, it was a miracle she'd suffered no other injuries. At least none that Jodie could see.

"Venus, are you okay?"

"I'm fine."

The answer cracked mid-sentence. The words were meant to have weight but were supported by a weak voice that couldn't carry them, much like Venus could barely carry herself.

Her green eyes had taken on the hue of pine needles and her focus seemed lost somewhere between a thousand yards and the distant past. She was not fine. It didn't look like a concussion and Jodie couldn't put her finger on what might be wrong, but the girl was hurt.

"I need to take her to the hospital."

"No."

Peña looked even taller up close, and dirtier somehow. He smelled of wet cigarettes and dust, and his eyebrows were like two caterpillars covered in soot. He was an emperor in rags, majestic and imposing in his domain. The city was his obedient kingdom. He towered over Jodie, twice as much when she knelt in front of Venus.

"Please. Something's wrong with her. I think she's in shock."

"She's fine. There's nothing a hospital can do for her."

This was a proclamation of fact, or so he wanted to project. His words were unwavering and he punctuated them by putting a possessive hand on Venus's shoulder.

This seemed to snap the girl out of her torpor. Her eyes found focus in Jodie, recognizing her, *really* recognizing her, for the first time. She reached out with a shaking hand and latched on to Jodie's wrist. Her frail fingers clutched tightly, pushing the shirt buttons into the constable's skin. In a weird way, she was completing the circuit, connecting all three of them in a chain of which Venus was the common link.

"I should go with her," Venus said, taking strength from Jodie's touch. "She's right. I'm not fine."

"We're not done our business, McKenzie," Peña answered, half growling. He could have bared a set of fangs and Jodie wouldn't have been surprised.

"I can't finish anything if I fall apart."

"You sought me out, girl."

"And I'll seek you out again! I just need a few hours. Make sure I can keep doing . . . doing what needs to be done."

A tense exchange of looks passed between the street shaman and Venus. Her head craned back to look at Peña, the hand holding

Jodie's wrist the only clue she even remembered the constable was there.

"I'm not negotiating with you," Jodie interrupted, using as much authority as her exhausted voice could manage.

"No. You're not," Peña replied, pulling Venus back to him by inches. "I'm negotiating with her."

Jodie wanted to interject again. Venus was in no condition to stand up to this sort of intimidation. She needed to be looked at, needed to get away from this man. Without a gun or a nightstick, Jodie had very little leverage of her own. Even without whatever trick of urban magic Peña might have up his soiled sleeve, she wasn't going to take him down, and Venus would be no help if she tried.

"There's a god to kill, McKenzie," Peña said. "You still have a lot to learn if you're going to be part of that."

"I know," she replied, pulling away from his grasp. "But I gotta do this. I gotta know."

"Four hours," he finally said. "I'll find you in four hours. Make sure there's no one standing between the two of us when I come."

With that last threat spoken, he let go of Venus's shoulder. Jodie's head throbbed at the memory of the accident that had brought Peña into their lives, and Venus stumbled, her left ankle apparently giving up on her.

VENUS

JODIE HAD TAKEN her back to Sacré-Coeur. The same hospital she and Peña had briefly stopped by earlier. Venus no longer believed in coincidences. This had to be yet another cog in one of Peña's machines. Or an echo from the past that resonated with her current circumstances. It didn't matter. She was powerless against whatever it was.

They'd sidestepped all of the waiting lines, the constable asking for favors wherever she could. Anti-inflammatories were quickly administered for the pain and to help bring the swelling down. Then Venus was wheeled from an examination room to the imaging room for an X-ray and then a different room for an MRI. She felt a little embarrassed to be sitting in a wheelchair when she'd walked into the ER under her own power, but after being on her feet for more than twenty-four hours, Venus welcomed the rest.

There had never been so many people poking and prodding at her at one time. They all shot her concerned looks that were more irritating than comforting. Nurses in colorful scrubs and doctors with starched white coats busied themselves looking for physically broken things under her skin, afraid she'd suffered a concussion, broken a rib, or punctured some organ.

Venus could feel the aftertaste of worry at the back of her mind. What good would it do to indulge it though? Besides, any fear she might have for herself had been crowded out by the heavier burden she carried.

The greater wounds weren't to her body. Guilt and fear and remorse had left deep gouges and were left to fester. She drained the pus and infection of them into the cold chasm left by the god's touch. While it kept her sane, Venus could feel the presence of the entity reaching out to her from the depths. A siren's call she loathed but felt compelled to answer.

Jodie seemed to see it too. Performing her own examination, the constable observed Venus with near-scientific concern. She, too, was looking for symptoms, but to a disease she knew was already there, as far as Venus could tell.

It was the shadow of Beatrice Bergeron. The television in the waiting room kept bringing it up. Either with images of Place Vertu mall or with the headline teased at the bottom of the screen, scrolling by to incite viewers to stay tuned. Jodie could do the math herself. She already knew about Saint-Ferdinand and the Bergerons. Her faith in coincidence was probably as shaken as Venus's. Peña had struck again, but this time Venus had been there.

A crack had been left open to the small examination room where Venus was allowed to change back into her own clothes, ostensibly so Jodie could peek in and make sure her young ward was still doing well. Had they deemed her a risk to herself? Would they even let her go?

While weighing whether she should put her left boot back on over her bandaged foot, Venus peeked through the narrow opening. She could barely see Jodie and had to adjust her angle to get a good look at her face. Her eyes were sunken from lack of sleep and a bruise leaked from a bandage's edge over her left cheek. Her hair was a mess and her posture, which Venus had seen as confident, was now slumped and defeated.

"Constable LeSage?"

Venus didn't recognize the voice calling from out of frame. It could have belonged to one of the myriad nurses and technicians who'd cared for her in the last two hours, she couldn't tell. But the conversation that followed was in hushed tones that her ears couldn't pull out.

Jodie's eyes conveyed quite enough, however.

Her features initially lit up, a smile breaching the surface of her weariness for a moment. It was quick to sink back under, swallowed by an even deeper anguish. Her hand reached up to cover her mouth and she seemed to choke back a sob. She was quick to pull together her composure. Whoever had brought her the bad news reached out to offer comfort, but Jodie nodded the hand away, mouthing a question instead.

Carefully, Venus slipped her boot on, tucking the laces instead of tying them so she'd be somewhat comfortable.

"Venus?"

They locked eyes through the crack. Jodie's were all determination while Venus assumed hers conveyed little more than confusion.

"You ready?"

Venus answered by shouldering her bag and limping out of the changing room. *Goodbye, my friend*, she thought toward the wheelchair, glad their acquaintance had been temporary.

"It's Ben," Jodie said. "He's awake."

As it turned out, Ben had been awake for some time. Doctors had wanted to talk to him and evaluate his cognitive abilities before allowing visitors. His family, whom Jodie had advised about the accident, were flying in from Vancouver but wouldn't be there until the next day.

It felt good to know that he was alive.

When Venus had first spotted Jodie on Thimens, she could barely register what she was seeing. She'd given so much of herself to the god's presence in her soul that it was a long time pulling herself back out. The cold hollow had swallowed more than her guilt and revulsion at what was being done to Beatrice. It had taken most of Venus with it, leaving nothing but an automaton in her stead. She could feel the alien presence of the god pulling her strings through the hollow, doing what she couldn't do on her own.

"I don't think I want to go," Venus complained as they made their way to the elevators.

Her heavy bag was slung over her shoulder. For the first time, she realized how much it aggravated her limp. Yet she wanted to be gone as fast as possible. The clock was running out on Peña's threat, but that wasn't what pressed her most.

"We can't stay long anyways, but the doctor told me seeing friendly faces would be good for him. He can't read or watch TV or he'll get a headache. He's all alone in his room with just the morphine drip to keep him company."

"That doesn't sound that bad," Venus said, attempting a joke.

"Never been on morphine, have you?"

Venus shook her head. The last two months in Montreal had been an interesting lesson on exactly how straightlaced of a kid she'd been. Not that Saint-Ferdinand boasted a thriving underground of sex and drugs, but for someone who'd always considered herself independent, she'd taken very little advantage of her freedom.

"It handles the pain, but it gives you nightmares. When all you have to pass the time is sleep, well, it kinda sucks. Here . . ."

Jodie took Venus's wrist and put something in her hand, closing her fingers around it.

"What's this?"

When Venus opened her hand again, she saw that the object was a cheap necklace with some sort of pewter seashell pendant.

"I saw it at the gift shop and thought of you. You can give it to Ben. Though I'm not sure he'll get the reference. He'll just be happy for the thought. I'll get him some chocolates later."

The pendant swung in front of Venus's eyes as she observed it up close. A scallop shell.

"Why this?" she asked.

"A Botticelli reference, I guess."

It took a moment for Venus to put it together, stuffing the gift into her pocket once satisfied that she'd gotten it.

They stood in silence as the elevator took them up a few floors. Venus was burning to ask more questions, but they weren't alone.

A doctor and a young intern had slipped in with them. They were quiet, almost bored, barely exchanging glances, despite going from one patient to the next, one crisis after another. Life and death come routine.

Venus looked at her blurred reflection on the brushed stainless-steel surface of the elevator doors but couldn't distinguish the empty place in her eyes. But it was there. Did the doctors also have something like that within them? Or was death so routine that they'd grown accustomed to it?

This wasn't going to happen to Venus. She wouldn't allow it. The god's gift, that ability to retreat into hollowness, was just a tool. Wasn't it?

Walking into Ben's hospital room immediately tested this resolve.

Constable Ben wasn't old. He wasn't riddled with cancer waiting for the next tumor to finish him off. Unlike Harry Peterson, he was young, healthy, and fit. Yet he was plugged into just about as many machines as Abraham's father had been the last time Venus had seen him. Tubes were hooked up to Ben's nose and arms, either pulling liquid out, dripping fluid in, or pumping oxygen. Monitors kept a close watch on his vital signs and relayed any abnormalities to the nurse's desk. His legs were covered by bedsheets, but she could tell there was something abnormal about them. The bumps in the covers were too large in some places, absent in others.

His entire left side seemed to be covered in bandages and his left arm was in a thick cast. That left side of his head was also bandaged up, including his eye. As Jodie and Venus passed the threshold, Ben had his right hand in a bucket of ice chips, idly picking at them as if they were a snack.

"They told me you were on solid food," Jodie said, the words testing the resolve of their camaraderie, hopeful it had survived the accident.

"I am, but I like these. It's like having a glass of water, but more fun."

"Of all the things that broke, why is your jaw still intact?"

He crunched his ice loudly and openmouthed as a reply. Jodie broke into a grateful smile and sighed. His body might have been shattered, but his spirit was unbroken. Or so it seemed, until he saw Venus, standing sheepishly behind his partner. Try as she might, she couldn't meet his gaze.

"Look at that. A revenant. I thought you were dead." Ben seemed genuinely pleased to see her.

"Likewise," Venus answered, trying on a smile. "How are you?"

It was a stupid question. She'd known that the moment it had left her lips, but she couldn't take it back. Fortunately, Ben seemed amused by her faux pas.

"I'm alive. The doctors tried to bum me out. Told me a bunch of depressing stuff, like 'Every bone below your belt is pulverized' and 'You have a minor skull fracture' and 'Your spine is severed.'"

The last mocking statement left a heavy silence in its wake. The implication was not easily masked by the jovial tone and Ben's voice faltered on the last words. Young, fit Constable Ben would probably spend his life in a wheelchair and go back to just being Ben. Making a parody of it was like spreading frosting on a moldy cake.

He saw her stunned, blank stare and pulled his smile back on and kept going with his list.

"But wait, that's not all. Rib punctured my left lung and they had to put metal pins in my arm so it would heal straight. Also suffered a pretty severe concussion, though I'm kind of thankful I lost consciousness. To top it off, I broke three fingers and I have a nasty cue ball fracture."

"Eight ball fracture," Jodie corrected him.

"What's an 'eight ball fracture'?" Venus asked, unsure if she wanted to know.

"Busted eye," Ben answered, pointing to his bandaged face. "Blood in the cornea. The doctor says it looks nasty but it'll heal fine."

Unlike your legs, Venus thought.

She walked up to the bed, fished in her pocket, and handed him the pendant.

"Here. It's a get-well gift."

The offering was hollow, her words stupid and obvious. What else did she have? *Sorry my quest destroyed your life*? There was no gift, no speech, that could make this better. Seeing familiar faces was supposed to be good for him, but how could hers be anything but a reminder of the mistake he'd made in trying to help her?

"Botticelli reference?" Ben asked, holding the pendent to his good eye with his good hand. He smiled and either blinked or winked at her.

How could he be so jovial? Shouldn't the pain make him angry or the morphine make him sleepy? Shouldn't he be pissed at his situation, at his life, at the world?

He should be mad at her.

She had done this to him. It would feel so much better if he could yell or curse at her instead of wearing this damnable smile.

"So? Did it work?"

"Yeah," Venus answered, uneasy with Ben's cavalier attitude toward his situation. "It worked. Peña reacted just like you thought he would, just . . . more violently."

The familiar guilt swam up from the depths of her. Some things were better left buried, but when face-to-face with the victim of her quest, even the power of the god and the hole it had left in her soul were impotent to quell the remorse.

The image of Beatrice, blubbering pleas for her life while trying to answer Peña's questions, vague and incoherent, was projected behind Venus's eyelids. Even as she shook the specter of memory away, the dying woman's final words, whispered and desperate, rang in her ears. *Audrey.* Beatrice had ended her life begging for her daughter.

"Venus?"

Jodie's voice, and then her hands, reached out to her, pulling her back. Venus's knees were on the floor, her bag lying next to her. When she opened her eyes, the hospital room was wet and blurry.

"Are you okay?" Jodie asked, calm and professional. "Do you need me to get a nurse?"

"I can just push this button . . . ." Ben added from his bed.

"I can't go back," Venus pleaded, the words spilling before she knew they were in her. "Don't make me go back."

Blinking away tears, Venus could see Jodie's face, but where she expected compassion, all she saw was business. The hands on her shoulders tensed, straightening Venus's back so they could lock eyes.

"You have to," Jodie said. "You heard what Peña said. If you're not back—"

"You can't be serious?"

It was Ben, from atop his medical dais. His voice had come out raspy when he'd raised it, and for the first time his discomfort was obvious to Venus.

"Peña said—"

"Screw Peña. Look at her. She's terrified."

"Peña said," Jodie repeated a third time, leaning into her cop voice for added authority, "that if Venus wasn't back with him in four hours . . . Well, he never specified what he'd do, but considering what happened to you, I don't want to go head-to-head with him again."

"Since when do we take orders from that guy?" Ben was nearly falling out of his bed, leaning dangerously over the side. "For all we know, this was an accident and he just took advantage of it."

"Now you're the skeptic?" Jodie sounded outraged. "He was behind the accident and, correct me if I'm wrong, traffic lights aren't the only thing he can manipulate."

"No." Venus shook off Constable Jodie's hold. "He can do a lot more, especially with a few hours to prepare."

"Is this about your sister?" Ben's one eye drilled into his partner. "Tell me this isn't about your sister—"

"She's going, Ben," Jodie interrupted. "We don't know who else will get hurt if she doesn't, and we know he wants her alive and well. That's how we serve and protect. We make sure no other innocents get hurt."

"God dammit, Jodie! You're willing to throw her to the wolves. That's not 'serving and protecting.' You're trading her life for Alice's!"

They went back and forth, arguing about her. The monitor next to Ben's bed registered his increased heart rate and the springs on his bed complained every time he waved his right arm in frustration. At this rate, nurses would be pouring into the room at any moment and both she and Jodie would be kicked out.

"He made me watch when he killed Beatrice Bergeron. I held her down while she bled out. He kept asking questions and she couldn't answer. I don't want to be part of this anymore. I don't want to go back."

"What kind of questions?"

The intensity in Jodie's eyes nearly burned Venus on the spot. Her tone was just as ardent as Peña's had been during Beatrice's interrogation. It was more demand than question.

"Christ, Jodie," Ben said. Even he sounded a little intimidated.

"Venus. What kind of questions?"

Venus tried to compose herself. Jodie was trying to help. She was the most levelheaded in the room. Ben was drugged for the pain and Venus was obviously distraught. The importance of knowing what had happened to Beatrice couldn't be overstated. Jodie was just being a cop and Venus had to be up to the task.

The cold hollow within her called out. She could almost hear the god's voice, demanding in a singsong manner that she return. When Venus reached within and touched the frozen hole inside her heart, the voice of Beatrice vanished from her memory. The blood in the dust, Peña's ever more manic questions, and the agonized begging all blurred into unintelligible mumbling, like voices heard underwater. Instead she heard the soothing rumbling of an unworldly breathing, like a leviathan snoring.

"He learned from Gauthier that the cult controlled the god by having someone sing to it," Venus explained after swallowing. "Then he needed Beatrice to tell him who sang those songs. But all we got from her was the name Martel."

The name had meant nothing to Peña. He screamed so much at the body of Beatrice once she'd breathed her last. It meant nothing to Venus, either, but it meant something to Jodie.

"You have to go back to him," she said, her voice suddenly numb.

"You know who this Martel person is?"

"Yes? Maybe? I'm not sure. It might be a huge coincidence, but the only way to know is for you to go back to Peña."

It was the same refrain but to a different tune. Jodie was no longer ordering—she was begging. It wasn't to the wolves that Venus was being thrown, but on a mission that she was being sent.

"I just can't."

"Venus. You're not going alone. You have your phone. You have my number. Just go back to Peña so he doesn't go through with his threat, get whatever you can from him, and come back."

Like it could be so easy. If looking for Peña had been difficult, running from him seemed impossible. He'd flexed his muscles enough that Venus knew to be afraid of him. In some ways, she feared Peña more than she feared the god from her shed. Both were brutal and merciless, but where the god's power seemed limitless, Peña's anger and thirst for vengeance was volatile and unpredictable. Much like Jodie's had been a moment ago.

"I'm not going," she said, trying her best to sound steadfast.

"He said he'd get you back, Venus. Do you want to be responsible for what he does if we stand in his way?"

"Why do you even want me to go back? I thought you were supposed to protect—"

The last word never made it out of her mouth. It was replaced instead by a collective gasp from everyone in the room, followed instantly by cries of surprise and whimpers of fear, creeping out of every room on the floor.

The lights had gone out, suffocating everyone with darkness, and Ben's heart monitor let out a disappointed whine before shutting off completely.

"Simon Martel," Jodie spoke in the dark. "He was my sister's music teacher."

The generators kicked in after what felt like an eternity.

Not everything came back online right away. Emergency lights and medical equipment flashed and beeped to life in quick succession, but televisions, radios, large fluorescent tubes, and other non-essentials remained dark.

This was Peña's doing. A warning that her time was up.

It wasn't much, all things considered, but hearing the equipment that kept an eye on Ben's vitals fade out of existence had sapped much of Venus's determination. If this was a reminder for her to come back, the schoolyard bell that told her recess was over, what would he do if she didn't show up? Sacré-Coeur must have dozens of intensive care patients who relied on a variety of machines to stay alive. Would Peña be so cruel as to turn those off as well?

She found him in the hospital parking lot. At some point, Lucien had managed to find a fresh pack of cigarettes. Venus would have much preferred he hadn't, but there he was, leaning on a lamppost, smoking with practiced nonchalance.

"Look who decided to show up," he said before exhaling a thick cloud of smoke.

"I was on my way. You didn't have to send me a message."

Venus wrinkled her nose at the billowing cloud that came out of his mouth. In a rare gesture, Peña glared at the cigarette with mild disgust and threw it away.

"Think of me as a lion," he said. "Occasionally I yawn, but it's as much to show my fangs as anything."

He pushed off the concrete block that served as a base for the lamppost. It had been yellow once, but the paint had long since chipped away.

They walked for a little while in silence. Venus tried to figure out where it was they were heading, thankful for the painkillers and compression bandage on her ankle. She wouldn't want to run, but at least walking wasn't the agony of the past two days.

"What do you even need me for anyways? I thought we'd hit a dead end."

Peña had been in a dark mood ever since the interrogation and murder of Beatrice Bergeron. Having pulled no usable answer out of her, he'd done nothing but grumble and mutter to himself until Jodie had found them. It felt like somewhat of a stretch to imagine, but Venus could have sworn the man regretted the pointless killing. Once in a while, as they walked the streets, she would catch a look on his face, soft and pained. Whether it was for the unrequited lover he still mourned or for his more recent deeds didn't matter; it showed Peña had a soul after all.

"It's exactly the reason I keep you around. Without you, I'm back to square one, McKenzie."

"Or, maybe, you shouldn't have killed Beatrice."

"You don't get it; we're at war with these people. And there's no room for pity if we're going to win. You're going to have to learn that if you want to be of any use to me."

In that, Venus knew she was no different to Peña than Beatrice had been. She was a tool in this war of his. Beatrice, along with Gauthier and the others, had answers to his questions. Meanwhile, she was the one who would fight the god. His own personal messiah, prophesied to bring about his victory.

"Some lion you are."

"Pardon?" He stopped in his tracks, turning toward her, frowning in irritation.

But Venus had already numbed herself to his intimidation, drawing from the hollow in her soul.

"You make a big deal of having sharp fangs, so how come you're pissing around Montreal instead of taking the fight to the Sandmen? Is the mighty urban shaman afraid of a bunch of lawyers, accountants, and housewives? Couldn't you just go in there and crush them with some fancy magic?"

"Mm-hmm. First of all, you know better than to think of it as 'fancy magic.' You've seen firsthand what's involved in cornering one of these fools.

"Second, this war goes back much further than you think. When the Sandmen figured out that I was going after them, they moved to where there is no city, and they made damn sure no one was going to build one around them either. Ipso facto, I am powerless until they walk into my lair."

The irritation faded from him with those last words. Instead, with a sigh and a shrug, he turned back to walking, stuffing his hands into the pockets of his coat.

"Besides, they have a god on their side now. All we have is a dead end."

Venus mulled this over as they kept walking. There was an after-taste of defeat in Peña's words. The blood of four of the Sandmen was on his hands, along with the stain of what he had done to Constable Ben. There might even be others who had suffered in the name of his unrequited love.

This could very well be the end for Venus. The last moment of a regretful association. She'd spent months looking for this man, but the last few days had proven that he was nothing like she had hoped.

Every time they passed by a streetlamp, his shadow swept over her. He was a brutal, angry, broken man. Back to square one, as he'd said, he'd likely start killing again, trapping other Sandmen to inter-rogate, moving from one victim to another on a trail of clues like bloody bread crumbs through a dark forest.

She could try to escape. If his power truly did stop with the city limits, she'd be safe back in Saint-Ferdinand. Back with Penny and Abraham, she could focus on another angle. Maybe look up another name from her grandfather's list of associates. Peña had talked of Sophie Courtier and Elijah Byrd. Maybe they would be of more help.

But then what? She had next to nothing to bring back from her long stay in Montreal and would immediately get mired in the tar pit of finding a foster home. She'd have to answer countless questions about her whereabouts. Much like Peña, she'd have to start every-thing from scratch, with barely any better understanding of what she was up against.

Perhaps, Venus thought, she was too numb to the situation. Maybe she'd always been. Ever since the death of her father, the dis-appearance of her mother, and the massacre at the circus, she'd bur-ied her feelings with increasing efficiency. The pit in her soul was all but too happy to swallow that pain for her. Venus knew this was the god's work and that it somehow connected her to it. The same way the fly was connected to the spider once stuck in its web. Trapped and slowly devoured.

The more she thought about it, the more "brutal and angry" felt right.

"I know who Martel is," she finally announced to an astonished Lucien Peña.

They arrived at Simon Martel's town house in NDG a few minutes before the music teacher did.

Tracking him had been easy. Simon still gave private music lessons for a living. His contact information was readily available to potential students on several websites advertising tutors and teachers. It wasn't hard to cross-reference that with addresses for all the Simon Martels in Montreal to find the right one.

The brown bricks looked almost black under the shadow of a huge maple tree in the front yard. White aluminum window frames the only features that cut through the penumbral darkness. The sun had almost finished setting by then and Lucien Peña had kept an unlit cigarette between his lips during the whole journey. They set up watch at a nearby bus stop, credible cover for their loitering around Martel's home. Venus could feel the ache of her injured ankle bite through the painkillers.

There was sufficient traffic on the small street. Dozens of people getting back from work at the same time, clogging the lanes as they jockeyed for parking spaces and turned into driveways. Fortunately, Venus and Peña didn't have to wait long.

"There." Peña pointed with his chin toward a white sedan gleaming under the orange streetlights.

It took a moment for Venus to figure out which car he meant, but the moment her eyes landed on the white Honda Civic, the breath went out of her.

Despite the lack of any particularly distinguishing characteristics, there was something about the vehicle that made it stand out. It was all the small details, the little things she could not remember, only recognize, that made it *the* Civic.

"All right," Peña said. "Let's go."

"Wait!" Venus grabbed his arm to slow him, but he just pulled her along a few feet. "Let the car drive off. Otherwise, we'll have to deal with the both of them."

Lucien gave her a look of approval and stayed put until the white Civic passed them again, going back in the other direction. Venus paid close attention and, just as her instincts had told her, there was Daniel Crowley at the wheel.

What was he doing working for the Sandmen, chauffeuring one of their key members around? Was that where he'd been this whole time, working for the enemy?

When he opened the door at their knocking, Simon Martel gave Venus and Lucien an appraising, then terrified look. There was something damaged and broken about him, something that rang familiar to Venus. Nothing like what she'd seen in herself, but rather a dullness that had stared back at her from the eyes of her own uncle when she'd visited him in jail. They were the eyes of a man defeated by forces far outside his control and barely within his comprehension.

"Please. No, I'm just a teacher . . ." Simon began to say before being shoved into his own home by Lucien's powerful hand.

The next few seconds passed at the weird speed in which most traumatic events seem to exist. Like the car accident that had crippled Ben, it was both incredibly fast and ponderously slow.

By the time Simon Martel had recovered from being pushed around, Lucien had already brought his imposing presence into the town house. Venus dutifully closed the door, separating them from the outside world.

"I just work for them. I don't have a choice," Simon pleaded, his voice weak.

Venus waited for Lucien to pull whatever cruel trick he had in mind. What did he have in store that would force the music teacher into telling them what they wanted to know?

Lucien's eyes darted around, taking in his surroundings for a second before settling on his weapon of choice. Without so much as bothering to remove the bland hats and two fall jackets that were on its hooks, he picked up and swung a massive wooden coatrack in an enormous arc in front of him.

The hooks caught Simon in the temple and jaw, sending the hapless teacher crashing into the entranceway table before crumpling to the ground.

By the time Lucien had set the coatrack down, neatly standing it about a foot from its original position, Simon was reduced to a quivering, gibbering mess. Not dead, but not all right.

His eyes were rolled back into their sockets and his mouth was agape, pink saliva foaming at the edges of his lips. A modest trickle of blood ran down the side of his face. Too little compared to the force of the blow.

"What are you doing?" Venus said. "Aren't we going to interrogate him?"

"Why?" Lucien answered, leaning down to pick up something from the floor. "You were right, McKenzie. I've been baring my teeth without biting for too long. Time to force their hand. Without this guy, their little singer's not going to learn any new tricks."

Venus lowered to one knee, uncertain what to do about Simon's convulsions but unable to take her eyes off him. He looked like he'd been short-circuited. "He's still alive," she said.

"Bah. Probably not for too long," Lucien answered, barely interested.

He stood up, holding a leather-bound book, random sheets of paper and notes pressed between its pages. Lucien seemed satisfied, almost giddy at his find. He opened it, voracious eyes devouring the contents in arbitrary bits.

"Got what I wanted. More, even." Peña brandished the book. "Come on. Let's get out of here."

"This isn't the city doing your killing for you!" Venus could feel the panic in her own voice, emotions creeping out of their hole. "We can't just leave him like this?"

Her question was answered by a heavy sigh followed by the snapping shut of the leather tome. Lucien then strode into the kitchen.

When he emerged after some rummaging, his cigarette was finally lit. In one hand he held the lighter he'd pilfered from his victim, in the other, a large carving knife.

"Here," he said, tossing the knife at Venus's feet. "Finish him off if it bothers you so much."

It was a terrible thought. To execute someone like that in cold blood. It was a step she couldn't bring herself to even contemplate. Her hand grabbed the knife, uncertain what to do with it next. It was tempting to charge at Lucien and stab him with it, avenging those he'd slain. The desire to do so was strong, urged on by cold voices in her mind.

Simon's convulsions were becoming increasingly violent. His head kept banging on the hardwood floor, and with each impact, something in the right side of his skull moved, like tectonic plates being disturbed under the skin.

A primal instinct, half fear and half panic, began to take hold, pulling aggressively at her fight-or-flight reflexes, demanding that she act. She couldn't just leave him like that. Could she?

Forced to find a way to cope, to coax a solution out of herself, Venus turned to the god's gift. She could almost hear the voice of the creature from her shed as she fed it more of her guilt. Ignoring her tears and gritting teeth, she grasped the knife handle in a white-knuckle grip and as she did so, something in her snapped. The cold place in her soul yawned open and from its depths a dark presence arose, taking hold of her.

ALICE

SHORT FINGERNAILS TRACED the cool and rough surface of the concrete walls. Their ragged ends stung with each bump and crevice.

Alice always did that whenever her actions earned her time in the Reflection Room. The darkness and the cramped space, the smell of urine and fear, everything about this room dug into her psyche to pull out her worst memories. Within minutes of being locked up, she had scraped her nails down to nothing, scratching at the door and walls in a frenzied panic.

Dark confines were her earliest memories, obliterating anything that came before. This was how she had come to the Sandmen, birthed from the womb of a car trunk where she'd been held captive. She had gestated there for hours, curled in a fetal position, tears and piss in lieu of amniotic fluid, all in preparation for her new life.

The Reflection Room was used to punish any member of the Sandmen who transgressed, but Alice always thought it was designed especially for her. The specifics of the penance crafted to trigger her nightmares. And it worked wonders.

The similarities weren't limited to smell, confinement, and darkness. Much like that dreadful car trunk, it was Francis who'd put her there, and Francis who pulled her out. He was her executioner and her savior. At first she hated him for it, but after a few years

Alice realized that she might as well have been angry at the car or the Reflection Room itself. Like Francis, neither of those things had any malice toward her. They weren't happy or glad to punish. Nor were they doing any of it against their will. They just were. Each an unfeeling tool in her chastising.

Apart from the thin gray line of timid light that crept under the door, there was nothing to see in the Reflection Room. That was the point. One was meant to "reflect" upon their sins and contemplate their mistakes, as to best not repeat them. Alice was more alone than most in there. Even the sound of her own voice couldn't keep her company. Mother made Francis gag her, so that she wouldn't scream her voice raw and be unable to sing.

Or so she couldn't sing her way out.

She could still touch, however, and her fingers routinely traced the bumps and divots in the concrete. By now she knew the pattern by heart. So much that Alice felt confident she could draw it on a piece of paper from memory.

It was music. Bars etched into the wall. She wanted to hum the melody, but the leather gag in her mouth was locked in place by a small but sturdy padlock at the back of her head. It had the added benefit of making lying down uncomfortable, giving her all the more time to think upon her errors.

But she didn't want to think about that. All she wanted was to sing the song carved in the wall.

"Hey."

A shadow interrupted the light under the door and Daniel's voice cut into her daydream. Despite being the one who'd put her in trouble by trying to take her away, Alice felt a lightness in her soul at hearing his voice again. He'd come back for her.

He'd get in trouble if they found him keeping her company. Giving any kind of help to those being punished was strictly forbidden. How was one to repent if they didn't suffer the full weight of their mistakes? This punishment was, after all, for her own good and the good of the family.

But it wasn't his voice that came next. No words of encouragement and support.

Instead it was the timid clicking of metal on metal, followed by the sound of steel biting into steel. Another moment of fussing with the door and a neon-blue flood of light poured in, spreading inside the Reflection Room. The dark corner of hell that was her prison transformed back into a vulgar closet.

"Are you okay?"

Daniel's comforting shadow obscured the light as he knelt next to her, a red and rusty bolt cutter dangling at his side. Gently, he turned her head to the side, fussing to remove the lock that kept her gag in place.

The thick rubber ball of the gag slid from between her teeth, pulling along with it tendrils of saliva and a ragged breath.

"What are you doing? Mother will be furious," Alice said, her jaw aching with each syllable. "You have to lock me back in!"

Either Daniel didn't hear her or didn't care what she had said. He ignored her instructions, helping Alice to her feet instead, supporting her hand and elbow as she stood.

"It's fine. No one knows I'm here. Mother is giving one of her sermons. She's on the rampage after what happened yesterday. It was easy to sneak out."

Alice shook her head. No good would come of this, she knew. Someone, probably Francis, would figure out Daniel was missing. And they'd be quick to figure out where he'd gone. How far could he stretch the immunity provided by his tie to Mother? How terrible would the backlash be when it reached its limit? Alice didn't like to speculate. She was used to this sort of treatment, but she couldn't bear to imagine Daniel going through it.

"You need to go. This"—she gestured toward the cramped room—"this is nothing. They'll do much worse if you get caught."

"Nothing? I saw them dragging you away. They have no right to do this to you."

"No, Daniel. I have no right leaving. You took me away for less than an hour and six people died. Mother is right: This is my destiny. No one else can do this. You can't save me from who I am."

The fluorescent lights in the hallway flickered for a moment, drawing her attention and making her heart skip a beat. Only after a moment, after she was satisfied that no one had come to get Daniel, did she continue.

"You should go."

It came as a surprise how hard the words were to say. If Daniel left the Sandmen, she would never lay eyes on him again. Alice would remain here, appeasing the god until the Sandmen found a replacement or she finally passed away.

In contrast, Daniel would go on to have a life and hopefully never think of her and the Sandmen again. Maybe he'd get a wife and have a family. He'd see them off to school and take them on vacations. All things that would be denied her. All things that he would have because of her sacrifice. That last thought made her smile.

"What?" he asked, confused.

"Nothing. Just a stray thought. Please, Daniel, you've got to go. I don't want more people to die."

But Daniel didn't budge. He stood in front of Alice, towering over her. He was trying to hold her gaze, but she couldn't maintain eye contact, turning away after only a few seconds each time. Whenever she returned to look at his face, he was still locked onto her.

"So I can't take you away from here."

Alice shook her head, all the while secretly hurt by the reality.

"But I can't leave you behind, either."

With that, Daniel crouched down and sat on the linoleum floor, leaning his back against the wall.

It was now her that towered over him, and for the first time she could see his vulnerability. In a way, he was the one asking to be saved.

With a heavy sigh, Alice leaned back on the doorframe, letting herself slide onto the ground to face Daniel. The floor was cold to the touch and felt almost humid through the worn denim of her pants.

"Why is it so hard for you to just leave?"

It was Daniel's turn to smile and avoid eye contact. He pressed the back of his head on the wall behind him, scrutinizing the ceiling. The way he pulled his knees up to his chest, clutching at them with his hands, made him look all the more vulnerable, melting Alice's heart.

"Because . . ." He trailed off, taking a deep breath before a second attempt. "Because I've failed to save everyone I love. This cult bullshit consumes everyone it touches. It killed my dad and my girlfriend. I thought I'd come here and find a way to get revenge, but . . ."

Talking about his father and girlfriend seemed to wound Daniel with each word. The boy who'd looked so rugged and strong now wiped a tear with the back of his hand. Alice wanted to crawl over to him and hold his head against her chest. Let him cry out his sorrow while she stroked his hair. But the very thought of it made her stomach turn to stone.

"There's no taking me away from this, Daniel."

"I know," he admitted. "You are the Sandmen."

"What?"

"Mother said that. You're the threshold between Heaven and Hell on Earth, or something like that. It's not this cult that needs you; it's the whole world. That's a big responsibility. I'm sorry."

He wasn't though, she could tell. He was angry. Angry on her behalf, at the Sandmen for putting her through everything she'd endured and for taking away his family. At himself, maybe, for being unable to do more.

Alice scooted over to be closer to him. Pulling deep within herself, she drew enough courage to put a comforting hand on his knee and lean her head on his shoulder.

He ignored both gestures.

"What is that?" he asked, nodding toward the back of the Reflection Room.

Under the blue light of the hallway's fluorescent lights, Simon's scratches on the wall became an eerie pattern of dots and lines. It looked like a code, carved into the paint and concrete. They might as well have been the claw marks of a desperate man on the underside of a coffin lid. Only the clear rhythm of the markings gave the impression that it was more.

"Back when Simon was more disobedient of Mother, he'd get locked in here too. Often. I think he carved this out to keep from going insane."

Alice mourned that the mutilated wall was more worthy of Daniel's attention than she was. However, the discovery seemed to have snapped him out of his own mourning.

"This is music?"

Alice nodded, struggling to understand why Daniel even cared at all.

"Can you sing it?"

"I've hummed it a few times," she admitted. "It's a really sad song."

Daniel crawled on all fours into the Reflection Room, rapt by the series of markings. He ran a curious finger over their surface, tracing the same pattern Alice had in the dark a few minutes ago.

"Do you think it means something?"

"Music always has some kind of meaning," she answered, crawling in next to him. "But I think only Simon would know what, though."

Mesmerized, Daniel sat in front of the wall. Being close to Daniel in the cramped space was intoxicating to Alice. She could smell the soap on his skin and see the tears still drying on his face. The proximity was almost enough to make her forget all the terrible memories of being locked inside this room. Her spine would still freeze, her legs twitching in a silent attempt to drag herself out and escape, but Daniel's presence lessened the intensity of it all.

"He wrote this for you."

Daniel had given no indication that he knew the first thing about reading music. Even Alice, who wasn't great at it herself, had barely recognized the code as a song. Yet, there he was, making broad assumptions about Simon's intentions.

"Don't be ridiculous. Why would he bother doing that? If Simon wanted to teach me a song, he'd have done so during our lessons."

"Except Mother gave him strict instructions on what to teach you. You said you were no stranger to this room? He must have known you'd eventually end up in here again. Who else would he have left this for?"

It was an unpleasant thought. Simon hadn't been locked in the Reflection Room in a long while. A few years at least. If it were true that he'd left this for her to find and understand, she'd failed him.

"What does it mean?" she asked, somehow expecting Daniel to have an answer.

"I don't know. How does humming it make you feel?"

Without answering, and as gently as she could, Alice pushed Daniel aside, leaving the back wall of the Reflection Room free of their shadows.

Committing the pattern to memory again, refreshing the mental image she'd built of the song in her mind, Alice closed her eyes.

She breathed in and slowly began to sing the song. It wasn't a perfect rendition. She got the tempo wrong at first and, not wanting to attract attention, kept the timbre of her voice to that of a whisper. In the back of her mind, she knew it was for the best. Whatever this song was, if she sang it as perfectly as she did lullabies, who knew what the effect on Daniel would be.

The music spilled gently from her throat, filling the small room. It was beautiful. Clumsy and unrehearsed, but melodious and sweet. It was such a short, fragmented piece, sung in the worst of conditions, but it tugged at her heart. It wasn't hard to see what this was meant to be, full of longing and adoration.

Alice went through the music once, getting a handle on how it should feel in her mouth. When she repeated the song, careful to mouth the wordless notes with her best inflection, she made the melody as perfect as the conditions allowed. It was becoming easier to give that flawless sheen to her songs.

"It's a love song," Daniel said, beating her to the punch.

"Why would Simon write me a love song?"

"Why does anyone write a love song?"

Daniel's tone was light, not mocking, and he gave her a tilted smile as he spoke. It was a tease. Francis teased too, but his were heartless jabs, usually making a point of how she'd been tricked or reminding her that she was a prisoner. His favorite was comparing food in the cafeteria to that of restaurants, asking for her opinion. Family members would politely chuckle and Francis would smile his empty smile.

"I'm pretty sure Simon doesn't think of me that way. No one does."

He leaned in, drawing his face to within a few inches of hers. His eyes narrowed as if he were looking at the brushstrokes of a painting, examining her features with the studied care of a curator. It made Alice uncomfortable and she wanted to peel her eyes away from his, but to little avail. His pupils were dilated and his breathing came quicker.

"You're being too hard on yourself," he whispered.

The hair on Alice's arms rose and her spine was grasped by a chill. The cool surface of the concrete became so cold as to bite into the palms of her hands. Icicle teeth gnawed through the fabric of her pants.

There was no understanding why this was happening, until Alice finally put the pieces together. It was the song! The love song had woven itself around Daniel's heart. This wasn't real love. She'd cast a spell on him. She'd bewitched the boy the same as she had Simon back in the woods.

Alice parted her lips to confess to what she'd done, to stop Daniel from further saying things he'd regret, but as she did so, his lips collapsed upon hers.

And she let it happen.

It wasn't bad, as far as first kisses were concerned. Though his lips were cold and she knew there was no real passion or truth behind the kiss. He acted exactly as she'd expect someone would if they were in love with her, because of course, he thought he was.

How furious would he be once the song wore off? Surely, he'd give up any plans of taking her with him. Though right now, going with him was all she wanted to do.

Their kiss lasted for a moment, or perhaps an hour, but the more their mouths touched, the colder their lips became. Neither seemed to care or notice until—

"Ouch!"

Alice recoiled, a stinging pain half an inch under her nose. She thought that Daniel had bitten her, but as she saw his face, there was a dot of crimson on his upper lip. His skin had become pale, but his nose and cheeks were rosy and flush. He looked like a child who'd come in from playing outside in the winter. Beads of sweat on his arms had formed into pearls of ice that fell from him as he moved.

The cold had frozen them together and he'd torn off a tiny piece of her lip when he'd pulled away.

Daniel seemed confused for a moment, a man waking from a dream. After blinking the hoarfrost from his mind, the expression turned to a mix of fear, pity, and disgust.

Instinctively, his tongue licked at the blood on his lips and a shock ran through him.

"Sasha," he whispered before stepping out of the Reflection Room and running away.

Alice didn't bother calling out after him. Nor did she try to catch up and explain. The spell had worn off faster than she'd expected. The sudden, unnatural cold probably had something to do with it.

Everything good that Alice had ever had eventually got taken away from her. Her television. Her snack-food privileges. Being able to look out the goddamn window without seeing bars. Everything. Gone.

As always, it was her own misdeeds that brought calamity on her. Daniel had offered her salvation and she'd refused. Oh, what a noble sacrifice! At least it felt that way when she thought of the lives she was saving, but now that she'd sent Daniel away . . .

She thought of those fleeting moments when she was just a little awake but also a little asleep, when she could remember being loved, really, truly loved. She'd had a father and a mother and a grandfather who'd showered her with affection on sleepy Christmas mornings. Her mother knew her lullaby and her father would carry her on his shoulders. Even her sister, who was often a tease, as older siblings were, showed her love by being overprotective. It was a blessing that she could barely remember it at all; it was enough to know that this had been taken away too.

Deep inside, Alice had built this fantasy, a fragile dream that she could barely stand to look at. It was made out of gossamer things. Hopes of finally going to school, of having a best friend, of building a family of her own. She even pictured a career in music. Standing before adoring audiences, using the gift no one could deny she had.

Instead she had to rot in misery under a dismal old school. Reduced to little more than a tool and a possession. This was her sacrifice. But it didn't have to be.

She *was* the Sandmen.

Mother had assembled her "family" with promises of fulfilling all their wishes. If only they waited, if only they had faith, she would deliver them a living god from whom they would pull mountains of gold and eternal life, or whatever they wanted most in this world. As long as each was willing to give up something of themselves.

She'd delivered the god, indeed. But it was not the god of love and life that had been promised. There was no such god. Alice had seen the soul of the thing and heard its song. All she could find was hate and death.

There was only one possible culprit for the cold that had first glued Alice and Daniel and then separated them so dramatically. She knew of only one source of supernatural power in the compound.

Either on purpose or in his rush to get away from her, Daniel had left his keys to the compound in the door of the Reflection Room. Alice grabbed them before tiptoeing through the hall and up to Room 004.

Once inside, after finally closing the door behind her, Alice realized she'd been holding her breath.

Sam's prison was like an altar. Others didn't see it, not like she did. They saw the worn couch sitting atop cold concrete, the ratty mattress, the dirty sheet, and, lying on it all, the frail old man. That was the stuff of the material world, however. Once one recognized Sam Finnegan as the avatar that he was, everything in the room took on a different light.

Releasing a long pent-up sigh, Alice allowed herself to drop onto the couch. She licked at her lip, tasting the dried blood left there and feeling the place where her skin had been pulled off.

"I wish I could destroy you."

Alice didn't expect a reply. Was there even a way to do such a thing? It didn't matter. When she set her eyes on the immobile corpse of the man that was Sam Finnegan, his clothes and skin covered in dried blood barely rinsed away, her heart wasn't in it anymore. They were too alike, it and she. Both were prisoners. Both were tools.

"How can you destroy that which never truly was?"

The voice was the echo of her singing. The same she heard come back to her when she lured the god to sleep with her music. Where the god's voice had been unsettling at first, a soundless song riding back to her on her own melodies, Alice was beginning to find comfort in it. It was something between camaraderie and respect but with undertones of fear and hate. There were no words to describe it, except perhaps in the language of the silent songs they shared.

"You're not what she promised," Alice said, with what could almost pass for nonchalance.

She wondered, in passing, what it meant that she was more comfortable in the presence of the Sam-creature than around human beings. She cowered in fear before Mother, and forgotten pains would come back to haunt her at Francis's slightest touch. Even Daniel did nothing but confuse her emotions, turning her into an awkward mess. But this god dressed in a man's corpse and coated in blood had ceased bothering her.

"You and I both share in the knowledge that the flesh lies."

It spoke ominous words, toying around with the mystery of what it was. It seemed to know and savor the fact that people like her—weak, little mortal things—couldn't comprehend the vast complexity of a being such as it was. Alice had glimpsed it. Through the haze of the music, in the dialogue that they shared, she'd seen how much larger than its prison the god of the Sandmen truly was. Unlike the others, though, she'd been shown the truth and was content to accept it.

"Is it you?" she asked, the question suddenly popping into her mind. "Is it you that froze the room when I got close to Daniel Crowley?"

A dumb, almost romantic notion crossed her mind that the creature was jealous. What would that be like, she wondered, to have a god be in love with her? There was a sort of mythological poetry to it. The ugly duckling with the voice of gold, charming the angry god into docility.

"*No.*"

No? The answer was cold and direct. If not the god, what else?

"Who?"

"*A dead girl,*" it said, implanting a new memory, formed out of nothing, in her mind. She could see plastic bags filled with flesh and blood split and spill into a puddle and from that, a beautiful woman rose. Nothing but bones at first but soon organs and muscles and sinew and finally dark sun-touched skin and hair like raven feathers. She was stunning, beautiful in a way that Alice could only envy. Alice could also see on her the touch of two Crowley men. One was the tender caress she'd so craved from Daniel Crowley. A dead girl whose memory Daniel had picked over her.

The other was the unfeeling attention by way of a knife from Francis as he took her apart, feeding her soul piece by piece to the god that now lay at her feet.

ABRAHAM

"MUMMY'S CURSE?" Abraham asked.

He knew that Dr. McKenzie did not like answering questions in the middle of a procedure. Abraham thought it had to do with the professional etiquette drilled into him by his years as a medical examiner. Or maybe it was out of some lingering respect for the dead. Whatever the case, Randy was having a hard time relaxing. His fists were clenched almost as hard as his jaw, and he never took his eyes off Abraham's actions.

They'd done this almost half a dozen times by now, though it was only the second opportunity Abraham had to accomplish the procedure himself.

"I don't know," Randy said in answer to the young man's question after a moment. "Probably not, but who knows? I've read that at least one of the god-kings of Egypt was one of them: Just like Sam Finnegan, a god tricked into a human body. Except back then they had the sense to embalm the beast and bury him in the largest tomb they could build. I somehow doubt that's what the Sandmen have in mind."

Randy had told Abraham about the last few moments before his escape from the local jail. How members of the Sandmen cult had shown up at just the right time and taken Sam Finnegan's body away. As if they'd known exactly when Randy had imprisoned the hateful god of Saint-Ferdinand. He'd also been answering Abraham's nonstop questions about other gods.

"Now, would you please pay attention to what you're doing?"

Abraham didn't understand Dr. McKenzie's skittishness around the dead. He could see someone like Penelope or Venus having difficulty with such procedures, but Randy should be used to it. Besides, they were doing something good. This was by far the most heroic act he'd ever performed. If only he could tell Penny about it, she'd be impressed with him, no doubt about it.

It was difficult and meticulous work, not to mention smelly and disgusting, but the results were well worth it. All these people who'd died and had their spirits hijacked by the god would finally find peace.

Randy had shown Abraham how to look for someone's soul in a body. It was a deceptively simple trick, though it required some level of subtle understanding. The kind that was often out of reach for him.

"You have to look into the eye until you stop focusing on it. Like stereogram pictures, but instead of your eye focus, it's your mind that has to let go."

That was how Randy had described it, though he'd also had to explain that a stereogram was one of those weird images that looked like television static until you stared at it long enough that an image emerged. Abraham had never been very good at seeing the hidden images in those things.

But he did eventually get the knack of spotting a soul. It wasn't that hard once you'd done it once or twice, but that wasn't the disgusting part.

No, the gross part was painting the psychopomp, or soul funnel, on the body.

First they needed the body, a task for which Randy was more than happy to have Abraham's assistance. The huge boy had little difficulty digging up graves and carrying corpses back to William Bergeron's Mustang. He'd gently lay the bodies on the back seat, then quickly cover the grave up before driving back to the Bergerons' garage.

Then they had to make the "paint." Of course, they couldn't just pick up a few tubes of oils from Harry Peterson's studio. That would have been much too easy and so much less fragrant.

Instead the "paint" had to be produced from the corpses themselves. For more recent bodies, like that of William Bergeron, there was a terrible abundance of liquids to work with. Though they had to avoid embalming fluids, so much of the tissue had liquified that it was a simple matter of collecting what they needed, filtering it, and then going about their nasty business. Older bodies were far more problematic. Desiccated remains, like those of David Reese, who'd been dead since Abraham had been a toddler, needed to have some fatty tissue removed and then dissolved and "reactivated," whatever that meant, in order to be used.

Only then could they paint the intricate spiral patterns that would pull the souls back to their bodies and, through that, hopefully, into the ether.

"There," Abraham declared, stepping back from his handiwork.

Randy moved closer and gave a long, careful appraisal of the pattern. Every few seconds he'd nod approvingly. Abraham allowed a touch of pride to skew his lips into a smile. If he were completely honest with himself, he'd admit that he was better at this than the good doctor. While he had large and clumsy hands, his fingers were unusually nimble and steady, something he'd picked up from his father. Painting, it seemed, ran in the family.

"Well done," Randy said. "That oughta do it. Hopefully good ole Iain here isn't wandering too far afield. It's getting late and I'm getting tired."

This was probably the part Abraham hated most. The waiting. Once the soul funnel was painted, they had to wait to know that the procedure had worked. It was, as Randy put it, the professional thing to do. This could take minutes, or it could take hours. Fortunately, the signs were unmistakable—the room would grow cold, making the graceful patterns upon the flesh of the dead freeze and crack. If the subject still had eyes, they could look into them to see the fleeting moment the soul passed through.

Abraham thought the bodies looked more at ease after the procedure was successful. Randy's exasperated sigh told him that he was imagining things, but Abraham didn't care. He liked to think that the people they helped were finally at rest.

"So," the large teenager said, "when the old lady said that Venus would be fighting the god, are we talking about something like Osiris against Seth?"

Another exasperated sigh escaped Randy's lungs. He wasn't even trying to hide his impatience anymore. He was tired of answering questions, but Abraham couldn't help it, and it was part of their deal.

"God against god? That idea has certainly been floated around." Randy leaned over to better inspect Abraham's work. "For a while, it was my father's whole plan. Finding another, similar entity, and leveraging it against the one we had here.

"They came close, too. He and Lucien and some other folks found legends of a god, a truly old one, thousands of years old, and connected to many ancient myths. What was peculiar about this one is that instead of hating people like the creature we had captive, it loved humanity. According to legend, he died to save us. Maybe several times."

Abraham was rapt. The telling of the story of another god, a benefactor to mankind, had him riveted. This was the god his father and Penny had been discussing.

"So what happened? Why didn't they find him?"

"I'm not sure. They traveled around the world. My father would vanish for months, leaving us with our mother the whole time. Then, one day, the trips stopped. In hindsight, I think maybe they did find what they were looking for, but it wasn't what they'd expected."

Even Randy seemed crushed by the idea. To find one impossibly powerful entity to pit against the devil in their backyard would have been a convenient solution.

"As for Katrina's prophecies, well, they were vague. Prophecies always are. If you avoid enough details, then people will make up their own stories about why the predictions are true. I could do without prophecies."

Abraham sat down on the hood of the Mustang, watching the body on the workbench in front of him. He crossed his arms, thinking. His line of questioning was always too scattered. Every time he left the Bergeron house, a dozen more important questions would pop up in his brain, as if the cells that governed them could only exit when they weren't needed. By the time he was back doing more work with Randy, he'd forget them all over again.

"What about the knife?" he asked. Randy gave him a blank look. Abraham continued. "The knife Penny used to stab the god with. The old guy at the circus said it had powers and, judging by what the god's blood did to Penny's hands, it must have done something to the knife, too."

"Well," Randy said, scratching his chin, "Cicero called it 'as fine a start as any.' I'm assuming he thought the damn thing could at the very least wound it. Actually wound it, I mean. And, if you can wound it . . ."

"You can kill it," Abraham concluded.

"Maybe, maybe not. But it is as fine a start as any."

Neither of them noticed the exact moment when the garage's temperature began to drop. It was only when they started to see their own breath in the air as they exhaled that they knew the procedure had worked.

The reaction was impressive and fast. The cold would go from a light shiver to freezing within a minute, but just as it felt like the degrees would never stop dropping, the homemade paint brushed onto Iain's skin turned to ice, cracking and falling off in paper-thin flakes. Then, just as fast as it had fallen, the temperature rose to what it had been before. The task was complete. Iain's soul had been put to rest. One more down, several dozen left to go.

All they needed to do now was bring his corpse home to the cemetery.

As Abraham loaded the body, which felt to him lighter and more at rest, he thought back to Daniel Crowley stopping him on his walk home a few weeks back. How he'd insisted Abraham take the knife in case he ever needed to get rid of Venus's cat. Or, it was implied, anyone else influenced by the god.

Abraham finished tucking the body inside the car, slamming the door shut to get Randy's attention. The medical examiner had been about to get in the driver's seat so they could be on their way, but he raised an eyebrow at Abraham's look.

"Randy. What if . . ." Abraham hesitated. "What if I told you I have that knife?"

Randy had yelled at him for the entire drive back to the cemetery. It got to be so loud that Abraham was convinced their passenger was going to get up, open the door, and make his escape. God knew he was thinking about it himself.

"Why would you not tell me all this immediately?" Randy demanded.

Abraham mumbled an answer about how it seemed more important to him that they put to rest the souls of the dead. That explanation was met with incredulity and even more anger. Randy went so far as to call him stupid, which rolled off Abe's ego like water on a duck's back. He was used to it. Self-deprecation was, after all, his specialty.

This time, however, he firmly believed in his moral responsibility to help the deceased find peace. In fact, he had a personal stake in mastering these skills. Sooner rather than later his father would pass, and the idea that Harry Peterson—after losing his beloved wife, raising a son on his own, and suffering nearly a decade at the hands of a series of cancers and tumors—would spend eternity wandering between worlds without knowing solace was too much to even conceive. Besides, they had yet to take care of Audrey's spirit and she was the very reason he'd become Randy's de facto apprentice.

"The knife," Randy had said while dropping Abraham off, just out of sight of the Peterson farm. "Bring me that knife tomorrow. Maybe . . . maybe we can finally end this."

Abraham complied with the request, having carefully wrapped the knife in the same grease-stained rag in which it had been given to him. It looked so ordinary. The blade was about nine inches long, relatively standard for a chef's knife, and it had a black lacquered wooden handle.

The knife was leverage. Abraham had no particular attachment to the thing. In fact, now that he'd taken his vow never to hurt Sherbet, the responsibility of having it weighed heavily on his shoulders. If Randy wanted it, he could have it. If he could find a use for it, even destroy the god with it, then all the better. In addition, there was something in Randy's voice when he said the words "finally end this." It was the unfamiliar sound of sincerity. The blade would be his, but only if it meant bringing an end to the god and all the terrible impact it had on Saint-Ferdinand.

Abraham steeled himself. Randy had so far been greedy with information and reluctant to take direct action. With the knife, Abraham hoped he could change that, but his plans were once more derailed. He'd repeated his questions on the walk to the Bergeron house and prepared what he would say to Randy as best he could. He'd be diplomatic but firm, ready to walk out, knife still under his care, should the situation warrant it. However, when Abraham showed up at the Bergeron house, Randy was nowhere to be seen.

He called the medical examiner's name while pacing the house, wondering where a fugitive like him could have gone to.

He checked the garage first, and then knocked on every bedroom and bathroom door. Eventually he wound up in the basement. He half-heartedly considered switching on the arcade cabinet. It was an old Ms. Pac-Man. A refurbished antique. Venus had lost her mind when she'd seen it the first time. The memory made Abraham smile.

Still wondering where his reluctant mentor had gone and when he'd be back, Abraham rattled the handle of the wine cellar as he passed by it. An absentminded gesture he'd performed almost as many times as he'd walked by it over the past few days. Except this time there was no rattle. This time the knob twisted gently in his hand until the latch clicked and the hinges squeaked.

Chilled air rushed out and Abraham's thoughts quickly went to psychopomps and ghosts, though he knew this was simply a climate-controlled room, designed to keep wine cool. Nothing supernatural about it.

Annoyed by Randy's absence, bored, and more than a little curious about what it was that had been kept locked in here, Abraham pulled the door open and took a tentative step inside the frigid room.

The chill didn't so much bother him; it was still warm by comparison to a Quebec winter. Penny had scolded him many times in the past about wearing a T-shirt too late in the season or forgetting to put on a coat in the middle of winter. Abraham simply didn't get cold very easily.

Smells were also seldom a concern. Working on a farm had made him immune to the vilest odors that man or nature could concoct. He'd spread manure in the fields, cleaned up carcasses—and now he'd emptied bedpans and mopped up vomit and bile. Yet there was something foul in the wine cellar. Putrid enough that even in a refrigerated environment, it made his stomach lurch.

He tried to paw at a switch to turn on the light, but for some reason he couldn't find one. It was lower on the wall and farther away from the doorframe than standard. The moment spent in the dark gave him time to imagine that perhaps Randy kept this room closed so he could hoard the wine and liquor. Had the medical examiner gotten so drunk as to pass out in the cellar and soil himself? Would Abraham find his mentor lying on the floor, drowned in his own puke?

His fingers found the switch at long last, and the lights came on, flashing to life in a series of flickers as cold fluorescent tubes tended to do.

That was when Abraham decided he'd have rather found Randy's corpse. In fact, he'd have rather found almost anything but this.

The cellar, as it happened, had been emptied of nearly every bottle. Presumably by Beatrice when she'd left town. Rows upon rows of shelves lay empty, surrounding what should have been a tasting table. Instead someone had brought in a large sheet of plywood and covered it with linens, a hurried, half-hearted attempt at making a comfortable bed.

Atop the makeshift cot lay someone's deformed and twisted remains.

It took a moment for Abraham to recognize it as a human being. At first glance he thought it was the near-hairless body of a particularly large dog or wolf, or maybe an emaciated bear. The joints were all wrong. There were too many of them and they were not where they should have been. After a moment he realized that the anatomy was asymmetrical and, to his horror, that the extremities had fingers. Fingers with fingernails. Fingernails with chipped burgundy nail polish.

Curiosity and morbid fascination drove his feet as he circumvented the bed, looking at the mottled pink-and-purple texture of the skin, trying to make sense of what had killed the poor creature. It was only when he got to the head that he recognized the face of Erica Hazelwood, the criminal psychologist who had come to town after Sam Finnegan had been caught. The woman who had been Penelope's therapist and Dr. McKenzie's friend.

Her naked chest and abdomen were covered with curves and spirals, painted in blood. The lines were shaky, as if applied by someone with a severe palsy or crumbling nerves.

The pattern wasn't what he'd expected though. It was similar in basic shape and theme to the one he'd painted on Iain's body the previous night, or to those he'd seen Randy paint on the other half a dozen cadavers pulled from the Saint-Ferdinand Cemetery. But there were also subtle differences. Not to mention that if the ritual had been done to allow Erica's spirit to pass on, why had it not frozen off like all the others? In fact, why did it still look warm and wet?

"Please . . ."

Her voice shattered the silence of the cellar like a sledgehammer on crystal. Pleading and sad, it was accompanied by the clumsy grasp of an inefficient and deformed hand, clutching helplessly at his flannel jacket. It had taken all of Abraham's self-control not to swat at the reaching fingers or scream and flee. No one this broken should still be alive, let alone be able to move.

"Make it . . . stop," she continued.

Erika's eyes snapped open, adding to Abraham's fear and revulsion. Despite being at different heights on her otherwise intact face,

Abraham had no trouble recognizing them or noticing the intense agony locked inside.

"Kill me," she said as Abraham tried to rally his wits.

Corpses were one thing. Dead things didn't bother him; after all, they were already dead. But what had become of Erica trailed near the far edge of sanity. She was connected to several tubes and Abraham had the experience to identify each one. An IV was awkwardly attached to her left arm, somewhere between the interior of her elbow and an odd twist in the bone of her forearm. A catheter ran underneath the bedsheet that covered her body, accompanied by several surgical drains.

"Please!" she hissed.

There was no nightmare in Abraham's mind that could have been constructed more perfectly. His phlegmatic nature broke down when seeing other people suffer. Especially those familiar to him. Taking in her form, the state of her body, and hearing her plea for release, Abraham was reminded of the fate of lame animals on the farm. That sometimes it was more humane to take a life than to allow it to continue with no other purpose than to suffer. Swallowing hard, he looked deep inside himself, searching for the strength to obey Erica's request, but no matter how far he dug, Abraham came up empty-handed.

"What the hell are you doing in here?"

Randy didn't wait for an answer. He didn't want an answer. The medical examiner stormed past Abraham, pushing the boy almost twice his weight aside like he was rushing through a cloud of smoke.

With unsteady hands shaking with nerves, Randy picked up a bottle and syringe off one of the wine racks, pulling it from among a plethora of other medical supplies stashed around the room.

It was a miracle that Randy managed to fill the syringe with whatever the clear liquid in the bottle was. More surprising was how quickly he was able to steady his fingers and plunge the needle into Erica's neck to inject the substance.

She made to protest, letting go of Abraham's coat to swat at Randy, but he'd already done what he had to do.

Within a few breaths, Erica's uneven eyes rolled back in their sockets. The same arm that had attempted to latch on to Abraham with such a vice-like grip went limp, slumping to the side of her makeshift bed in an awkward position. Her body was soon motionless again. Even her breathing was difficult to perceive, its rhythm slowed to a glacial pace.

Dr. McKenzie stared at his handiwork. He clutched the syringe and bottle in the same hand, gripping them so hard that the tube on the needle gave out an audible crack. His other fist, knuckles the color of bone, unfurled and reached out to touch strands of her brown hair. His attempts to collect himself seemed unsuccessful, the tremors coming in waves that rocked him from chest to extremities.

"What the hell was that?" Abraham asked with his customary level of tact.

Randy's eyes went from staring at the table, at Erica's face, to crawling up to look at Abraham through his eyebrows. For the first time since running into this new version of Dr. McKenzie, Abraham was in genuine fear of the man. Whatever he was up to, Venus's uncle was clearly capable of darker things than Abraham had assumed.

"This," Randy began, his voice level but charged with a rage of such complexity that Abraham knew the depths were out of his reach, "is why I haven't left Saint-Ferdinand."

"I thought she was dead."

"She is. She isn't. It's difficult to explain."

Abraham let the silence speak for him. He'd have loved to come up with something clever, like "Try me," but he simply wasn't that quick on his feet. Randy sighed.

"I didn't tell you the whole story about what happened in the jail this summer. She . . . Erica was there too. Just a bystander, really, but she was there when . . . it arrived. She wasn't even in its way.

"It just . . . willed her into this. Reshaped her body on a whim with about as much attention as you and I would give to swatting a fly."

Abraham looked down at Erica. He could see what passed for a chest slowly rise and fall, the effects of the sedative and cold working to slow down her metabolism. How was she even still alive? Was it the markings? The soul funnel keeping her spirit from leaving the body and moving on?

"I'm keeping her alive by any means I have at my disposal. Keeping the body working and the soul anchored," Dr. McKenzie explained. "But also sedated. There's no reason she should know what she's become."

Swallowing hard, Abraham looked down at the tortured woman on the makeshift bed. He nodded, but his lips were thin and white, his jaw tense, speaking of struggle within.

The first time Abraham was forced to put an animal out of its misery, he'd been about twelve. His father had tasked him with going around the perimeter of the field and straightening the metal posts of the wire mesh fence. Halfway through the chore, Abraham started hearing a sharp, desperate, and gut-wrenching cry. It was clearly an animal, but there was something of a human quality to the high-pitched keening. He figured that some critter had just met with a predator and was about to become a meal. It happened. Circle of life and all that. However, the closer he got to the sound, the more furious it became. When he eventually found the source, Abraham saw that it was an American cottontail, something like a hare with brown fur save for a pronounced white ball of a tail. It had a large gash on its left side that ended in a bloody stump where the back leg should have been.

As it turns out, bunnies are as cute as their screams are terrifying. This particular little guy wasn't so much crying in pain as it was expressing infinite anger at a universe that would allow the outrage of its wounds to happen.

Abraham's first thought was to take the animal home and nurse it back to health, but as he crouched to pick it up, the smell hit him. And then he saw the maggots. For the first time in his life, Abraham recognized that there was a certain point where a life simply wasn't worth saving anymore. That it was more humane to help it move on.

The feeling of a tiny neck snapping between his fingers haunted him while he finished inspecting the fence. He kept quiet after that, aside from the occasional sniffle as he wiped off tears.

There was no conceivable world in which Erica would survive, or want to survive, in this condition. Her short waking moment had been nothing but agony. She was half a corpse. Nature hadn't had a hand in this, and no matter how much human assistance it got, nature would not fix it either.

"This is why you want the knife," Abraham said, clutching the rag-covered blade tighter. "This is why you've been studying those psychopomps. You're looking for the god so he can undo this."

Burning intensity ignited in Randall McKenzie's eyes, all but confirming what Abraham was claiming. The medical examiner's head bent forward and his fingers curled in front of him in a maniacal, grasping gesture.

"If we can threaten its life, its very existence, we can finally leverage the beast into doing what we want."

Abraham took a step back, moving the hand with the knife behind him, farther from Randy, as if he expected him to lunge at it and take it away.

"You can't be serious. You said it yourself, that only a god can kill a god! And isn't this how all this started anyways?"

Abraham was incensed. Anger didn't come quickly to the lumbering boy, but the idea of perpetuating a cycle that had already proven to be, across multiple generations, a fool's gambit, stoked a rare fury within him.

"Abe . . ." Randy insisted, taking a step of his own. "I can save her. We can put Audrey's spirit to rest. You can even save Harry. You can save your father. The god wasn't always evil. We made it that way, and with the right tools, we can correct that mistake."

DANIEL

IT WAS AS if Sasha were there, back in the flesh. She was whole instead of the liquifying remains Daniel's mind kept conjuring. It could have been his imagination, except that every attempt at re-membering Sasha had so far backfired, always circling around to the bags he was told she was buried in. Even through the cold of the Reflection Room, Daniel had sensed, or imagined, her warmth. The same dichotomy played in his heart. The choking joy of looking in her eyes, fighting the suffocating pain of her loss.

Why had he leaned in and kissed Alice? Daniel suspected he knew the answer: it was the song. Did she plan this? Alice didn't push him away, nor was she under the spell of her own music. Accident or not, she looked disappointed, hurt, and confused by his sudden departure. Daniel wasn't fond of abandoning the girl he'd moments before tried to save, but how prudent was it to hang around someone who could manipulate him like that? Especially if it could happen by accident.

As he tried to put it all together, Daniel had to ask himself: Did Alice conjure Sasha's image, or was that a separate phenomenon? Or was it the god, only a few dozen feet down the hall?

The god had claimed to have had no direct hand in killing Sasha. While Daniel didn't trust this devil-made-flesh, he had no reason to think it would lie about this. The Crowleys were "in good standing" after all.

Imagined or not, Sasha's spirit was calling out for him to right the scales and give her peace. If that was the case, then who, if not the god, had killed her?

Daniel had avoided talking to Francis since the bloodbath in the cafeteria. Brother or not, the man made him nervous. The amused detachment with which he navigated life. From their first meeting up to his cavalier reaction to the god slaughtering half a dozen Sandmen. He might as well have been watching a Little League baseball game, so bored the whole affair seemed to make him.

It had been Francis who'd brought the sad news of Sasha's death to the Crowleys' door. In fact, Francis always seemed to know more than he let on. More than he should know. Whenever Francis showed up, things took a turn.

He was one of the few among the Sandmen who had his own room. In fact, apart from Mother and Alice, no one had their own accommodations or the privileges of privacy. Even Daniel had been given a bed in one of the many common quarters shared by members of the Church: six to a room, each with their own tiny bunk. It was crowded and sometimes uncomfortable, but it might as well have been a five-star hotel compared to the apartment he'd left behind in Brossard.

The door to the room opened up a crack moments after Daniel had knocked. Surprise registered in Francis's eyes when he saw his brother standing in the frame. Not a human level of shock, but rather an astonished form of mirth.

"Daniel? I thought you'd be at the sermon," Francis said, pulling the door open. "Please, come in."

Even alone in his own room, Francis still wore a full black suit and jacket, accented with a red tie. His shoes were polished and his starched shirt a crisp white. Not a hair on his head was out of place. The room itself was no different. Though it lacked the expensive look of his uniform, it was obsessively neat, the single bed made with military precision and not a lone piece of clutter on the desk to the far side. The walls were decorated with framed pictures of generic landscapes, the kind one might find at a garage sale. Even the curtains on the tall windows looked freshly pressed and meticulously arranged, yet drab and soulless.

"Mother's sermon was getting a bit heated. I didn't think anyone would mind if I slipped away."

"Mother will mind. She will mind a lot." Francis shrugged. "I'll tell her that I needed your help with something."

He followed the statement with a smile and waved Daniel inside his room.

Looking at his older sibling, Daniel was suddenly reminded of all he'd learned about Alice. The soothing effect of her singing was lifting from him, and the memory of her living conditions, the punishments she'd endured, the dark solitary confinement of the Reflection Room, and her lost family flooded back to him. His fists clenched.

"Thanks," he said, finding it hard to dig up gratitude under the circumstances.

Francis took a few steps deeper into his room, slowly turning around to run a finger over his desk, looking for dust that wasn't there.

"So, what can I do for you? Or are you just looking for a place to hide from Mother's rant? What is it this time? Unity? Faith? Unwavering devotion to the cause or does she just want more money?"

He turned and smiled, still rubbing index finger to thumb critically.

"Actually, I was wondering." Daniel closed the door to the room behind him, looking for privacy. "Who did you say killed Sasha again?"

"The god, of course." Francis's smile widened, as if he were enjoying a joke only he knew the punch line to. "Does it make you nervous to live under the same roof? Don't worry—once we get Alice to assert full control over it, well, things are going to get interesting, aren't they?"

Something about the smugness of his attitude grated on Daniel's nerves. He was reminded of the first time Francis had introduced himself, pretending to be someone else and asking to see his father.

Francis had known about the god that day. He'd known about their father's involvement with the Sandmen of Saint-Ferdinand. He'd been the one responsible for everything that had gone wrong for Daniel ever since that sunny summer day.

"Francis," Daniel asked, stepping forward. "Who killed Sasha?"

Eyes riveted on his brother's perfect smile, Daniel already knew the answer. It didn't matter what would come out of Francis's mouth—it would be a lie. There was no doubt who had tortured and killed his girlfriend. Who would be so callous as to kidnap an eight-year-old girl from her family? Who could lie without so much as blinking an eye? Only a complete sociopath would be able to do any of these things all while wearing a smile.

"I told you. The god did it," Francis said, his lips thinned as he stretched his smile even farther.

Whatever residual calm Alice's song had left on Daniel faded away like smoke in a stiff wind. Only the Crowley anger remained. Images of his father's crimson face as he scolded him or gave one of his subordinates a dressing-down flashed before Daniel's eyes. He could feel his fingernails biting down into his palms as he balled his fists. His heartbeat was like a war drum in his ears, his own music egging him on toward violence.

"Daniel?" Francis asked, his smile only diminished by a fraction, but his voice was drowned out by the sound of the blood rushing through Daniel's veins.

The right hook flew almost of its own accord. Daniel's fist, powered by years of athletics and training for football and hockey, found its mark, ramming into Francis's jaw with an audible crack. For the first time, Daniel could feel what his father had felt on those occasions when he would succumb to the Crowley anger. It was pure satisfaction, devoid of shame or guilt. An immediate reward for indulging in his base instinct. It tasted like justice and demanded repetition.

Francis didn't retaliate. In the heat of the moment, Daniel had imagined his brother would have some trick up his sleeve. Perhaps he'd pull out some curved blade from his jacket, or maybe he wore the suit to hide a shoulder holster and would draw a gun on him. Daniel was ready for either scenario, stepping back, poised to unleash more of his fury.

But Francis just laughed. Quietly at first, wiping at his mouth and inspecting the hand for blood, but soon much louder and almost genuinely.

"You killed her," Daniel said, finally putting voice to the accusation.

"It had to be done," Francis insisted.

Satisfied that his split lip wasn't bleeding too much, he straightened up again, fastening the top button on his jet-black jacket.

"You cold-blooded son of a bitch! You killed her and you lied to me about it!"

"Tsk. Don't call mother names like that, Daniel." His smile was returning, though marred by a sliver of crimson coating a few of his teeth. "If it makes you feel better, she died for a higher cause. And besides, with her gone, there's nothing to stand between the two of us."

"What 'two of us'? What the hell are you talking about?"

"The Crowley Boys! It's what you and Dad called it."

Daniel tensed at hearing the term. It had been his father's name for the two of them. A mark of solidarity between them after his mother, Stephen Crowley's wife, had abandoned them both. Francis wasn't part of that. He had no right to it.

Whether he was being provoked further or his brother had some other purpose for mentioning the Crowley Boys, Daniel didn't care. All he wanted was to hit Francis again. And again. And again. To completely succumb to the fury that was his birthright.

He could hear footsteps in the hall. Someone opening the door behind him. The Church had heard the commotion and was coming to rescue Mother's shadow.

"Everything is fine, Mr. Dover," Francis said over Daniel's shoulder. "A misunderstanding between brothers. You know how it is."

Still, Daniel didn't hear the door close behind him. Sean Dover, and maybe others, were watching, waiting to see how the situation would play out. Strange calculations came to Daniel's mind. Could he kill Francis before the congregation descended upon him to prevent it? How many Sandmen might be behind him, and could he fight them off? Could he stand it, killing his father and now his brother?

Daniel started to back out of the room and toward the assembled crowd, unwilling to take his eyes from Francis, but also apprehensive of what might be waiting behind him. His fingers were knotted into fists and his joints ached at the tension, ready to unleash should he feel but the lightest touch.

"Let him leave," Francis said, waving one hand while the other touched his bruised face. "It's okay. Just let him go."

The assembled Sandmen, only six or seven of them in the end, parted around him as Daniel backed out. From the dark hall, the light of the room was like a halo around Francis's silhouette, the frame of the door like that of a painting with the wounded brother as its only subject. Once clear of the Sandmen, Daniel shook his head to dismiss the image, turned on his heel, and sprinted down the hall.

Perhaps there was a better way to put Sasha's spirit to rest.

Daniel sat in the driver's seat of his parked Civic. He inspected his balled-up hand in much the same way one might admire a finely honed sword.

Running out of the compound and to his car, Daniel had felt the eyes of at least a dozen more Sandmen, all pressing down on him as he passed the threshold of the Church's home for what could be the last time. Word of the altercation would make it to Mother and surely that would be the last straw, or perhaps the excuse she needed to send him into exile again. It was becoming clear to Daniel that his mother's disdain had nothing to do with protecting him. She probably knew about Sasha's death and that Francis was responsible. Maybe she'd even ordered the deed done. None of it mattered. Daniel's purpose was now clear.

Vengeance featured high on his to-do list, and hitting Francis had given him a moment of clarity above the overwhelming satisfaction. His path was now more obvious than it had been in months. The road map so simple to see.

To give Sasha the peace she deserved, he had to get back at her killer. To do that, he had to kill their god; and to do that, he needed a weapon.

The same way he'd seen Sasha's face as he touched Alice's thin lips to his, he'd heard her voice calling his name. She wanted this. Of that Daniel was certain.

Penny had mentioned the presence of ghosts in Saint-Ferdinand. Little Audrey's spirit lingered long after her body's grisly discovery on Finnegan's property.

The blue glow of his phone's screen lit up the interior of the Civic. On it, the name PENELOPE LAFOREST was cut out in white letters, the call button silently taunting him. In his mind, he'd call Penny and they'd talk. She'd immediately forgive him and then help him understand whether he was really seeing a ghost or simply losing his mind.

But then he remembered her crystal-blue eyes, their cerulean purity so clear that they almost defied the shadows of her bangs. In them, he'd seen a terrible fear after he'd threatened Sherbet, the cat. That more than anything convinced him to leave her house, though the shattered mug over his forehead had been another compelling argument.

His finger gently touched the healing scab over his brow before going back to tap on the glowing screen. Penny's name was replaced by that of A. PETERSON. He'd talked to Abraham briefly after getting kicked out of Penny's house. The two boys were essentially on the same page when it came to how they should handle Venus's cat. Maybe he could help him get back into Penny's good graces. Besides, he'd given Abraham the knife.

"Hullo?" Abraham said.

"Abe? It's Daniel Crowley."

"Oh. Hey, Dan," Abraham answered. "You okay, man? Haven't heard from you in a while. Where are you?"

His voice had the electronic echo of someone using speaker-phone, and the various noises, bumps, and shuffling confirmed to Daniel that this was the case. It sounded like Abraham was cooking while he talked.

"I'm okay," Daniel said, looking at the school behind him, the lights of the gymnasium shining brightest in the twilight. "Actually, no. I'm not okay. Listen, I need to talk to Penny. You think she's still pissed?"

Daniel knew about Abraham's long-standing crush on Penelope. He knew it, she knew it, dogs knew it. Everyone was aware, yet Abraham thought it was his best-kept secret. Nobody was callous enough to contradict him. Yet it did color his asking to talk to her somehow.

"Penny doesn't hold grudges," Abraham said. "I mean, she'll make you pay for threatening Sherbet, but she'll hear you out. What's the problem? Maybe I can help."

"Oh good! Great! Okay." Daniel was glad for the answer and immediately wanted to hang up to call Penny, but something in the way Abraham was asking compelled him to at least give a cursory answer. "Remember how Penny said she saw Audrey Bergeron's ghost?"

What followed was a long pause on Abraham's part. When he spoke again, much of the lighthearted bumpkin attitude in him was gone, replaced instead by a serious, even somber tone.

"Yeah. I remember. I've seen her too. There's been a lot of ghosts in Saint-Ferdinand lately. Why?"

Daniel proceeded to explain everything he could about seeing Sasha. Of course, he couldn't do that without also talking about Alice, and with Alice came talk of the god and the Church of the Sandmen and Simon. The only thing he omitted were his direct family ties to the cult, skirting around Francis and Mother's involvement. By the time he was done, Abraham was dumbstruck and Daniel's phone battery was down to less than 10 percent.

Then a different voice came on the line.

"Wait," said the voice of Randy McKenzie. "Go back to the music teacher."

Driving down the highway, Daniel replayed the conversation with Randy through his head. Daniel had wanted to ask so many questions of the medical examiner. Had he known about Sasha? Francis? His mother? What was he doing with Peterson? Where was Penny?

"What about Simon?" Daniel had asked.

"You don't just get to teach perfection out of nowhere, Dan. If he's instructing that girl, Alice, on how to manipulate a god, then he has to know more than he's letting on. Maybe he doesn't have the voice for it, but someone taught him the theory."

"Does it have to be a person?"

Randy's excitement could be heard over the phone's speaker as Daniel described the leather-bound book that Simon always carried around. Even though there were few details he could give—the book was about an inch thick and a little smaller than a textbook, covered in worn leather the color of aged oak with no discernible markings that he could remember—they were enough to ignite Randy's curiosity like a child eyeing piles of gifts under a Christmas tree.

"That sounds like Neil's notebook. You have to get it," Randy had demanded. "And the music teacher. Can you do that, Daniel?"

"No. I'm driving down to Saint-Ferdinand. I need to speak to Penny," he'd argued. "I think I'm being haunted by—"

"Yes, yes," Randy had interrupted. "By your girlfriend. Don't drag Penelope into this. Bring me that book and this Simon and I'll handle your ghost."

He'd sounded so confident that it left Daniel little room to argue the point. He'd dropped Simon off at his home only a few hours prior. It would be but a small detour to get him, and considering the rising tension at the Sandmen's compound, it may very well be safer for Simon to disappear for a little while.

A quick drive-by revealed that the lights in Simon's house were turned off and there was no discernable activity.

It was late enough in the night that the only other pedestrians were students streaming out from the Loyola campus of Concordia University. The people coming out of the library or from practice at the sports center across the street would have been his peers the next year. Football season was in full swing and Daniel should have been playing for his school's team. Maybe, when all this was over, he still could, but the notion seemed absurd in the moment.

Up on Rosedale Avenue, where Simon's town house was located, there was hardly a soul left awake. One older gentleman was out walking a gray schnauzer while smoking a cigarette he was probably not allowed to have indoors, or at all. The two were quick to disappear around a corner, leaving Daniel alone with the distant sight and sound of cars occasionally patrolling the larger arteries.

It might have been just another fall evening, freshly fallen leaves crinkling under Daniel's feet as he walked up to the town house's door. The faded orange glow of an aged doorbell stared back at him like a cyclops, and he was about to push its eye in when Daniel noticed that the door was ajar.

Crime scenes were nothing new to Daniel. The first time he'd strolled onto the site of a murder, he'd been no more than ten years old. He'd seen his father's car by the woods on the bus ride home from school. Eager to see his old man, already his only parent at the time, Daniel had ridden his bicycle all the way to where he'd seen the police truck, lights flashing even in the afternoon sun.

When he arrived, sprinting under the yellow tape, yelling gleefully for Stephen Crowley to see him, the boy was greeted with nothing short of the Crowley red-hot fury. Daniel rubbed at the arm his father had grabbed to drag him back to his truck. Daniel could still see the red mud on his white sneakers as he struggled to touch the ground.

Since then, he'd been to too many such scenes and had learned to recognize the signs.

The door, open by just a crack, was only the first clue. There was also a smell, one that seemed to linger like an afterthought, long after a location had been scoured and cleaned. Something deep in the human psyche could always pick up on the scent of blood, and there it was.

Daniel looked around, hoping the old man and his dog weren't back, or that a cop car wouldn't choose this moment to drive by.

What a remarkable coincidence would it be to catch the son of mass murderer Stephen Crowley at the scene of another crime?

Fumbling for a moment, Daniel pulled his phone out.

After flicking the flashlight on, the very first thing the phone illuminated was a coat rack. It looked strikingly like the one they had in the entranceway back in Saint-Ferdinand. Not one of those modern hollow-tubed monstrosities that his father couldn't stand, but rather a thickly lacquered solid wood near-antique. The kind found in the homes of old families or in rural houses. One of the metal hooks near the top was bent in and glistening, wet with what might have passed for strawberry jam.

Daniel panned the beam of light all the way to the floor, looking for whatever had been hit by the coatrack.

His father could have read the scene in an instant, just from the position of everything that was out of place. He'd notice the entranceway table knocked aside, its contents partially thrown to the ground. He'd have seen the blood splatter at the foot of the table, an array of red drops splashed over the hardwood floor. He would mention how a body had lain there, evidenced by the drag marks in the blood and how a rug was moved. Daniel only knew that these elements were there, mixed into the clutter, but he was slow to add it all up.

He could, in his mind, see his father looming over the scene, giving his evaluation and professional opinion in a tone that straddled the line between sadness and anger, the cocktail of which came out as weariness. For a second Daniel could have sworn his father was right there. A tall, wide, and angry presence stepping from the darkness. The very shadows that had consumed Stephen Crowley after being stabbed releasing him back to the living. The illusion didn't last. Before Daniel could so much as blink, an immense hand grabbed him by his shirt, picking him up and slamming his back into the wall. The town house shook.

Daniel's phone dropped to the ground, a thin cracking sound escaping the device before it went dark.

Daniel was athletic and strong, the star of his school's football team, but the man who held him pinned to the wall might as well have been a grizzly, huge and covered with dark hair. A thick paw that smelled of cigarettes slapped on to Daniel's mouth to silence him, nearly dislocating his jaw in the process.

"You," a familiar voice called from the shadows.

The faint light of a streetlamp filtered through a window, but it wasn't enough for Daniel to identify who the voice belonged to. It was so flat and emotionless that it reminded him of Francis. Except it was from a girl and it was nowhere as practiced.

"You betrayed us?" the voice came again, a shade of doubt over the otherwise flat question.

"You know this boy?" the owner of the cigarette hand asked, low but with authority.

Daniel wanted to scream and bite and fight, but the monstrous hands of the bearded giant held him still. His arms strained as he thrashed to get away, and another hand closed around his neck. He wasn't as strong as his assailant, but surely he was faster. All he needed was a moment, the blink of an eye when he could slip free and make a run for it.

"Don't. I'll take care of it," the girl in the shadows said.

Suddenly Daniel relaxed. In fact, he almost laughed at the mis-understanding. Headlights on a passing car illuminated the girl who spoke like she knew him. She looked like she had as they'd driven to Sherbrooke a little over two months ago. Similar headlights flashing over the same red hair as she sat, small and reserved in the passenger seat of his car.

Venus!

He said it, the words muted and distorted by the hand that kept him put. He was saved.

Except, he wasn't.

The light faded as the car kept going. Bright white headlights were replaced by dim red taillights. Hope turned to pain as Daniel felt something sliding into his stomach, gliding and scraping on his bottom right rib. The taillight faded out of existence, but the red in his vision remained.

The bear let him go, but Daniel was out before hitting the floor.

VENUS

"WHAT THE HELL did you do?"

For the first time, Lucien Peña did not have control.

Daniel's body fell to the ground as Venus's companion of the last few days let him go. His huge fingers trembled, either from rage or shock.

What the hell did I do? Venus's thoughts echoed the words.

She knew what she had done. Nothing. Absolutely nothing. Not of her own volition anyway. It was her hand holding the knife as its blade slid through Simon's neck, puncturing the carotid artery and trachea. It was her fingers that had become slick with his blood as it gushed from the wound in rhythmic spasms and her palm that had pressed against his forehead, waiting for the convulsions to stop.

But it was not Venus who had done those things. It was the god, or rather a side effect of the wound that it had left in her soul. Through their communion, it had gouged a piece of her and left it empty, but Venus had soon filled it with all the regrets that pulled at her conscience.

What she did not realize, what Venus could not see, was how, with each bit of remorse she meticulously hid, her humanity was pushed further away. In turn, she was pulled closer to the god.

So, when faced with Simon's torment, his agonized death throes that were so unbearable to watch, she willingly gave the reins over to that dark, lingering presence, and through that small crack, it had taken over.

From that point forward, the knife hadn't left her hand and the dark hunger of the god hadn't left her heart. At least, not until she'd plunged it into Daniel Crowley's gut.

Daniel's face, contorting in pain and going from relief to shock to fear, was painted with red hues in her memory. Her hand punching into his side remained etched in perfect detail in her memory. The whole scene was a museum that she was forced to visit in her mind as Lucien pulled her away from the scene.

But she wasn't the artist behind this tragedy. If anything, she was the brush and the god had been the one to wield her. It was done with Daniel, with the whole Crowley line. She was tying up the god's loose ends in its name.

"Which one's his car?" Lucien demanded, frantically gesturing at the row of vehicles that lined the street in front of Simon's town house. When she didn't answer, he grabbed her arm in his fist and tried to shake the answer out. "Which one is it?"

He must have picked up Daniel's keys because he was looking at the one covered with thick black plastic, a large H embossed on both sides. In his other hand, Peña had the leather-bound book he'd collected from Simon Martel.

"The white Civic. There."

Venus's voice came out flat and naked of emotion. She could feel the terror and shame inside her like a meal crawling up her throat and threatening to spill from her mouth. Instead of vomiting or crying like she wanted to do, Venus moved like a puppet, motivated entirely by outside forces.

Pulling her by the wrist, Peña shoved her into the passenger seat of Daniel's car. In the seconds it took him to go around and settle behind the wheel, his huge frame barely fitting into place on the seat, she'd realized her fingers were still wrapped around the knife's handle.

Venus's breath caught in her throat as she let the murder weapon fall to the floor between her legs.

Trembling fingers stained with blood found their way to the seat belt, buckling it more out of habit than purpose. The car growled to life, then purred as Lucien pulled out of its parking spot and onto the street.

The god's presence was starting to ebb. Like a receding tide, it left behind the debris of its passing. In the case of Venus's soul, it was the vestiges of guilt she'd been storing away, now laid bare for her to see.

It felt like déjà vu. She'd done this before—been silently driven toward yet another piece of her so-called destiny.

Before, she had been with Daniel Crowley in his white Civic as it sped toward Sherbrooke Hospital. It was the same car but a different highway and a different driver.

The orange glow of the streetlights that ran along Highway 15, one of the main arteries that cut through Montreal from south to north, eventually leading to Laval, highlighted the blood on her fingers. She tried to wipe the hand clean on her pant leg, but the blood wouldn't go away.

"What the hell came over you, McKenzie?" Lucien demanded.

Her eyes remained dry but her vision was tunneled. It was like looking at the world through a straw and her concentration was entirely focused on remembering to breathe.

"Do you know who you just killed?"

"Daniel Crowley," she answered, tempted for a moment to explain that she wasn't to blame. Saying his name, however, brought tears to her eyes.

"No. You killed Daniel *Lambert*-Crowley. Marguerite Lambert's son. Edouard Lambert's grandson."

The grandson of the man Lucien had loved. The one he was doing all of this for. Peña's composure was showing cracks. His knuckles were white on the wheel of the car and his jaw was set so tight that Venus thought his teeth might shatter. His focus, which had usually been relaxed and able to take in everything about his beloved city at once, was now on the rails, his eyes locked on to the road ahead.

He pressed the car's horn with a sudden punch to the wheel, startling Venus as they merged onto Highway 40, going east. They were going much too fast now.

"She won't ignore this. Especially not if she's got the power of a god under her thumb. We have to strike first. Before she even knows what happened."

His hand patted the leather cover of Simon's book, resting on the dashboard, to punctuate his intentions.

"We have to go back," she said, the words barely making it past her swallowed guilt.

"No, we don't."

"Dan might still be alive. We didn't check that he was dead! If he's still alive, we have to do something. We have to—"

"He's dead, McKenzie. If he wasn't when we left, he will be before we get back. You killed him." Lucien's narrow focus shifted as he locked eyes onto her. She'd never felt so small in her life.

"I didn't . . ." Venus started, but Daniel's blood was still on her hands. She could remember a deep hatred toward Daniel and a desire to see him, his father, and everyone associated with him dead. But those weren't *her* thoughts and emotions. They were desires, dark and angry, that rose from the hollow in her soul. Driven to her limit, she had fed the cold place too much and something dark had taken hold. "You! You pushed me into this. You made me stab Martel and . . ."

"And what? Martel was collateral. He's a tool we broke before we could use him. Just like you're a tool that's waiting to be used. What made you think I needed you to stab Daniel Crowley? Do you have any idea how useful he could have been to us?"

The fury drained from Lucien. His eyes darted around, manic and paranoid, but the anger was gone. Venus could recognize features familiar to her: those of grief. For a moment she wondered if Lucien really had questions for Daniel, or if he simply wanted to somehow protect the grandchild of the man he'd once loved.

Lucien gripped the steering wheel as if he hoped to crush the life out of it. The longer she let the silence hang between them, allowing him to mull over his fears, the more intensity seemed to come over him.

Venus reached over to the dashboard to pick up Simon's book. Peña gave her a reproachful side-glance but otherwise didn't interfere.

The book didn't look like much. One might have mistaken it for a fancy address book or faux-aged diary.

Leafing through the pages, illuminated by the intermittent orange glow of the passing streetlights, she saw that the book wasn't what she'd expected. To be fair, she didn't know what she'd thought might be written there. Probably musical bars, since they had taken the book from a music teacher.

Instead the whole thing was cover-to-cover madness. One page had diagrams depicting detailed anatomical renditions of the human eye, while the next was covered in chicken-scratch notes. Then she fell on a page with drawings of long rows of nails and another one with a sketch of a stone archway covered in spiral patterns similar to those made by the god while it had been her prisoner.

All of it was in her grandfather's handwriting.

Finally her attention was drawn to the pages inserted after the fact. Those that were, presumably, added by the music teacher. Venus had never learned to read music. The series of dots overlaid on lines looked complicated and impossible to play on a single instrument, let alone by a human voice.

Yet, despite her ignorance, she could feel something unsettling about the way the music was written. Even with just her eyes brushing against the orange-lit scribbles, the presence in her soul, hidden inside her like a barracuda in a cave, stirred.

Then it hit her.

Steal the god.

They weren't going to the Sandmen's home to finish things. Whatever use Lucien had for her wasn't to kill the creature and get his revenge for the suffering his beloved Edouard had endured. They were on their way to try to take control of the beast, perpetuating the very same foolishness Venus's grandfather had started with the leather-bound book.

A fresh calm came over Venus. Lucien Peña wasn't an ally. He wasn't fighting against the god. Revenge wasn't what he sought.

What he wanted was to bring back Edouard. To undo what had already been done.

History was about to repeat itself and Venus wanted no part of it. She had become a passenger on Lucien Peña's grief train, and her own goals had been left at the last station.

She watched him for a moment. Studied his intensity and single-focus determination. Then she saw it. How could she have not noticed before? In his eyes there was something missing. A dullness, like a piece of his soul had been surgically removed. She knew that missing spark.

There was a cold place inside him, the same one that was growing within her. How many years had it been there, devouring him from within? He thought he had a plan, but Venus recognized him as little more than the knife on the Civic's floor. Just a tool for the god.

Before she could convince herself otherwise, Venus yanked the gearshift to the letter *R* and pulled violently at the car's hand brake.

The accident didn't happen the way she'd expected.

Venus thought the car would stop dramatically, perhaps destroying the transmission in the process, but otherwise everything would be fine. She'd jump out and make a break for it with the book.

Instead Daniel's Civic swerved right with a jolt. Lucien overcompensated, jerking the wheel sharply to the left. Then the night turned into a hundred headlights of oncoming traffic shining through the driver's-side window.

Once that shattered, a hundred headlights turned into a million, reflected in the shards from the shattered glass.

Somewhere during the accident, Venus hit her head on the dashboard. While they'd swerved? When that dark blue SUV had crashed into them? The ringing in her ears made it hard to comprehend what was going on.

Opening her eyes, Venus could see that Lucien was in bad shape. Automatically, she felt guilt and fear. *What have you done?* The question came back; except, this time, she had an answer. She'd done whatever it took to get away. Spasms replaced Lucien's breathing.

"Are you okay?" A voice, manic and scared, broke through the ringing. "Don't move . . . accident . . ."

She ignored the voice. She needed to get out of the car, to walk, to get rid of this goddamn ringing.

Bystanders clutched at her as she pulled herself from the wreckage. She shrugged them off, far too concerned with escaping. Looking back at the Civic, she wanted to apologize to Daniel for wrecking his car before remembering that he, too, was dead.

"I'm fine. I'm fine," Venus repeated, over and over, swatting at the concerned silhouettes that hovered around her like so many flies. "Please check on my friend. I'm fine . . ."

Venus leaned on the concrete median that split the eastbound and westbound traffic on the 40. The headlights were blinding and the neon signs of restaurants and businesses off the side of the highway made her nauseous. She wasn't fine.

Pulling out her cell phone, Venus struggled to remember the phone number she needed. The screen was so bright and so blurry, there was no way she could navigate through the menus.

Closing her eyes, Venus pushed the home button on the device and held it down until she heard a distant chime.

"Call Jodie," she instructed.

The phone acknowledged the request with its emotionless female voice. Venus lifted the thing to her ear, dreading the noise so close to her brain and feeling every ounce of the device. Her arm hurt, she noted, but it also seemed to still function. Pain could wait.

"Jodie?" she slurred into the microphone.

"Venus? Are you okay? Are you in trouble?"

"I messed up, Jodie." Venus could feel tears welling in her eyes but immediately wanted to suppress them. She wanted to use the god's blessing to ignore the pain. As tempting as it was, she knew to resist the urge. "I need help. I messed up bad."

"Where are you?"

"There's this accident on the 40. Westbound. No! Eastbound. Just before the ramp to the 15 North to Laval, but a little before the Rockland Centre. That's my accident. I made that. I'm here."

"Okay," Jodie answered, calm and professional. "When the cops show up, find one and tell them Officer Jodie LeSage—"

"My battery is low and I'm not sticking around."

The ringing was almost completely gone and her eyes were finally starting to find their focus. The trade-off was a massive incoming headache, approaching like black clouds on the horizon, but at least her thoughts were coming together more clearly now.

"Venus? Stay put. Wait for the cops. Tell them I'm coming. Whatever you did, I'll help you through it. Okay? Venus? Venus!"

Someone was lighting flares to help traffic go around the accident. The crash she caused just so she could escape Lucien Peña. How many cars had been involved aside from the Civic? Two? Three?

"Oh my god. Those poor people," she said, loud enough to be heard over the phone.

Venus could hear noises on the other end, keys being picked up in a hurry, the rustling of a jacket being thrown on, a lock being turned. Jodie was on her way and Venus's hearing was getting better.

"Stay where you are, Venus. Are you listening?"

"I think I've figured out where I am," Venus said, her voice distracted, her neck craned to look around and over the edge of the elevated highway. "You know the Starbucks at the corner of Lucerne and De Liesse?"

"Venus! Don't you dare. Stay where you are!" Jodie was screaming into her phone now.

"That's where I'm going to be."

With that, Venus pushed herself from the concrete divider and proceeded to start walking back to the on-ramp and off the highway.

Venus was sipping calmly from a chocolate chip espresso Frappuccino when Jodie stormed through the front door of the coffee shop. The two baristas and a handful of patrons jumped at the violent interruption of the otherwise calm, easy-to-digest alternative-pop music that floated between the bags of pre-ground coffee and branded travel mugs. Everyone except Venus, who sat calmly at a corner table, barely registering a single thing around her.

"Ma'am!" one of the baristas said, calling out to Jodie in disapproval. He must have been about two years older than Venus, his Irish-green apron and faded fuchsia hair landing him all the authority of a school crossing guard.

Jodie glared at him, flipping open the right side of her jacket to show off her badge. Her expression softened, then melted when she saw Venus at her table.

"Oh god. Venus? Are you okay?"

Venus had been looking at herself for almost half an hour now, studying her reflection in the dark glass windowpanes of the coffee shop. The right side of her face was already a mass of bruises, and there was a line of blood from a cut over her eye. But worse than the wounds, her eyes had a haunted look that she couldn't shake. It looked like the nightmare that was her inner struggle, the piece of hate left over from the summer, was oozing out of her pores.

"How long does it take for someone to die from a stab to the stomach?" she asked, barely lifting her head to look at Jodie. If she looked at Jodie, she knew she'd start crying.

"I don't know. It depends," Jodie said, trying to sound compassionate but just as desperate to get to the truth. "Venus, what happened? Why didn't you stay put like I told you? Did you stab Peña?"

Jodie reached out, careful not to touch any of the purple skin, and pushed Venus's chin to the side so she could take a better look at her face and force her to make eye contact.

"You've got to have someone take a look at you, baby."

"They'll arrest me when they find out what I've done. But I've got to do something first. I can't afford to go to jail right now."

"The accident? We can handle that, but not if you've got a concussion or worse. Venus?"

Venus struggled to maintain eye contact. She focused instead on what she felt she had to say. Like a deathbed confession.

"No. Not the accident. I hope no one else got hurt, but if it nailed Peña, then it's worth it. Jodie?"

Piercing through the million questions Jodie had, Venus could see the spark of recognition at Peña's name. A quick glance at her radio and Venus knew everything she needed to know. Jodie had monitored the chatter about the accident. She knew the outcome.

"Yes," Jodie said, her efforts at comfort ravenously consumed by the much louder concern.

"I stabbed a boy earlier tonight. In NDG. I'm pretty sure he's dead. And . . . I know what you're going to say, but I can't go to the police, not yet. I gotta finish something first, but I can't do it alone."

Jodie shook her head, eyebrows furrowed in deep worry. She was giving her that look Venus had seen given to all the kids in Saint-Ferdinand who'd lost a parent. The look Erica Hazelwood had given Penny when she'd learned about her mother. The look everyone gave Abraham when discussing his father.

Penny had hated that look, and Venus could understand why. Her friend had no use for pity, and neither did she.

"Sorry, Venus. All this has gone too far. I'll arrest you myself if I have to, but I'm putting a stop to this. For your own good."

"I know," Venus said, breaking eye contact again. She reached down to the seat next to her and pulled up the worn leather book she and Lucien had retrieved from Simon Martel's home.

Jodie suppressed a gasp at seeing Venus's blood-stained fingers flipping through the yellowed pages, skipping to the end of the book to fish out some of the more recent additions.

"Lucien killed Simon," explained Venus, still going through the notes. "These are the notes the teacher kept about his activities with the Sandmen."

The book slid across the narrow table, guided by Venus's hand. A finger with crusted blood drawing a brown line under the nail, tapped twice over a line of handwritten text.

"'Alice put me to sleep today. Just by singing. I think she's ready,'" Venus recited the line from memory. "Alice. Alice LeSage. That's your sister, isn't it?"

ALICE

ALICE USED TO have her own set of keys to the Sandmen compound.

It had been an uneasy compromise on Mother's part to give Alice her own set of keys. Even though it was a necessity, one that had long been on the horizon, it was a shred of trust that had simply never sat well.

On the first day she had been called upon to put a god to bed, Alice had received the symbol of trust, which, at the time, had made her feel like a real part of the Sandmen. There were only a few keys to the ring, but each put a little bit of her life back in her hands. If she was to be the guardian of the Sam-creature, and if she would be the one to cajole it to sleep whenever necessary, then she needed full access. The day she'd been training with Simon had driven that point home. What if she couldn't get to the part of the compound where she needed to be while the creature was on a rampage? No, it was much safer to allow Alice freedom to roam.

Though it wasn't really freedom, was it? She had the keys to all the important doors in the compound and could, if she wished, walk out the front and be on her way. Mother knew that Alice would never go through with it. Since her arrival, she'd fed the girl nothing but a steady diet of isolation, pain, and captivity. It was no coincidence that these were the exact ingredients to the god's existence. It wasn't just about tearing down Alice's humanity, shackling her to the Sandmen, but also building a bridge between herself and the monster inside Sam.

Alice couldn't leave because of who she'd been trained to be and who the god already was.

So long as Alice had things to lose, she would remain a prisoner of the Sandmen. The fewer privileges she had, however, the fewer reasons she'd had to toe the line; the more power she discovered was in her hands, the closer her breaking point got.

Even when everything had been removed, even her keys, there had still been Simon and after that, there had still been Daniel. Fun, beautiful Daniel. For a brief speck of time, she thought maybe he cared.

Now Simon was gone and who knew if Mother would ever allow him back to train her, and Daniel had run off after kissing her. For a time, she imagined that it didn't mean much. In fact, who better than her and her soothing voice to help Daniel through a difficult time? There was an anger in him, buried mostly, but burning at the surface on occasion. She could cool that anger. She could help him forget all about his dead girlfriend, whatever her name was.

The god, cruel but honest, was quick to remind her of the facts. He showed her that the girl Daniel loved had been beautiful, clever, intelligent. They'd gone to school together, dances and sporting events. Damn! She probably played sports! It didn't take more than a glance at his arms to see that Daniel must have loved sports. No. Mother, Francis, the Sandmen, and now even a god had made it clear: Alice was no prize. She was no beauty and she was no genius. She was her music and little more.

Having nothing left to lose, Alice saw that, when all you had was a voice, everyone started to look like an audience. And the Church of the Sandmen had quite the auditorium.

With fingers as clumsy as they were bony, Alice went through her key ring, opening each door that led her first upstairs, then through the cafeteria, and finally to the main hallway of the compound. Black and white squares of linoleum shrouded in dim light carried Mother's sermon like so much flotsam on a river.

Mother had been going at it for a while. Her voice had become raspy, the pauses between sentences lasting longer. Alice could hear the anger behind each word, even though they were carefully wrapped in disappointment.

Disappointment was always Mother's go-to when she wished to admonish the family. Anger would scare off members, but disappointment made Mother the victim and the family the aggressor.

"It saddens me!" Mother said, moving on to the third act of her presentation. "You may think it's frustration or indignation, and I am agitated, but what you see in your mother isn't rage. No, no, no, my children. It's heartbreak. To have loved so much and given so much only to be cast aside when the hurdles become too high and the hills too steep."

Mother would go on like this for another hour if no one was there to stop her. She'd explain to the flock how they, by simple virtue of their staying by her side, were made superior to those who deserted. That whatever share of salvation was meant for those who had left, would now be distributed among the devoted faithful. As if divine love was a pie to split among those that remained come the end times.

"You!" Mother's voice boomed through the auditorium speakers, drowning out the very thoughts of those in attendance.

"Are the true believers. The ones chosen for their conviction and clarity."

Alice hadn't been to a sermon in ages. She remembered them being a source of inspiration. Often she'd be trotted out to the stage and allowed to sing, which delighted the family. Other Sandmen would clap after each performance and Mother would lean in and whisper in her ear: "See how much they love you? You'll never be as loved as you are here, Alice. Never and nowhere."

It was hard to contradict or deny. The entire Church had been under her spell back then. But one day she'd sung her last song in front of the Church. It was one of the lullabies she'd been practicing with Simon, one at which she was beginning to excel. That day, she had nailed it. Not only did it sound perfect coming out of her throat, but for the first time, she had felt every part of the music. She could touch and control all the instruments built into her anatomy.

When she'd opened her eyes, there was no uproarious applause to greet her. No cheers or gentle compliments or mentions of admiration. Only the single, slow but enthusiastic clapping of a solitary admirer. Francis. Everyone else, including Mother, had fallen into a deep slumber.

From that day forward, she was only allowed to train outside or in what would become Sam Finnegan's prison. Never in front of the Church. Never another cheer.

"Some have fled," Mother continued as Alice stepped into the auditorium. "Their souls were not up to the task at hand. I'd be petty if I called them unworthy, but I'd also be lying if I didn't." There was a low, half-hearted chuckle from the audience. "Others have died, and to them we owe our inevitable salvation. They knew the value of what the Sandmen stand for. They knew that, in death, they served a purpose greater than in life, and they knew! They knew deep in their hearts that they would ultimately be rewarded.

"Now, I know there's doubt in your souls. I see it. Maurice, don't be afraid, admit it. You're unsure. It's painted on your face. But it's okay. It may not seem that way tonight, but I assure you, ours is a god of life, and a god of love."

The audience murmured an approval. Alice went through the music sheets she'd brought with her, the hasty scribbles left behind on the wall of the Reflection Room by Simon, along with several of her own compositions. To some it might have looked like the ramblings of a madwoman. A crazed manifesto written in incoherent melodies. To Alice, it was an arsenal. She just had to pick the correct weapon. She knew she'd put it in there somewhere.

"But our god is displeased," Mother continued. "Not with us but with this world. With how it has been treated. Imagine a creature of such magnificence being kept in a cave, shackled by primitive, gruesome means. Now imagine this torture lasting for a century or more."

Alice let out a chuckle at the hypocrisy of Mother's statement. As if the conditions the Sam-creature was kept in here and now were any better. What was more disturbing, and perhaps a bit amusing, was how no one in the auditorium was ignorant of that fact, yet they hummed in agreement.

Alice's laughter was ill timed, however, as it fell between the timid support of the assembled Sandmen and Mother's speech and was, thus, landing on a patch of near silence where it could be heard by everyone.

Including Mother.

"What do you think is so funny, Alice?"

The authority in Marguerite Lambert-Crowley's voice acted like a bullet to Alice's convictions. It pierced them, wounded them, and made them bleed, but Alice would not be cowed. Not this time.

"How many times do I have to order you to your room? You're damn near an adult, Alice. Why do you make me treat you like a child?" There was vitriol far above the threat in Mother's voice. If asked, Alice would have guessed that the only thing keeping the matriarch of the Sandmen from kicking her out, or worse, was that she still needed her. The Church needed her to sing.

So, Alice thought, she would oblige.

Taking a final glance at her music sheet, Alice took in a deep breath and, after but a short pause to close her eyes and settle her nerves, she began.

There was no warm-up, no lead-in. The very first note was already full of power. Perfect in pitch and depth and tone. It was a warm song, a loving song. The melody wasn't meant to soothe its listeners into slumber like all the lullabies in her arsenal, nor was it meant as a weapon to fell the members of the cult, though she knew such a song could exist.

No.

What Alice had in mind wasn't hurting the Sandmen. They were, after all, family. They had never hurt her, not directly or of their own volition. What Alice wanted was the one thing she'd always been denied. Despite being taken, trained, and hurt for the sole purpose of leveraging control over others, she had never been allowed any control over herself. She didn't mean them any harm, but she wanted them as her own. Including Mother.

Opening her eyes, Alice could see that it was working. The sounds of her voice were washing over them and, like waves over a sandcastle, the music eroded their will and removed all their initiative. She could see it in Mr. Denis's round face as it went slack and in Melanie Nelson's eyes as they stopped blinking and turned their devoted focus from Mother to Alice.

It was also in Mother.

The all-powerful Marguerite Lambert-Crowley, the pillar at the center of her congregation and sole decider of Alice's fate, stood like a mannequin. Her precious microphone dropped to her side. Fingers barely clutching at it as the will bled from her.

Alice had the whole Church under her thumb.

"Ahem!"

Or perhaps not the whole Church.

"Could you, perhaps, not do that?" Francis asked, stepping calmly over the legs of the rapt members of the congregation, making his way toward her.

He was cool and completely in control. He might as well have been deaf for how much her singing affected him.

Francis may not have had the sheer athleticism of his brother, but he was taller than Alice was and there was no reason to think he was weak under that suit.

Alice slowly shook her head at him, taking a few steps back. The volume of her voice increased and the intensity of her song with it. Nothing. It did nothing to him.

Music was about reaching into one's soul and pulling at the emotional strings within. A perfect song exerted perfect control over one's feelings. But what about someone who didn't feel? Someone like Francis.

"All right," he said, rolling his eyes, imitating what he thought annoyance should look like. "You're not leaving me much of a choice."

Hopping over one last row of theater seats, Francis came at her. Then, with what seemed like the first genuine emotion she'd seen from him, he smiled.

"You're not going to hit me," Alice said with more bravado than she'd thought herself capable.

The last notes of her interrupted melody still seemed to drift through the air, echoing from forgotten nooks and crannies in the gymnasium. Music completing its circuit bouncing off the tall ceiling and reverberating between the rafters. Before the last sound had even finished its return journey to her ears, Alice could see the Sandmen already shaking off the effects of her song.

Francis started to meticulously remove his jacket, carefully laying it on the back of a chair. "Alice. You wound me. I thought you knew me well enough by now to know that what you're saying isn't true."

"You can't . . . . You need me to sing," Alice said, still trying to stand firm despite her increased heart rate and shortness of breath. She wondered, through her fear, if she'd ever seen Francis without his jacket before.

"I've been waiting for this for quite some time," he said, pulling at his red silk tie. "Mother wouldn't listen to me, but it was inevitable. You can't raise a lion without having to get a sturdier cage, eventually."

He stopped a few yards from her, having closed the gap enough that if she tried to run, he'd be on her in a second. With an air of regret, as if saying adieu to an old friend, Francis unbuttoned the cuffs of his pristine white shirt and began rolling up the sleeves. Every fold in the fabric seemed to cause him physical discomfort.

"If I can't sing, you'll all die."

The math was simple. Cause and effect. He'd seen it himself only a couple of days prior. If Alice wasn't there to sing the god to sleep, it would go on a rampage. The body that trapped it was nothing more than a tool and a weapon. Sam Finnegan didn't need to be alive and the god within didn't need the corpse to remain intact.

Yet Francis didn't seem to care.

"If I can't sing, she'll die," Alice said, specifying with a thrust of her index finger that she was referring to Mother. They'd all die, of course, but Francis's mom was, if anything, the only thing he cared about. There was a momentary flinch in his posture. A pause or hesitation that did little to slow him down but spoke volumes about his attitude toward Marguerite. As Alice had suspected, there was some sort of residual care, an alien affection that only those who couldn't truly feel would experience, but it wasn't enough to stay his hand.

"The problem with your assertion is," Francis started, putting a final fold into his left sleeve, "I don't need to kill you or break your pretty voice box to keep you contained. We just need you to sing. Not walk around causing trouble or reading books to keep yourself entertained. When all's said and done, we don't even need you to be able to see or even feed yourself. There is so much I can do to you that will guarantee your obedience without keeping you from singing. In fact, my theory is that if singing is all you have left, you'll be more than happy to oblige whenever we allow you."

"You wouldn't. Mother wouldn't let you."

Francis glanced back at his paralyzed mother. He shrugged.

"I'm not sure what you expect she'll do about it." He turned his gaze back toward Alice. "Though I suppose I should hurry before she comes to her senses."

He punctuated the threat by cracking his knuckles, a sound that carried through the auditorium.

This left Alice with only one final option.

Alice wasn't quite sure what she was doing when she closed her eyes and started singing again. She knew her actions, down to the ratio of air inhaled and expelled and the position of her uvula, and she knew her intentions, but what the results would be was far more nebulous.

She'd had no time to practice. No opportunity to test. The song was an angry thing. Where the soft songs that cajoled the listener to sleep were silk ribbons placed upon the mind, tying them in gentle knots that barely tickled at the senses, this song was a chain. Heavy and brutal, there was nothing in it to calm the nerves. It was meant for a waking audience or, failing that, shocking the sleeping awake.

The volume was ear-shattering. How such a small chest with whatever limited lung capacity it might have could shake the concrete walls of the gymnasium with such force seemed to surprise even Francis. Enough at least to give him pause.

The leftover Sandmen looked at one another, waiting and fearing for the effects of the song. Moments ago Alice had sung their will away, chipping at their ego with each note until their initiative, their fears and desires, were taken from them and delivered to her. To not only lose the hold on their bodies but on their minds must have been terrifying, even though the song itself had been sweet and disarming. What currently shook their jawbones and made their eardrums buzz like the wings on a dragonfly was something else. It wasn't meant for them. It was a song of hate and death.

Mother was the first to realize what was happening. Her own voice came in through her precious speakers, loud and ugly in contrast with Alice's singing.

"Stop that!" she said. "You have no idea what you're doing, you stupid girl!"

Ah . . . thought Alice. *The sweet song of fear.*

She was familiar with that particular refrain. Except, she was usually the vocalist behind it. It was the first song she'd learned living with the Sandmen. Except, the only power it had was satisfying Mother. Alice could see the appeal. It was delicious to hear others sing it.

"I've seen better people than you try," Mother continued, hints of manic terror seasoning her electrically enhanced words. "None have succeeded. None have survived, Alice! That's how my father died, and let me tell you—it wasn't a pleasant death. You can't control it! You aren't ready!"

Except Alice didn't need any assurances. She already knew. The creature inside Sam Finnegan had sung back to her. It had told of its deeds and it had told of its plans. Alice didn't agree with all of it, but for now their purposes were in harmony. They wanted the same thing. What had been denied them for the majority of their time in this world. Freedom.

There was no need to look. They all heard the basement door burst off its hinges. Alice felt the hush of cold terror as the beast stepped into the room a few heartbeats later. It must have paused. A fleeting second in which it took stock of the gymnasium, long enough for the assembled Sandmen to know what they were facing. She only opened her eyes at the sound of the first scream.

The song shifted. The harsh and violent discordance necessary to wake the dead was no longer needed. The door of that particular cage had been opened. The Sam-creature already knew the Sandmen. It already hated them. It hated everyone, even Alice. So her music had to change accordingly.

Alice improvised a short coda to bring the current piece to its end, picking up immediately with a slightly different song to keep the god's hate under control. Left unchecked, who knew how much the Sam-creature would lay waste to?

So she sang a song of discipline. Something with an almost military cadence that wouldn't soothe the rage but instead allow her to constrict the flow of it. In a way, she hated putting a fresh chain on her fellow prisoner, but Francis was right. A lion needed a cage.

Upon opening her eyes, voice still ringing from her perfect concert, Alice could witness the fall of the Sandmen. Unleashed, the Sam-creature was nothing short of a demon.

It was satisfying to see that both Mother and Francis had already vanished. The former had stepped out of the spotlight and disappeared into the shadows, loathe to die with the rest of the cattle she called her congregation. Francis was more difficult to predict, but his jacket and neatly folded tie had been left on the seat where he'd carefully placed them. Was it fear or an automatic sense of self-preservation that had driven him?

The rest was a ballet of violence. Like the red-orange spots in her eyes had danced for her when she'd sung to the sun, the torn limbs of the Sandmen seemed to align with her chant, transforming into a graceful choreography.

Blood fountained in majestic arcs that caught in the spotlights. Entire torsos would be flung skyward, arms akimbo in their ascent, like angels ascending toward Heaven. Every death was a movement. Every splatter, a painting.

The god had told her that, too, but only now did she understand. It was beautiful.

DANIEL

A SINGSONG MELODY burst from the silence. A buzzing not unlike an electric razor accompanied the music. After five seconds, the electronic song, designed to be just obtrusive enough, went silent again, swallowed up by the night.

A few struggling heartbeats later and the song played itself again for another five seconds, then silence.

Daniel could see his phone, the musician, through his right eye. The left was too close to the floor, almost touching the ceramic tiles he rested on. He kept that one shut. Not that he could be sure he had the energy or will to reopen it.

The knife had been short, but so had the path to his lung. There was no way of knowing the extent of the damage, but judging by the liquid bubbling in his breath, it wasn't good. Daniel knew he needed help. That his only chance of survival lay in reaching out for his phone and getting someone on the line. All he had to do was pick it up and answer. Child's play.

After a moment the song stopped repeating and the phone ceased its vibrating.

It was a relief, in a way. Daniel considered what surviving entailed. If the agony he was suffering and the exhausting struggle of breathing were any indications, the fight to stay alive was going to be difficult and painful. Recovery would be demanding. It wasn't that Daniel wanted to die; he simply didn't want to go through the trouble of staying alive. If he could just pass out again, everything would be perfect.

The stupid phone, however, persisted in keeping him awake.

Once again it sprang to life, singing and dancing and putting on a light show.

Can't a guy die in peace? he asked himself as he reached for the phone.

Regret was almost immediate. The hole in his torso burst with fresh torment. The pain was one thing, unbearable and searing, but the sensation of blood weighing down his lung, his diaphragm feeling somehow severed and sliding against itself, was even more terrifying.

Pulling the phone closer to his face, he saw the glass was cracked. Now he'd need to buy a new phone. Yet another argument against survival, he thought, suppressing a chuckle.

A. PETERSON the display read.

Daniel had hoped for Venus. If nothing else, he would have liked to know why she had stabbed him.

Trying to take a deep breath but settling for a wet, shallow rasp instead, Daniel tapped the screen to answer.

"Hey," he said, pushing down a cough that probably would have knocked him unconscious again.

"Daniel? I can barely hear you."

"Yeah. You'll probably want to listen close then."

He swallowed, tasting blood. *Great.*

"Daniel. I'm with Randy, Venus's uncle?"

Abraham sounded excited and nervous, which weren't attributes he'd known the boy to have.

"I've still got that knife you gave me."

"Oh yeah?"

Daniel could remember how dangerous the knife was, thinking of what it had done to his father. The image of shadows consuming him made death suddenly less appealing.

"And Randy thinks we can use it to kill the thing from Venus's shed. We're going to end this once and for all!"

Awesome, Daniel thought, *about time someone did something about that monster. Wish it could have been me, though* . . .

"Good. I hope it goes well."

Consciousness was fleeting. He wanted to pass out again so very badly. At least then there would be no pain, and breathing wouldn't be so difficult. But Abraham's voice kept tugging him back from the brink.

"Actually, we could use your help for this."

"I'm a little preoccupied right now."

"You okay? You sound like a wounded animal."

Of course the farm boy would make that parallel.

"If you must know," Daniel said patiently, "I was recently stabbed in the gut. By Venus."

"What?" Abraham cried out before turning away from his phone. "He says Venus stabbed him? That doesn't make any sense. Daniel? Where's Venus now?"

Daniel wanted to shrug. Shrugging was easier than talking, but just as painful.

"I don't know. She attacked me; she was with this huge hairy guy. We didn't get much of a chance to chat."

"Dan? What hospital are you at?"

"None. I'm not very mobile right now."

The only reply was a sigh and more mumbling on the line. He did make out the word *delirious*, which made him want to laugh, but he wasn't delirious enough yet to forget how much that might hurt.

"Dan? Dan!"

"Still here."

"Where are you? Randy's going to call 9-1-1 and get you some help. Meanwhile, give me the address to this Church of the Sandmen you were talking about earlier."

That sounded like the single most reasonable course of action Daniel could have conceived. Send the able-bodied Abraham and the more knowledgeable Dr. McKenzie to handle the Sandmen, his mother, and Sam Finnegan. At the same time, he would receive the professional medical attention he desperately needed. No argument. This was what he should do.

"No can do. I can give you the address where I'm at, but no cops, no ambulance, or anything. Just come and get me."

"That's insane. You said you got stabbed. I thought it was bad?"

Daniel thought about the pain in his gut that came with every breath and the fact that he hadn't moved a limb since answering the phone call, too afraid to worsen the damage. Was it that bad? Such a short blade. It felt pretty bad.

"It's bad," he said, "but I can't let you do this without me. I gotta see this through."

"That's very heroic and all, but no," Abraham said, sounding awfully sure of himself.

"No heroics. I just have unfinished business there."

"Listen. You can keep the location of the Sandmen hostage if you want. We'll figure it out, but we're getting you help. Give me the address you're at. We'll send 9-1-1 over and go."

So much for that plan.

Thinking was beginning to be difficult. Daniel wasn't sure if it was lack of oxygen or the tendrils of unconsciousness pulling at his reason.

He still had one ace up his proverbial sleeve, though he was loath to use it.

"I gotta do this Abe. My mom's there. She's part of that Church. With that monster there . . . I don't know how long they've got and I don't know how things are going to shake out when you guys get there. These Sandmen are fanatics. They aren't just going to let you walk in and kill their god. I want to make sure my mom doesn't get caught in the crossfire."

Family. Abraham Peterson's own personal Achilles heel. There was no way the lumbering, softhearted guy wouldn't fall for that. Still, for good measure, Daniel added:

"Also, I have the keys to the compound. With those, we might be able to slit that monster's throat and be out before anyone even knows we're there. I know where they keep it. I've seen it myself."

There. His hand was revealed and all he had to do was wait to see what Abraham was holding.

It took a moment. There was heated deliberation on the other end of the line. The words were formless, liquid, electronic. Nonsense filtered through a phone that felt too far away and was getting farther with each of Daniel's faltering breaths.

"Okay."

Abraham's voice snapped Daniel back to wakefulness. Had he passed out? How long?

"You've got a deal, Dan." Abraham sounded like he'd been asked to get rid of his dog. "We'll come get you, you take us to the Church, but as soon as we're done there, we're taking you to a hospital. You understand?"

"Uh-huh."

"Randy's going to bring some painkillers and some first aid stuff. Maybe the wound ain't that bad."

Daniel swirled his tongue inside his mouth. Copper-flavored saliva was accumulating near his gums. It forced him to swallow, sending spasms of pain through his abdomen, tracing the outline of every inch of where the knife had pierced his body.

Oh, it was bad all right.

It was like getting stabbed all over again. Except slower and without the benefit of immediately falling into shock.

Daniel didn't remember hanging up on the call. Oblivion must have claimed him again at some point. The waking up was terrible. Someone was flipping him onto his back, careless of his wounds. Too weak to defend himself, or even complain properly, for that matter, he had no choice but to let himself be manhandled. Warm blood pooled anew onto his belly as the laceration reopened. The only thing to greet his gaze was a light that seemed as powerful and blinding as the sun itself.

"He's bleeding again," came an older, impatient voice. "Here, push on the wound with this."

Dan's shirt was ripped open with the help of scissors. Something a little wet and a little cool was pushed onto the hole in his gut, causing him to breathe in sharply. The cold touch, the pressure on his wound, and the sudden expansion of lungs and rib cage made Daniel want to pass out again, but as reason was flooding back into his brain, he recognized what was happening and who was torturing him.

"I think he's awake," Abraham said, his voice unexpectedly soothing to Daniel. Abraham Peterson wasn't his first choice as someone to administer medical aid to him, but he could do far worse. After all, Abraham was calm under pressure and had been tending to his ailing father for years.

"I'm fine," Daniel lied. He felt and sounded like he was drowning.

"Well, if you're still alive after all this time, it's a good sign." The old voice, which he assumed to be Dr. McKenzie, continued. "On the other hand, your pulse is weak and you almost certainly have some internal bleeding. You need a hospital, Daniel."

Randy sounded different. Tired and used up. Daniel couldn't help but think of him as leftover food. Dry. Wasted.

"They have hospitals in Laval," Daniel said. "C'mon. Let's go."

He tried to get up, clenching his abdominal muscles in the process. It hurt. Not as bad as other stupid maneuvers he'd performed since Venus had put a knife in his gut, but enough to force him back to the floor.

"A little help?"

Abraham and Randy, reduced to shadows and silhouettes hidden behind the burning LEDs of their flashlights, seemed to exchange a look of quiet acknowledgment.

"Are you sure about this, Daniel?" Randy asked. "You could die if we take you with us."

"I've seen worse."

And he had, of course. Just two days prior he'd been mopping up blood for hours after Sam Finnegan, fueled by the malevolent entity within, had torn through half a dozen Church members. Cassandra Poole had survived half a day with a leg torn off in the middle. If she could endure for a few hours, surely Daniel could do the same.

He gritted his teeth, ready to be helped to his feet. Ready to go back to the Church and . . .

And what? Finish off the cult? Save Alice?

With any luck, seeing their god destroyed would tear the Sandmen apart, annihilating the final vestiges of those who'd killed his girlfriend and destroyed his father.

As for Alice, the poor girl had long suffered at the hands of the Sandmen. Like him, everything in her life had been taken from her. Surely, she was worth the effort? The sacrifice?

"Dan?" Abraham interrupted his reverie. "We're gonna pull you up, buddy. But, uh . . . Dr. McKenzie says there's a solid chance you'll pass out."

"I can take it."

"I'm sure you can, but what if—"

"Give us the Church's address," Randy interrupted. "If you pass out, we'll get you to the car and put you in the back so we can be our way. Hell, it'll probably be easier on you if that's how it goes down. It's not like we have a stretcher or anything."

Daniel's thoughts were already whirling. He could tell they weren't telling him the whole truth, but he also couldn't decide what they were hiding. Were his injuries worse than he thought? Did they intend to leave him for dead?

Still, the memory of the pain of being flipped over remained fresh. Being carried by a clumsy yeti of a farm boy and a fragile old man, then dragged into whatever car they had, wasn't appealing.

"What about the painkillers Abe mentioned?"

"Those?" Randy said, patting a pocket on his jacket. "Those'll knock you right out. But with your blood pressure, I don't want to risk them unless they become absolutely necessary."

"All right . . . all right," Dan said, trying to collect himself somewhat. "You're right."

Bracing himself for more pain, Daniel pulled the keys to the compound out of his pocket. Gripping them in his left fist, he recited the address to the school.

"It's off an access road on the Nineteenth North. You'll have to drive pretty deep. You need to go through an abandoned residential development. It's the only place with lights. Can't miss it."

He then raised the key chain and put it in Abraham's large paw. Abe took the keys and gave Daniel's hand a squeeze. A subtle act of compassion. What the fuck did the big guy know?

"There's a girl in Room 003, in the basement. She's not one of them. You need to help her out. Room 004 . . . that's where they're keeping Sam Finnegan. All right . . . I'm ready. Should I be biting on something?"

The two looming figures looked at each other again and, even through the glare, Daniel could see them nod to each other.

Then Abraham pulled out a phone.

"Oh no . . . No, no! You bastards!"

"Hi. I've got an emergency." Abraham started talking to the person on the other end of the line, presumably a 9-1-1 operator. As he walked out of Daniel's line of sight, so too did his voice drown out.

"Don't do this to me, Peterson!"

"Daniel?" It was Randy, leaning over him. The medical examiner's face was a mere few inches from Daniel's. He was so close that the glow of the light no longer obscured his features.

Randy wasn't just thinner, but gaunt. His eyes were a little sunken and very crazy. Much more than his voice let on.

"Listen, Daniel." Randy fidgeted with the boy's ruined shirt, pulling it back over his chest to cover him as much as possible. The cold, coagulating blood in the fabric felt like the skin of a fish. "I'm going to take care of it. Your mom's going to be fine. We used to know each other. I can talk to her. But this girl . . . the singer. You have to tell me what you know about her."

"I swear, Randy . . . don't you leave me here."

Daniel could feel the Crowley anger swelling up inside him. It had never burned with such fire.

"Tell me about the girl, Daniel. I'll make sure Marguerite makes it out okay. Can the girl control the god? Can she do that?"

Daniel grabbed the medical examiner by the front of his hoodie, pulling the middle-aged man up to his face. The pain was excruciating. Enough to make Daniel see sparks of white fire in his eyes and clench his teeth so hard that one of his molars cracked noisily.

Just as he was about to use his left arm to grab the doctor's neck and suffocate the bastard, sparks exploded into atomic blasts of light and pain. The muscles in his hands, his arms, his entire body, were drained of everything. A marionette without the strings. Sound without air.

Randy removed his finger, bloody and cruel, from within the hole in Daniel's chest before getting up. The silhouette of the medical examiner looked down at the son of Stephen Crowley with an expression that spoke of nothing but pity.

"I'm sorry, Daniel," he said. "I hope I didn't make things worse."

Daniel didn't hear, however. His unblinking eyes were focused on a detail in the ceiling that the darkness hid from him. Every breath was a herculean task and its own circle of hell. Everything short of pushing his lungs was impossible.

As blood left his veins, settling either on the tiles of Simon Martel's entranceway or in some abdominal cavity in his gut, Daniel could feel the cold encroaching. The floor, then the air around him, everything was taking on a chill. He counted his irregular breaths, always expecting the next one not to come, until eventually he noticed that he could see the air he exhaled.

"Shhh . . ." A calm, comforting voice echoed through the room. It was a beautiful sound. What it lacked in the practiced perfection of Alice's singing, it made up for in comforting familiarity.

"Sasha . . ." he whispered.

The name seemed to conjure up her image. She appeared, sitting at his head, cradling his face in luminescent hands. She glowed, an aura of beatific light emanating from her skin yet taking nothing away from her copper complexion or silky black hair.

"Don't talk, Danny." She parted his hair, brushing her fingers against his forehead.

"Is it over?" he asked.

She shook her head slowly, sadly.

"No."

"Sash? I'm sorry I kissed that girl. I—"

She put her index finger on his lips, the spittle and blood crystallizing almost instantly.

"I'm dead, Daniel. I can't really tell you how to live your life anymore."

Frozen lips curled into a comforted smile for a moment, but quickly, it melted into concern.

"Sasha?" he asked, voice trembling from cold, pain, and fear.

"Shhh . . . They're almost here. Listen."

He could hear the sirens, but instead of relief, Daniel could feel the sands of time, the opportunity itself, slipping through his fingers.

"Sash? I know who killed you."

The glowing apparition frowned, digging into her memories. The furrowing of her eyebrows didn't go away, but a slight setting of her lips signaled that she had the answer to his question.

"I know. It was that reporter. The one from out of town. He was . . . talking on the phone while he did it. Arguing with someone."

"Someone?" Daniel asked, watching the light of the ambulances cast through his girlfriend's apparition.

"Yes. His mother, I think."

ALICE

ALICE FELT LIKE a princess and this was her ball.

She walked slowly onto the stage, her head held high and each step deliberate. Her gown was an oversize T-shirt and a pair of baggy jeans, her crystal shoes little more than beat-up sneakers. Instead of a tiara, she wore a used-up hair elastic that held her black locks under tenuous control.

When she got to the spotlight, Alice remembered the last time she'd performed for the Sandmen. How the only one to applaud at the end had been Francis. Not out of admiration for her singing, but rather for how it represented an important milestone on the road to the Sandmen's ultimate destiny. Years of patience training her to become this perfect instrument. He was applauding himself, the Church, and Mother. Alice the person was little more than an incidental.

Tonight there would be no clapping at the end of her performance, but Alice had transcended the need for the admiration of others. She had moved on. Approval only needed to come from one place anymore: herself.

So she sang. Eyes closed to the light raining down on her. Alice put on the performance of a lifetime. Twirling to the music as the sounds of carved flesh and tear-filled screams cheered her on. This was her party. Her ball. Her night.

A spray of blood misted over her left cheek, the wind blowing over ocean waves. A limb stripped of all its skin landed at her feet, a bouquet of roses from an admirer in the audience. The screams and wet tearing of meat were her applause.

Alice's memories turned to the night Sam Finnegan had been brought to the compound. How she'd been too slow to stop him from killing three members of the Church, including Victor Poole. A sticky wetness in her hand reminded her of pushing Victor out of the way, of keeping his blood on her palm and fingers until the god had been driven to sleep.

Tonight she knew that stopping the massacre would be as simple as switching her inflection by a fraction, but she kept on singing.

"This is your family you're killing."

It was the voice of authority. The voice that had forever held fear close to her heart. Alice had thought the woman dead or that perhaps she had run away, but somehow Marguerite was right there, right next to her. A captain brave enough to go down with her ship.

"Open your eyes, Alice! Look at the consequences of your actions. I thought I had brought you up better than this. I truly believed you understood what the Sandmen stood for."

Alice opened her eyes and looked around. Her song faltered.

Marguerite Lambert-Crowley was there, scant few feet away. Whatever fright the woman might have endured at the moment when Alice had unleashed the god upon her congregation, it had been reined in. Despite the carnage raging all around, she was once more Mother, matriarch of the Church of the Sandmen. Seeing her followers torn asunder in a shower of blood did little to take that power away from her. In the end she was responsible for these people.

Mother, annoyed, kicked aside a scrap of flesh that had landed on her otherwise impeccable shoe.

"We were going to build a better world, a world of love and life. You were going to be the figurehead of a new order. The curfews and rules and punishment, they were all meant to train you for that. Why would I be so strict with you after all? *This!*" Mother waved her arm, indicating the ballet of hate and death. "Because I knew you were capable of this!"

On cue, the stage's spotlight died out and the powerful gymnasium lights hummed to life. Their low buzzing spreading through the air as they illuminated everything beneath them.

It was a ghoulish sunrise over a slick red hellscape. The warm glow revealing ever more details of a scene bathed in death. To Alice's surprise, her divine servant had only gone through nine or ten of the remaining Sandmen. The screams and cries, the sounds of ripping flesh and cracking bones had all come from less than a dozen victims. Brutal at first, the Sam-creature's fury was channeled into pure carnage. But as Alice's song got more theatrical, so did its terrible ministrations. Currently it sat on the naked back of Eric Lecourt. Carving out intricate spiral patterns into his skin, pulling off thick layers of epidermis in the process. Maria Di Stefano's body, less artistically disposed of, was instead pulled limb from limb. Still, her remains had been positioned so that she looked like a bloody and elongated classical painting. Others had had their bodies opened up, ribs splayed open like the wings of birds, organs strewn around them like bright red and fetid-yellow feathers.

The survivors huddled near exits, but judging by the savage display in front of the fire escape and the door leading to the main hall, anyone trying to run had been punished for their attempt.

Just like in "Cinderella," midnight had struck. The fantasy was broken. This was not a beautiful ballet, and Alice was no princess.

Bile rose in her throat, silencing her song. Her hands shook and her knees buckled as a cold sweat broke out all over her.

"That's right," Mother said, somehow soothing and accusatory all at once. "Now sing your monster back to sleep. Bring your little outburst to an end and we'll see how lenient we can afford to be for your actions. Accept your place in this family."

Alice shook her head.

"No?" Mother's surprise bordered on outrage.

"No," Alice said, raising her head, the bile now burning at the back of her throat. "Look around, Mother. None of this blood is on my hands. Your god is going to come for you. It might go through me first, but after that, who'll sing it to sleep for you?"

They'd all seen what the Sam-creature was capable of. All been witness to what a pitiless butcher the creature was when given slack on its leash. Every Sandman had learned in the last few days to properly fear the beast they worshipped. However, what Alice found in Marguerite's eyes went somewhere beyond. She had a different, new kind of fear. One that spoke to a deeper understanding of exactly what the Sam-creature, or rather the beast within it, was truly capable of.

"Sing," Mother said.

It was not an order or a demand. She was begging for Alice to use her gift.

And Alice, to her credit, did try. But her voice came out faltering and wrong. Mother had succeeded too well in rattling her. Sobs of fear kept interrupting, and the images of torsos splayed out like butterfly wings and blood splashed onto the floor in perfect mirror pools kept interfering with her focus.

Alice envied the luxury of breaking down and awaiting her fate. Of being free of the responsibility of having caused the carnage and being tasked to stop it.

She almost had it once, when her concentration was broken once more by the earsplitting cries of a group of survivors, the ones closer to her right, though she did not have the courage to open her eyes and witness their fate.

Eventually Alice did regain control. Though tears streamed down her face and her shoulders convulsed in sobs that she would not, could not, allow her lungs to share, she sang.

Not a lullaby, not a song to chain and shackle and subdue. In fact, she didn't know what she was singing; she was simply stringing together the melodies like she had done for Simon. Her only concern was to connect with the thing that wore Sam Finnegan like a suit.

"*I should have destroyed you,*" she said, the words nested into her song. A secret message tucked into a bottle of sound that only the god could open and read.

And the creature replied, its voice still terrible and familiar.

"*You can't. You can't and you won't. We see ourselves in each other.*"

Then it showed her.

The god opened Alice's eyes to the realm in which it dwelled. Peering through its eyes, she saw an unreality, dark and empty. She could understand that the souls of the living were like glowing beacons. They begged to be owned, to be loved, to be destroyed. To be experienced. But behind all the luminous shadows and the dark, cold sun above, the whole of reality was permeated by a single inescapable presence. To be in this world was to swim in the ocean, and the thing caught in Sam Finnegan's flesh was the water. It was everywhere and inescapable.

Singing had gone from being a refuge to being yet another prison.

It was the final wall of the fortress Alice had been building since she was a child. It was built as a means to shut out the outside world, but now it was collapsing onto her.

She had tried to shore it up as best as she could. Her fondness for Daniel, which she had foolishly allowed herself to think was reciprocated. The new sense of power her singing had given her, which only served as a new layer of responsibility. Being able to communicate with an actual god and learn of its secrets.

She saw now that each was an illusion. Insubstantial things unable to hold up the forces pressuring her inner sanctum. It wasn't the first time her emotional refuge had been torn down, but it seemed like this would be the last.

With tears streaming down from tightly shut eyes, Alice couldn't understand where she was supposed to find the strength to rebuild. There was no hope and no joy. In the end, Mother had been right about everything. Alice was meant to be a tool and her only use was to keep an angry god in chains. If not this particular monster, then it would have been one of countless others. Hers was a hopeless life, as once the curtain was pulled back on the stage of reality, it revealed a hopeless universe.

Carefully, she again dared to open her eyes by a slit. Light flooded her retinas, washing away the image of a god so vast, it might as well have been the ground she walked on. A reality as maddening as a four-dimensional kaleidoscope. To keep staring at the home of gods was the path to insanity.

The Sam-creature had made its way to the rafters, hiding behind the burning floodlights that illuminated the gymnasium. It had long since stopped being human, twisting its host into a creature of sinew, bone, and blood.

Time might as well have stood still as she sang and communed with the divine, for nothing had changed. Marguerite still held Alice with her gaze, commanding her to keep her song going, to enslave the god and put a stop to the carnage. Francis stood next to the switches that controlled the lighting in the gymnasium, still floating between boredom and amusement. The other survivors stood like antelopes in the savanna, waiting for the lioness to pounce from the tall grass.

Wiping the tears from her blurry eyes with her right forearm, Alice managed to focus again on the real world. Taking stock of the things available to her, she struggled to keep her singing consistent, beautiful, and awash with meaning while also leafing through the pages of the music she had brought with her. Her arsenal.

She knew multitasking didn't lend itself to perfection, and her voice began to falter again. Each time it did, the connection with the Sam-creature frayed. Despite the flaws in her tone and cadence being nearly imperceptible, her mistakes were made obvious by the noises the Sam-creature made with every severed link to its shackles.

"Do you see?" Its voice was a hiss at the back of her mind, meshed into the music she sang. *"We are still so very much alike, you and I . . . tethered and chained."*

Alice could feel it stalking above. How long, she thought, before it decided to kill her and free itself of its only remaining chain?

Sweat-stained pages fell to the ground one after another as Alice flipped through each. Desperately, she read the music in her hands while maintaining the impossible melody that prevented the god from striking her down.

She faltered yet again, allowing part of an unfinished lullaby to slip in, breaking the spell for a second. The stray notes infected her song of control and dominance.

An explosion of noise startled her as the Sam-creature landed on the stage between her and Mother.

It was as gruesome as it was magnificent. So little of Sam Finnegan remained. The inhuman form of the entity seemed to push from within and, with every moment of freedom, reshape its prison into something more suitable to its purpose. Its limbs were like twisted branches more than arms or legs. Where only bone had shown, tight, ropy muscles had taken root. Instead of looking through its eyes, which were still pierced with forbidding black iron nails, the creature kept its face upward, craning its neck, sniffing and sensing at its surroundings, looking for any clue to its prey's whereabouts.

"Alice . . ." Mother murmured, begging somehow to be saved.

The red shape of what had once been Sam Finnegan would advance toward Marguerite Lambert-Crowley whenever there was a flaw in Alice's singing, and the flaws were getting more frequent as the performer's alarm grew.

"Always . . . trying . . . to bind me, Lambert," the creature spoke. Its voice was human, borrowing that of the old man, but the words were fractured and strange in his mouth. As if each were from a different language. It supplemented the statement with a hiss.

"Alice . . . please," Mother said, redefining the meaning of fear.

For a second Alice was tempted to just let go. As long as she held her voice, she couldn't find the song she needed to completely bind the entity. If she stopped singing, the creature would make good on its implied threat. Alice had to choose between saving Mother or herself and the other Sandmen. Why should this be a difficult decision? When had she chosen that she should be the hero?

The decision was ultimately stolen from her. Before Alice could make her choice, a hand, cold and dry, clamped down over her mouth. An aborted cry of panic was all that escaped before she was silenced. With the music stopped, the air felt like it had been sucked out of the room.

The only thing Alice allowed herself to notice, before going back to furiously leafing through her arsenal, was that even the god seemed surprised by her decision. Mother didn't so much as have time to blame Alice for what happened next. The god, now hewed into a merciless killing apparatus, an engine of hate and death, set upon Marguerite. Whatever her fears of the god might have been, she would now have to face them. Alice cocked her head as Mother's screams burst forth from across the stage.

Through the cries, the cracks, the begging, and the ripping, Alice finally found the page that had been eluding her—Simon's song.

Simon had explained once that anyone could sing, but it took a true artisan to tap into emotions and amplify them. To make ephemeral feelings grow beyond the limits of reality. A lullaby could put a god to sleep. A commanding melody would bring it to heel.

And a love song—a love song might reshape its heart.

A brief look at the sheet in her hands and every detail of the melody came flooding back. This was the song she should have started with. If she was fast enough, maybe she could still save Mother.

Alice tried to shrug off the hand that silenced her. She knew that this song wasn't for her and it wasn't for the Sandmen. She was singing for the world.

The hand covering her mouth tightened. Alice struggled, but it was no use. Another hand closed on her forearm with a familiar, dreadful grip. She wanted to sing and let the power of Simon's song ring through the auditorium, but only the sounds of a thrashing and dying Marguerite Lambert-Crowley filled the silence.

That, and the whisper of Francis in her ear.

"Shhh . . . You were right. My attachment to Mother was an unfortunate weakness. Why don't we let this play out?"

ABRAHAM

ABRAHAM HAD NEVER been a car guy. He'd always thought that might be part of his problem making male friends. Every boy his age who lived in Saint-Ferdinand had been into cars. Cars, sports, and girls. The last two might be fun, but cars represented freedom. They were the ticket out of the village, an easy way to the big city. Or to Sherbrooke, at least, which was the next best thing. Even so, Abe had never really seen the appeal.

He could have a conversation about the ins and outs of taking apart a tractor engine—specifically the one rusting slowly in the Petersons' barn—but that was where his automotive expertise ended. He wasn't much use when it came to anything with an electronic fuel injection, a "continuously variable transmission," or, God forbid, an onboard computer.

But sitting in the passenger seat of William Bergeron's refurbished 1977 Mustang, Abraham was beginning to regret his disinterest.

In fact, there were a few other things he regretted: leaving Daniel behind, for instance. While they couldn't take the wounded boy with them, it felt wrong to leave him alone like that. What if he didn't make it? Abraham would have to carry that on his conscience for the rest of his life.

Assuming he lived through the night.

After all, they were racing to confront a god with little more than a set of keys and a kitchen knife. He and Randy would be lucky to see the next morning.

There were so many things he still wanted to do. Abraham had fallen in love with the idea of going to cooking school over the last week or so. He could imagine himself becoming a modest baker or even a great chef. But now it was likely that he'd never find out which.

What he regretted most, however, was Penny. Abraham had always assumed she knew how he felt, but he'd never had the courage to tell her. It was his assumption she'd turn him down. Now, on his way to meet an uncertain fate, he wished he'd at least given it a shot.

It was too late for any of that now. Chances were, these opportunities had slipped his grasp forever, leaving only room for regret.

Abraham had grown increasingly frustrated by the medical examiner's driving. Randy had somewhat hurried on the way from Saint-Ferdinand to Montreal, likely urged on by Daniel's dire straits. Now, as they were working their way toward the Sandmen compound, trying to go around an accident on the highway, his hesitation had become almost palpable.

"Daniel made it sound like we should hurry," Abraham said, hoping Randy might go a little faster once they were through this patch of traffic.

"Won't get there any faster if we get pulled over. And would you put that thing away?"

"That thing" was the chef's knife. The Knife. It felt and looked like any other kitchen utensil. It wasn't even the most menacing of blades. A boning or carving knife would have been scarier, in Abraham's opinion.

Yet this thing was supposed to be magically imbued. Able to do what no other weapon on Earth could. It seemed unlikely.

Randy was right. Police and ambulance lights, along with the bright pink glow of road flares ignited the night around them as they crawled between cops and EMTs. It would only take one curious officer to notice he was playing around with a ten-inch blade to put a wrench in their gears. A fugitive behind the wheel of a stolen car? Dr. McKenzie had a reason to be nervous.

Abraham put the Knife on the car floor and peered out the window, trying to get a better look at the accident.

The crash must have happened some time ago. Ambulances were on their way out and the wrecked cars were being tied down onto flatbeds. Had they arrived ten minutes later, there probably would have been nothing to look at.

One of the cars looked like a light gray or white Honda Civic. It reminded Abraham of Daniel, and a fresh wave of guilt washed over him. Would it have killed them to wait for the ambulance and make sure Daniel was taken care of?

"You really think Venus stabbed him?" Abraham asked.

The question had gnawed at him ever since the accusation had left Daniel's mouth.

It seemed impossible. Venus was the kind of girl who'd pick up and nurse a baby bird that had fallen out of a tree. She'd never been a fan of the sight of blood and, despite a fascination with medical science, would turn a special shade of green at the sight of roadkill. Even when bullied, she never fought back.

To Abraham, she was still the city girl who'd moved to Saint-Ferdinand four years ago. To think that she would, in cold blood, stab Daniel Crowley. It didn't make a lick of sense.

"I don't know. She's your friend. You tell me."

"She's your niece."

He didn't answer.

Venus hadn't just been his niece; she'd been his favorite. They had the kind of relationship that reminded Abraham of the one with his father.

They had to stop for a few minutes as one of the flatbed tow trucks merged into traffic ahead of them and, with orange lights blazing atop the cab, took off in the far-right lane. After a moment, an officer wearing a bright fluorescent yellow security vest waved them through with a flashlight.

As soon as they were through, Randy shifted into first gear, then second, and sped ahead of the crash site.

"Finally!" he said, impatience seething through.

"Oh, now we're in a hurry?"

"We'll attract just as much attention going too slow as we would going too fast."

"Don't see us getting there at all if we get in an accident ourselves," Abraham said.

Randy shot him a withering glance, taking his eyes off the road in a way that made Abraham nervous. They were surrounded by like-minded drivers, all frustrated for the wasted time, all in a hurry to make up for every lost minute. All driving that much more recklessly as a result.

"Do you know how long the sedative I gave Erica is going to last?"

That one question explained everything.

Abraham, as always, had forgotten something important. Of course the drugs wouldn't last forever. Erica would wake up, the same way she had when he'd found her, and she would be in terrible agony. The fear, pain, confusion, and unfathomable helplessness would return in force. This time with no one around to help alleviate it.

"You shouldn't be keeping her alive," Abraham said, trying to put authority and wisdom behind the words.

"I know," Randy said, showing remorse instead of the impatience Abraham had expected. "I just can't let her go. Not as long as there's hope. Of anyone, I thought you'd be one to understand."

The initial reflex was to lash out. That was always the go-to response whenever anyone mentioned Harry Peterson, especially those who suggested simply letting him go. "Trust me. I understand," Randy continued, cutting off the onslaught. "The dead and I? We go way back. At work I cut them open and try to figure out their stories. Then at home I study the epilogue to those stories. What happens after they die? Death has been my one constant companion since I started to learn all this arcane garbage from my own dad.

"I thought I'd be able to pull the trigger on just about anyone if it came to it. For Christ's sake, I let my own brother walk to his death under the pretext that it was his destiny."

"So, what?" replied Abe. "You think you can save her? Then what? She'll forget the months of torment you put her through, fall in love with you, and you'll both live happily ever after?"

For the first time since finding Randy in the basement of the Bergeron house, Abraham saw a smile draw itself on the medical examiner's features. It was a wistful expression, longing and sad. Again, Abe understood. That wasn't the plan at all. Randy just wanted to fix her.

He'd lived most of his life thinking the same way about Penelope. Wishing for more, but satisfied and glad to just see her happy.

Leaning down, Abraham picked up the knife from the car floor. Flipping it around between his fingers, he aligned it so he could see his own face and, sure enough, he was wearing the very same weary smile.

"You really think we can force a god to fix our sorry lives with a kitchen knife?" he asked.

"Why not? Others have tried with far weaker tools."

Abraham had known they were going to what used to be a school. But he didn't expect that it would still look exactly like one.

They call themselves the Church of the Sandmen, after all. Shouldn't the converted school look more . . . churchy?

The design reminded him of his grade school, down to the eighties architecture and brown brick exterior, and he hated it. The appended gym, visible as a black silhouette on a dark indigo sky, was particularly familiar, a reminder of being bullied during gym class for both his size and lack of coordination.

Even without these memories, the compound retained a forbidding air in its isolation. It felt like there had been terrible things done in this place, with the promise of more to come.

It wasn't hard to find which of Daniel's keys fit into the lock at the gate. The largest key in the large lock. The gate itself swung open effortlessly, suggesting it was frequently used.

"Leave it open," Randy called out from the car window. "We might have to make a quick escape."

Abraham nodded at the ominous request. He then started making his way toward the school on foot, pointing at the main doors to indicate his intention.

The Mustang emitted a low growl as it rolled off to the side, taking position in a spot well away from the other vehicles.

Stopping for a moment, Abraham fished his phone out of his pocket. Running the tip of his thumb over the cracks that still textured the surface, he considered making a call. The phone came to life, lighting up at his touch.

Unbidden, his fingers danced over the cracks to summon Penelope's number. Her listing came up with a photo that never failed to squeeze his heart and an icon demanding to be tapped.

Abraham considered it. Wanting to tell her that he was about to finally put an end to everything. That he was doing this for her, so she could be free. Maybe he'd even find the courage to tell her more.

But he couldn't bring himself to do it. She wouldn't reciprocate his feelings or even wish him luck. Abraham simply couldn't imagine such words coming out of her mouth. She'd express concern in her own way, by calling him an idiot and comparing his plan to one of Venus's harebrained schemes. Then they would all go back to Saint-Ferdinand and come up with something less rash.

The phone went dark and he slipped it back into his pocket with a sigh. His feelings, as always, would have to wait.

"Do we even have a plan of attack?" Abraham asked, hearing Randy's footsteps on the gravel draw close behind him.

"Dan said they were holding the girl in the basement with the god directly next door, right?"

"Rooms 003 and 004. Got the keys right here." Abe held up the key chain, a massive bundle of metal.

"There's gotta be what? Maybe two or three dozen people in there? I say we have a look around, make sure we know what we're dealing with. Everything seems dead but the gym. Maybe they have something going on."

"You really think we can save Erica?" Abraham asked.

"That thing is always trying to make a deal, but it never fails to backfire on everyone who tries. But now? We have the upper hand. And if all else fails, we'll have the girl."

It didn't feel that way to Abraham. All they had was a simple chef's knife. Even if it was imbued as Randy claimed, it seemed like inadequate leverage to hold over a god.

"This thing," Randy continued, "it's not like us. It's as alien in psychology as it is in anatomy. We assume we're speaking the same tongue, but really, we're just throwing words at it and it throws them back. Pain, however, is a universal language."

"You think that's a one-time deal?" Abraham asked. "I mean, could we get it to save other people's lives?"

They'd made their way behind the school, looking into whatever windows they found, paying more attention to the basement ones. Away from the parking lights and streetlamps, both were engulfed in darkness. Enough that their eyes had adapted somewhat. Abraham could see the gray outline of Randy's face when he stopped to look at him.

"By 'other people,' I'm assuming you mean your dad?"

"Yeah."

"Listen," Randy said.

It was the same *Listen* that doctors would often use before telling Harry Peterson the odds of him enjoying another Christmas or seeing his son graduate high school. Abraham had heard that same *Listen* from William Bergeron one day at a barbecue his father was supposed to attend. It was the *Listen* that introduced bad news. *Listen, dreams don't come true.*

"I don't know that we can turn this god into a wish factory," Randy continued, putting a hesitant hand on Abraham's huge shoulder. "It's going to fight us and I don't think we're going to get many turns at bat."

Abraham braced himself for the bad news. *Listen.*

However, Randy's tone changed somewhat. Something on the edge of his voice shifted.

"If"—Randy hesitated—"*when* it fixes Erica, we'll do everything we can to have it cure your dad."

They kept going until they got to one window that, like the others, had the lights off. What made it stand out, however, were the bars bolted into the frame outside. It was the only window with bars in the entire school.

"Bet this is where they keep the girl," Randy whispered.

Abraham could remember when the girl was kidnapped, the thought chilling his mind. It had been a big deal, even all the way out in Saint-Ferdinand. He could remember her face from the posters, but her name escaped him.

Moving on, they soon reached the back of the gymnasium. This part of the structure seemed tacked on, a lazy afterthought to the design.

On this side of the property, the only source of light aside from the moon and stars was a small exit sign glowing red above an emergency doorway. If they looked toward the roof of the building, they could also see the electric glow in the windows that lined the gymnasium like a crown.

What their eyes couldn't tell them, however, their ears reported with eerie clarity.

Music.

Music without instruments, yet pristine. Hearing it, even through forbidding blocks of cement and a layer of bricks, felt like seeing the sun rise. A glorious event, pure and majestic.

"I think we know where the girl is," Randy said, incapable of suppressing his awe.

Abraham was about to say something, but he didn't want his voice to corrupt the perfect beauty that already tickled the edge of his hearing. He was awestruck. The music was too beautiful, too captivating, to interrupt.

But it didn't last.

As suddenly as they heard it, the music stopped. In the empty silence that followed, Abraham felt his heart go up his throat as if it were trying to escape. The floor had been taken away and gravity had reclaimed him. It felt like his wings had been cut off.

The screech of metal that followed was an ugly and jarring sound after such beauty. The jumbled footsteps and screams of a dozen human beings spilling into the night was just as horrible to hear in contrast.

When it did hit Abraham that these frantic, bloodied, and fleeing people must be members of the Church of the Sandmen, he tried to wave one of them down to ask what was happening.

"Don't." Randy grabbed his arm, shushing him. "The fewer of them the better."

Abraham soon regretted not running with the escaping Sandmen.

Once the coast became clear, he and Randy made their way to the open door, taking their first look inside the Church. What they saw redefined the meaning of *massacre*.

The deaths at Cicero's Circus had been caused by gunshots and bullet wounds. Granted, some of them were close-range shotgun blasts with all the gruesome damage implied. And there had been the horrible display of Stephen Crowley being devoured by shadows.

Here was a beast of a completely different species.

The floor of the gymnasium was slick with blood, an easily overlooked detail lost between the incomprehensible mess of bodies. Abraham would have been hard-pressed to count the number of victims. The air in the gymnasium was thick with evaporating bodily fluids and their accompanying stink. Most of the victims had been dispatched in what could only be described as an artistic fashion. Even the many splatterings of blood showed a strange, expressive flair.

Beyond the field of flesh, the gymnasium had been outfitted with a raised stage surrounded by theater-style seats. On the dais was a girl as small as Abraham was large. With dark hair and big watery eyes, she struggled against a man, tall and dark, who held one hand over her mouth and another crushing her arm. It took a moment for Abraham to recognize him without his jacket and tie, but he finally identified the man as Chris Hagen, the reporter he'd traded jokes with at the ice cream parlor during the summer.

Replacing the music were the screams of a woman. Another victim who, judging from the near-animal pitch of her tormented cries, was either being skinned alive, disemboweled, or both. The sound alternated between something that reminded Abraham of the gurgle of a drowning man and the cries of a dying American cottontail.

VENUS

"OKAY. I'LL ADMIT. This is spooky," Jodie said as she stepped out of her car.

Her attention was barely on her hands as she buckled her duty belt, securing her sidearm, radio, and other gear to her waist. There was no question in Venus's mind that Jodie meant business, despite her obvious doubts.

The constable checked her radio and shook her head, probably still wondering why she was even here. Venus closed the car door and heard the telltale scratch of the radio on Jodie's belt.

"Hey. What are you doing?" the teenager asked.

"My job." Jodie picked up the receiver for the device and brought it to her mouth. "Ten-thirty-nine?"

"Ten-four," the radio scratched back.

"All right . . . radio's working. I am way out of my territory," Jodie said, satisfied and visibly relieved to be still in contact with the authorities.

"You could just leave me here."

"Are you kidding? You baited me here with stories about my sister. With all the crap you put me through, either I'm seeing this to the end, or I'm cuffing you right here and dragging you back downtown."

Venus nodded, glad to have the constable with her, but also enduring the guilt of all she'd done to get to this point. Between

Ben's injuries, the risks Jodie was taking with her career, and the way things had ended with Simon, Lucien, and especially Daniel, the weight was almost more than she could carry.

"I just needed to get here. I can handle the rest if you'd rather go."

"Wrong," Jodie said, making sure to lock eyes with her. "You've done things that can't be taken back, Venus. There's going to have to be consequences. I'm here because these are the people who kidnapped Alice. I have to believe this is all happening for a reason. That Ben and I trusted you for a reason. Whether I'm here to make sure you face those consequences or to save my sister is still up in the air, but I'm here."

The constable brought her hand to her face, pinching her skull at the temples. "If I'm going to be honest with you," she continued, "I'm here because I worry about you. I want to believe you're a good kid, but that's only true if there's a point to all of it."

Venus gave this some thought. There was an emotional numbness that had come as a side effect of ignoring her guilt for so long. Yet she could still feel some warmth at hearing these words from Jodie. Aside from Abraham and Penny, when was the last time someone had cared enough to worry about her? Even her parents had shielded themselves from such concerns. Her own mother had skipped town the moment things had gotten too complicated.

"Are you sure?" Venus asked, uncertain what she was hoping for as an answer.

Jodie raised an eyebrow and unstrapped the Maglite from her belt, shining it into Venus's face, paying close attention to the massive bruise that had formed there. It was blinding, but Venus suffered through it quietly.

"Positive. What are we looking for anyways?"

"Actually, if you're going to stick around, I was hoping you could tell me," Venus answered. "What does Alice look like?"

"Right," Jodie said. "That was over eight years ago. So she might be different, but Alice always looked a bit more like Mom. Paler skin and a mouth like mine but with thinner lips. Big brown eyes and black hair. I . . ."

Something seemed to break. A wall was collapsing, exposing old ruins beneath. A piece of skin tearing and letting old blood spill forth again.

Jodie pushed the words out. "She had a unique smile. Thin, but so wide you'd think it would split her skull apart. I don't think that's what we're looking for though."

"Maybe." Venus struggled to find the right words, pushing hard against the fog of apathy that obscured her feelings. "When we find her, you'll see it again."

The Maglite switched off suddenly, plunging the two of them into darkness. After a second, Jodie sniffled loudly. Venus couldn't see the tears, but she could feel them. The effect wasn't unlike having ants in her leg after sitting on it for too long. Her emotions, like the limb, beginning to feel again. Empathy was returning and although it carried a heavy burden, she was glad. The call of the hollow remained loud, but she felt human again.

They walked past a black Mustang with a pair of white stripes on its hood. Venus recognized it as the Bergerons' car, teasing at her guilt over Beatrice's death. She wanted that guilt gone too and was tempted to feed it to the hollow of her soul, but that would put her back on the same road that had led to stabbing Daniel Crowley. Instead she allowed the remorse over her actions to run its course.

"Jodie?" Venus asked, trying to distract herself. "About the pendant you made me give Ben."

"The pewter shell? You know, I bought him a watch for his birthday two years ago. A good one too. Citizen. Solar powered. Great watch. He's never worn it, not even once! But he was still wearing that cheap piece of junk when I left his room today. I'm not jealous or anything, but he certainly took a fancy to you."

"Why the whole Botticelli thing?" Venus said, ignoring Jodie's nostalgic complaint.

"I don't know. You've seen that painting: *The Birth of Venus*? Naked goddess standing in a giant scallop shell surrounded by other gods? Probably Botticelli's most famous piece. I just made the connection with your name when I bought it."

Venus understood. The connection to her name, that of a Roman goddess.

Only a god can really kill a god, Peña had said. Venus's parents had known the predictions about her fate long before she'd been born. Was her name even part of it? Was it enough to be named after a goddess? Or did she have to somehow become one if she had any hope of coming out victorious?

The front door of the Sandmen's compound was locked. In fact, apart from security lights within, the whole place appeared to be abandoned. Venus looked inside, hands cupped around her face to study the interior. A long hallway stretched in both directions and a small desk stood alone like an island in front of the doors. Jodie looked around, fingers skittish on her Maglite.

"Looks like the party's in the gymnasium," she said, nodding toward the second-floor windows.

"Can you shoot the lock so we can go in?" Venus asked, backing away from the front door to let Jodie take the shot.

"God no. That's what idiots do. Even if it worked, discharging a firearm isn't the most subtle way of gaining entry, and then there's the risk from shrapnel or a ricochet. Besides, this is private property and I can't go in without probable cause or a warrant. Is there a door-bell you could ring?"

Venus was about to point out the glowing button on a black plastic box attached to the wall next to the door, an old-style inter-com, when a sound of screaming metal cut the night. A small group of crazed people emerged, running in a frenzy from the fire escape of the gymnasium building.

"How's that for probable cause?" Venus said.

Some of the escapees sprinted as if their very lives depended on it, while others limped awkwardly behind, slowed by their wounds. One woman was being urged along as she clutched her elbows, her body racked by spasms and convulsions. Another man hopped along on one foot, pulling a broken leg behind as he went.

All of them were red with blood.

"Jesus," Jodie hissed between her teeth, already moving toward the group and clutching at her radio. "Station?"

She waited for the ten-four before requesting backup. Venus wanted to interrupt, to tell her not to get more of the authorities involved. The exchange of police codes and jargon was too fast. By the time she'd caught up and grabbed Jodie's attention, the officer was already halfway through giving the Church's address.

"You." She grabbed Venus by her left shoulder, careful not to touch her bruises. "Get in the car and stay there. Copy?"

Venus nodded, but as soon as Jodie's attention had turned to the escaping Church members again, she was off running toward the emergency exit.

"Venus! God dammit!"

The plan was to sneak in through the open door, get her bearings, and find Jodie's sister—hopefully without running into the god.

As Venus ran toward the gym, she imagined what lay waiting for her. Did they have a room with dozens of cameras, borrowing from how she'd kept the god captive back in Saint-Ferdinand? Or did they have a rotation of people to keep an unblinking vigil on the creature? More chilling was the question of whether the god had broken free. That kind of power and cruelty unleashed would explain the fleeing people, along with their wounds and confusion. The thought did nothing to slow Venus down; in fact, her pace hastened, either pushed by the hand of destiny or morbid curiosity.

She reached the gymnasium door just before it closed, hitting a wall of foul humidity. With any luck, Jodie would be busy corralling the panicked Church members and coordinating with the colleagues she'd summoned long enough for Venus to find this Alice.

Whatever it was she'd been expecting—rows of zealous, robed fanatics, an impassioned sermon delivered by a Jim Jones–type leader—this wasn't it.

The scene was beyond belief. A nightmare that stretched her imagination but also felt all too familiar.

Her hearing reported the scene before her eyes could process them.

Screaming, inhuman and awful, reached her before she crossed the threshold of the door. Venus knew she was walking toward something terrible, something that might make even the Saint-Ferdinand Circus Massacre seem like a day at the beach. But of all the sounds, it was that of her boot squishing in a puddle of blood that made it real. Her foot landing in someone else's fluids made the events unfolding before her undeniable.

The full scene flooded into her with all its bizarre details. The gymnasium had been converted into a makeshift auditorium, complete with lighting, speakers, and a stage. There, two figures were playing out a strange scene. The man she knew as Chris Hagen held a small girl roughly Venus's age against her will.

The path that led to the stage from where she stood was paved in gore. The first plague of Egypt imposed upon the floor of a basketball court. It was a terrible image, but one with a familiar tone to it. Venus could recognize in the cuts and splatter the care with which certain bones had been removed while others had been broken and crushed, a unique artistry. The same way an expert might recognize the brushstroke of Van Gogh, she could see a specific signature upon this massacre.

And the artist was still at work.

Between the stage and the path of blood, a creature of flesh and bone and little else was at work pulling the screams from the living remains of a woman. It struggled to do as much damage as it could without allowing its victim the solace of death. Probing a wound whenever she started sinking into sweet, painless oblivion.

Venus wasn't prepared for this. All she wanted was to get the singer and leave, crippling the Sandmen and hopefully gaining a powerful tool and ally. If these were the conditions set by fate for how she would be going toe-to-toe with a god, she knew now that her destiny was to fail and to die.

A maelstrom of emotions battled for supremacy over Venus's mind. She felt revulsion and disgust toward the twitching, bleeding mess that littered the ground at her feet. She felt the freezing terror of a monster she knew all too well, thrashing into the body of a fresh victim. At the center of it all, a burning anger toward the man she'd known as Chris Hagen busy restraining some poor, helpless girl.

The alien part of her, the cold place that promised solace but delivered only hate, called softly, offering relief from her emotions again. More than that, it seemed to welcome her to the abattoir. How efficient could she be if the guilt, horror, and revulsion that pulsated through her heart with every beat could be put to rest? *Deal with it all later*, she told herself. *Let the cold place feast on them.*

But she could still hear the gurgle in Daniel's voice as he called out, confused and afraid, asking why she'd stabbed him. The god's gift ate up her unwanted emotions, but in return it dispensed only hate.

Instead of succumbing to the growing voice in her mind, Venus followed a different instinct. Without taking her eyes off the scene before her, she allowed her shaking knees to bend. She embraced the pain in her right side, feeling the bruises on her face more vividly than she had since the accident. Even her sprained ankle ached back to memory.

With mechanical reverence, she put her right hand flat on the gymnasium floor, suppressing her gag reflex as she let the cooling blood stick to her skin and seep between her fingers. The memory of Daniel's blood soaking through his shirt and onto her hand came flooding back with picture-perfect quality. It was a stark and implacable reminder of what she risked becoming if she allowed the god to conquer her from within.

Instead of putting the emotions aside, or surrendering completely to them, Venus leveraged her fear, leaning into the adrenaline rush, choosing fight over flight.

Her feet left the ground without her noticing. Venus couldn't afford to run. Between the pain in her right leg and her still tender left ankle, there wasn't much room for error and, if her hand was any witness, the ground was slick and slippery. She'd make a poor savior if her first action was to lose her footing and fall into a pile of dismembered bodies.

Her hesitant jog brought her around the stage and behind Chris Hagen. He held the girl in a vicious grip. His hand was pressed so hard onto her face that her neck arched back into his shoulder.

It was Alice, Venus understood. He was keeping her quiet, allowing the god to go about its grisly work unrestrained. The psychopath wanted the creature to have the freedom to enact its depraved fantasies onto the flesh of the Sandmen.

Bracing for the inevitable agony, Venus pushed herself onto the steps to the stage, every muscle and every joint in her right leg begging her to stop, but the need to take Hagen by surprise overwhelmed the pain.

She threw her right fist at the first convenient target: not Hagen's face, or his groin, though that would have been both effective and satisfying, but instead directly into his kidney.

Before he knew what was happening, Chris Hagen's legs folded under him. His prisoner was quick to react, slipping from his grip but also turning around. By the time Hagen's knee hit the stage with a loud thud, the skinny girl with the black hair and large angry eyes was kicking him in the face with all of her strength, the ball of her foot connecting with his jaw and sending his head jerking to the side.

In a perfect world, Chris Hagen would have been knocked out cold, but the asshole was resilient. While not completely ignoring the onslaught, he seemed more offended by the stain Venus had left on his pristine white shirt with her blood-soaked fist.

"McKenzie?" he said, rubbing his jaw, an air of incredulity painted over his usually bemused features.

Venus, her leg on fire, tried to adopt some kind of fighting stance. She knew it was probably ridiculous and ineffective, and Hagen's expression seemed to support her impression. He was going to throttle her.

The singer threw a punch at him, connecting nicely with his face again, but lacking the power to do any significant damage.

"All right, Alice, I've been patient enough," Hagen said, turning on her like a viper.

Like a man who'd been waiting his whole life to unleash the violence he had studied and practiced, Hagen administered two quick and powerful punches, catching the girl square in the face. One in the nose, the other on the left side of her jaw.

Hagen turned toward Venus but was interrupted by a loud retort.

From the door she'd walked in, Jodie was standing, sidearm pointed to the air, having fired a warning shot. For all her short height and compassionate manners, at that moment she was the second most imposing presence in the room. Not because of the gun, but simply by virtue of her confidence. In the middle of Hell's very own butcher shop, she was an unblinking force of authority.

"Hands behind your head," she said. "Now!"

Constable Jodie lowered her firearm to take aim at Chris Hagen.

"Hands!" she said only half a second later.

Hagen hadn't moved, satisfied with smiling his arrogant smile.

"Why does no one listen?" she said, intent on firing. But before the trigger got pulled, something else entered stage right.

In a single effortless bound, the ghoul-like god stood between Jodie and her target.

Recognition came slowly to Venus. The creature had made a mockery of Sam Finnegan's features. It moved its tortured head in arbitrary jerking motions, relying not on its broken eyes but rather on ears and nose and perhaps other senses beyond those of mortal beings. The grinning face of the Saint-Ferdinand Killer sniffed at the air, crouched and poised like a predator searching for prey.

"Edouard? But I just killed you again," it said, setting its gaze on Chris Hagen. "How many times do I get the pleasure?"

"Yes," the black-haired girl said, pointing at Hagen. "That's him. That's her son. Kill him too."

Then something weird happened. The creature gave the girl a *look*. A familiar, revolting, yet alluring twist of the neck that denoted familiarity between the two. Familiarity and belonging. Her words were filled with anger a decade old, and the kind of hate that Venus had only seen when looking deep in the god's very own soul.

The creature gave a slow, knowing nod to the skinny girl before turning back to Chris Hagen. If Venus didn't know any better, she could have sworn the man had fear in his eyes.

Jodie fired again.

The bullets hit the the god in the back, between the shoulders, ripping out chunks of old, desiccated flesh. Jodie might as well have been shooting into a pile of dried-up onions, their parchment skin exploding into confetti.

It did nothing to stop or even slow down the creature. Instead, in a familiar display, the bits of flesh were quickly reabsorbed into the body. Venus had seen this before. This was how Stephen Crowley had achieved his all too brief invulnerability.

The Sam-creature wheeled around, malice and annoyance writ large on the once-human features. Knobby fingers flexed with unnatural strength as it turned around to face the new assailant.

"Hey!" Venus screamed, surprised by her own bravado. "Here! Remember me?"

"Neil?" the god said, the familiar pins and needles of its voice etching into her mind.

"I am not my grandfather!"

Venus took a step forward, putting herself between the singer and the monster. The black-haired girl wheezed out a few notes, apparently trying to find her singing voice, but was yet unable to make a decent sound.

If only Venus could buy her some time. Hopefully, the girl would sing something to put the god to sleep. That was her role in all this, wasn't it?

Fortunately, the creature didn't see the ruse. Unfortunately, it remembered how Venus had kept it imprisoned in her backyard shed and how much it had longed, desired, and even lusted to kill her, not only in body, but in soul. Carving out a piece wasn't enough.

Before Venus could take another step, the creature was on her, hand around her neck, lifting her from the ground, holding her, and her life, in its inescapable grasp.

ABRAHAM

THE DOOR IN which Abraham stood, dumbfounded, was not the only fire escape to the gymnasium. Opposite him, another door had been flung open, a red carpet stretching between its threshold and the stage that dominated the auditorium.

What stunned him, however, beyond even the tortured wailing that bounced between the walls of the gymnasium, was that it was his friend Venus standing in that opposite threshold.

She looked different from what he remembered. The jean shorts and T-shirts had been replaced by army pants and a jacket. She seemed to have lost some weight and her face was badly bruised. What stood out most was her posture and the look in her eyes. Her fists were clenched and her knees bent. Her focus was cast of cold iron and her body language spoke of being ready for a fight.

Her gaze was set on Chris Hagen and the skinny girl he held against her will. *Someone should help her*, he thought, still stunned by the enormity of all that lay before him.

Before he could make the decision to act, Venus was already on the move. Limping toward the stage and vanishing behind it, she reemerged suddenly, striking at Hagen from behind. A heartbeat later the skinny girl was kicking her assailant across the face.

It was a little surreal to see the two girls, his friend and a stranger, attempting to beat up a man he'd casually befriended only a few months prior. Still, Abraham knew what side he was on. He moved forward, balling his fists and setting his jaw, ready to join in the fight. He may not have known the black-haired girl, but he knew Venus and he trusted that if she was beating the shit out of someone, they probably needed the shit beaten out of them pretty bad.

"Don't."

Randy McKenzie reached from behind and grabbed Abraham's arm, aged and bony fingers strong with urgency.

"I gotta help—"

But Abraham's protest was cut short. The inhuman cries of desperate pain were interrupted and replaced by a loud thud. Feedback from a microphone left on the stage screeched in accompaniment.

It was Sam Finnegan. Not as Abraham remembered him, thin but wiry with an affable smile, his skin red from the sun and eyes a pale gray, colored with senility. Rather, this was a nightmare version of the old man. Stretched and sinewy yet skeleton thin, he stood with a menacing hunch, looming over Venus, Hagen, and the black-haired girl.

The beast spoke in a gravelly, unearthly tone. The name Edouard bled out of its mouth and Abraham immediately recognized the voice.

It was shadows and blood given sound. Liquid darkness from that night in Venus's shed when Penny had almost given her life to avenge her mother. Venus had invited Abraham to show him "something" in her backyard. She'd explained as best she could, but there was no way to take her seriously. A demon trapped by a camera? When he'd seen the beast for the first time, every animal instinct within him had switched on. Primal memory of the things that lived in the night and preyed not on human flesh but rather on their essences. Now that the demon had arms and claws, legs and teeth, it could partake of both.

With a jerk of his shoulder, Abraham shrugged off Randy's hand. His senses were on high alert. He could smell the blood of every victim that surrounded him, along with the contents of their stomachs and bladders. He was aware of the puddle of blood under his right foot and the wood flooring of the gymnasium under his left.

"That's your niece, Randy," Abraham said, his tone flat.

"There's nothing you can do," Randy answered. "Maybe this was her destiny all along."

The fatalistic words were barely out of Randy's mouth when the creature attacked, snatching Venus from off the ground with a strike reminiscent of an asp.

Her feet dangling from the edge of the stage and her face turning red as claws closed around her neck, Venus's eyes rolled back in their sockets. Whether dead or dying or simply in some sort of trance, she was now completely at the creature's mercy. And Abraham knew all too well that even death was no escape.

Abraham's fingers closed around the handle of the kitchen knife, his palm dry on the varnished wood. He was keenly aware of the two rivets that held the blade in place, cold to the touch.

One step of hesitation was all he allowed himself. Pulling the knife from his jacket, dropping the piece of cloth that was wrapped around the blade, Abraham broke into a dead sprint.

It took only a handful of steps and one bounding leap for his tall legs to bring him onto the stage and close enough to thrust the blade forward.

Powered by fear, adrenaline, and years of grueling farm work, the knife punctured the back of Sam Finnegan's skull, pushed its way into the soft brain matter, and exploded on the other side, through the left eye socket.

For a moment the only noise that could be heard across the gymnasium was that of Abraham's breath, punctuated by the metallic sound of a nail bouncing on the floor.

The god's hand relaxed its grip from around Venus's neck, letting her fall unceremoniously to the floor. When she shook her head and staggered back to her feet, Abraham allowed himself a sigh of relief.

He'd done it. This was the prophecy Venus had talked about. She would fight the god, and she did, but in the end, it was he who had delivered the final blow. Whatever had transpired before his and Randy's arrival was the battle, the piles of dead bodies testified to that fact, but at one second to midnight, Abraham Peterson had been the one with the right weapon at the right time to strike down the malicious god.

Penny would see him as a hero now. He'd transcended from the useless schlub she'd grown up with into something more. Someone worthy of her.

Perhaps her hands would be warm again.

Victorious and vindictive, Abraham pulled the knife back. It slid from Sam Finnegan's ruined skull, drawing with it blood the color of dark wine and the texture of motor oil. The blade seemed to eat at the viscous liquid, drinking it in. Like water spilled over a hot rock on a torrid summer day, the god's blood vanished, almost without a trace, until Abraham could see his face in the metal again.

However, where he expected to see Venus looking up at him with gratitude and the distorted body of Sam Finnegan slumped to the ground, he was met with his friend's washed-out and bruised features, healthy skin white with horror.

Finnegan still stood upright. A shudder went up through the creature as if a thousand beetles had repositioned under his skin. Then, in a slow and deliberate motion, one that Abraham had only seen when the god was still locked in Venus's shed, it turned around to face him.

From the hole that had once housed Sam's left eye, a cloud of oily black smoke seeped out, dropping toward the ground in quickly dissipating billows. All the while, red streaks crept down the old man's cheek, like thick crimson tears. Blood and shadows.

The god did not waste time with Abraham the same way it had Venus. He'd struck it with a weapon that had hurt its flesh and rented its essence. For the first time, to Abraham's knowledge, it had been hurt, and there was no world in which such insolence would go unpunished.

In one fluid motion that could have fit between the beating of a fly's wings, Sam lunged forward. His right arm extended, claws and sinewy hands piercing through Abraham's abdomen, like a fork through cake.

Abraham could feel the fingers tear his skin and then intermingle with his upper intestine, sliding in just under his stomach. They then clenched around a handful of whatever organs were closest and pulled back out again, taking a shower of blood and chunks of random viscera.

The ceiling of the gymnasium came into view as Abraham toppled backward, the shock and pain having knocked the strength from his legs.

The god had overdone it, though. If its plan was to torture Abraham's flesh, it had gone too far already. As agonizing as each passing second was, it would be a quick death. In fact, Abraham didn't expect to be conscious long after hitting the ground.

As he fell, an object fell alongside him. His phone had been torn from his jacket while his guts had been torn from his abdomen. Whether real or imagined, Abraham could see the picture on the lock screen. A souvenir from happier days.

"Penny," Abraham rasped, pushing one last breath out of his lungs.

An instant later his back slammed into the gym floor, but he couldn't feel a thing. He didn't even hear his body crashing onto the ground or the sound of singing and screaming that now filled the auditorium. All he could hear in his final moment was the crack of his phone as it died right alongside him.

ALICE

THE RED-HAIRED GIRL wouldn't stop screaming.

Alice understood. She'd been surprised at the girl's courage in the first place. She was her savior, striking Francis hard enough to break his hold on her. In turn, Alice had managed to get in a satisfying kick, knocking the contented smile right off his face.

For that split second Alice had felt a kinship with her savior, whoever she was. They were united in purpose, and the girl's blood-soaked fist reminded Alice of her own first day meeting the Sam-creature. Whatever circumstances had brought the stranger here, the two of them were, for that brief moment, one.

Even when the Sam-creature leaped onto the stage and grabbed the redhead by the throat, Alice could see in her eyes and in the god's body language that there was more to its assault than mere fury. Silent but for a few words, Alice could tell that the girl and the god had history.

Alice tried to return the favor. To save her savior. But her throat felt raw and her mind was a jumbled mess of songs and melodies. She tried to decide which song she could manage with her hoarse trachea. She felt like a surgeon unable to decide which wound to treat first, skipping from one injury to the next without fixing anything.

Precious time was slipping between her fingers. Not only did the redheaded girl have little of it, but if Alice was to have an opportunity to stop Francis before he got away, she needed to rein in the god as fast as possible. But what in her arsenal could she sing that might have the desired effect?

When the decision came to her, so clear it should have been obvious from the beginning, events had already taken a new turn.

A boy, one she'd thought to be a man until his features became clear, had rushed the stage. In a dramatic, almost heroic fashion, he'd stabbed the Sam-creature through the skull.

Alice was stunned. She didn't think such a thing was even possible, but for a second she believed that this desperate attack had been enough to kill a god.

It hadn't. The god faltered, but recovered, wheeling around to take swift revenge, gutting the would-be hero on the spot.

Alice had seen enough of the god's handiwork that even this level of violence didn't faze her. She wanted to close her eyes and start singing, to get things under control before they could deteriorate any further. Mother was dead, she could see Francis limping toward the door, and the Church of the Sandmen lay in bloody ruins all around her. She'd done what she'd set out to do. It was time to put a stop to the carnage.

But the redheaded girl wouldn't stop screaming.

She screamed and cried what Alice assumed to be the boy's name. Abraham. Alice wanted to tell her to shut up. That she needed to concentrate, to focus, but the screaming wouldn't stop.

The god seemed frozen in time, gently squeezing at the handful of viscera it had extracted from this Abraham, looking much like a painter deciding where to put his next brushstroke. It was a brief respite in the chaos, but it wouldn't last. Who knew where it would strike next? It could go for the redheaded girl again or turn on Alice, effectively shutting down the only person to have any hope of controlling it.

When the music finally came to her, it was not a song of destruction to try to finish what the boy had started. It wasn't a lullaby or the song of control she'd used upon walking into the auditorium. Alice instead went back to the song Francis had kept her from singing—Simon's love song.

Alice had sung a snippet of the melody to Daniel Crowley. A handful of notes had been enough to quell his rage at the Sandmen's treatment of her. They had even been sufficient to make him kiss her, if only for a moment.

Like Daniel Crowley, the god was also filled with rage. It unleashed its fury by wanton killing, each death tearing at the fabric of reality that kept the god from their world. The god had claimed that it couldn't be destroyed, but perhaps it could be charmed.

Alice pushed Simon's serenade through her larynx. Her thin lips hitting the perfectly pitched notes and lilting melodies. Her large brown eyes wide open so she could see that even those for whom the song was not meant were mesmerized.

The cop who moments ago had been shooting at both the fleeing Francis and the Sam-Creature held her weapon in limp hands. Alice's redheaded savior stared, slack-jawed, stunned, and confused by the music.

And the god . . . the god was enthralled. Alice could tell that it was no longer blind. That through the broken socket of its fleshy eye, leaking shadow and blood where a cruel iron nail had been a moment earlier, it could see her. Not as she appeared to other mortals, but as only a god could see. In the roiling shadows that floated from the hollow, Alice recognized a look she had seen in so many of her fellow Sandmen as they had lavished their worship on Mother. She saw adoration.

Alice let the final note of the song trail off, echoing through the auditorium as if the melody itself refused to die. The charm had worked. She had outdone her purpose and reached into the soul of the soulless, beyond the curtains that separated life from death, and touched a heart colder than ice. What she left there was but a hint of warmth.

For a moment the song didn't seem to take. The Sam-creature snapped out of its reverie like a shark that had suddenly smelled blood in the water. It went from placid and calm to baring its teeth and frantically swinging its head. It wasn't long before the god's attention was on the redhead again.

"No! You're mine!" Alice said, angry and jealous.

The god hesitated for a moment, a span of time just wide enough for fear to squeeze in. Would it listen? Would it care what she had to say? Was it even in its capacity to care?

The Sam-creature twisted around, setting its shadowy gaze upon Alice and tilting its broken head as if it were discovering her for the first time. It turned to look at the cop and the redheaded girl, hissing at the former in warning, but exchanging a look of understanding with the latter, as if the two had unfinished business that would have to wait for later.

"We have to go," Alice continued, calmer, satisfied that her hold on the god was firm.

Inhaling deeply, the stink of carnage passing through her aching throat, Alice stepped down from the podium, trusting the god to follow behind her, tame as a dog.

Mother's carcass lay on the floor, largely intact apart from the nerves expertly pulled from her body and limbs. Bloody strands extended from the corpse, laid out in dizzying spirals. The work was incomplete, but Mother hadn't survived the process.

It was difficult for Alice to decide how she felt about Mother's death. In all the wrong ways, she'd loved Mother. She'd been her protector, her savior, and her spiritual guide. Mother had delivered on the biggest promise she'd made. She'd given Alice purpose.

But Mother was also pain.

In a sense, this was a suitable end for Mother, both in timing and execution. She'd died at the hands of the god she'd feared, but she'd also fulfilled her own purpose of bringing it and Alice together.

Satisfied with her conclusion, Alice nodded farewell to the body. Whatever it was the god and Mother had intended for each other was now irrelevant. A few more steps would put her on the threshold of the compound. For the first time since she was eight, Alice would walk outside with no tethers to draw her back to the Sandmen. At long last, she would be free.

But someone was still blocking her path.

"Alice?" asked the policewoman.

VENUS

"DID YOU ENJOY my gift, McKenzie?"

Cold and angry, Sam Finnegan's grip crushed Venus's throat. Meanwhile, like a welcoming embrace, the god's immaterial grasp closed in on her soul.

The butcher shop gymnasium was replaced by spots of light and dark in Venus's vision. The first symptoms of asphyxiation, the air in her lungs unable to be recycled, blocked at her throat. Unconsciousness should have followed, her brain no longer able to function, starved of oxygen.

In contrast, Venus's mind went in the opposite direction. While her hold on reality collapsed, her inner awareness burst open, throwing her weeks into the past.

Once more Venus had left the physical world behind and instead found herself in a vortex of shadows. Perhaps she was already dead or dying, the god having finished what it'd started. If that was the case, the monster was keeping her alive, as it seemed to enjoy doing with its victims. Much like the first time they'd met, she had fallen completely under its power, at the mercy of its whims.

"Get it over with," Venus said.

The words didn't spill from her lips, but they rang clear as bells through the private little reality that existed between her and the god. With them came the bottomless exhaustion of the situation. *"Why the hurry? Don't you want to savor your death? Your kind only gets to experience it once."*

There was no overt anger or threat in the creature's voice, except when it lingered on the words *your kind*. Over a century of hate pooled into those words, expressing a contempt for the whole of the human race.

A familiar fear crept up Venus's spine. She didn't know as much of the god's nature as she needed to. Every bit of information was a crumb here and a fragment there, all trying to be part of a coherent whole. It amounted to little leverage to stop the apocalypse.

Because that was who was at the other end of this conversation. The god had been trapped by a promise it had made to Nathan Cicero decades ago. Now it seemed trapped in the body of Sam Finnegan, but the bars on that cage were bending.

"No need to fear, McKenzie. I gave you a place to put your fear away. Did you not appreciate this gift?"

"Yes," Venus answered.

Maybe she was dying. Perhaps these were her last stray thoughts as her brain starved and withered. But she felt renewed confidence.

"Your gift," she continued. *"Reminded me how much I need my fear, my guilt, my regrets."*

"Why would you want to hold on to things like that?"

"They keep me from becoming something like you."

Could a god be insulted? Would its ego be bruised because a puny human didn't want to be anything like it? Venus was left waiting, wreathed in shadows marbled with blood. The god went silent for what seemed like hours. It was long enough for her to wonder if perhaps this was her death—a purgatory of swirling darkness.

The thought terrified Venus.

"I want to make a deal," she said, remembering Cicero's bargain and the god's propensity for taking oaths.

"You've broken promises in the past, McKenzie. I gave you a taste of godhood and you deemed it inadequate. You have little to offer anymore. Let us be done with each other."

As ominous as the statement was, nothing followed it up. If she was dead, then her afterlife was shaping up to be more boring than torturous. If she was still alive, she had to keep fighting.

"I promise to honor my word this time!" she screamed into the shadows. *"Answer me!"*

Nothing came, not even a stray thought from the creature. Spiraling winds howled in her ears, but nothing intruded into her mind.

"Please," Venus begged. But how many had used that tactic before, hoping for a shred of mercy from a creature that knew no such thing?

In fact, why was she being kept this way? None of the god's other victims had benefited from even a shred of respite. If the god knew anything aside from death and hate, it was pitiless savagery. The gymnasium painted a clear picture of that.

"Me," she said, venturing the word. *"You can have me."*

Whatever the relationship had been between Neil McKenzie and the god, she had somehow inherited it. Whatever vengeance the creature had in store for her grandfather, Venus would volunteer to suffer its fury.

Either her words or her thoughts got the god's attention.

"Perhaps," it whispered at the edge of hearing. *"We can talk."*

Venus swallowed hard, preparing herself for whatever the god might demand of her, and how she would try to leverage it into salvation.

Saliva was difficult to push down her throat. Her esophagus felt narrow and bruised. Gravity took hold of Venus once more, pulling her to the ground as her body struggled to draw in more air. Her wounded ankle exploded in fresh pain when her feet hit the ground, and every bruise on her right side burned with fresh agony.

For better or for worse, she was alive. Alive and free of the god's hold, both physically and spiritually. Had they struck their bargain?

The Sam-creature stood above her, silhouetted by the gymnasium lights. The clawed hand that, a second ago, had held her by the throat now shivered and spasmed. An iron nail, stained in aging blood and crusted with brain matter, rolled next to her feet.

From its left eye, the Sam-creature bled shadows.

"Abraham?" she rasped.

There was no way of counting how many times Abraham had come to Venus's rescue in the past.

In the four short years they'd known each other, after Venus had moved to Saint-Ferdinand and they'd met at school in Sherbrooke, Abraham had become a kind of guardian angel. Venus had always been prone to being bullied. Between being the new kid and her unusual upbringing, she was often singled out as the weird child and got pushed around for it. Except when Abraham was there.

The big kid with the goofy smile stood out too, but few were brave enough to taunt him to his face. Abraham had always been glad to extend that clout to cover Venus when he could.

Scaring off bullies and taking on a god were different things, however; but somehow he seemed to have done it.

With the closest thing to a flourish Abraham could manage, he pulled the knife out of Sam Finnegan's head. He smiled at Venus, glad to see her alive but unaware of what he had done.

The beast shuddered, and twisted to face its attacker.

Everything that happened after was a blur.

Though she'd always been privy to the aftermath of the creature's actions, Venus had been spared many of the atrocities the god had perpetrated. From the morbidly artful displays on the wall of her backyard shed to the abattoir of the gymnasium she stood in, it was all gruesome epilogues to her. Even her father's death, she'd only heard about from the mouths of others.

To Abraham's death, she had front-row seats. Vicious and pitiless, the Sam-creature wasted no time disemboweling her friend. This wasn't a kill for sport or entertainment, as so many others had been. There was no art or ritual to it. The god traded vengeance for efficiency, opting to take out the threat swiftly. That did not make the murder any less of a nightmare.

Forgetting fear, forgetting danger, Venus threw herself at Abraham, her knees crashing to the floor of the stage. Copious amounts of blood soaked through her pants and tears stained her face. Her hands hovered, trembling, searching for something to do that might help save Abraham, but half of his intestines were strewn across the stage. If he wasn't already dead, there was little she could do.

"Abe?" she asked, hoping that, if there was a hint of life left in him, she might see a reaction. "Abe!"

The screams hurt her crushed throat, but they were all she had. Abraham's eyes stared at the ground next to him, where his phone had fallen.

"Hold on, Abe. I . . ." She hesitated, not knowing what to promise.

There was nothing. Venus knew only the basics of first aid she'd learned in swimming lessons, and those were wholly inadequate to the situation. The only thing that could reverse the damage inflicted was the creature who'd inflicted it, and there was no longer any bargaining with that monster.

Overwhelmed, Venus could feel the tendrils of emotional collapse closing in on her. She could hear her screams becoming more hysterical with each word. This was Abraham, and there was nothing she could do to save him. As a last resort, she tried to reach to the hollowed-out place inside her. If the god wouldn't help her save her friend, she could use its so-called gift to her advantage.

But it was gone. There was no hollow, no cold place. Her emotions were hers to deal with.

Hoping for no less than a miracle, Venus reached into her pocket, pulling out her own phone.

"Please, please, please . . ." she begged, but she was again met with disappointment. Instead of the welcoming photo of two girls on a summer day, the icon of an empty battery flashed for a moment, then vanished.

"No!" she shouted, tossing the device across the gymnasium. It clattered in the distance, the faint sound of glass shattering on impact, marking its demise.

Venus didn't bother looking, her eyes already set on her next best hope. But Abraham's phone was broken, the crack on the screen

having split farther, the frame bent in from its own fall. No amount
of pushing the home button would bring it back to life.

"Jodie!"

Jodie had a radio. She'd called in backup. She was a trained
policewoman. She had to know first aid.

"Jodie!" Venus repeated, pleading across the bloodied auditorium.

Her stomach sank. Constable Jodie LeSage was already walking
away and toward the door through which they'd entered, accompanied by the forbidding presence of the Sam-creature. Together
they flanked a girl with jet-black hair and pale skin. The girl who'd
gone missing eight years ago. Alice, the singer they'd come to rescue.
Jodie's sister.

She turned around, halting her steps. Jodie's eyes were full of pity
and compassion, but little else. She did mouth something to Venus,
parting words before abandoning her with Abraham's body. It could
have been *thank you* or *I'm sorry*. It didn't matter. Her last hope was
leaving, having found what she was looking for.

Betrayed by everything around her, Venus bent over her friend's
inanimate form. Small fragile fingers wrapped behind his neck and
head, lifting him from the floor and onto her lap. The blood on her
hand mixed with the sweat in his hair as she cradled him with all the
gentleness of a doting mother.

"You big, dumb hero," she whispered into his ear. He was listening. He could hear her. Ghosts were real and they paid attention to
the living. That much she'd learned.

Once more, time vanished. Venus wanted to stay there, with her
friend, and let reality fade from both of them. How was she going to
tell Penny? Or Abraham's father? This would surely kill poor Harry
Peterson, accomplishing what a decade-long battle with cancer had
failed to do.

"For a second I thought he'd done it," a voice whispered from
behind her. "Big, dumb hero indeed."

Venus looked up, knowing who she'd see standing over her.

Randall McKenzie hadn't changed much since last she'd seen
him in Saint-Ferdinand, except perhaps for a worn-out determination in his eyes.

"You," Venus spit, remembering her hatred for the man who'd been her favorite uncle. "You brought him here."

He didn't bother contradicting her. Instead, extending a hand, offering to help his niece to her feet.

"You can hate me on the drive out," he said, a bit of an apology in his voice. "But unless you want to be the one explaining all this to the cops, we have to go."

Reluctant but defeated, Venus put her hand in his. She didn't meet his eyes, however. Those she kept on Abraham, who she was loath to abandon.

"Wait," Randy said before lifting her up. "The knife. Take the knife."

DANIEL

"WELL, WELL. IMAGINE my surprise when I found out you were here."

The voice cut through Daniel's anesthetic reverie. It was soft and cool and somewhat comforting. A tone and cadence practiced to elicit trust and lull listeners into letting their guards down.

Daniel could have slept forever. It would have been preferable to what awaited him on the other side of slumber. Though his unconsciousness was drug induced, somehow, in that middle ground between sleep and wakefulness, he could still remember clearly what had brought him here.

Venus had stabbed him in the abdomen. Abraham and Dr. McKenzie had abandoned him after taking his keys and whatever information they'd needed. Most of all, he remembered a beautiful, delirious vision of Sasha urging him to hang on, to survive, and to avenge.

Familiarity dug its hooks into Daniel, pulling him from his sleep. The new voice, though weary, carried with it something that resonated with Daniel. It was the soothing comfort of family. The one that had listened to his woes on his darkest day and said: "Come home."

"Lucky call, really," the voice continued. "Came here to get a bullet wound treated and overheard one of the nurses mention how much I looked like another patient. A certain boy named Crowley. As you can imagine, the moment I heard that name, I just had to investigate."

Daniel forced his eyes open. No day at football practice had ever exerted him so much as lifting his own eyelids in that moment. It was both a physical effort and a spiritual sacrifice. He now had no choice but to confront the reality of his situation.

At first there was nothing to see but blinding light. Red for a second but soon bursting into a burning white. Objects blended into a blurry mess. He was about to say screw it and pass out again, when tubes began to take shape. Tubes and ceiling tiles.

Daniel attempted to talk, but it felt like there was a garden hose shoved down his throat. He tried to spit it out, but all he got for his effort was choking pain.

"Yeah. You'll want to keep that in. I think it's one of those that keeps you alive. Anyways, I'm afraid I come bearing tragic news."

The dark shape beyond the tubes refused to come into focus, retaining a vaguely humanoid form. It moved with a bruised nonchalance, trying very hard to be fluid and carefree, but halting whenever it took a step.

Daniel must have made a face or twitched in some way that spurred the shape into continuing its one-sided conversation.

"Mom didn't make it, Daniel. She's dead."

The declaration came with no emotion. A flat statement of fact. It struck Daniel as unfair that the person who wanted, needed, to express grief couldn't, paralyzed by drugs and restrained by tubes and wire. Meanwhile, the blurry bringer of ill omen refused to mourn.

Francis, Daniel thought. Of all people, Francis was the one who'd found him in the hospital. Had Randy and Abraham even tried to locate him after they'd left him for dead? What about Penny? Or Venus? Why had Venus stabbed him? he wondered again.

Daniel braced himself. Soon Francis would get bored at his own soliloquy and proceed to the real reason he'd come up to Daniel's room. Francis was going to unplug something vital or smother him with a pillow in revenge. To make matters worse, he wouldn't even have the decency of feeling anger while doing it.

"It wasn't a quick death either. But it also wasn't as long as it should have been. You'll forgive me if I don't pull any punches here, won't you? Good.

"In the end, it was all Alice's fault. Maybe a little bit yours? But don't worry. I don't blame you. I think she fell for you pretty hard, and when you left, she went a little berserk. I have to give it to her: she was much more advanced in her singing than I gave her credit for. I'm telling you, Dan, she was a sight to behold."

He remembered wanting to kill Francis, a fury that went far beyond his plans for revenge. Between the pain, the fogginess from the drugs, and an unbearable thirst, Daniel could only really think of how infuriating his brother was for remaining so blurry. Why wouldn't he just come into focus?

While Francis seemed bent on blaming Alice for everything, Daniel was beginning to build a particular hatred for the tube in his mouth. It kept him from talking and drinking. If he could drink, his throat would feel better and he wouldn't be thirsty anymore. If he could talk, Daniel could tell Francis to get closer so he'd stop being so blurry. He tried his best to tell Francis that.

"Mm? Yeah, I'm pretty broken up about Mom too," Francis said, clearly not meaning it. "I've seen . . . Hell, I've done some pretty damn horrible things in my life, Daniel. Being a Sandman is a lot more work than we let you think. But I've never seen someone get the 'business' like what that thing did to Mother."

The constant callousness kept pulling at Daniel, dredging him up from the semiconsciousness he still labored under. There was something about it that made his weak pulse go faster.

Blurry Francis came a little more into focus, revealing a freshly sutured wound running vertically down his chest.

"I'll be completely honest, Daniel: I didn't stay for the grand finale. You see, Alice and I, we didn't get along all that well. I mean, it's no secret where she's from, but did she tell you that I was the one Mother sent to abduct her?

"A sixteen-year-old boy with a fresh driver's license, and she sent me to go commit what became one of the most high-profile kidnappings in the province's history. Let that sink in if you're still feeling sorry for Mother."

Why was he saying all this? Did he think Daniel was his confessional? That perhaps his little brother would pull the tube from his own throat and give him absolution for his sins?

"In hindsight, I can't say I blame her, ya know?" Francis continued. "The family was small back then. I don't think Mom trusted any of the others with that sensitive a mission. God knows it did not go well with everyone at the school. They all thought the police were going to be knocking at our door any day. Some poor fool even threatened to rat Mom out! Can you imagine?

"She made me take care of him, too."

Francis, his image clearer with every moment, seemed to pinch his pants at the knees to yank them up before sitting at the foot of Daniel's bed. Despite his cavalier talk of kidnapping and death, his actions were impossibly gentle, careful not to rock the bed or touch any of the medical equipment.

"There was a lot going on when I left. A cop showed up, your little friend Venus almost got choked out by Finnegan . . . . Don't know how that went down after I skedaddled."

Francis gave a mock shiver. "Not sure I want to either, if you get what I mean."

Was Venus really dead? Daniel wondered. Seemed unlikely. If so, he might never know why she ran him through with a kitchen knife. Of all the people he'd encountered who had faced the Sandmen's god, she was the only one to survive. She had been destined to survive.

"Anyways, buddy, I just wanted to check in," Francis said, getting up from the bed. "I'm glad I ran into you. Oh, and that you're still alive. That goes without saying. Not sure how I would have found you otherwise. Luckiest bullet wound in history, if you ask me."

Something flashed in Daniel's mind. Like a spark, briefly illuminating a hidden part of himself. It could have been caused by a rush of cold air coming from the door, or perhaps his increasing awareness of the pain in his body.

Sasha.

"Oh! Speaking of bullets. I walked out when they started asking too many questions. They're probably already looking for me."

Sasha was killed by Chris Hagen.

"So, if you don't mind, assuming you remember any of this when you wake up, don't let them know I was here. Does that sound good?"

Chris Hagen is Francis Crowley.

"Fantastic. I knew I could count on you, brother. The Crowley Boys! I know you don't like me saying it, but that's us now. We're all that's left. Think of it as the new Crowley Boys. How does that sound?"

Daniel wanted to tear every tube out of his body. To lunge at Francis and wrap all of the wires around his neck and strangle him. Even if it killed him, he wanted his last act to be fratricide. Let them both bleed and choke to death together. The Crowley Boys indeed.

But he couldn't do it. The most agitation he could muster was a flickering of his eyes and a twitching of his jaw. Even tears wouldn't come up.

"Good. Get better quickly, Daniel. You and I have a lot of work ahead of us. Don't worry though—you're not in this alone. I'll be back soon. We'll get through this together."

Daniel watched as his brother moved away, going out of focus again before vanishing. The last thing he heard Francis say before he disappeared and before the drugs took Daniel under again was "the Crowley Boys," followed by a laugh.

EPILOGUE

THE MAGIC HAD taken time. Almost nine weeks for this particular ritual. Though, it could be argued that there was a lifetime invested in casting the spell.

Harry Peterson had spent decades perfecting his art. He'd always dabbled with paints, but apart from the occasional landscape to pass the time, there had been little devotion to the brush and canvas.

He'd only picked up the hobby at his wife's behest, but when Edith passed, Harry had kept it up. It made him feel close to her despite having stepped on the other side of the grave.

Then the cancer came and the painting gave him something to do while he recovered. It occupied the space between this surgery and that chemo treatment, filling the void that might have otherwise been taken up with vomiting and self-pity.

When one is sick as often as Harry had been during the last two decades, one gets a lot of time to practice a hobby. But practice was only part of it. The other part was Amanda.

She had what Harry called "the knack." Her paintings were on a level that transcended talent. She mostly dealt with abstracts, which were magical in a more mundane way, doing what most paintings do, only more so. They'd tug and play on emotions and memories, throwing the viewer into near-fugue states when looking at them. One critic once described a piece as "singing" to him. However, when Amanda put her mind to painting something real, it broke the limits of perception.

Harry hungered for that degree of skill and she attempted to feed that hunger. She taught him how to paint birds because how bad could bringing a few birds to life be? It became an obsession for Harry. It outweighed his farm, his friends, and even his health. The only thing that measured up to the desire to bend reality just once before he died was his son.

It never happened.

The birds would stir and chirp, but imperfections would tether them to their frame. There was magic in those attempts, but it was crude and vulgar. Parlor tricks, as Neil and Edouard had called them.

This last painting was not a bird.

Harry could feel the end looming. He'd been told that he would meet his end in Saint-Ferdinand and now, after his last trip to the hospital, he knew he'd never leave this godforsaken village.

Screw birds, he told himself.

The bristles of his brush teased the canvas one final time, tickling on a touch of basalt gray into the shadows of the stone archway.

It had been a few days since the painting had come alive, but while animated and vibrant, it was still nothing but a vivid illustration. A fancy moving picture that would draw gasps of wonder from an unbelieving crowd, and questions from unbelieving skeptics, but nothing more. Days did not change and events repeated themselves on an endless loop within the confines of the frame.

Until Harry put on that final touch.

There was no flash, no shower of stars. Harry didn't have to speak any Latin or wave any wand beyond his paintbrush. The only hint that he was done came as the canvas seemed to vanish and suddenly he was applying pigment directly onto the rocks of the stone gate.

"Whoa!"

Penelope's exclamation confirmed that Harry wasn't hallucinating. Considering how medicated he was these days, battling a fever that would simply not capitulate, anything was possible.

"You see it?"

"No," she said, extending her arms, fingers splayed. "I feel it. Don't you?"

He did. The scarce few hairs on his sunken head swayed, caught in the thrall of a cool wind inside his studio. None of the windows were open. The fans were turned off. The gentle breeze, scented with a hint of salt, came from the painting.

The brush in Harry's hands trembled, following the sudden palsy in his fingers. His lower lip quivered as he struggled to find the proper words to express his own awe.

"You've done it," Penelope said. There was a joy in her voice that he hadn't heard in months. His son's friend had every reason to be greedy with her exultations. The summer had been cruel to her, taking everything away, from her mother to her sense of humanity.

Harry had tried to give the girl whatever bits of knowledge he had regarding the cults and magics in Saint-Ferdinand. They were meager treasures, scarce and unstitched, but it helped give Penelope's agile mind something to play with other than her fears. It was a trick not unlike how painting had gotten him through his own worst times.

Steadying his hand on his work stool, Harry lifted himself to his feet, every inch a struggle. Once he finally stood, still leaning for support, Penelope wrapped him in a delicate embrace. She squeezed him gently lest his bones break with her effort, and they both gazed in wonder at the impossible achievement.

"Do you think it leads somewhere real?" she asked.

"I don't know. I painted it based on a sketch Neil McKenzie showed me. So it is certainly based on a real place, but I wouldn't know where that is."

"Maybe it's only real within the painting's frame? Like a tiny world that you made with your brush?"

Harry shook his head. His breath was still short from the excitement of making real magic at least once in his life.

"I hope not," he said, reaching to adjust the oxygen output on his tank. "I'm hoping whatever it was Neil found there, we can find it again, and maybe it'll help you."

Penelope gave him a squeeze of gratitude before letting him go and taking a step back. Harry could feel the cold of her hands even through the leather gloves she now wore. Her condition was worsening and although he'd done nothing short of a miracle this day, there was no way of knowing if it would change anything for her.

"Abraham is going to be so impressed," she said, eyes still riveted to the painting. "This is going to floor him."

"I hope it doesn't floor him too hard. Someone needs to go through that thing and see if I painted it for a reason or not, and that sure ain't gonna be me."

He rattled his oxygen tank for emphasis.

Penelope took a step forward. The night outside the studio was dark and forbidding, but the powerful fluorescent tubes on the ceiling kept the shadows at bay. They also brought out the pure cerulean blue in the girl's eyes. Her irises had taken on an increasingly crystalline sheen. They picked up light in a way that made them glow for themselves in an almost bioluminescent gleam.

Careful, as if testing the water before diving in, she poked a gloved finger through the painting. She met with no resistance, her hand moving farther and farther into the painted world beyond. Each breath came quicker to her as her excitement grew. The air in the studio felt charged with possibility.

"What are you doing?"

Harry's words were raspy and a little more panicked than he'd intended.

Penelope was leaning into the frame, kneeling as she did so with half her upper body fully within the painting. When she pulled back, there was a small purple flower in her hands. Harry remembered brushing on dozens of them as he'd toiled over his masterpiece. Now there was one, delicate and bright in Penelope's leather-clad palm.

"It's real, Harry,"

"I know."

Her enthusiasm was such that she dropped her prize, letting it flutter to the floor as she stood. Her smile took on a manic figure made all the more worrisome by its tremor. There was an electricity within her that couldn't be contained.

"Where is Abraham anyways?"

The question was impatient and jittery. Harry could tell that while she cared about his son's whereabouts, this was about going through the painting.

Unable to wait any longer, Penelope reached into her jacket pocket, fishing out her phone. With nervous jerks, she pulled at the fingers of her right-hand glove, dropping it to the ground, crushing the tiny bluebell underneath.

Her hand was still pink and could have passed for warm at a glance, but Harry knew better. With each touch of her fingers to the phone's surface, he expected the device to become covered in hoarfrost or crack from the cold.

She held the phone between the tips of her fingers, close to her ear, waiting. Her foot tapped the wooden floor and her left hand played with the sleeve of her jacket as she waited.

"He's not answering," Penelope said, pocketing the phone with impatience.

"Don't worry. He'll be home soon. The boy won't let his old man go one night without some supervision."

It was day on the other side of the painting and the sun was finding its way into the studio, bright and warm. The light played with Penelope's blond hair as it danced in the wind, but she didn't seem to notice or enjoy any of it. Instead she was fixated on the horizon beyond the stone gate.

"Don't," Harry warned, watching his son's friend raise a booted foot and extend it into the frame.

"I can't wait for Abe."

"We don't know what's on the other side of that. What if Neil found something terrible? What if there're some wild animals there? Wait for Abraham. You can have each other's back while I wait here."

Penelope hesitated but put her foot down beyond the threshold of the painting. The simple act seemed to relax her, satisfy her.

"I'm just going to take a quick look," she said. "I won't step out of frame. I just want to see where in the world your painting leads. Don't you?"

"I've waited this long, I can wait a little more. Abraham will be here soon, and you should prepare before going."

"Prepare how?"

Penelope had almost her entire body through the gate now, twisting her torso and neck this way and that, trying to get an idea of where the painting led.

"I don't know. Bring a weapon? Some food?"

"It's fine. It looks beautiful out here."

She took another step, immersing herself fully into the image. Her boots sank into the grass and moss and her hair was being tousled wildly in the breeze. Penelope turned her face to the sun, closing her eyes and letting the light warm her skin.

"Penny? Come back. This isn't safe."

She didn't answer, instead taking another step, deeper into the landscape. She twirled once, her scarf swinging around her in an arc.

"Penny!"

Harry could feel his heart quicken and his lungs struggle. He tried to twist the oxygen valve again to increase the flow, but his hand became numb with the effort. Panicking, he jerked the knob, but it only served to make him lose his balance.

"Pen—"

The word was cut short, interrupted by a sharp pain in Harry's chest. The strength went out of his entire body, yet every muscle seemed to contract at once.

As he tried to remain upright, Harry only managed to push the oxygen tank to its tipping point. The heavy metal container toppled over, falling to the ground with an earsplitting thud accompanied by the sound of fabric tearing.

Clutching at his failing heart, Harry also fell to the ground, unable to do much to slow his collapse. Too short, the tube that connected him to the oxygen was pulled from his nostrils, leaving him to lie on his side, gasping for air.

Over his head, the canvas of his masterpiece fluttered in the aftermath of the wind that had come out of it moments before. The painting had been torn by the green tank, breaking the spell.

Harry Peterson's miracle had come to an end moments before his life did, leaving a shattered frame and a torn canvas.

When authorities would find his body, the paramedics and cops would see an old man, dead eyes staring in unseeing horror at the painting of a blond girl dancing in the light. Her blond hair golden in the sunshine and her eyes an unnatural shade of blue as she twirled, her smile frozen in place, among the bluebells.

THE END

LIST OF PATRONS

Amy Frost

INKSHARES

INKSHARES is a reader-driven publisher and producer based in Oakland, California. Our books are selected not by a group of editors, but by readers worldwide.

While we've published books by established writers like *Big Fish* author Daniel Wallace and *Star Wars: Rogue One* scribe Gary Whitta, our aim remains surfacing and developing the new author voices of tomorrow.

Previously unknown Inkshares authors have received starred reviews and been featured in *The New York Times*. Their books are on the front tables of Barnes & Noble and hundreds of independents nationwide, and many have been licensed by publishers in other major markets. They are also being adapted by Oscar-winning screenwriters at the biggest studios and networks.

Interested in making your own story a reality? Visit Inkshares. com to start your own project or find other great books.